MW01609832

Also by the Author

Children of Monsters:
An Inquiry into the Sons and Daughters of Dictators
(Encounter Books)

Peace, They Say:
A History of the Nobel Peace Prize, the Most Famous and Controversial Prize in the World
(Encounter Books)

Here, There & Everywhere:
Collected Writings of Jay Nordlinger
(National Review Books)

DIGGING IN

Further Collected Writings of

JAY NORDLINGER

For further information, please contact

National Review Books
215 Lexington Avenue
11th Floor
New York, NY 10016

Library of Congress Cataloguing-in-Publication Data

Names:	Nordlinger, Jay, 1963-
Title:	Digging in : further collected writings of Jay Nordlinger / Jay Nordlinger.
Other titles:	National review.
Description:	New York, NY : National Review Books, [2016] | Includes index.
Identifiers:	ISBN: 978-0-9847650-4-1
Subjects:	LCSH: United States--Politics and government--21st century. | United States--Social life and customs--21st century. | Manners and customs. | Language and culture. | Music—Social aspects. | LCGFT: Essays.
Classification:	LCC: PS3614.O733 D54 2016 | DDC: 810.9/355--dc23

Jacket and book design by Luba Myts

PRINTED IN THE UNITED STATES OF AMERICA

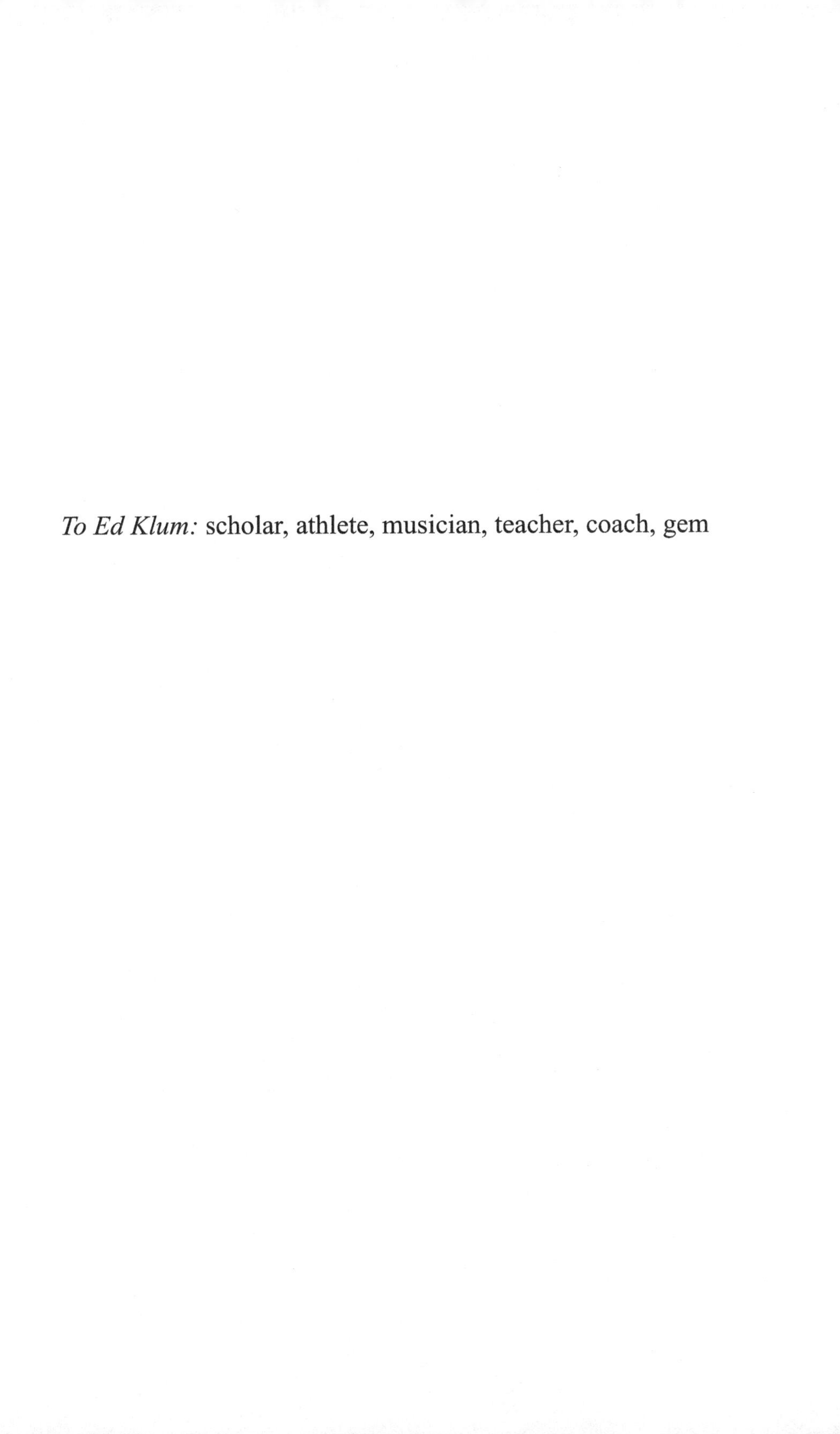

To Ed Klum: scholar, athlete, musician, teacher, coach, gem

TABLE OF CONTENTS

PEOPLE

AMERICA—SOME SNAPSHOTS

ABROAD

ISSUES AND ESSAYS

LANGUAGE

MUSIC

Preface

In my years as a writer and editor, I've titled thousands of pieces—and blogposts and a few books. I have a rule, at least in my head: No titles that are subject to multiple interpretations. I think titles ought to be straightforward and clear in their meaning. I don't like those cleverish titles that "work" on several "levels."

And here I've gone and titled a collection "Digging In." My "rule" is not so much a rule as a guideline, or inclination, or preference.

"Digging In" can be understood at least three ways. You dig in to life, or to a book (maybe particularly a collection of diverse pieces). Think of attacking a feast. Also, "digging in" means getting below the surface of something. And it means increasing one's resolve. You're not weakening or retreating. On the contrary, you're digging in.

There is a saying in politics: "If you're explaining, you're losing." Well, I *am* explaining, but I hope I'm not losing, too badly.

My previous collection was called "Here, There & Everywhere." For this new one, I thought of "Here, There & Everywhere, Volume II." But that takes up a lot of acreage on a cover, especially when you consider the subtitle ("Further Collected Writings of Jay Nordlinger"). You don't want to exhaust the reader before he begins.

The first collection had eight chapters; the present one has six. The first one had a chapter on politics, whereas this one does not. And yet politics infiltrates the book (not wrongly, I trust). The first collection had a whole chapter on golf. This one does not, but it has two pieces about golf: They bookend the chapter called "Issues and Essays." The first one deals with President Obama and his golf habit; the second, the closing one, describes a visit to Augusta National.

That first collection, *Here, There & Everywhere*, had a chapter called "Personal." It was about things pertaining to . . . well, me, the author. *Digging In* has no "Personal." Yet it has plenty of personal. Let me amplify this by telling a couple of stories.

Several years ago, I was writing a history of the Nobel Peace Prize (*Peace, They Say*). A friend of mine—a fellow writer—said, "I hope there will be plenty of you in it. I mean, I hope that it will have your personal touches. I hope you will let something of yourself come through." That was very nice, but I said, "No way. This is a work of history. I'm writing neutrally, objectively, and impersonally. But I'm afraid I will slip through, regardless."

I then told my friend a story about another friend—Patrice Fowler, who was from the South, and an excellent southern cook. One day, she served a meal, and I said, "Pat, is this southern?" She thought for a second and said, "No. But by the time I get through with something, it's southern."

Occasionally, people say to me, "I like your writing style." (They also say they dislike it.) I object to this, believe it or not. I deny that I have a style. I think a writer applies a style—or a sensibility, or an approach—to the subject at hand. Also, the venue may make a difference. (The magazine, newspaper, or website.) There can be no single style. A reporting piece will take one style, a concert review another style, a personal essay another style, and so on.

Consider the musician. The pianist, in particular. When he plays a Clementi sonata, that calls for one style, and when he plays a Scriabin, another.

So, I will explain this to people, and they'll smile at me, indulgently—as though thinking, *Jay is deluding himself. He has a style.* I will let readers—other readers—judge for themselves. If you think that I have a style, across the board, please don't tell me.

Here, There & Everywhere was published in 2007. All the pieces in *Digging In* were written after that time. In selecting them for inclusion in this second volume, I thought about what would make a good variety. A nice bouquet. As for the order, I have not gone chronologically. How have I gone? By feel, frankly. You could have ordered these pieces—and chaptered them, and, for that matter, selected them—in any number of ways.

The opening chapter is "People." You never run out of people, as a journalist. They supply endless and rich material. Bill Buckley used to quote someone (whose name has been forgotten, at least by me): "Ninety-nine out of every hundred people are interesting, and so is the hundredth, for he is the exception."

I'll give you a taste of how these "people" pieces come about. In 2008, I read a news article about an officer in the Special Forces, who had been badly injured. Blinded, even. Yet he had insisted on remaining in the Special Forces—and they let him. I wanted to meet him. I wanted to ask him questions. And I did. And was very glad of it.

In 2013, I attended the funeral of a friend in Salzburg. A man, the head of the local Jewish community, spoke. Someone said to me, "You know, that man is 100 years old. And he survived four concentration camps. He says, 'I could write a Michelin guide to the camps.'" I definitely wanted to meet him. And was glad I did.

Two years later, I read that Julie Kent was retiring. Like the rest of the world, I had always loved this ballerina. Wouldn't it be nice to meet and question her? And wouldn't her retirement make a good excuse, or "peg" (as they say in journalism)? It was a most pleasant hour or so, across a table. When I left the building, my feet barely touched the pavement (not that I'm as nimble, or floaty, as Julie Kent).

After "People" comes "America—Some Snapshots." North Dakota was experiencing an oil boom, a fascinating story: an economic story, yes, and a political one. But mainly a human one. People who hadn't worked in *years*—and had virtually given up *ever* being able to support their family—were working there, in North Dakota.

So, that is one "snapshot" (or series of snapshots, actually). I also went to explosives camp. Explosives camp? Yup, in Rolla, Mo. A friend had told me about it. At this remarkable camp, youngsters learn how to blow things up—responsibly, of course. But still . . . When the campers were sitting at tables, making firework shells, I said to a counselor, "It looks like arts and crafts." True, she answered: "arts and crafts with an edge."

As there are snapshots from around America, there are snapshots from around the world, in "Abroad." The opening piece of that chapter is about the Iraq War. Re-reading that piece, years later, I thought, "How that war has been mythologized, in the years since its ending. How quickly things get twisted, to suit different 'narratives.'" Anyway, readers can ponder this for themselves, and reach their own conclusions.

Of course, that is true at every turn, right?

In the 1960s and '70s, there was a TV program called "Issues and Answers." I think that must have been in the back of my mind when I titled the next chapter "Issues and Essays." In this one, you have subjects from A to Z. Most of the essays, I think, were prompted by current events—or at least by something I read or observed, which tickled my brain, and made my fingers itch (to write). I'll give three examples.

A conference I was to attend—the Oslo Freedom Forum—was postponed at the last minute. Because of a hotel-workers strike. Some months before, Opening Night at Carnegie Hall had been canceled. Because the stagehands union had a grievance. (These guys are rich, by the way.) My fingers itched to write about labor unions, and my mental wrestling with them over the years. So I did.

In December 2013, a pro-Obama group put out an ad promoting ObamaCare. It pictured a young man in pajamas, who became known as "Pajama Boy." People on the conservative side of the aisle said that he simply "looked liberal." So, I wrote an essay on looking like your politics: looking liberal, or looking conservative. Can you judge a book by its cover? (Sometimes yes, sometimes no.)

A year and a half later, I was reading an article about higher education, in which the author made a blunt declaration: Anthropology was "the most pathetic college major" whose name "doesn't end in the word 'studies.'" So—an essay on anthropology and its decline since the glory days. A "lament" for a field.

The next chapter consists of essays too—but they are all on one subject, language. I figured they should have their own chapter. Linguistic issues come up constantly, at least in my mind. My fingers frequently itch to write about language.

In an editorial, the *New York Times* described the Supreme Court's Democratic appointees as "moderate liberals"; the Republican appointees were "conservatives" (no modifier). This led to an essay by me about labels, political or otherwise. I noticed that Vice President Biden was referring to the president, in public, as "Barack." So I wrote an essay about the (tricky) business of first names. Obama said that, henceforth, the mountain in Alaska would be known as "Denali," not "McKinley." From me: a meditation on "the rise and fall of names."

Is that a linguistic issue, properly understood, or more like a name issue? How about the "Barack" essay? I am speaking of language broadly.

In the concluding chapter, "Music," you will find essays. And profiles, of musicians. You could have put some music pieces in "Issues and Essays," and some of them in "People." In any event, music, like language, gets a chapter of its own.

The first two pieces are about two composers as different as it's possible to be, American though they are: Lee Hoiby and Elliott Carter. Curiously enough, I mention Carter in the Hoiby piece, saying that Hoiby once forwarded me a spoof on Carter. Each man was highly interesting, in his distinctive ways.

Some of the music pieces, like other pieces in this volume, were sparked by events. At Obama's second inauguration, Beyoncé sang the national anthem. Or rather, she lip-synched it. Which led to "Faking It and Making It."

Preparing this volume, I of course re-read the pieces. One notices one's tics. And there is repetition in this book, which I have done little or nothing to obviate. In two different pieces, I mention Milton Babbitt and the title of his famous, or infamous, essay: "Who Cares If You Listen?" (1958). But each mention belongs in the particular piece. I also tell a story about Harry Reid—twice, in two different pieces. Again, the story belongs where it is, each time.

When it comes around again, maybe you can pretend you haven't heard it before?

Also, I say that I'm from Ann Arbor—over and over again. After the third or fourth time, you probably register that. And yet my pieces are littered with Ann Arbor, which I trust you won't mind, or will forgive.

Then there is WFB—William F. Buckley Jr. I quote him over and over again. I have a bad case of Buckleyitis. I quoted him just a minute ago, didn't I? More precisely, I quoted his quoting of somebody else. I do some of that in *Digging In*. I quote him quoting someone else. I quote him quoting the same quotation in two different pieces. And, I hate to tell you, those pieces aren't placed very far apart either.

Friends and colleagues sometimes say, "Practically anything can remind Jay of something Bill said or did." Which reminds me of the time he . . .

This is my defense, to the extent I need one: I spent chunks of my life reading him. Thoroughly. I spent a lot of time with him (personally). He just seeped in. Plus, he's quotable, isn't he? As there is something Biblical or Shakespearean for every occasion, there is something Buckleyan.

In this book, there are no photos. But I hope you'll be able to picture people and places regardless. There are no audio recordings either. But I hope you'll hear the voices! *I* heard them, as I re-read the pieces, and that was easy because I had heard them in the first place.

Take Lorin Maazel, the conductor. I asked him, "Why do people sneer at Puccini and Tchaikovsky" (to name two composers)? "Envy," he said, dismissively. I think he even waved his hand a little. I wish you could have heard him: the mixture of pity and contempt for people who make themselves feel good by sneering at people whose talents they can barely fathom.

I wish you could have heard Gene Genovese, the historian—that sharp Brooklynese, directed with deadly aim at various targets. His voice, his speech, was one of the most impressive and delightful things about him.

And I must confess, I laughed out loud on reading my piece about Angela Gheorghiu, the Romanian soprano: "Prima Donna Assoluta." I could just *see* her and *hear* her! In addition to her singing, she is known for her diva antics and episodes. Let me quote from my piece:

> There are books of opera anecdotes, and I suggest to this soprano that books in the future will have whole chapters devoted to her. Yes, she says, "and I'm not finished yet!" I ask her about one of my favorite stories: Did she really demand hair and makeup for a radio interview? No, she says: There was a photo-shoot the same day as the radio interview. Too bad, I say, it's such a good story. Yes, she says, "but I have lots of others."

As I remember, she brightened when she said "but I have lots of others." I think she was trying to cheer me up. And she knew she was dishing up a good quote. She is smart as can be.

I'd better stop now, and let you get on with the book (let you "dig in"). Early in my career, I worried about where my next piece would come from. I soon stopped worrying. There are zillions more pieces than there is time to write them. The world gives a journalist a Niagara. There is horror, there is joy. There's a lot in between.

I feel a paean to journalism coming on, but I said I'd stop . . .

PEOPLE

Captain Extraordinary

Ivan Castro of the U.S. Special Forces

Fort Bragg, N.C.

Captain Ivan Castro will tell you he's an ordinary man, basically. You may wish to disagree. He is an officer in the U.S. Special Forces, and blind. He was blinded while fighting in Iraq about two and a half years ago. He did not then leave the military. He persevered, to an astonishing degree. He has attracted interest all over the country, as well he might.

He was born in Hoboken, N.J. (same as Frank Sinatra), in 1967. His parents were from Puerto Rico. His dad was a cook and other things, and his mother was a factory worker and other things. How he got that interesting name, "Ivan Castro," he doesn't know. His sister's name is Olga! The family moved to Puerto Rico when he was twelve.

He wanted to be a policeman, a fireman, a soldier—"something with action," as he says. He went to a military high school, and joined the Army when he was 20. He expected to stay for four years. He fought in the Gulf War—and continued in the military. "I had done so much in those four years," he says, "it just didn't make any sense for me to get out."

After the Gulf War, he was in Bosnia, Colombia, and other places. And then he was back in combat, this time in Afghanistan. He was a platoon leader in the 82nd Airborne. In due course, he was in Iraq. It was in September 2006 that the mortar blast came. His injuries were extensive: his right eye gone, his left eye beyond repair, his lungs collapsed, etc. There is a long list of injuries and problems. "Believe it or not," he says, "we keep discovering things that are coming up—injuries we weren't aware of."

I have come to see him in his office at Fort Bragg. He is a personable, gregarious man, the kind who puts people at ease. There is also about him the air of command. He's the kind of soldier about whom people say, "Officer material." A white cane leans against the wall. On another wall is a picture of Captain Castro and his wife with President Bush. There is also a letter from Bush.

And Captain Castro has a specially equipped computer—one that reads him his e-mail, for example. He'll tell you, "I used to hunt and peck. But when you're blind, you can't do that. So I had to learn to type."

When that mortar round went off, "I was fighting to stay alive, fighting not to give up. That's all I remember. I knew I didn't want to die. I knew I wanted to come back to my wife and son." He was unconscious for six weeks. Then he woke up and began his recovery. His wife and mother-in-law never left his bedside.

After his surgeries and rehabilitation, the 82nd was "going to send me to the Warrior Transition Battalion"—that would ease the transition out of the military and into some other kind of life. He would begin life as a disabled vet. "But that was not my intent. My intent was to stay in the Army, to continue my service. I had been doing it for more than 18 years. Why should I give it up now?" (Others might have thought of reasons.)

He told Special Operations that "I wanted to serve as long as they gave me the opportunity, and I wanted to be productive. I didn't want to be sitting down licking envelopes and shredding paper." They agreed. His group commander said, "I'm going to treat you like everyone else, like every other captain here. And I'm going to expect a lot out of you"—which is what this captain wanted.

Why did he not simply give up, and slink away? "My mother, my dad—they were really hard workers. My mother was a survivor. They divorced when I was five, and she worked really hard for everything she had. And she taught me to work hard as well." Castro worked a lot as a kid, and "I was the man of the house. When something broke, I had to fix it. Had to figure it out." His military training made him tough, too: Ranger School, the Special Forces Qualification Course. Those are not cakewalks.

Also, he feels he has an example to set: for his peers, for the soldiers who were under his command. About those soldiers, he says, "They kind of look up to me. I can't let them down." There is the public to consider, too: "When I don my beret, and go out with my cane, people stop and stare." He can feel it. And "if you're a Special Forces Ranger, everyone expects more from you. You're never cold, you're never hungry, you're never tired."

Plus, "I got a son who's 15. I got bills to pay. I'm a husband. Just because I'm blind or injured doesn't mean I don't have to pay my mortgage or stuff like that." His wife, Evelyn, was a speech pathologist in a public-school system. Now she works with injured service members in an Army hospital. Castro describes her as his hero. For one thing, "she never expected to be married to a blind guy."

He also has laudatory words for military doctors and nurses: "We think about the soldiers that get hurt, and we don't think of the doctors and nurses who every day have to see the trauma and suffering that service members go through. It's tough on them. I'm pretty sure they have some post-traumatic stress as well."

Last year, Ivan Castro ran five marathons. (Best time: 4 hours, 11 minutes. He hopes to break the four-hour barrier this year.) He also did a triathlon. And climbed Grays Peak in Colorado (14,270 ft.). He lives life with gusto, whether running a marathon or visiting a museum: "I went to the Air Force Museum in Dayton. I didn't see it with my eyes, but they let me put my hands on the aircraft. Incredible." At Fort Bragg, he oversees the Spanish-language lab and carries out various administrative and logistical tasks, "making sure that soldiers are ready to deploy."

He wanted to command an A-team, but "that wasn't meant to be, so maybe, by taking this job here, I can clear somebody from having to do this job," and let such a person "do the things that I wanted to do: go out and lead." (Have you heard anything nobler than that lately?) "Right now, my main focus is what I can do to help other service members, and anyone else. It's not about Ivan."

He speaks before groups all over the country: various associations and organizations. He does a lot of teaching, too, particularly of those who face severe challenges, physical and mental. And he wants to accept no limitations. "If someone tells me I can't do something, I have to keep myself from punching him in the nose. Instead of saying that I can't do something, let's figure out a way for me to do it."

And how are his spirits? "I'm not going to lie to you: We all have our good times and bad times. I'm just like anyone else." When the doctors told him he would never see again, "I was extremely, extremely bitter. I was at the point where I asked the Lord above, 'Why me?' I was bitter with the Lord, angry with the Lord."

One day, "my wife came in and told me, 'Ivan, if you could only see the hospital ward: You just don't know how fortunate we are.' It's sad to say, but other service members have had to make a huge sacrifice. I have to be grateful for what I have, instead of dwelling on what I don't have. I miss not seeing, I'm not going to lie to you. But I have two legs, two arms, I can talk, I can eat, I can laugh. I have my memory."

Further, "I'm a military guy, and I speak in military terms: God has a mission for me. A plan, an operation."

Castro has what he calls his "demons in the darkness," or "demons in the closet." And "the closet is my brain. I don't see anything. I'm totally blind. I have no light perception. And when the demons want to take over, as soon as they try to, I try to keep them out. I think about all the things I'm grateful for: my wife, my son, the Lord above, His mission for me." There are days "when I walk into the wall, both literally and figuratively. I try to take a step back and not get angry and figure out a way to go around things."

And "you know the best thing about being blind?" (I couldn't imagine what the answer would be.) "I saw for 39 years. So I was able to see the world for 39 years. I've traveled around the world. I saw the good, the bad, and the ugly. The good thing about now is: Everything is beautiful, in my mind. The grass is always green. There's never graffiti on the walls. There's no trash. Everybody looks good—everybody's in shape, everybody's a movie star or rock star." And race is out the window: "There's no brown, white, or black."

A visit with Ivan Castro will teach you, or remind you, not to complain. It will remind you what a free people owes its warriors. And it will remind you to be in awe of those who do the awe-inspiring.

—February 9, 2009

UP FROM LEFTISM

A visit with the historian Gene Genovese

Atlanta, Ga.

"The first time my name appeared in the *New York Times*, I was described as 'an obscure associate professor,'" says Eugene D. Genovese. "I've always thought of myself that way." He's the only one who does. Genovese is an American historian, specializing in the Old South. In 2005, Benjamin Schwarz, an editor at *The Atlantic*, described him as "this country's greatest living historian." One could certainly make an argument. Genovese is definitely one of the smartest and most interesting people around. He made a spectacular journey from left to right: from Communism to anti-Communism, from faith in Marx to faith in God. He made this journey in tandem with his wife, another historian, the late Elizabeth Fox-Genovese.

A son of New York, he lives in Atlanta, in a handsome, quiet neighborhood of brick houses. I say to him, "I guess it's appropriate that an historian of the South should live in the South—though I understand that Atlanta is not a southern city." It's not, says Genovese. But "it's just southern enough so that life is more pleasant. People are more courteous, things are more civilized . . ."

Genovese encountered *National Review* long before a visit from me, one of its editors. He wrote an essay for the magazine in 1970—when he was in the full flower of his Marxism. The essay was for *NR*'s 15th anniversary issue. Our editors wanted a piece from a liberal point of view—it was written by Charles Frankel—and a piece from a Left point of view. (In those days, the difference between liberalism and leftism was far better understood.) Genovese's piece was titled, simply, "The Fortunes of the Left." *NR*'s James Burnham paid Genovese what he calls one of the highest compliments he has ever received. On reading the piece, Burnham said, "It's good. It's very good. It's much too good for my taste."

In the essay, one can see clearly the conservatism brewing inside Genovese. For one thing, he zestfully bashes the New Left and the counterculture. "The Weathermen would be laughed out of the Left," he writes, "were it not for the sobering thought that these pitiable young bourgeois will get themselves and some other people killed before the newspapers and TV, which invented them, stop finding them cute." He also mocks "the terrified elements of the Right and Center who interpret their own inability to discipline their children as the beginning of the end of civilization," adding, "I suspect that it is, in fact, only the beginning of the end of the quaint notion that children can be raised without occasional spankings."

As you might be able to tell, Genovese's essay is laced with humor—which, at least in my experience, is not a hallmark of the Left. He tells me, "Even my worst enemies always acknowledged that I had a sense of humor. My party friends did not always appreciate that." You know which party he means (the Communist). Moreover, he has always been a cultural conservative, he says, having no use for the slovenly, jejune, or vulgar. The Communist party of his youth had been "a very puritanical party," he notes. "If we had gone to a meeting not properly dressed, we would have heard about it later."

Before I came down here from New York, I asked Genovese, "Can I bring you anything from your hometown?" He answered, "Maybe a few heads." He was born in 1930 and grew up in Dyker Heights, Brooklyn. To this day, you could cut his Brooklyn accent with a knife. All his travels, worldliness, and scholarship have not dimmed it an iota. His parents were Italian-American, his father a dockworker, his mother a homemaker. The Depression was very hard on the family. "The year 1938 was particularly brutal," says Genovese. "I was eight years old. I will never forget it." Incidentally, the family pronounced their name JEN-o-veez. In his twenties, the historian started pronouncing it *all'italiana*: Jen-o-VAY-zay. He has never been "Eugene," except to his elementary-school teachers. People call him Gene.

He went to Brooklyn College, while working a full-time job. It's easy if you can manage on four and a half hours' sleep. Not wanting to waste his education on "baby courses," as he says, Genovese sought out the toughest and most rewarding teachers. One of them was Arthur C. Cole, an authority on the Civil War. Genovese learned a lot about the South in his undergraduate years. He had grown up with the notion of southerners as either bumpkins or sadists. But he soon realized he had been "swindled": The southern intellectuals, at least, were a very serious lot. General attitudes toward the South are still "idiotic," says Genovese, even "childish."

The undergrad went on to Columbia Graduate School, where his teachers included Dumas Malone, "a fine old gentleman." What about Malone's famous six-volume biography of Jefferson? "A great work." Another professor was Frank Tannenbaum, a renowned Latin Americanist. "He knew the inner life of Peru, the inner life of Mexico, to an extraordinary degree," says Genovese. Once an anarchist—a follower of Emma Goldman who had spent time in prison—Tannenbaum had become very conservative. And "there I was, sitting in his classroom as a Marxist. He could not have been more encouraging to me. His attitude was, I was going to grow out of it."

Genovese is a great mimic and raconteur, with a phenomenal memory, and he entertains me with impressions and stories. How many people today can do Max Shachtman? We're talking about a Trotskyist leader, a fairly big deal once upon a time. Genovese attended the legendary debate between Shachtman and Earl Browder, the deposed Communist chief. "Shachtman had a face like a pig," Genovese says, "and he talked that way." He was also a fantastic rhetorician.

But Communism wasn't all fun and games, as Genovese would be the first to tell you. In 1994, he wrote this terrible truth: "At the age of fifteen, I became a Communist, and, although expelled from the party in 1950 at age twenty, I remained a supporter of the international movement and of the Soviet Union until there was nothing left to support." In his living room, Genovese explains to me something about his younger self: He was under no illusion that Stalin wasn't killing people left and right. It was simply that he had "absorbed the notion that this was a period we had to go through," in order to form a more perfect union, so to speak. People have a tremendous capacity to rationalize, especially when infected by ideology.

In the course of his professorial career, Genovese would teach at several universities, among them Rutgers, Rochester, and Emory. He makes a very funny remark, although one he doesn't intend to be funny, at all: "In the old days, many departments wouldn't take me because I was on the left." Then, when he wasn't so Left anymore, "the Left had taken over the departments." Timing is everything, as they say.

He caused a big, national stir in 1965—that was his "15 minutes of fame," he says, though he has had many more minutes than that. At Rutgers, he stated that he would welcome a victory by the Vietcong. Therefore, he became an issue in the New Jersey gubernatorial campaign that year. Former vice president Richard Nixon and other Republicans said that Rutgers ought to fire him: A professor at a public university was openly in favor of the enemy in time of war. Rutgers refused to fire him. I ask Genovese—not 100 percent sure what the answer will be—whether he thinks the university was right. He does. He points out that he never proselytized in the classroom. Besides, there was academic freedom to consider. He further recalls that, while the Young Republicans on campus were in favor of his firing, the Young Conservatives, to their right, were not. They too stood on academic-freedom grounds.

In coming years, Genovese would win the highest honors in his profession. First came the Bancroft Prize, for his quickly canonical book *Roll, Jordan, Roll: The World the Slaves Made*. Then came the presidency of the Organization of American Historians. In rising to this position, Genovese made a little history himself, because he was the first Marxist president of the organization. But as the years wore on, he moved rightward, until the collapse of the Soviet Union and its empire forced a major, decisive reexamination.

In 1994, he published a bombshell of an essay in *Dissent* magazine. (I quoted from it earlier.) The essay was called "The Question," and the question derived from Watergate: "What did you know, and when did you know it?" What did you know about the atrocities of the Communists, and when did you know it? Genovese wrote that "in a noble effort to liberate the human race from violence and oppression we broke all records for mass slaughter, piling up tens of millions of corpses in less than three-quarters of a century. When the Asian figures are properly calculated, the aggregate to our credit may reach the seemingly incredible numbers widely claimed. Those who are big on multiculturalism might note that the great majority of our victims were nonwhite."

Genovese wanted his fellow Marxists to take stock of their assumptions, prejudices, and careers, as he himself had. But few were willing to go along. As a class, Genovese's colleagues were furious with him. I ask whether, in writing the essay, he had the sense of writing a professional-suicide note. (I don't mean to shock you, but they don't take kindly to anti-Communists in academia.) He says he knew he was saying goodbye—he was writing a farewell letter. "A lot of my friends broke relations, which I always thought was stupid. To break relations over political matters, you have to be an idiot. You must remember that today's enemies are tomorrow's allies, and vice versa. You might as well retain civil relations."

It was a stroke of luck, or a stroke of grace, that Genovese and his wife, Betsey, moved to the right and moved toward religion—Catholicism, specifically—at the same time. Neither left the other behind. "We had different temperaments," says Genovese, "but our brains were almost as one. We very rarely disagreed on things." One disagreement, whether intellectual or temperamental, was on Wagner's music: She hated it, he loves it.

In the field of politics, the two once thought that America could have a different kind of socialism, a socialism consonant with the American traditions of liberty and democracy. They came to the conclusion, however, that this was impossible. Oppression was baked into the socialist cake. Genovese is unwilling to call himself a free-marketeer, believing that the "logic" of the free market "leaves an awful lot of people in the gutter." But he would support most free-market measures, because "the alternatives are dreadful." The policies of such politicians as Mitt Romney and Chris Christie strike him as sensible.

One issue he is perfectly firm on is abortion: He is against. So was Betsey, the creator of the leading Women's Studies department in the country, no less. (It was at Emory.) In 2009, Genovese published a beautiful little volume called *Miss Betsey: A Memoir of Marriage*. He writes, "She gagged on abortion for a simple reason: She knew, as everyone knows, that an abortion kills a baby."

At some point in our conversation, we discuss Israel, a country that Genovese is now very much for, another of the changes that have occurred in him. I bring up Edward Said—the late Palestinian scholar and rationalizer of terror—and quote something that Paul Johnson said about him: a "malevolent liar and propagandist, who has been responsible for more harm than any other intellectual of his generation." Who else, in Genovese's estimation, has done significant harm? He suggests Michel Foucault, the philosopher. "But, you know, these Frenchmen, they come and they go." I ask about Noam Chomsky. "I don't understand him," says Genovese, "because clearly God gave him a very good brain, and yet for decades he has written the most rigid and knee-jerk stuff."

Genovese thinks that American education is in sorry shape, and he bases this opinion in part on what he saw with his own eyes: In his last years in the classroom—the early 1990s—his graduate students came to him knowing all too little. They had not been adequately taught in elementary school, junior high school, high school, or college. It's not that the students were any less bright than they had ever been: They were simply ignorant.

Turning to the president of the United States, I ask Genovese to classify him for me. What is Obama? A McGovernite, a social democrat, a socialist, a pinko, a red? Genovese says that Obama is redder than people suspect, even his conservative adversaries. Obama's instinct, he says, is to take the most radical position he can get away with. What's more, he is "probably the vainest president I can remember, and the least competent. What surprised me was the incompetence. The first time I laid eyes on this guy—I heard him make a speech—I said, 'He's a demagogue.' One more. More skillful than most. I mean, he is clearly a good speechifier. I say 'speechifier' because, in a classical sense, an orator he's not.

You just have to read Demosthenes and Cicero to know what an orator is. He ain't it. Churchill yes, him no. And furthermore he butchers the English language. Gets away with it. But he does."

All his life, Genovese had been hoping for a black president and a woman president. So, "we got a black president—thanks a lot." Still, Genovese allows, Obama's election was an historic occasion, symbolizing the huge progress we have made as a country. I ask whether he is hopeful or depressed about the future for black Americans. He regrets that he is more depressed than hopeful. "Look," he says (and he begins a great many sentences with "Look"): "They have a thoroughly corrupt leadership, and I don't just mean the politicians, I mean the intelligentsia too." He cites Cornel West, who, he says, had the choice to be a serious and useful scholar or a rabble-rousing clown, and went down the wrong path.

Genovese is far from a picture of despair, however. There is fight in him. He once chided the great Irving Kristol for saying that the "culture wars" were over and that the Left had won. "The culture wars haven't even been fought!" Genovese says. "It's not at all inevitable that the Left is going to win. I'm not convinced that the present madness will last forever. Some of the damage will remain, though."

Here at his home in Atlanta, Genovese continues to work. He has just come out with a book started jointly with his wife and finished by him: *Fatal Self-Deception: Slaveholding Paternalism in the Old South*. He has no e-mail, fax machine, or cellphone. He has a home phone, whose number is unlisted. He follows baseball, he watches Fox News. He gets along fine, as near as I can tell.

And there is a heroic aspect about him. Writing about Genovese in 1995, William F. Buckley Jr. said, essentially, that the 20th century—the bloodiest on record—was a hard teacher. Genovese had learned his way through. "Is this learning to be compared with 'learning' that the earth is round, not flat? No, because the physical features of the earth are not deniable. But it is different in the social sciences. Everything is deniable, or ignorable." The terrible costs of Communism and its cousins, including socialism, Genovese could not deny or ignore. He said goodbye to a Left that had loved him and lionized him. His truth-telling exposed him to their total wrath and condemnation. Genovese is not only brilliant, he is brave. A hell of a lot of fun, too.

—November 14, 2011

Über-Survivor

Marko Feingold flourishes at 100

Salzburg, Austria

Marko Feingold has a very good memory. His memories begin in 1916, when he was three. The Feingold family lived in Vienna. There were four children, all boys. One of them was a baby, Emil. Their father was off at war. Their mother habitually rose at 4 to stand in line for milk and bread. She took her ration card, and she took her baby. Women with babies got to the head of the line faster. That was important, because sometimes the city ran out of bread and milk.

It was cold in the winter, and the baby caught pneumonia and died. The way Marko Feingold puts it today is, "Three of us lived, because our brother died." There was milk and bread for the children at home because their mother took the baby.

Feingold has vivid memories of that first war—and the deprivations of Vienna. He remembers exactly what the bread looked and tasted like: It was all crumbs, not able to hang together. He remembers when his sister, Rosa, came along in 1918. The other kids were put out of the house while she was being born.

Marko Feingold was born in May 1913—more than a year before the war began. He would experience the next war too, of course. He survived four concentration camps: Auschwitz, Neuengamme, Dachau, and Buchenwald. He has been known to quip, "I could write a Michelin guide to the camps." Today, he is the president of the Jewish community here in Salzburg. It's hard to believe he's 100. He is fit, sharp, active. He walks at a good clip. The words come easily: He's in full command of facts, names, dates. He seems not to tire. He has almost a full head of hair, and much of it is dark. It doesn't look dyed, either. He is a handsome, dashing gent, with a twinkle in his eye. With his mustache, he looks almost raffish.

Before World War II came the Depression, of course. In Vienna, people were sleeping on bridges. Feingold and his brother Ernst went down to Italy, where life was sweeter. They were there from 1932 to 1938. Feingold says those were his six fat years: his best years. In early '38, he and Ernst returned to Vienna, to get their passports renewed. The Anschluss took place on March 12. They were nabbed by the Nazis, and an unimaginable ordeal began.

Never believe, says Feingold, that Austria was the "first victim," as propaganda once had it. That the country was unwillingly occupied by the Germans. Most Austrians rejoiced in the Anschluss. "The country welcomed the Germans with open arms," says Feingold. He grew up with plenty of anti-Semitism, and was discriminated against, like others. But did he ever suspect that his neighbors and countrymen would turn against the Jews, murderously, genocidally? No.

He and Ernst were the first Austrians to be confined at Auschwitz. The camp was still under construction. From Auschwitz, Marko was sent on to one camp after the other. About every day in these camps, he says, "you could write a whole book." He has written his memoirs (available only in German). Their title might be translated "When You've Already Died, You Feel No Pain."

Needless to say, Feingold endured much torture, starvation, and other evils. I will mention a single detail: He and other inmates were forced to dig a canal with their bare hands. Ernst died in 1942. The fates of the other two siblings—Rosa and their brother Nathan—are unknown, specifically. They can be presumed killed in the Holocaust. Marko was still in Buchenwald on April 11, 1945, when the Americans came in. With other Austrians, he walked the few miles to Weimar, got on a bus, and headed home.

How did Feingold survive the camps? Was it luck, bravery, cleverness, some combination? He smiles and says—more like sighs—one word: "Zufall." That means chance, coincidence, happenstance, amazing turns of events. For example, he was classified as "gassable" at Neuengamme. But the crematoria at the camp were not ready yet. Meanwhile, he was shipped to Dachau . . .

After the war, he could not return to his hometown, Vienna, because the authorities there would not allow Jews back in—or anyone else who had been imprisoned in the camps. These people would know who did what, when. And the Jews might want their property back. By unlikely twists and turns—*Zufall*—Feingold wound up in Salzburg.

Those guilty of war crimes got off lightly, he says. The Nuremberg trials took care of a few, but just a few. He says, with great specificity, that officials of the Catholic Church and of the Red Cross helped Nazis escape to South America. In Austro-Germany, the standard line was, "The SS men were bad, yes. But everyone else was merely swept up in the madness."

Feingold spent the first three years after the war—1945 to 1948—engaged in the Bricha. This was the movement to smuggle Jews into Palestine, soon to be Israel. ("Bricha," in Hebrew, means "escape" or "flight.") The work was illegal and dangerous. According to Feingold, there were about 250,000 Jews in the Salzburg area: displaced persons. About 150,000 of them wanted to go to America, Canada, or Australia, where many had relatives. The other 100,000 wanted to settle in Palestine.

Feingold helped them get down to Italy, where they would take ships—leaky, barely seaworthy ones—across the Mediterranean. These bedraggled, wretched Jews from Eastern Europe and Russia knew nothing about the Alps. Few had proper shoes or warm clothing. They were afraid of heights. Feingold led them at night, so they would see less. He told them to hug the mountainside and not look down.

He himself did not go to Palestine. Why? With a smile, he shows me an old photograph: "That is why." The photo is of himself and a blonde woman, his first wife, Else. He met her two months after he got out of the camps. She was a Catholic Salzburger. They were married until she died in 1992. In 1998, he married his present wife, Hanna. Feingold feels like an Austrian, by the way. He always has, through everything.

Austrian though he may be, he knows a lot about Israel, and cares a lot about it. He scorns the world's scorn of it. I ask a hard question: Does he believe Israel will survive? He doesn't really answer, instead saying, "It has to survive." Where else would the 6 million Jews there go?

In Salzburg, he owned a clothing store, then two: "Wiener Mode," or "Viennese Fashion." He retired more than 35 years ago, in 1977. But his other work—from which he will never retire, I'm sure—has been to tell people about the Holocaust. Since 1945, he has been to something like 6,000 schools in Austria and Bavaria. He has been to other institutions too, including prisons and churches. Most people are receptive to what he has to say. He makes a common observation, however: Germany has been more forthright in acknowledging the past than Austria has. Much more. In Austria, people are "still lying," says Feingold: lying about the Austrian role in Nazism.

I decide to ask a timeworn and unanswerable question: How do you explain anti-Semitism? Why does the world hate Jews? Feingold answers quickly and confidently: "Envy. Jealousy." He goes on to say, among other things, that Jewish families were always close-knit. Family members helped one another, and they prospered. This made others resentful.

"Slowly, slowly," says Feingold, anti-Semitism in Austria is lessening. It is stronger in the countryside than in towns and cities. He makes an observation that is somewhat lighthearted: These days, everyone says, "I had a Jewish great-grandfather," or, "I had a Jewish aunt," or, "My father was half-Jewish." There once was a time when no one, ever, admitted to a Jewish relative.

Feingold says that he and the archbishop of Salzburg are "like brothers." The archbishop calls him "my elder brother"; he calls the archbishop "my younger brother." Feingold is a very liberal-minded and ecumenical person. "I work with Muslims, Catholics, atheists, anybody," he says.

In a typical day, he gets up at 5. "I check to see if anything hurts. If it does, I say, 'Okay, I'm alive.'" He has breakfast and reads the papers. He arrives at his office by 8—he works in Salzburg's synagogue. He deals with his correspondence and phone calls. He attends all sorts of events: He is a pillar of the general community, not just the Jewish one. He has received many honors, local and national. There are about 70 Jews living in Greater Salzburg. Feingold knows maybe 30 of them. The rest? Many opt to keep their heads down.

A believer in Holocaust remembrance, Feingold has returned to all four of the camps in which he was confined. At home, he has helped to lay "Stolpersteine": little stones that commemorate victims of the Nazis—not just Jews but Gypsies, Jehovah's Witnesses, homosexuals, and others.

I ask Feingold whether he has ever suffered from survivor's guilt. No, he says. "Anyone who thinks like that is crazy." Does he believe in God? Yes, but he is not especially religious, or observant. Does he have any bitterness toward his persecutors? No. Does he forgive them? "It's difficult," he says, "because those people aren't living anymore. How can I forgive them?" But then he says, "For myself, I forgive. But for others, I have no right to forgive."

His main concern is "never again." He warns incessantly against dictatorship. There must be no brainwashing of the young, no dictatorship in any form: "not from the left, not from the right, and not from religion."

Naturally, he does not have a wealth of peers left. A Holocaust survivor in Bad Ischl, about 25 miles from Salzburg, died recently at 106. Toward the end of our visit, I ask Feingold a boring, standard question—one that every person of advanced age must face: "To what do you attribute your longevity?" He smiles, glances upward, shrugs a little, and says, "Zufall."

—September 16, 2013

The Anti-Che

Felix Rodriguez, freedom fighter and patriot

Miami, Fla.

Felix Rodriguez seems fated to be linked to Che Guevara. This is not entirely just. Rodriguez loves freedom, and has worked tirelessly for it; Guevara loved tyranny, and worked tirelessly for it. "Two sides of the same coin," some people say. Maybe—but only in the way that light and dark are two sides of the same coin. Rodriguez had a role in stopping Guevara. He was there, in the Bolivian mountains, in 1967. He was the last person to talk with Guevara—a man who did so much to tyrannize the country where Rodriguez was born, Cuba.

The story of Guevara's last day has been told many times, in many ways. Rodriguez told it in his 1989 memoir, *Shadow Warrior*. It is told in a book published earlier this year, *Daybreak at La Higuera*, by Rafael Cerrato, a Spaniard. La Higuera is the village where Guevara met his end. Cerrato's main sources for the book are Rodriguez, who was working for the Central Intelligence Agency, and Dariel Alarcón Ramírez, whose nom de guerre was Benigno. A Cuban, Benigno was Guevara's lieutenant in Bolivia. He was also a member of Fidel Castro's inner circle. He defected in 1996—and now he and Rodriguez are friends.

Just a week ago, Rodriguez made a donation to the CIA Museum: ashes from Guevara's last pipe. But he has a few more of those ashes here, in his Miami home. His den is chock-a-block with mementos. On the wall, for example, is a bond signed by José Martí, Cuba's national hero. In this den, we talk about events past, present, and future. Rodriguez is an excellent talker (as well as doer). He is large, sharp, and commanding.

He was born in 1941. His hometown is Sancti Spíritus, in central Cuba. His father was a storeowner; his mother helped out in the store and tended the house. Rodriguez's earliest memory is of being with his mom while she talked about what Hitler was doing in Europe. The little boy was scared that the Nazis would come to Cuba. Among his forebears are notable figures from Cuba's wars of independence. One of these figures is Alejandro Rodríguez Velasco, who would become the first popularly elected mayor of Havana. In 1895, Máximo Gómez sent a letter to Alejandro's wife—who had asked whether her husband might come home from the field. Gómez wrote her a tender letter about the value of fighting for freedom. This letter is one of Felix Rodriguez's treasures.

And who was Máximo Gómez? Cubans know: He was an officer from the Dominican Republic, who went to Cuba to help that country win its independence from Spain. For Cubans, he is a Lafayette. In the 1980s, Felix Rodriguez went to El Salvador, as a private citizen, to help that country defeat a Castro-backed Communist insurgency. The alias he adopted: Max Gomez. Here in his den, he reads out the letter from the original Gómez—and chokes up.

When he was about twelve, an uncle offered him the chance to study in the United States. Felix was reluctant at first, because he loved his life in Cuba. But another uncle, who had studied in Paris, said, "Think hard about this. This is a rare opportunity, and if you pass it up, you'll regret it." Felix heeded this advice. And he chose a school in Pennsylvania, because he wanted to see snow. The school was called Perkiomen, in Pennsburg, not far from Philadelphia. When he was a junior in high school, his country experienced its cataclysmic event: the takeover by Castro and his fellow revolutionaries. Felix's parents were on vacation in Mexico. (It turned out to be a long vacation.) Felix, just 17, determined to fight the Communists, as soon as possible.

It was possible through something called the Anti-Communist Legion of the Caribbean, being formed in the Dominican Republic—which itself was ruled by a dictator, Trujillo. Felix joined up against his parents' will. He arrived in Santo Domingo—or Ciudad Trujillo, as it was then—on July 4, 1959. He hoped that this date, the Fourth of July, would be as auspicious for Cubans as it had been for Americans. The Anti-Communist Legion staged just one mission into Cuba, a disaster: Castro was waiting for them, and all the troops were killed or captured. Rodriguez had been excluded from the mission at the last second. A friend of his, Roberto Martín Pérez, was captured and spent the next 28 years in Castro's prisons. Rodriguez vowed to keep doing what he could.

One of the themes of his life is that too few people know what it is to have your country seized by totalitarians. In a *60 Minutes* piece, aired in 1989, Mike Wallace asked Rodriguez why he was helping the Salvadorans. "What is it, are you a war-lover? Is that it? Are you constantly in search of adventure?" Rodriguez replied, in short, that people in general are clueless. You can read about Communism, but until you have experienced it for yourself, you have no idea. Also, there is the experience of exile: to be ripped from your country and family and friends, and not be able to return.

Many people think of Castro and his brother as Northern European–style socialists who occasionally get a little rough—or as traditional caudillos who flavor their speech with Marxism-Leninism. In reality, they are in the mold of Hoxha or Ceauşescu, monsters. And the Castros' grip on Cuba is monstrous. Like many Cubans and Cuban Americans, Rodriguez often refers to Fidel Castro simply as "he" or "him." Equally often, he refers to him as "the son-of-a-bitch."

At the beginning of 1961, he had an idea: He would assassinate the son-of-a-bitch. It would avoid or shorten the coming war, he reasoned. He and a friend volunteered their services—and the CIA accepted. The Agency equipped Rodriguez with a German rifle, which had a telescopic sight. The Agency also added a radio operator to the team. Three times, this team headed to Cuba on a luxurious yacht, whose captain was American and whose crew was made up of tough, hardened Ukrainians and Romanians, bearing East Bloc weapons. Rodriguez later heard that the yacht belonged to Sargent Shriver, President Kennedy's brother-in-law. All three times, something went awry, and the Agency changed its mind about the assassination mission. In late February of '61, Rodriguez was sent into Cuba as part of an infiltration team, whose mission was to help the Cuban resistance in advance of the invasion: an invasion that would be known as the Bay of Pigs.

Rodriguez's mission was, of course, harrowing, with many close calls. But it was not without its amusing elements. One day, Rodriguez and a companion approached a beach. Not thinking, Rodriguez said to a militiaman, "Is it okay to use this beach or is it private?" The militiaman said, "*Compañero*, where you been? There aren't any private beaches anymore. They all belong to the people!" "Oh, right," said Rodriguez. "Thanks, *compañero*. Power to the Revolution!" But Rodriguez was soon warned away from a particular stretch of beach: which was marked off for Fidel Castro himself.

In his Miami den, Rodriguez gives a detailed account of the Bay of Pigs, an operation that earned the name "fiasco." The blunders of the American planners are almost unbelievable. The Cubans had confidence until the end, says Rodriguez: America was John Wayne. And John Wayne never loses. Until he did. After the Bay of Pigs, Cuban hopes sank, and Castro cemented his power. Fear gripped the island. People shrank from resistance, understandably. Rodriguez managed to get to the Venezuelan embassy in Havana, where he was sheltered for five months: He left Cuba in September 1961. He would not be sheltered in the Venezuelan embassy today: The government in Caracas regards the Castro dictatorship as a model. Venezuelan oil helps sustain the Castro dictatorship. As Rodriguez sees it, Venezuela's president, Nicolás Maduro, is loyal to the Castros, like a son to a father (two of them). Maduro's predecessor, Hugo Chávez, was likewise loyal.

Rodriguez married a Cuban girl he met when he was 14—"It was love at first sight." He and Rosa had two children, Rosemarie and Felix Jr. The family settled into American life—but not entirely. They were between countries, in a sense, as so many others in South Florida were. Then, in 1967, came Felix's rendezvous with Guevara.

The old Argentinean guerrilla was in Bolivia to lead a revolution, to impose on that country what he had already helped impose on Cuba. The "old" guerrilla was 39; Rodriguez was 26. He was assigned by the CIA to assist Bolivian forces in tracking Guevara down. What was his role in the ultimate success? We can say this: Rodriguez's skillfully gentle interrogation of a young guerrilla prisoner helped the Bolivians home in on the guerrilla leader. On October 9, Rodriguez met this leader face to face, in the mud-brick schoolhouse in La Higuera. You can imagine some of the emotion. Guevara had killed many people, personally, back in Cuba—mainly at La Cabaña, his fortress headquarters. Before they died, the Cubans shouted, "Viva Cuba libre!" ("Long live free Cuba!") and "Viva Cristo Rey!" ("Long live Christ the King!"). And now Rodriguez had him at his feet.

Guevara was a cocky killer, but he was not so cocky at this moment. Still, he had an air of command. Said Rodriguez, "Che Guevara, I want to talk to you." Said Guevara, "No one interrogates me." But talk they did—about philosophy, life, and death. Rodriguez asked him about the people he killed at La Cabaña. Guevara said they were all "foreigners." He himself had been a foreigner in Cuba, of course. And as Rodriguez pointed out to him, he was a foreigner in Bolivia. Guevara answered, "These are matters of the proletariat that are beyond your comprehension." Rodriguez asked how he, an Argentinean physician, could have become president of the Cuban national bank. Guevara told him a funny story: One day, Castro said to his top cadres, "Who here is a dedicated economist," or *economista*? Guevara thought he had said *comunista*—and raised his hand. That's how he became president of the national bank. Rodriguez thought he might be kidding—but later, Benigno, the Cuban defector, confirmed the story. He had been present, sitting right next to Guevara.

Rodriguez's orders from Washington were to do everything he could to keep Guevara alive. Then, the prisoner would be transported to Panama, to be interrogated by the Americans. But the Bolivians had the authority in this matter. It was their war, their country—and they wanted him dead. Rodriguez gave the prisoner the news. "It's better this way, Felix," said Guevara. "I should never have been captured alive." Rodriguez said to him, "*Comandante*, do you want me to say anything to your family if I ever have the opportunity?" After an interval, Guevara said, "Yes. Tell Fidel that he will soon see a triumphant revolution in America" (i.e., South America). "And tell my wife to get remarried and try to be happy." The two men embraced. Then Rodriguez walked out of the schoolhouse. (He was never to meet Guevara's family.)

The Bolivian officer in charge, Joaquín Zenteno Anaya, had offered Rodriguez the chance to finish Guevara off. Guevara had done Rodriguez's country so much harm, Zenteno said. It was only right that he have the opportunity. But he declined. It was left to a Bolivian sergeant. Rodriguez has always maintained that Guevara died with courage and dignity. He admired him for it, and still does. But that's as far as his admiration goes.

He remembers meeting a woman some 30 years ago, whose son had been executed at La Cabaña. He was 15 years old. She went to the fortress to beg for his life. Guevara received her. This was on a Monday. He called an assistant and said, "When is this prisoner scheduled to be executed?" On Friday, he was told. The prisoner's mother thought Guevara was going to grant a reprieve. Instead, he said, "Get him and execute him now, so his mother doesn't have to wait until Friday." She fainted. Says Rodriguez, "He was a very, very cruel man."

What does he think when he sees Guevara's face on all those T-shirts? What does he think of the people who wear those T-shirts? Mainly that they are ignorant, having no idea who Guevara was or what he did or what he stood for. One day, Benigno and his wife saw a young Frenchman in a Che shirt. His wife asked him, "Who is that fellow on your shirt?" The young man answered, "A rock singer."

Rodriguez became an American citizen in 1969. And he volunteered for Vietnam. From 1970 to 1972, he was in special operations. He told the Vietnamese with whom he worked, "I've already lost *my* country," meaning his original country, "but it's not too late for *you*: You can fight for *your* country." One Christmas, after he was back home in Miami, he received a card from a Vietnamese comrade named Hoa. "Do you think the United States will ever abandon us?" asked Hoa. Rodriguez wrote back and said no. In his view, the U.S. did in fact abandon the Vietnamese, in 1975. He is of the school that says the U.S. won the war militarily but lost it politically, and shamefully. After their triumph, the Vietnamese Communists killed about a million.

In 1976, Rodriguez left the CIA, for several reasons. One had to do with security. In May of that year, Zenteno, the Bolivian, was gunned down in Paris. He had been serving as his country's ambassador to France. Claiming responsibility was a group that called itself the International Che Guevara Brigade. Not long after, Rodriguez received a call at home. In Spanish, a man asked for "Felix Ramos." Then he said, "You're next." That name, Felix Ramos, had been Rodriguez's alias in Bolivia. (Unlike "Max Gomez," it had no political or historical significance.) The Agency offered to give Rodriguez and his family new identities and move them to a different state. But Rodriguez decided against: too disruptive. So, the Agency added security enhancements to his house, bullet-proofed his car, and took some other measures. They also gave him a very high award: the Intelligence Star, for valor.

For some years, the Cuban dictatorship had a price on Rodriguez's head. From Benigno, Rodriguez learned that Raúl Castro had a special interest in him. There were at least three plots against Rodriguez. Is there still a price on his head? He thinks not: "The Cuban government has enough problems without worrying about me. But it's always possible that some crazy guy will try to do something to congratulate himself."

Rodriguez has a lot to say about the Carter years—none of it good—but we will skip ahead to the Reagan years. In 1985, Rodriguez went to El Salvador, as a private citizen, and as Max Gomez. He flew hundreds of combat missions with Salvadoran forces, applying what he had learned about counterinsurgency. He told the Salvadorans exactly what he had told the Vietnamese: "It may be too late for Cuba, but it's not too late for you." El Salvador remained out of Communist hands and took a democratic path (however stony). Like all astute observers, Rodriguez sees a general threat to Latin America today: The threat is from little Castros who are elected democratically—once. Then they go about Castroization. Rodriguez cites Evo Morales, among others: He will rule Bolivia for a very long time, presumably.

While in El Salvador, Rodriguez received a request from a White House staffer, a man soon to become famous: Oliver North. Would Rodriguez help with the resupply of the Contras in Nicaragua? They were fighting the Castro-backed, and Soviet-backed, junta in Managua. Rodriguez agreed—but fairly rapidly became disillusioned with the whole "Enterprise" (as North called it). Equipment for the Contras was shoddy and unsafe. Operational security was shaky. What really stuck in Rodriguez's craw was war-profiteering. In 1987, he testified at the Iran-Contra hearings, without a lawyer, and without holding back. That was the end of his involvement in scandal, he thought.

But a month later, there was an eye-popping story in the *Miami Herald*: A convicted money launderer for the Medellín cartel had accused Rodriguez of soliciting drug money for the Contras. This was a leak supplied by "unnamed congressional sources." And who might they be? It was no mystery. In the Senate, John Kerry was chairing a subcommittee known to one and all as the "Kerry Committee." He was keen to establish a link between the Contras and drug-running. He was especially keen to link the vice president, George Bush, to any such drug-running. Rodriguez had a tie to Bush, because the vice president's national-security adviser was Donald Gregg, who had been Rodriguez's superior in Vietnam. Rodriguez wanted to testify before Kerry's committee in an open hearing, so he could clear his name. But Kerry insisted on a closed hearing.

Toward the end of that hearing, Rodriguez said to Kerry, "Senator, this has been the hardest testimony I ever gave in my life." Kerry asked why. "Because," said Rodriguez, "it is extremely difficult to have to answer questions from someone you do not respect, and I do not respect you and what you are doing here." The senator was not pleased. "Boy, did he blow his top," Rodriguez says. But after almost a year—and considerable Republican pressure—Kerry apologized to Rodriguez and acknowledged that the money launderer's accusation was false. Fine, says Rodriguez. But if you Google his name, you will find plenty of references to the Medellín drug cartel. The endurance, the permanence, of the 1987 lie rankles Rodriguez.

While Kerry had Rodriguez before him, he took the opportunity to question him about Che Guevara and Bolivia. For one thing, had he really done all he could to save the guerrilla's life? Kerry was sarcastic in this questioning. It seems to Rodriguez that Kerry, at that time, had sympathy for Guevara, and the Sandinistas, and Castro. In 2004, when the senator was the presidential nominee of the Democratic party, Rodriguez spoke against him at a rally on Capitol Hill organized by Vietnam Veterans for Truth. Today, of course, Kerry is secretary of state—which pains and disgusts Rodriguez. "I despise that guy. He is a phony. He was a phony during the Vietnam War. He's a self-promoter." His voice trails off: "I don't like the guy at all . . ."

Cubans such as Felix Rodriguez expected the Castro dictatorship to last a year, two years, maybe three. He was 17 when Castro took over; Castro, with his brother, still rules the island, and Rodriguez is 72. Communism in Cuba has lasted longer than Communism in Eastern Europe, by ten years and counting. Obviously, this is more painful and disgusting to Rodriguez than John Kerry's current status as U.S. secretary of state. Cuba was no Jeffersonian democracy when Castro took over. But it was nothing like the totalitarian hell he and his partners made it. And it has had no chance to evolve in a democratic direction, as the Dominican Republic and lots of other places did. When will it end? When will the Communists fall? Cubans are weary of answering this question, after almost 55 years. Rodriguez, though, points to the Castros' friends in Venezuela: If the oil ever stopped coming, the brothers would be in trouble. Needless to say, Rodriguez is unsure whether he will see Cuba again.

Twenty-five years ago, he wrote in his memoir, "Sometimes I feel a little bit like Ulysses. . . . Like him, I am from an island nation. Like him, I went to war. And like him, I am having a hard time getting home." How about today? Does he still feel that way? Is he still trying to get home? Where's home? "It's complicated," Rodriguez says. Yes, it is. It is complicated for virtually all Cuban Americans of his generation. Rodriguez is a patriotic Cuban. He is also a patriotic American. Under normal circumstances, this would be a bald contradiction, but the circumstances of the Cuban exile are peculiar, not normal. Rodriguez says that the Cuba he knew has been destroyed, over these 50-plus years. He doesn't know anyone over there anymore. The Communists long ago expropriated his family home in Sancti Spíritus. If the regime fell, he wouldn't claim it. But he might like to negotiate to buy it, "for sentimental reasons."

The *60 Minutes* piece done on him in 1989 is an exercise in soft-Left condescension. It portrays anti-Communism as some kind of mental disorder, or at least a sign of immaturity. Of Rodriguez, Mike Wallace says, "He has never lost his love of war nor his anti-Communist ideals." Rodriguez doesn't love war: but he is willing to fight in order to keep or gain freedom and peace. At the end of the segment, Wallace wonders, "What does the future hold for this 48-year-old foot soldier in a fading Cold War?" Arthur Liman, who was chief counsel to the Iran-Contra Committee, says, "I think that Felix Rodriguez will probably end up—and I hate to say this—in an unmarked grave in some faraway place, fighting the remnants of Communism." Wallace responds, "A little bit like Che Guevara."

William F. Buckley Jr. once came up with a formulation: Say that Smith pushes an old lady out of the way of an onrushing bus. Then Jones pushes an old lady *into* the way of an onrushing bus. It would be absurd to say that these are two men who push old ladies around. Felix Rodriguez will always be linked to Che Guevara, and they both fought. But they are not alike. Rodriguez's face will probably not grace a T-shirt. He is what they call a "right-wing Cuban exile." Guevara is a "romantic revolutionary" and "idealist." His face sits on a billion T-shirts. Pilgrims flock to La Higuera, to worship at his shrine there. But of the two men, Rodriguez and Guevara, only one deserves honor.

—August 5, 2013

Writing Brave

A conversation with a staffer at *Charlie Hebdo* magazine

Oslo, Norway

Does Zineb El Rhazoui ever think of going off and leading a quiet life, maybe teaching school somewhere? Must she remain in the fray? "It's too late for me, regardless. There is a Sword of Damocles hanging over my head." Wherever she went, whatever she did, her opponents would try to hunt her down and kill her.

Besides, "I owe something to my colleagues. I can't abandon them," not after so many were killed. "It's my duty as a survivor, I think."

Rhazoui is a journalist, a staff member with *Charlie Hebdo*. This week, she is participating in the Oslo Freedom Forum, the annual human-rights conference here in the Norwegian capital. She is a chic, even a glamorous woman in her early thirties. There is also a sense of purpose about her. She's an intense communicator.

Charlie Hebdo is the proudly left-wing and atheist satirical magazine in Paris. Among its many targets have been Islam and Islamism. Last January 7, two Islamists, Saïd and Chérif Kouachi, went to the magazine's offices. The Kouachis were Parisian-born brothers of Algerian parentage. They murdered twelve people, afterward yelling the usual triumphant slogans. Zineb El Rhazoui was not present that day. She was on vacation in Casablanca.

She was born and raised there. Her father was Moroccan, her mother French. Zineb came to her political ideas—secularist, nonconformist, individualist—early on. "In childhood, I started asking myself about my condition as a girl and as a future woman in Morocco, a country where women don't have the same rights as men, a country where your whole status is ruled by religion, or by laws inspired by religion." A woman, she says, is "condemned to be a half-citizen." She formed a desire to "contest" this system.

After high school, she went to Paris, where she studied languages. She eventually earned a master's degree in the sociology of religion. She wanted to understand the world from which she sprang, the better to contest it.

In 2007, when she was 25, she returned to Morocco, becoming a journalist. She worked for *Le Journal Hebdomadaire*, an independent magazine. (*Hebdomadaire* means "weekly," and *hebdo*, of course, is its shortened form.) Rhazoui wrote about religion and irreligion, seeking out underground atheists, for example.

She also co-founded an organization—a clandestine organization—called MALI. That is the French acronym for the Alternative Movement for Individual Liberty. *Mali*, in Moroccan Arabic, also has the sense of "What's wrong with me?"

In September 2009, the group tried a little civil disobedience. Muslims were observing Ramadan, the month of fasting. In Morocco, it is forbidden to eat publicly during fasting hours. In fact, it's a jailable offense. So, MALI staged a picnic. Rhazoui explains, "We wanted to say, 'We are citizens and we don't fast.' There were also people with us who do fast but who oppose this unjust law. No one should go to jail because he's eating a sandwich."

The picnickers did not get very far before being arrested. And the country's theological council issued a fatwa against Rhazoui. The council declared her an enemy of Islam. Rhazoui maintains, "The picnic was not an action against Islam but an action for freedom."

In the months and years to follow, Rhazoui was subjected to near-constant threats and harassment. The newspaper, *Le Journal Hebdomadaire*, was shut down by the government. It was virtually impossible for Rhazoui to work. She finally left the country, winding up at *Charlie Hebdo*. It seems to be a spiritual home for her.

On January 7, 2015, however—as I have said—she was back home in Casablanca. She woke up early that morning. She e-mailed her friend and editor, Stéphane Charbonnier, known as "Charb." She had an idea for her next piece: The Islamic State had just issued regulations for the buying and selling of women. The regulations answered such questions as "Can I buy two sisters? Can I sleep with both of them?"

Rhazoui went back to bed. A few hours later, a friend called, in a panic, saying that there had been reports of a shooting at *Charlie Hebdo*. Rhazoui figured it was nothing. "I was sure at that moment that the atmosphere at *Charlie* was funny and jokey. I couldn't imagine that anything horrible had happened. I thought I would call them and they'd say, 'Oh, don't worry about it. There was one guy, and he broke a couple of windows.'"

Throughout the day, Rhazoui learned who had survived and who had been killed. Charb, her close friend, was killed. Another close friend, Simon Fieschi, the webmaster, was very badly wounded. The receptionist, Angélique, had been spared because she had gone out for a smoke.

"I didn't know whether I would have the courage to buy a ticket and fly back to Paris," says Rhazoui. "I was on my sofa, hiding under a cover, just crying. And then when I heard that Simon was still alive, that gave me the courage to go." She flew back the next day, January 8. At the airport in Paris, security agents were waiting for her at the door of the plane. They were there to protect her. Such agents have been with her ever since.

The next day, January 9, the surviving members of *Charlie Hebdo* got together. Rhazoui told them, "I never thought I'd be so happy to see you again." There was much joking, of the darkest kind. And the team planned the next week's issue.

Since that time, Zineb El Rhazoui has received countless death threats, from Islamists and jihadists. These men are angry that Rhazoui was not killed in the January 7 attack. Their threats are highly specific, and completely in earnest. The killers, or would-be killers, have vowed that they will not rest until this woman is dead.

She has been living the life of a vagabond, going from friend's sofa to friend's sofa, and from hotel to hotel. She has never stayed in a hotel more than a week. Usually she changes every day, or every two days. "I have had to invent a new life and try to find a significance in it."

As a journalist, and as a sociologist, Rhazoui prides herself on understanding the world, or at least trying to do so. But, like the rest of us, she is perplexed by much. "I grew up inside Islam. I know the Koran and the Arabic language better than the Kouachi brothers, who killed my colleagues, but I don't understand what's happening in the world today."

She can't understand how the Islamic State has gained so much ground—literal ground, in several countries. "How come all the modern countries, with all their science and all their armies, can't destroy a bunch of madmen who don't even have showers and believe you can heal cancer by drinking camel piss? I don't understand how we cannot win this war."

I point out to her what she well knows: that many people fault *Charlie Hebdo* for being "provocative." What does she have to say to them? Many things, of which I will relate a few.

First, these critics "may have a lack of culture." The satirical press is an old tradition in France, and "it is not meant to please the one who is cartooned. By definition and necessity, it is provocative. But that does not mean that, if you provoke, you deserve to be killed."

Second, "we are a French atheist magazine. Why should we accept a rule of *their* religion?" (By "rule," she is alluding to the Sunni taboo on depicting Mohammed.) "In France, do we work under sharia law or French law? Just tell me!"

Third, "you don't have to buy *Charlie Hebdo*. It's not a compulsory product."

Fourth, "the monsters who killed my colleagues in the heart of Paris are the same monsters who kill in Nigeria, Syria, Iraq, Afghanistan, and many other parts of the world. In Paris, they killed because we depicted the prophet, but in other places they kill you because you're drinking a beer or because you're not covering your hair or because you don't go to mosque. They even kill innocent children, for no reason. They will *always* find a pretext to kill, so I don't accept this argument from those who say we are provoking."

Rhazoui further has no patience for those who say that she and her colleagues are "racist" and "Islamophobic." She points out that Islam controls many countries, politically. If you criticize Islam in one of those countries, you are liable to be imprisoned or worse. "They have legal tools to shut your mouth." But in a secular country—a liberal democracy—they have no such tools. So, to shut your mouth, they cry "racism" and "Islamophobia."

In the last ten years, says Rhazoui, *Charlie Hebdo* has run 523 covers. Seven have dealt with Islam; 19 have been about Christianity; and the rest have been about French politics, the Right, culture, sports, and so on.

The "real racism," as Rhazoui sees it, comes from those white Westerners who say, for example, that equality between the sexes may be well and good for their own countries, but not for other people's countries (such as her native Morocco).

Near the end of our discussion, I ask Rhazoui the most clichéd question in the business: "What would you like people to know?"

"I am not merely threatened," says Rhazoui, "I am condemned to death. I live under protection, and this protection is paid for by the French state. But I don't think it's to protect me personally. My life is not worth that much. It's to protect freedom of speech and to protect a model of society that we want to build and preserve. So people must understand that if people like me are threatened today, tomorrow their own rights and freedoms will be threatened, if they do nothing."

Zineb El Rhazoui is a brave and admirable lady. I tell her so, of course. I also say, "Atheist though you may be, I'm going to say, 'God bless you.'" She smiles warmly. I then say that I hope she'll live to be a very old lady. Still smiling, she says, "For that, I have to stop smoking."

—June 22, 2015

AN ENTREPRENEURIAL LIFE

Pictures from struggling, wonderful California

Fresno, Calif.

As some people have a talent for sprinting or dancing, Richard Spencer has a talent for entrepreneurship. Like most talents, this one manifested itself early. And, like many an entrepreneur, Spencer had the chance of a little capital.

Before he graduated from high school, in 1962, his great-aunt May asked him, "What are you going to do this summer?" He said, "Deliver furniture, same as last summer." She said, "How would you like to do something more interesting?" The two of them went down to the Hall of Records. They leafed through some books and found a home about to be foreclosed on. May bought the home for $5,200. She also gave her great-nephew $800 for supplies. The plan was, he would fix up the house, and then they would sell it, splitting the profits.

At the end of the summer, he had another idea: How about renting it? They did. In the meantime, the young man had noticed a vacant lot, zoned for four units. As the owner of a house with a renter, he could borrow $4,000, to buy the lot. He did. To make a long story short, he has not stopped working and growing since. He presides over several enterprises, employing something like 400 people.

His city, Fresno, needs the employment. This is one of the most depressed areas in the country, dubbed "the Appalachia of the West." Unemployment is now 14 percent, although recently it was 17 percent. In some of the small surrounding towns, unemployment is as high as 35 or 40 percent. "We are the agricultural center of the world," says Dennis Woods, a leading banker in Fresno, "yet people are starving."

It is indeed a strange and frustrating paradox. Fresno has long been famous for raisins, and it also has tomatoes, onions, peppers, cotton, oranges, pistachios—you name it. Almost anything can grow here. Armenians were once the prominent minority in the area (as immortalized by William Saroyan, Fresno's literary light). The descendants of these immigrants are still here, but the prominent minorities are Mexicans, Punjabis, and Hmong.

As for Richard Spencer, he is nothing special, or so he says. But the type he represents is undoubtedly special: the person who comes up with an idea, comes up with another idea, takes risks, finds his way around obstacles, employs others, and prospers. "He's always thinking," says Mike Conway, a friend of Spencer's, and a fellow entrepreneur. "He takes an intellectual approach. I'm more seat of the pants"—and Conway has done well by those pants, for himself and others.

Spencer is at the head of Spencer Enterprises, which builds houses and apartments. He also heads Harris Construction, which builds schools, hospitals, and the like. Then there is a parts business, and a company called CMEC. The latter builds aerial work platforms: boom lifts, scissor lifts. Spencer also has an almond ranch and a winery (the Cru Wine Company). He has had lean times and fat. He keeps going through the lean times, knowing that investors, employees, and others count on him. Business life is constant adjustment.

I think of something Bill Buckley often said, quoting Whittaker Chambers: "To live is to maneuver."

Spencer is not a complainer, but he is nevertheless willing to tell me about the follies of government. Take the matter of engines. You have to buy new engines now, because older ones are deemed too polluting. The new engines are very expensive, too. Just last week, Harris Construction lent a water truck to the almond ranch. The people at the ranch wanted to water their dirt roads, in order to keep the dust down. The EPA demands this. But this same EPA demanded that the water truck be taken off the road, because its engine is too old. Harris will now have to scrap the truck.

That's a relatively small matter, among many. Here's another: Spencer is building 160 apartments in Fresno. He has to pay the EPA a fee of $220,000. Why? Because people will live in the apartments, and people take trips—to and from work, or to the movies, or even out of town. They live; therefore, they pollute. And Spencer must pay. Naturally, he will build the fee into the tenants' rent. And what will the EPA do with his $220,000? He has a good guess.

Over the years, he has noticed something about government: Often, its offices will charge fees, impose penalties, and so on simply to keep themselves in business. They justify their existence this way. They can say, "See? We pay for ourselves"—by generating money from the regulated, or overregulated.

Incidentally, this is a big part of what turned Thomas Sowell, the famed economist and writer. He became a libertarian-conservative when he was a young man working in the Labor Department. He saw that the bureaucrats around him were more concerned with perpetuating their jobs and keeping or expanding their powers than with the public interest.

Spencer, in his various enterprises, has a lot of EB-5 investors. "EB-5" refers to a provision of immigration law, a provision that allows foreigners to make a substantial investment in certain U.S. businesses in exchange for a green card. But there is a problem, says Spencer: The rules shift under your feet. And you can't talk to anyone in government about it. You deal with "nameless, faceless websites." You are at the mercy of anonymous regulators who can hold up an application or otherwise gum up the works—and you have little recourse.

To add insult to injury, says Spencer, the immigration service now employs "entrepreneurs in residence." "By definition, a government employee is not an entrepreneur," he says. But do they know what they're doing? Are they of use? "I don't know," he says, "because we haven't been able to meet with one or talk to one, despite our best efforts."

Like other businessmen, Spencer now faces ObamaCare—and so do his employees. At first, they were relieved to hear, from President Obama and others, that they would not have to give up their existing health care, if they were satisfied. But that has proven untrue. Spencer's CFO at CMEC has devoted many hours to figuring out the new world of ObamaCare—hours he could be spending on more productive work. This much is certain: Spencer will pay more for his employees' health care, and so will they. Whether the health care will be better is doubtful.

In the almond business, Spencer is small-time, he says, but he takes me to see someone big-time: Tony Campos, a veritable almond king. He wasn't born a king, or prince, however. He came to America in 1952 from the Basque country, with nothing. He took a bus from New York to Wyoming, where he would work as a shepherd. Eventually, he and his brothers tended sheep in California. Then they moved into farming, finally hitting on almonds. The Campos brothers did hard, tedious manual labor.

Now Tony—the sole remaining brother—has a sprawling, gleaming operation, with equipment that seems out of Willy Wonka's chocolate factory.

Business has never been better, he says. That's because of a global market: He sells to 62 countries. Still, he could be doing a lot more. His company spends endless money and endless hours on regulations—particularly those relating to food safety and labor. Campos acknowledges the need for regulation, but says that much of it is absurd. Just a giant waste. Money that could be going to expand business goes instead down a rathole. When he speaks of this, his face registers both disgust and amazement. Why would a country want to do this?

Here is a regulation that may be coming soon, a regulation in the pipeline: Say a kit fox wanders into your orchard and defecates near a tree. You have to quarantine off a sizable area and destroy the trees within it. You can't keep Mr. Fox out in the first place—because he's an endangered species. The government can tie you up in knots, in myriad ways.

Back to Dennis Woods, the banker—and more than a banker, a business impresario. He has started about 40 businesses, of various types. He is a banker who hates bankers, he says: They are risk-averse, practiced at saying no. And you can't build anything with no. Woods likes to say yes, helping entrepreneurs get started. He lends them money and guides them through regulations, to the extent one can. The biggest barrier to entrepreneurs today, he says, is not taxes—though we could argue about tax policy. The biggest barrier is access to capital (a lack thereof). That and the morass of regulation.

It bothers Richard Spencer that men such as Tony Campos have to bow before regulators, and be yanked around by them: people who have no relevant experience, no relevant knowledge, and no accountability. Businessmen rise and fall, but a regulator is seldom fired.

But Spencer does not want you to feel sorry for Campos, or Dennis Woods—or Spencer. They're all doing great. They're big boys, well established, and they can hold their own with government, at all levels. Nor do you have to worry about their children, says Spencer. (He and Karen, his wife of 46 years, have six children.) They have resources. They also have resourcefulness. They have seen entrepreneurship in action, and they'll figure out a way.

Spencer worries about those without resources, or with few resources: "the entrepreneur who never was," as he puts it. The guy who could never get going, because the barriers were too high. "That is the sinister and obnoxious effect of overregulation," he says—stopping people before they can get started, choking dreams in their cradle. If he were starting out today, he says, he could not accomplish what he has. The environment is too forbidding.

On top of everything else, businessmen have to put up with being demonized—with being the villain in countless movies and countless politician's speeches. Spencer especially objects to the insinuation, or outright assertion, that people like him came by their money dishonestly. He belongs to "the rich," I suppose, or "the 1 percent." But he has also worked his tail off, paid millions in taxes, given millions to charity, provided goods and services that people need or want, and employed thousands.

He doesn't mind paying taxes, by the way. "Happy to do it." He does think that a welfare state may not help the people it intends to help.

Despite the unpleasantness of recent years, Spencer is optimistic. His California is in bad shape, as everyone knows. But it is still a golden state. "There's still magic here," says Spencer. And magic across America. "People from all over the world want to come here, and invest here, and have their children educated here. We're tarnished, but we're not through."

Spencer may be nothing special, as he says—"Please don't make a big deal out of me"—but, again, the type he represents is special. If we who are not entrepreneurs dump on the entrepreneur, and overtax him and overregulate him, we are only harming ourselves.

—March 25, 2013

De Soto's Excellent Path

A visit with Peru's economist and global activist, Hernando de Soto

Lima, Peru

Sitting here listening to Hernando de Soto, I think, "How am I going to avoid describing him as a 'force of nature'?" That is one of the laziest clichés. But de Soto is, I'm afraid, a force of nature. He seems to be thinking constantly, and the thoughts come out in great waves of speech. They are big thoughts and little thoughts, grand concepts and details. As he speaks, de Soto draws on huge reservoirs of reading and observation. He seems to remember everything he ever encountered. Sometimes, he will think for a minute or two, before releasing the waves of speech. This is unusual, in my experience—a long period of silence before the talking begins.

De Soto is a talker and a doer. He is an economist, one of the most influential intellectuals in the world. He is also an "economic activist," as someone once put it. He has an organization called the Institute for Liberty and Democracy. De Soto is a classical liberal, a free-marketeer, a capitalist (pick your term). He is best known for his advocacy of property rights and the general rule of law. He has spent many years trying to lift the poor out of their poverty. In his career, he has been everywhere, met everyone. He has been praised by U.S. presidents starting with Reagan. Of course, he has won a slew of awards, from governments and private groups. Three of those awards are named for Adam Smith, Friedrich Hayek, and Milton Friedman. That gives a strong flavor of de Soto's thought.

I have come to deepest, darkest Peru to talk with him about several things. This is a phrase that he himself uses—"deepest, darkest Peru"—and he reminds me of its origins: the Paddington Bear stories. Paddington is a native of this country, an immigrant to England. De Soto lives here in Lima in a beautiful home complete with lush gardens. It is something out of a South American fantasy—and it gets more fantastic when you see the alpacas, gazing at you from their pen. (An alpaca is a smaller cousin of the llama.) De Soto's walls are covered with more than the usual number of books, photos, and mementos. The photos are mainly of statesmen and intellectuals. Two in the latter camp are Hayek and Friedman: De Soto brought both down to Lima, to talk up classical-liberal ideas. As far as I can tell, security is light, but not nonexistent. There used to be a need for a great deal of security: De Soto was a key enemy of the Shining Path, the Communist guerrillas who killed about 40,000, and terrorized many more, before they were finished.

On my agenda are three main subjects: de Soto's life, his latest documentary, and some of the big issues in economics—especially the perpetual struggle between socialism and capitalism.

His parents had the conquistador in mind when they named him: The first Hernando de Soto was born some 450 years before the economist. The economist was born in 1941, in Arequipa, a town in southern Peru. His father, Alberto, was a diplomat, and his mother, Rosa, was a local beauty. After a military coup in 1948, the family went into exile, living in Geneva. In that international community, Hernando learned many things, including utterly idiomatic American English. He visited Peru frequently and returned to live in 1979. Here, he found himself haunted by a question: Why did his native country lag so far behind Europe and the rest of the developed world, when Peruvians were just as talented as anybody? He concluded that the system was rigged against the majority, working only for a privileged few. In 1980, he set up a think tank with Mario Vargas Llosa, the writer. This was, is, the Institute for Liberty and Democracy, or ILD.

For seven years, de Soto walked the shantytowns and other "outsider" areas of the country, and thought. He then came out with his first book, a blockbuster: *The Other Path*. The alternative he presented was the path of—well, liberty and democracy, as opposed to the Shining Path and its Communism. Prior to publication, it was clear to de Soto that the guerrillas would come after him. He took some security precautions. He also decided to change the title of his book—to "The Path of Liberation."

Maybe the guerrillas would take less offense to that. But a few days later, de Soto was shaving, looking at himself in the mirror, and he said, "You coward." He changed the title back—and was entirely, permanently committed to the fight.

In 1990, there was an epic presidential contest between Vargas Llosa and Alberto Fujimori. Fujimori won—and adopted many of the recommendations of the ILD. Indeed, ILD implemented those recommendations, carrying out its own program, for Peru. The country liberalized, bringing more and more of the poor and dispossessed into the mainstream legal and economic frameworks. The Shining Path persisted, of course, including against de Soto: No fewer than 17 guerrillas were assigned to kill him. Shining Path bombed the ILD in 1991, wounding two. They bombed them again the next year, this time killing two, though not the principal target, and wounding about 20.

During the 1990 presidential campaign, de Soto and Vargas Llosa had a falling out. (More about that in due course.) And, for two years, de Soto was close to the president, Fujimori. They met every other night, in the presidential residence, from 10 or 11 to 2 in the morning. They talked about whatever challenges were at hand. De Soto says that Fujimori had enormous self-confidence, chutzpah. In getting elected, he had bucked the system, all the elites, on left and right. He was a very quick study, says de Soto, assimilating ideas and then acting on them, or having them acted on. He was also brave, very brave, especially against the Shining Path. More than once did he provide an example of sangfroid. So, those are good sides to Fujimori—but there proved others, including egomania, corruption, and gangsterism. De Soto broke with him in 1992. At one point, Fujimori told de Soto, "*Doctor*, I live under a lucky star." He apparently thought himself a man of destiny, invincible. But the star went out and Fujimori has been in prison since 2007.

It was in 2000 that de Soto came out with his second book, another blockbuster, *The Mystery of Capital*. It has been translated into some 30 languages and has sold more than 2 million copies. The ILD has been very busy, fulfilling its mission, which is "to assist emerging nations in integrating their poor majorities into the economic mainstream under a single rule of law." De Soto and ILD have been "called in," as de Soto puts it, by about 30 heads of state, not all of them nice democrats, but dictators, too. It seems to me that de Soto has a wide streak of realism, to go with his idealism: He will work with nearly anyone, as long as it means improvements for the poor. His rule is, ILD will work in any country that is accepted by the "world community"—wherever a U.S. embassy and a U.N. representative are found.

De Soto has made three documentaries with the Free to Choose Network, based in Erie, Pa. The latest of them is *Unlikely Heroes of the Arab Spring*, now airing on PBS. This "spring" began in January 2011, when a Tunisian fruit vendor named Mohamed Bouazizi committed suicide in a public self-immolation. De Soto sent an ILD team into the region. He says, "I'm a researcher, really. It's kind of like Joe Friday in *Dragnet*: 'Just the facts, ma'am.'" He wanted to know why the Middle East in general was ablaze, from the lips of the very people doing the blazing.

The team discovered that, in the two months after Bouazizi self--immolated, 63 more men and women had done the same. They did it in country after country. Like Bouazizi, they were entrepreneurs, or would-be entrepreneurs. ILD talked to their families, and they also talked to survivors: Thirty-seven of the 63 failed in their suicide attempts. In the documentary, one of these 37 shows the scars all over his body. "I tried every possible way to get my rights in society, to find work," he says. "I tried a thousand things," with no success. He felt trapped, finished.

De Soto testified to the U.S. Congress about the Middle East last year. In an understatement (as I see it), he said, "Mass suicide in defense of property rights is hard for the modern Western mind to understand." Why would someone like Bouazizi kill himself over the confiscation of some fruit and the scale with which to weigh it? But Bouazizi's act was motivated by a lot more than that, de Soto has explained—to Congress, in his film, and to me: Bouazizi was under the whim of local authorities, who could choke off his every avenue. There was nowhere to go, no other authority to appeal to, no veritable rule of law. His last words, before he lit the match, were, "How do you expect me to make a living?" ILD asked

Bouazizi's family what they thought he had died for. They answered, "For the right to buy and sell."

To Congress, de Soto said, "The average Arab entrepreneur needs to present 57 documents and faces two years or more of red tape to obtain a legal property right over land or a business." In Egypt, the legal opening of a business "requires dealing with 29 different government agencies and navigating 215 sets of laws." Arabs, like the majority of the world's population, lack basic property rights and related rights. They feel left out of the good life, unable even to strive for it. In his film, de Soto says that the Arab Spring amounts to "a huge shout for inclusion."

He is also entitled to say something about terrorism, I think. The Middle East is plagued by it, as are other regions. He told Congress, "Not so long ago, we at the ILD saw with our own eyes . . . how the entrepreneurial frustrations of ordinary Peruvians could easily be whipped up into terrorism."

I want to ask de Soto about the word "capitalism." Where I come from, it is a dirty word, usually said with a scoff or a sneer. De Soto is quite practical about the matter: "If the word is in bad odor, avoid it. Words are what people want them to mean, and if 'capitalism' is a bad word, I can think of a lot better uses of our time and talents than to defend it." When he first arrived back in Peru, capitalism (or whatever we wish to call it) was known as "la economía de la selva"—"the economics of the jungle." Well, what word does he himself use? It depends on where he is, he says. It depends on the local vocabulary. "Private property," to some, means "what the rich have"—not the materials a humble fruit vendor has. In the Middle East, the term "property rights" may not mean anything (de Soto and ILD found). But people know the word "expropriation"—they have been victims of expropriation. In any event, says de Soto, "Never go die for a word, if what is important is the idea behind the word."

He is not one who believes that the free market or "Western values" are for some and not others. He is more a universalist. He recalls a crisis in the Peruvian Amazon, where people were rebelling violently. He spoke with them, and they said, "Sir, your ideas are absolutely alien to our ethnicity. There are things that are Western that are not made for the rest of us." "Oh?" said de Soto. "Like penicillin?" And "how about soccer"? He then went through the list of demands that the rebels were making of the government in Lima, pointing out all of the items that were "Western"—including computers. De Soto says, "There is no such thing as a Western thing or an Eastern thing: If it works, everybody wants it."

Furthering his case, he brought Alaskans to the Amazon, "in full regalia." One of them said, "My name is Bobbi, and I am an indigenous woman from the U.S. I am now running a $2.3 billion company, and I tell you, I'm not ethnically averse to it." Her counterpart, or would-be counterpart, from the Amazon said, "My name is Irene, and I'm a Bora [a member of a particular tribe], and I have no legal property, and I'm poor as all hell." Obviously, de Soto grants that there will be local or national adaptations of universal ideas and mechanisms—the Japanese do capitalism in a Japanese way, for example. But he does not accept that economic freedom is suited to some and not others. Pleas about culture can be excuses for the status quo, including the protection of privilege. If you want to know what the poor really want, you should ask them.

William F. Buckley Jr. often asked, "How do you explain the continuing success of socialist politicians in the Third World, and elsewhere, when socialism is manifestly a failure and capitalism the opposite?" He got a variety of answers. De Soto says that capitalists make gross mistakes, and socialists capitalize on them (so to speak). Socialists present themselves as checks and balances on capitalism. The capitalist he sees in Peru, says de Soto, may talk the language of economic freedom, the way plain old dictatorships adopt the rhetoric of Marxism—but he is really concerned with his own interest, regardless of others'. "By 'capitalism' or 'economic freedom,' he does not mean what Bill Buckley, you, and I mean." That is a problem.

In the United States, President Obama is making inequality of income a big issue, and it is a big issue elsewhere, too, of course. De Soto notes that there is some "human need for leveling." And people are sensitive to enormous and unnatural-seeming gaps between rich and poor. In Peru, he says, there is a lot of money to be made in mining, "which is perfectly legitimate." (De Soto himself was a businessman in mining.) But what do you have to do to be involved in this field? You need a concession, which means that the state has to give you some kind of property right over the subsoil. You have to pay significant fees and jump through many hoops. The native people living on top of those mines, or around them, are not likely to get a concession. And they are ripe for the Marxist language of exploitation. "How do you beat socialism?" de Soto says. "You make sure that everything you do that helps business reaches everybody." Drawing on his bottomless fund of American idioms, he continues, "Make sure that what's good for General Motors is also good for the Peruvian Indian, and we'll wipe them out"—not the Indians, but the socialists.

Since 2008, and the onset of the financial crisis, the capitalist idea has had a hard time of it. But the trends are still with us, says de Soto. "Outside of North Korea and Cuba, everyone accepts that a competitive economy, without privileges, is what is best for the poor" and society at large. What the Left falls back on, he says, is a lack of political viability. They say, "The people are just not ready for that kind of thing yet." Then there is the curse of "romantic nationalism," as de Soto calls it—nationalism of the kind represented by the late Hugo Chávez in Venezuela.

I bring up a potentially painful subject, and I introduce it this way: For 20 years, there were exactly two anti-Communists east of the Hudson River (I exaggerate a little): Richard Pipes, the historian of Russia at Harvard University, and Solzhenitsyn (who lived in Vermont). And they were at odds. This was unhappy for admirers of them both. In the whole of Latin America, there are exactly two classical liberals (again, I exaggerate). They are both Peruvian, and they are both from Arequipa, and they are even distant cousins (I learn from de Soto). I am talking, of course, about de Soto and Vargas Llosa. De Soto says he never thinks about their split, until curious people like me bring it up. It happened so long ago. He takes me through the story step by step. He and Vargas Llosa were close friends and comrades. Since the split, there has been occasional sniping between them. They have not seen each other in almost 25 years, except fleetingly: De Soto has spotted Vargas Llosa on the street a couple of times; Vargas Llosa has gone in another direction. I have only one side of the story, of course. Will these two titans ever reconcile? I could not say, but it would be a reconciliation to cause smiles worldwide.

I have talked with de Soto late into the night—late into two nights, actually—and I ask him the big question concerning the United States, which also concerns everybody else: Are we going down the tubes? Is the sun setting on us? Nonsense, says de Soto. We are so far ahead of everyone else, second place is not even close. The U.S. is still a model to peoples all over. We have done better than any other country in "bringing people in," which is to say, including them in our legal and economic systems. We can show other countries how to achieve liberty and democracy and the resulting prosperity, and save them some steps: The United States has evolved a great deal since the Revolution or the Wild West or some other period you might name. Poor countries can take intelligent shortcuts.

De Soto has his detractors, as everyone does, and some of this detraction is probably driven by envy: De Soto is famous and laureled, and regarded by many as a guru. But he is clearly doing work of extraordinary value. He is like a physician who knows what ails the patient and the medicine he needs. And if the patient won't take it—or some government won't let him have it—that is another problem that needs working on.

—February 24, 2014

Wife and Soldier

The continuing story of Natalia Solzhenitsyn

Over the course of 40 years, Natalia Solzhenitsyn worked hand in hand with her husband, Aleksandr Solzhenitsyn. He died in 2008, at almost 90. Mrs. Solzhenitsyn continues to work. She is in charge of the Solzhenitsyn Archive, a vast project. Solzhenitsyn was a great man, of course: a symbol of freedom for Russia and the whole world. But he was also a great writer, and a prolific, versatile one.

Mrs. Solzhenitsyn's "priority task," she says, is to complete the publication of her late husband's collected works. They will run to 30 volumes. At least three of them will consist of previously unpublished works.

She notes that Solzhenitsyn will be one of the last writers to leave a manuscript archive, in the original sense of "manuscript." This is an archive of documents written by hand. He wrote by hand from boyhood to the day he died.

Speaking of his boyhood writings: At age ten, in 1929, he devised a magazine called *Twentieth Century*. He wrote all the articles, for every section, under a variety of names. The sections included "news and events," science fiction, and games and puzzles. The boy Solzhenitsyn was the editor, the subscription manager, and everything else.

The "treasure" of his archive, says Mrs. Solzhenitsyn, is a manuscript of *The Gulag Archipelago*, the work that did so much to break the back of the Soviet Union. It was "saved by friends and lay buried in the ground for 20 years." It was presented to the author when the Solzhenitsyns returned to Russia in 1994, after 20 years of exile.

Natalia Solzhenitsyn had a key role in her husband's writing life, or rather, series of roles: She was editor, sounding board, assistant—constant helpmate. The two would pass drafts back and forth, making notes on them all the while. When he wanted to accept a suggestion of hers, he would make a plus sign; if not, a minus sign. He always explained himself (as she did, when making her suggestions).

Twenty years younger than he, she was born in 1939, in Moscow. A World War II childhood was a daunting beginning. Natalia was 14 when she realized there was something wrong and abnormal about the Soviet Union. She resolved to work for changes, although she could not know what form her work would take.

In college, it would have been natural for her to study literature, philosophy, and other such subjects. She was inclined in that general direction. But, to study those subjects, you had to join the Communist party, and that, she refused to do. So instead, she studied math.

And, before long, she became a "soldier of the samizdat," as she says:

a worker in that underground world of dissident literature. "I was a very fast typist and spent a lot of time at the typewriter," preparing the forbidden articles and books. She helped in their distribution, too. All of this was highly dangerous.

Eventually, she had four sons, and she now has a passel of grandchildren. She lives once more in Moscow, where two of her sons are also living.

Solzhenitsyn was exiled in February 1974; the family followed six weeks later. You might think this was a great blessing: The writer would now be free to work openly, without fear of arrest, imprisonment, and worse. Yet Solzhenitsyn considered his exile a tragedy, and so did his wife.

She was well aware, she says, that, without exile, her husband would have died in short order. (He had this same awareness.) He would have died even if he had not been sent back to the camps. His health was very poor; the pressure he was under was tremendous. But, says Mrs. Solzhenitsyn, "we were faced with the prospect of having to raise our kids in a foreign country. Of having to say goodbye to our country forever." That was indeed tragic, in their eyes. "It seems to me now that for the first two or three years in the West, my mother, my husband, and I unlearned how to smile. It seems we never smiled. We did not feel ourselves."

Mrs. Solzhenitsyn is a big-city girl, but she found herself living in rural Vermont, outside the town of Cavendish. Did she feel she was in Siberia, so to speak? Did she long for brighter lights? "Not at all," she says. "Our life was so intensive, because of our work—it felt like the office of a major literary magazine." Solzhenitsyn's main activity in exile was to write *The Red Wheel*, his epic, multivolume novel of the Russian Revolution. He did much other writing as well. "If we had ended up in a large city," says Mrs. Solzhenitsyn, "that would have slowed down our pace considerably. We couldn't have kept up the crazy pace we set for ourselves in Vermont."

She adds, though, "When I did find myself in a big city, it gave me pleasure."

Readers of this magazine may like to know that the Solzhenitsyns subscribed to *National Review*, read it avidly and appreciatively, and saved every issue, for almost 20 years.

It was on Christmas Day 1991 that the Soviet Union expired. The Solzhenitsyns did not go back to Russia until May 1994, however. There was work to finish up in Vermont. And there was the matter of finding a place to live in Russia. (Mrs. Solzhenitsyn went on a scouting trip in 1992.)

I ask what their homecoming was like: "Thrilling? Shocking? Saddening? Gladdening?" All of the above, says Mrs. Solzhenitsyn. "But also, I had an enormous sense of gratitude," to be returning to "my country and my language and my people."

Another question: Has she been able to forgive the Soviet persecutors, either individually or collectively? "Not one of them ever asked for forgiveness of me"—except for some journalists "who had participated in one way or another in the campaign against Solzhenitsyn." Did she forgive them? "Of course," she says.

And then she elaborates: "One could forgive only if one dealt with individuals. Then we could talk about forgiving and not forgiving. My husband and I perceived these people as parts of a machine—as cogs in a giant totalitarian machine. Some of them took no pleasure in participating; others probably or certainly did. But we never had any personal animus against them. It's the machine, the system, that cannot be forgiven."

She does not see old persecutors and apparatchiks on the street, she says. They're not walking around. If they're still alive, they ride in limousines with dark-tinted windows.

Though she admires many of the old dissidents, she is willing to name three who stand out. The first is Aleksandr Ginzburg, "who was a beautiful, luminous person." He was arrested three times and sent to the camps three times. The third time was "for helping to manage our fund for political prisoners and their families." Solzhenitsyn insisted that all the proceeds from *The Gulag Archipelago*—which has sold 30 million copies worldwide—go into this fund.

Mrs. Solzhenitsyn then names Vladimir Bukovsky, "a man of extraordinary personal courage." She says that "we weren't as close to him" as to Ginzburg, "but I have just as high an opinion of him."

Finally, there is, of course, Sakharov—who "traveled that difficult road from privileged elite to below the level of an untouchable." Andrei

Sakharov was one of the most honored scientists, and honored people, in the whole country. He was on top of the Soviet heap. And he threw it all away to campaign for human rights and democracy.

Many of Solzhenitsyn's writings are available in English, and many are not. Which writings in the latter category would Natalia Solzhenitsyn most like to see translated? "I would put *The Little Grain* at the top of the list." This is Solzhenitsyn's memoir of his years in the West. "But second, how is it possible that a great, vast, and important country such as the United States has not yet seen *The Red Wheel* in its full form?" (Only two of the four "nodes," as Solzhenitsyn called them, have been published in English.)

She does not have a favorite Solzhenitsyn novel, poem, story, or other work. "Whichever one I'm working on at the moment, that seems to me the best. I find myself in love with whatever I'm reading or working on. This is hardly a blind love—I'm aware of weaknesses. But that's how I feel."

Solzhenitsyn almost never answered criticism, and there was much of it directed at him. He could do his own work, or he could answer the critics. There was hardly time to do both. He put his shoulder to the wheel: *The Red Wheel*. Does Mrs. Solzhenitsyn wish he had defended himself more? "It's true that I reacted to criticism. I took it much more personally than he did. But I supported his stance, because he was right."

She does not feel the need to look after Solzhenitsyn's reputation—she figures history will take care of that. "But naturally, every chance I get, when I'm asked to provide information or context, I do." There is this thought too: "When a widow such as I goes into battle to defend her husband's reputation or set the record straight, that does not carry much weight. Therefore, I don't take the initiative." But "when someone asks, I'm happy to speak."

Mrs. Solzhenitsyn returns to America every now and then, to see family here. She says that she is most struck by the self-confidence of the people, from all walks of life. "Your average American seems much more confident about who he is and where he is than the average Russian." The American, she continues, "is not expecting something bad to happen, every moment. Not expecting the proverbial brick to fall on his head. Not expecting to be cheated, not expecting his neighbor to do him wrong."

There is not a feeling of anxiety or wariness "minute after minute, hour after hour, day after day."

She has a sharp criticism of America: that it has been clumsy on the world stage, and that it has botched U.S.-Russian relations in particular. She also says that the Russian government can and should be criticized on a number of fronts.

One thing I wish to know is how people in Russia react to her, when they see her on the street or in a store. Solzhenitsyn means a great, great deal to many people. She says, "These are awkward moments. I'm bathed in a kind of sea of well-wishing and admiration on the streets of Moscow and environs. Sometimes people say nothing. They just stare, or shake my hand. Or say, 'Thank you, thank you.' Nothing but 'thank you.'"

Sometimes they say more, Mrs. Solzhenitsyn acknowledges, but she is reluctant to repeat what they say. "Too embarrassing."

—December 17, 2012

THE 'SPIRIT OF STRUGGLE'

An interview with a blind Cuban dissident

Washington, D.C.

The man sitting across from me has a mouthful of a name, but it's worth knowing: Juan Carlos González Leiva. He is a Cuban dissident, and he has much in common with his fellow dissidents, both in Cuba and around the world. He has endured imprisonment, torture, beatings, psychological torment—relentless persecution. He is impossibly brave.

One thing that sets him apart from most dissidents, however, is that he is blind. He has a counterpart in Chen Guangcheng, the Chinese dissident, who fled to the United States in 2012. Both are blind, and both are lawyers, specializing in human rights.

González Leiva tells me that, if he had not been blind, he probably would have been "a pilot for the government or a farmer. But I don't think I would have become a human-rights defender."

People in the Cuban democracy movement are in awe of González Leiva, and it's easy to see why: He is smart, articulate, personable, resolute, and compelling. We are sitting in the Washington, D.C., home of supporters of his. González Leiva has not fled Cuba. He is on a tour, drumming up support for the democracy movement, and telling people about the dire human-rights situation on the island.

Why has the regime let him out? As a rule, he explains, they like to keep about 100 dissidents outside the country, at any given time. This keeps the country calmer. It eases pressure on the regime. Well, would they like him to go into exile? Oh, yes, he says. "They have done everything to get me to go into exile. If I did, they would probably hold a national celebration."

Even now, while he is away, his home is being subjected to *actos de repudio*. The regime is harassing his family and friends. One friend, the regime has arrested, with the usual violence. At González Leiva's home, they arrested Omara Rodríguez Aparicio, a journalist. Though she offered no resistance, they put her in a chokehold and beat her up.

Actos de repudio are "acts of repudiation." In these charming instances, a government mob stands outside a dissident's home, screaming obscenities and threats, throwing rocks, assaulting people who come and go, and generally intimidating.

González Leiva says, "They are trying to implant terror so that I don't return." But will he? Yes, indeed, very soon. "I have a commitment to my country and to Jesus Christ." And what is that commitment? "To work so that people in Cuba have a better country."

Well, why doesn't the government simply expel him? Exile him? The government seldom uses forced exile as a tool, says González Leiva. They have other tools at their disposal, which they prefer. "For example, house arrest, as in the case of Antúnez. Or physical elimination, as in the case of Oswaldo Payá. Or prison."

"Antúnez" is the nickname of Jorge Luis García Pérez, a prominent democracy leader. Payá was another prominent democracy leader, almost certainly killed by the regime in 2012. He was in one of those car accidents that are not really accidents. Stalin used to order these, too.

Juan Carlos González Leiva is a year short of 50, born in 1965. The seeds of dissidence were planted early. His father would get up and make coffee, before going to the fields to work. While having his coffee, he would listen to an exile radio station, and also to the Voice of America. He thought his son was sleeping. Actually, he was listening.

Did Juan Carlos ever have a flirtation with Communism? Did he ever believe? When he was about 20, he says, he was involved with a governmental organization for the blind. During a few activities, he screamed, "Long live Fidel!" like everyone else. Every Cuban has these moments, he says.

Like Castro, González Leiva went to the University of Havana law school. (I tell him he is a better representative of the school.) In the beginning, his family read his law texts to him. "Some of my nephews learned to read by reading my law books," he says. He allows that he has a phenomenal memory (when I ask him). Eventually, he learned Braille. "But the revolution came for me with the computer," and a Windows program designed to help the blind read. "I was able to have access to all literature like any other person. I had a big banquet."

How is it that he turned to dissidence? How did he come to embrace it as a way of life? "I had read the Bible a lot, and also the works of José Martí" (the Cuban writer and hero from the second half of the 19th century). For González Leiva, dissidence was an "obligation." There was "a disaster in the country, with so many abuses, and so much poverty. So many people in need. As a Christian, I had to do something."

The last straw, he says, was July 13, 1994: the Tugboat Massacre. In this atrocity, the Cuban government killed 37 people, most of them women and children, as they tried to flee the island. The killing was accomplished this way: State agents swept people off the deck of the boat with high-pressure water hoses; then they rammed the boat until it sank.

Over the years, González Leiva has founded many organizations, including the Fraternity of the Independent Blind of Cuba, the Human Rights Foundation of Cuba, and the Council of Human Rights Rapporteurs. For two years and two months—starting in 2002 and ending in

2004—he was in prison. His torturers sprayed a chemical on him, which burned his skin and caused hallucinations and other problems. He was imprisoned with common criminals—murderers—as political prisoners usually are. They threatened him day and night.

In 2008, something quite satisfying happened: The president of the United States paid tribute to him, at a prayer breakfast. That was George W. Bush. I ask González Leiva whether the regime reacted badly to this. Oh, yes. "They were always furious when Bush talked about any of us Cubans," says González Leiva. He further says, "I would like to take this interview as an opportunity to thank Bush."

Last January, González Leiva and nine other activists, including his wife, Tania Maceda Guerra, were savagely beaten. One agent held González Leiva's hands behind his back while another agent pummeled him with his fists. Then they choked him until he passed out. During this episode, he was naturally trying to help his wife, who was also being attacked.

I ask him a slightly odd question—one I have asked other dissidents and victims: "Do they say anything to you as they are beating you?" Yes, they always do, says González Leiva. They say "gusano," meaning "worm"—Castro and his supporters, at home and abroad, have always called their democratic opposition "gusanos." They say "counterrevolutionary." And they say, "We're going to kill you." (Sometimes they do—kill them.)

Where can these people be found? Where can you find people willing to pummel a helpless and innocent blind man? Aren't they ashamed or embarrassed? González Leiva cites *Animal Farm*, George Orwell's parable from 1945: Napoleon the Pig, who is the Stalin figure, trains dogs to be his enforcers—his Chekists, his secret police, his brutes. Castro has done the same.

Not all agents are equally enthusiastic, however. González Leiva remembers an episode from 2002: A lieutenant named Amauri was giving him one of the worst beatings he ever received. The man was pistol-whipping him about the face. All the while, the man was screaming, "Long live Fidel!" González Leiva heard the voice of another agent, also screaming, "Long live Fidel!"—but in a tone that suggested disapproval of the beating.

According to González Leiva, almost no one in Cuba believes in Communism anymore, and that includes the leaders. "All that they're interested in now is to continue in power until their deaths." Opposition to the government is increasing, and the government is responding furiously. In the first six months of this year, some 6,000 people were arrested (with the accompanying violence). In the past ten years, more than a thousand people have died in prison, from maltreatment.

Opposition on the island lacks money, says González Leiva. But "there is a tremendous spirit of struggle. The people are disposed to confront anything. We breathe a glorious air, an air of combat"—moral and political combat.

The Castro brothers will go to their reward, someday. What then? González Leiva says that many people abroad, including here in Washington, believe the dictatorship must continue, to spare the island a "social explosion." This is false, he says. "After the deaths of Fidel and Raúl, no one will be able to maintain or save that government. I think there are people in Cuba who are capable of putting together a national salvation front, taking the people to a constitutional convention, and holding free elections."

Before I leave, I put another question to him, sort of theatrically: I like comfort and dislike pain. Why does he stick his neck out? Why not opt for a less risky life? Where does this spirit of sacrifice come from—love? "I'd like to stay in Miami," he smiles. "I like air-conditioning." But "if everyone leaves Cuba, who's going to struggle? Martí said that human beings have to participate in politics. Because if people who have human feelings leave politics, you only leave behind bad people, who want to devour the country." He also notes the example of Jesus—who said, "Let this cup pass from me"; but then, "Not my will, but thine, be done."

I have a final question, perfectly standard, almost a cliché: "Is there anything else you would like people to know?" Yes, says González Leiva. "I would like them to know that Cuba will soon be free. And that Cubans will have a prosperous country. Happy. And that people will want to leave Miami for Havana."

—December 22, 2014

An American Story
The rise of Harold Hamm, Algeresque oilman

Oklahoma City, Okla.

Harold Hamm is a major oilman, the biggest in the United States. He's also a significant contributor to our national debate over energy policy. But beyond those things, he's an amazing story. Horatio Alger would blush to include him in one of his novels. Hamm was born the 13th and last child of sharecroppers in Oklahoma. Today, according to *Forbes* magazine, he's the 90th-richest person in the world. (Remember, there are more than 7 billion of us.) Even foes of oil, and of capitalism generally, must smile a little, if only inwardly.

Hamm is the chairman and CEO of Continental Resources, a company that evolved from one he started in 1967. Continental is now in 20 states, and on the New York Stock Exchange. Hamm is an Oklahoman through and through, and his company is based here in Oklahoma City. Yet he is probably best known as the major player in North Dakota—a state that has experienced an oil boom for the last few years. With Montana and a couple of Canadian provinces, North Dakota is home to the Bakken formation, a fount of oil. In a conversation with me, Hamm says that a particular section of the Bakken "turned out to be a very, very nice field."

He says this quietly, almost offhandedly. And this statement is indicative of Hamm's personality (insofar as a personality can be assessed in an afternoon's conversation). He is understated, soft-spoken, unflamboyant. Anyone expecting or hoping for a swaggering oilman is likely to be disappointed. Hamm is bookish and somewhat shy. He's a bit of a science geek, with a love of geology. He enjoys showing the rocks and fossils he has collected. I ask Hamm's daughter Shelly, "Did you ever think your dad would get so big?" She says, incredulously, "No! No, no." Hamm, again according to *Forbes*, is worth about $12.4 billion. That makes him No. 33 in America.

I meet him, and his daughter as well, in his office. He moved the company to Oklahoma City from Enid last year. (Enid is 100 miles to the northwest.) Behind Hamm is a picture taken in Tel Aviv—showing him with Benjamin Netanyahu, the prime minister of Israel. "He's a great leader," says Hamm. Early in our conversation, I ask him, "Did your parents live to see your big success?" "When you say 'big success'—any success was big for them." His mother died while he was in high school; his father did live to see him get established in business.

Hamm was born outside Lexington, in central Oklahoma, in 1945. (He will be 68 in December.) His parents never owned land or a home. They picked cotton and did other farm work. So did their children. "We went wherever the cotton was good," says Hamm. The harvest could have been in Blair, Okla., or Littlefield, Texas. "Usually, whoever you were pulling cotton for had some kind of housing. Some folks lived in tents. We'd pull cotton till Christmas or the first snow, and then we were out of there." The Hamm family would return home, and the kids would start school (very late, of course). Did Hamm like it? School, that is? Yes: "It was a lot easier than pulling cotton."

When he was 17, the family moved to Enid—this was a new environment, oil country. At Enid High, he was part of a distributive-education program, which meant you got credit for working. Hamm worked 50 or 60 hours a week at a truck stop, the Potter Oil Company. He'd go to school until 1:30, run home and grab a bite to eat, then go work until 11. Then he would study, into the early morning. He would also work on Saturday and Sunday.

There is a story he has often told, and he tells it to me: One morning, he dragged himself to homeroom, then to a school assembly. The speaker was John Frank, an artist from Sapulpa, Okla. There on the stage, he demonstrated pottery, and he had some watercolors on easels. He spoke of his love of art. And he said, "You've got to find your passion in life. Figure out what you care about, what you're most passionate about, and pursue it." Sitting there, young Hamm thought, "Well, what have I got to be passionate about? Pumping gas, washing windshields, fixing tires?" That's what he was doing at the truck stop. But there was something—something to be passionate about: oil exploration. Enid was booming, and there were larger-than-life oil types around. Hamm wanted to be involved in that world. Indeed, he wanted to be an explorationist.

For "D.E. class" (distributive education), he wrote a paper on oil and its leading figures. He shows it to me, here in his office. It's nicely typed and replete with illustrations. He wrote about J. Paul Getty, Harry Sinclair, E. W. Marland, Bill Skelly, H. H. Champlin, Frank Phillips—the largest of the larger-than-life figures. Hamm was interested in the following: How did these guys find this ancient wealth, i.e., oil? How did they land the big fields? What talent, or edge, or know-how did they have? These were men who had not only done well for themselves: They built up the state of Oklahoma, through their businesses and their philanthropy. Young Hamm thought, "I'm gonna do that." It may have been an audacious thought for the 13th, or any, child of sharecroppers. But Hamm tells me he never felt trapped by his circumstances, never felt that he could not break out and succeed.

He wrote his paper under a teacher named Jewell Ridge, a pioneer in vocational and technical education in Oklahoma. He had been in the war, one of those dropped behind enemy lines. In other words, he had uncommon mettle. "He was one tough dude," says Hamm, "but he was also as good as gold." Hamm delivered a eulogy at his teacher's funeral. His eyes brim over as he recollects the teacher, and what he meant to an eager student.

After graduating from high school, Hamm went to work in the oil business, gaining a "toehold," as he says. Before long, he had his own company, the Harold Hamm Tank Truck Service. ("Real innovative," he says of the name.) His old boss at the truck stop, Charles Potter, signed a note for him at the bank—$1,000. "That was enough for me to operate on," says Hamm. The only equipment he had was a bobtail Ford truck, a vehicle that is at the center of Harold Hamm lore. In 1967, he started the Shelly Dean Oil Company (named after his first two daughters). This is the enterprise that grew into Continental Resources.

Hamm looked for oil, reading everything he could, learning everything he could, stretching his imagination as far as he could. Another part of the lore is that he hit a "gusher" on his second well. (I suspect that "gusher" is a term used only by non–oil people, not oil people.

Hamm confirms that this is so. Oil people are apt to refer to a "flowing" well.) Hamm says that this is true, about the second well. But he makes clear, without any immodesty, that the first one wasn't exactly a loser. It delivered 20 barrels an hour, and "that wasn't bad on your first shot." The second one came in at 75 barrels an hour—and "that puts you home quick."

The "beauty part" of this success, says Hamm, is that, suddenly, he could afford to take a breath. "So I did. I took a breath and went to college." At this point, Hamm was in his late 20s. He has been known to say he did things in the reverse order: fortune first, college second. He went to Phillips University, in Enid. (The university, which closed in 1998, was not associated with Phillips Petroleum. It was an institution of the Disciples of Christ church.) "I did not go for a degree," says Hamm. Instead, he took some courses in order to improve his "skill set." He studied petroleum geology, dear to his heart, and important to his career, but also literature and other subjects he was drawn to.

Later on in life came the Bakken. (The name of this formation is pronounced to rhyme with "rockin'," by the way. They have a bumper sticker up there: "Rockin' the Bakken.") The Bakken was "a real tough nut to crack," as Hamm says. People had been trying to crack it since 1951, when the oil was discovered. Hamm has been in the Bakken since about 1988. Many people have heard of hydraulic fracturing, or "fracking"—the technique by which oil or natural gas is forced from rock. Erle P. Halliburton, another Oklahoma oilman, performed the first frack jobs in the late 1940s. Fracking has certainly played a role in the Bakken, as elsewhere. But the big thing, says Hamm, is a much newer technique: horizontal drilling. "It turned everything around. It's what made possible the renaissance we're having today."

Like almost everybody, Hamm and Continental absorbed blows in 2008, when the recession hit. But the company, thanks to planning, was more resilient than others. And Continental soon had phenomenal growth: 85 percent from December 2010 to May 2012.

The oil business is the most demonized in America, or one of them. Hamm has thought long and hard about this. It could have to do with the early wildcatters and "Joe Roughneck," he says. I counter, "But aren't those things kind of romantic?" They should be, says Hamm, but they aren't to all. Also, he continues, "there's always one bad operator who fouls things up for the whole industry." On balance, he says, oil is a clean and safe industry, in addition to an exceptionally helpful one. (People depend on oil more than they know. It's in their cars and planes, of course. But the list of petroleum products is long and varied. Petroleum is a component of sneakers, lipstick, balloons—even the wind turbines so beloved of the environmentalist Left.)

I bring up a popular show from the 1980s: *Dallas*, the night-time soap. It was a story of Texas oilmen. Was it realistic? "Not at all," says Hamm. "It was the biggest piece of unreal garbage." And it set the industry back, he says. People thought of oilmen as endlessly conniving and rapacious. He allows that the show was entertaining, though. Last year, there was a Matt Damon movie, *Promised Land*, whose purpose was to scarify fracking. Hamm notes with satisfaction that the movie flopped. "Eventually, the American people get the story straight." They can't be fooled for long, he says.

Hamm is a staunch advocate of energy independence for this country. He points out that the 40th anniversary of the OPEC embargo is upon us. In his view, America has been "held hostage" to Middle Eastern oil, and energy independence will free us in a number of ways. It will give us more options in foreign policy, he says. He believes that American boys have been dying for oil. Hamm is the co-chairman of a group called the Council for a Secure America, which aims at energy independence. It was on the council's business that he was in Tel Aviv, when the photo with Netanyahu was taken.

A question: Is energy independence possible under the current regulatory regime—without the Keystone pipeline, without a loosening? Yes, says Hamm. Even under present regulations, we can "get there." But if the regulations get tighter, "it's going to be tough." Hamm says that the feds "keep trying to impose things that would basically shut us down." Well, if regulations get no worse, when can we expect energy independence? By 2020, Hamm figures. And it won't be windmills and their kin that achieve that independence: It will be oil and natural gas.

This phenomenon is highly interesting, to some of us. Oil is supposed to be old news, yesterday's energy. But it's the hot new thing, spurring job creation and economic growth (such as we have them). Consider North Dakota alone: It has the lowest unemployment rate in America, and the fastest rate of economic growth. There are people in North Dakota from all 50 states, and many of them hadn't worked for years, before the oil-and-gas "renaissance" arrived. The United States has just overtaken Russia and Saudi Arabia as the top oil and natural-gas producer in the world.

I ask Hamm to tell a story he told to Stephen Moore of the *Wall Street Journal* two years ago. It concerns a meeting with President Obama in the White House. Hamm told the president about the renaissance, and the prospect of American independence. He wanted to be sure the president knew about this. Obama replied that we would have to rely on fossil fuels for the next few years—but he had been assured by the secretary of energy, Steven Chu, that we would have a battery capable of powering our cars brilliantly. We would have it in five years. (The president held his hand up, showing the number five.) I ask Hamm, "How are we doing? Has it been five years?" No, not yet: Hamm talked with the president in March 2011. It was a depressing, incredible conversation for Hamm. The next year, he supported Mitt Romney for president. Indeed, he became chief energy adviser to Romney. And he gave almost a million dollars to a pro-Romney PAC.

Hamm's parents were Democrats, as most Oklahomans were. But he himself registered as a Republican. Then he switched to being a Democrat, when state politics led him in that direction. Finally, he switched back to Republican—"because of Washington, D.C., because of national politics." I ask whether he regrets helping Romney, given the election results. "Oh, no. No." He admires Romney and says, "He was a better candidate than we deserved"—"we" meaning the country. "It's a shame he couldn't get there," he continues. "Some things just go against you." He cites Hurricane Sandy, which battered New Jersey in the days before the election and gave Obama a chance to look healingly presidential.

(On Election Night, an MSNBC host said, "I'm so glad we had that storm.")

It bothers Hamm not at all that Romney was born rich—some people are, most people aren't, and what matters is what you do with what you have. I ask Hamm a slightly odd question: What's it like to be rich? Are there burdens as well as pleasures? In his answer, Hamm talks mainly about the Vietnam War.

"I grew up in the Vietnam age, early on in it. There weren't a whole lot of people going over there, but when I registered in '64, I knew I was going. But I wound up not going. When they weren't taking married people, I was married. When they weren't taking people with a kid, I had a kid. And so on. I didn't go join the Guards to get out of going to Vietnam. I just didn't go. And a whole lot of people went and died. In the Ringwood-Ames area, where I lived at the time, they lost nine boys. Good kids. We knew them all. Anyway, for the people who are left, there's a responsibility to carry on and do the right stuff. We're blessed. We didn't die. We didn't go over there and fight a war. So we have a great responsibility to contribute in whatever ways we can."

Hamm is a believer in giving away your money while you're alive, so that you can see what happens with it. "A lot of people wait till they die, and they don't get to see anything." One of Hamm's causes is diabetes (he was diagnosed with the disease in 2000). At the University of Oklahoma, there is a Harold Hamm Diabetes Center. Another cause is education. He talks about the "cycle of poverty" and how to break it. "I saw it personally. A lot of families just get into it and are never able to get out of it, those poverty conditions. It continues generation after generation." He feels sure that education is a ticket out of poverty.

One problem, he has found, is that people aren't able to travel from rural areas to go to college, owing to restrictions or responsibilities at home. College is out of reach both financially and physically. So he has made it easier for people to study where they are. He was involved in setting up a two-year college and a four-year college in Enid: branches of

Northern Oklahoma College and Northwestern Oklahoma State University. These institutions have made the hoped-for difference, he says.

Hamm is part of the Giving Pledge, a project spearheaded by Bill Gates and Warren Buffett, the richest people in America. It was with these givers that he was at the White House, meeting Obama. When you take the pledge—congratulations, you're a billionaire—you promise to devote more than half your wealth to philanthropy. I can't help telling Hamm that I disagree with his friend Buffett about the estate tax. The Sage of Omaha (Buffett) is a great fan of this tax. He is not such a fan of bequeathing an estate to one's children. Hamm laughs and says, "We all disagree with him on that!" The estate tax was especially disgraceful, he says, before recent reforms: when it caused relatively humble family farms to go under.

Hamm himself has five children, from two marriages. (He is in the process of a divorce right now. The prospect of the most expensive divorce settlement in U.S. history is titillating some in the media.) Several years ago in Washington, D.C., Hamm's friend Bert Mackie, an Enid banker, introduced him to David Rockefeller. Mackie explained to Rockefeller that Hamm was in the oil-and-gas business. Rockefeller said, "Our family has done pretty well by it." Like the original Rockefeller, Hamm has enabled a good number of other people to get rich (certainly richer). This is an effect of entrepreneurship. In North Dakota, there are many people who were once modestly off, if not downright poor, who are now millionaires—because they had land rights, for example, or, even better, mineral rights. Does Hamm get a kick out of helping other people get rich? Yes, he says. But he also notes a human tendency: "There are some who forget pretty quick who helped them . . ."

A terrible question sits on many minds today, especially Republican minds: Is the country going down the tubes? Hamm says yes and no. We will not go down the tubes "if we have real leadership, in all the places we need it." It is urgently needed in the Oval Office, he says. People like to blame Congress for budgetary impasses and other problems. But we could use a strong dose of executive leadership, says Hamm. "I wasn't the biggest fan of Bill Clinton, but Bill knew when to go to the middle of the road and make things happen, get things done." Moreover, Hamm fears that we're on a path to the sort of populism that has blighted South America. Then there's the question of foreign wars. "In the paper this morning," says Hamm, "there's a report about a boy from Edmond, Oklahoma, who was killed. That boy's life is worth so much more than everything they've got going on over there," in Afghanistan. "We've gotten numb to it all. We hear about 15 killed, 20, and we're just numb."

For all his concerns, Hamm is essentially an American optimist. "This country is so good," he says. "We have so many positive things going on here." He believes that there are still opportunities, still openings for entrepreneurs, for dreamers, for those willing to work and dare. Government may get in their way, more than it has in the past. But they can work around it. He quotes an old Enid oilman, Jack Hodgden: "There are more deals than there are people." There are more opportunities to be had than there are people stepping up and taking them.

Leaving Oklahoma City, I feel a little buoyed. Not every sharecropper's son can make the *Forbes* list (global or national). Not every poor kid can make Horatio Alger blush. But it would take a transformation more fundamental than anything we've seen to squeeze the life out of America.

—October 28, 2013

An Iranian's Life

How an exile journalist has coped with the currents of his time

When Khomeini created his Islamic dictatorship in Iran, he also created an Iranian diaspora: Some 3 million Iranians now live abroad, in various countries, on various continents. Many of them do what they can to ameliorate the situation back home. They are especially interested now, as the "green revolution" mounts a serious challenge to the dictatorship. Exile journalists play an important role, in two basic ways: They inform the world at large about Iran; and they inform those Iranians they can reach about both their own country and the greater world. Iran can be an area of darkness.

One exile journalist, among many, is Manuchehr Honarmand. He operates a website called *Khandaniha*, found at www.Khandaniha.eu. It is a "Voice of Democratic Iran," as the homepage says. Honarmand has had an eventful life, an all too eventful one. He spent two ghastly years in a prison of Hugo Chávez, the Iranian regime's close friend. A Dutch citizen, he has witnessed the rise of what some call "Eurabia." He has been caught up in some of the most daunting currents of his time.

Honarmand was born in Tehran in 1946. His father was a civil engineer. The family's name means "artist," incidentally. Part of the boy's education was French: Honarmand went to a French primary school in Isfahan (home of the famous roses). His university education was in Tehran. After graduation, he worked for some French contractors, and he also did some journalism on the side: a little translating, a little writing.

When the Khomeinist revolution came in 1979, Honarmand was arrested, as so many were. "They arrested anybody who looked respectable," as he says. They beat him up, stole his car, stole the air conditioner out of his home—and jailed him, for 15 days. Like so many others, he looked for a way to leave the country. And he eventually found it, when his wife had a medical need: They got permission to go abroad for treatment. They have never returned.

They went to France, where they stayed for a year, with Honarmand doing odd jobs. Then they went to Abu Dhabi, in the United Arab Emirates. There, Honarmand opened a restaurant, working 20 hours a day. After a year, they burned it down. "They"? Almost certainly agents of the Iranian government, says Honarmand, although there is no proof. The regime has a major presence in Abu Dhabi.

After the arson, Honarmand's idea was to go to Canada. He paid $15,000 for some false visas: four of them, for his entire family, which now included two daughters. They had to travel through Yugoslavia. And, the falsity of their visas discovered, they were arrested, right there in Belgrade's airport. But they were able to make a run for it: They ran out of the airport, leaving everything behind. And they found a smuggling contact in the city—a man who arranged to get them to Holland.

They were penniless, but they managed to start over once again. They got refugee status, they learned Dutch, they obtained citizenship. After some years, Honarmand and his wife were divorced, and Honarmand went to London: to work for *Kayhan*, the Iranian exile newspaper. It was, and is, liberal and democratic, and so is Honarmand. He is a Muslim who believes that religion and government "should not interfere with each other." He wants for Iran the kind of freedom that many in the West are able to take for granted.

The year 2000 was a brutally hard one. The Honarmands' younger daughter, 16, was killed in a car crash. The older daughter, who has Down syndrome, lives with her mother in Holland.

It was in 2002 that Honarmand found himself in Venezuela—vacationing. Two Iranians approached him in the Caracas airport. He was pleased to chat with them, giving them his business card. They turned out to be agents of Tehran. Quickly, Chávez's police were on him, beating him, arresting him, and making him sign something in Spanish. The relationship between the Venezuelan government and the Iranian government is a highly interesting and chilling story. Suffice it to say that Chávez has been to Tehran about ten times, and that Mahmoud Ahmadinejad has been to Caracas about five. The two governments work together on oil, nuclear capability, and international terror.

Honarmand was imprisoned in Venezuela for two years, on trumped-up charges of drug smuggling. His prison was an infamous one, known for depravity and murder: Los Teques. Honarmand recalls that three or four prisoners in his cellblock were killed every week—by other prisoners. They were armed with knives, pistols, other things. One evening, Chávez's men did some killing themselves. They came in and executed a man, by beheading him. They left the body and the head in the cell, for the dead man's wife to find the next morning.

How did Honarmand survive? "By money," he says: by paying off all who required to be paid off. He got the money from friends and family. Either you paid or you were killed—simple as that. Eventually, an agreement between the Dutch government and the Venezuelans sprang him.

Once again, he was penniless, in Holland, starting over. He took a position with Radio Zamaneh, the Persian-language outlet set up and funded by the Dutch government. Things took a bad turn, however, when Honarmand found that the director was all too cozy with the Iranian regime. For example, he would fly to and from Iran, something no dissident or democrat could do. Honarmand resigned, making a big stink. A public scandal ensued. In due course, the director was fired, for myriad reasons, stated and unstated. But Honarmand did not return to the radio.

He started his website, *Khandaniha*—and he repeatedly had trouble from Islamists around him, who threatened him. One night, walking home from the subway station, he was jumped and stabbed by two men. Was it political? He can't be sure. In any event, he found it wise to leave Holland, his adopted country, the country of his citizenship. He is now in a country whose identity he would prefer not to broadcast—he has had enough trouble and done enough running.

He thinks, incidentally, that Holland will one day succumb to Islamic fundamentalism. The government is too polite, he says, too worried about being thought discriminatory. And Islamists are using the freedom of Dutch society to subvert that society and make it unfree.

Khandaniha provides news, opinion—a little of everything. The site is in Persian, although it comes with a Google translator that works reasonably well. What about the name of the site? As Honarmand explains, it means, roughly, "Interesting Things to Read," and that was the name of the publication of Ali Asghar Amirani—who was the first journalist killed by the Khomeini regime (after much torture). The site is blocked in Iran, and must be reached by roundabout ways. But some 45 percent of its readers are in Iran. Honarmand does the site by himself, with no employees. He has very little financial support. He lives, essentially, hand to mouth.

Three times, he says, his site has been hacked. Asked whether this has been done by the Iranian government, he chuckles: "Who else? I am not a bank. Who else has the interest to hack a poor website like mine?" The hacking indicates that *Khandaniha* has gotten under the regime's skin; so do mentions in the official press.

The role of technology in the green revolution is "fantastic," Honarmand says. "I am an old man, but I admire this technology, because, without it, no one could communicate." And "the green movement has no other weapon than the Internet." So, will the regime fall? It is impossible to tell now, says Honarmand. At the moment, the regime has the upper hand, mainly in the form of the security forces. But if the West will impose "real sanctions," the regime will be in trouble, because it will lack the money to pay those security forces. And if Iranians in general see the government in such a bind, "they will have more courage."

Honarmand is opposed to military action against Iran. But he favors those "real sanctions." And he says that some money for democratic forces wouldn't hurt, either.

The 1979 revolution was dislocating, in more than one sense, for many, many people. They have dramatic stories to tell, and, as we have seen, Honarmand has had more than his fair share of drama. "Before the revolution, I was a normal guy," he says. "I was earning a living." But then, everything became chaotic. The world slipped from its track. "I had gone to a French school, remember, and I had a free and liberal spirit. Under the Iranian revolution, I could not fit in for even one hour. At my age, I should be retired somewhere, walking in the park, enjoying myself. I am living as a refugee and . . ." His voice trails off. It has been an unexpected, unsought, and unwanted 30 years. But he can be assured that he is making a contribution, as his country tries to get on the track of a better life.

—March 8, 2010

N.B. Later, Mr. Honarmand found it necessary to change the name of his website, just slightly—to Khaandaniha, *which has that double "a" in the beginning.*

Witness from Hell

The bravery of a North Korean escapee

Oslo, Norway

It was not until 2010 that I met a North Korean. I met Kang Chol-hwan at the Oslo Freedom Forum. Kang is the famed defector who wrote a memoir called *The Aquariums of Pyongyang*. Shaking his hand, I had a strange feeling: I felt I was meeting someone from outer space. I had the feeling of meeting an emissary, an escapee, from the largest, most terrible prison imaginable.

North Korea is called "the Hermit Kingdom," because it is uniquely isolated. No one comes in and no one goes out (as a rule). This is too cute a name, however. North Korea is a "psychotic state," as Jeane Kirkpatrick said. It is a cruel Communist experiment, run by a dynasty of dictators named Kim. It is a place of mass mesmerism, mass murder, and mass misery. With apologies to Syria, Somalia, and a few other countries, it is the worst place on earth.

Since 2010, I have met some more North Koreans, mainly through this same Oslo Freedom Forum (the annual human-rights conference in the Norwegian capital). There are two defectors or escapees at the forum this year: Yeonmi Park and Hyeonseo Lee. They are both young women, and they are stars of the North Korean defector circuit, so to speak. They are pretty and personable, which no doubt contributes to their "stardom." They are also incredibly brave and steely.

I will write about just one of them—Yeonmi—though their stories and views and abilities are equally compelling and impressive.

My first question is, "When did you first realize that your country was unlike other countries? That it was highly abnormal?" Yeonmi says it was when she was in her early teens: She saw the movie *Titanic*, in a bootleg copy. This movie not only tells the story of the famous tragedy at sea. It invents a love story between a young man named Jack and a young woman named Rose. In the end, Jack sacrifices his life for Rose.

Yeonmi was stunned. In North Korea, there were no love stories. "There is no *Romeo and Juliet*," as she says. The only "love" is for the

Communist party and the Kims. There is nothing more honorable than to die for the Kims. Dying for another person—someone you genuinely love—is unthinkable. As she watched the movie, Yeonmi wondered whether the director and actors would be killed. The movie was a criminal act, in North Korean terms.

The act of watching the movie "transformed my thinking," says Yeonmi. "It was mind-blowing. It gave me my first taste of freedom. I realized that there was something else out there, that not all the people in this world were living like us. It was a really important turning-point in how I saw the Kim regime."

There was an event earlier in Yeonmi's life that left a mark on her: an experience of terror. When she was nine, she and her classmates were made to witness public executions. One of the victims was her best friend's mother. She was shot, with the others. Her offense was to have lent a James Bond video to someone else. The regime could not let alien ideas take root and grow. Yeonmi stood next to her friend—the victim's daughter—as the woman was killed.

Death was a constant in Yeonmi's life, as in the lives of North Koreans in general. Kids died on the street all the time, of hunger. Yeonmi did not quite know to be sad or horrified. It was simply normal. So were the corpses that she saw floating in the river. Probably, these were North Koreans who had failed in their attempts to cross over to China.

Yeonmi Park is an articulate young woman, even in imperfect English. And she is obviously smart as a whip. But I ask her this question, because I suspect the answer is yes: "Do you find it hard to describe North Korea to outsiders?" It is impossible, she says. "I cannot find any words to describe my country, or the feelings I had while I was in North Korea." She does her best, however.

I will relate some fragments—further fragments—from her life. She was born in 1993 in Hyesan, on the border with China. The Yalu River separates the two countries. Sometimes, Yeonmi could smell food cooking on the other side. It was fatty, oily food, and absolutely mouth-watering. The Chinese would call over the river, taunting the North Koreans: "Are you hungry over there?" The North Koreans would yell back, "You bad Chinese!"

Like other North Koreans, Yeonmi was convinced that the Kims could even read her thoughts. They were all-pervasive. When Yeonmi was four, her mother told her, "Don't even whisper. The birds and the mice will hear you. The birds will hear you during the day, and the mice will hear you at night." The mother was trying to protect her daughter "from the terror," as Yeonmi says—from terrible consequences. A wrong word could get you and your family into fatal trouble.

The family was one of privilege. Yeonmi's father was a party member. But "my world came crashing down when I was nine," says Yeonmi: Her father was arrested and imprisoned (and of course tortured and broken). Her mother went to prison too for a time. Yeonmi and her sister had to fend for themselves, more or less. They were unable to attend school.

"Were you hungry?" I ask. "Oh, my gosh, of course," Yeonmi answers. The girls ate dragonflies, frogs, tree bark, and grass. You could eat grass only before June, because, afterward, it was poisonous. "We had to survive," says Yeonmi. "We had to feed ourselves. It was our work." Sometimes, people ask her, "What did you do in North Korea, without the Internet or anything? Were you bored?" Yeonmi tells them no: When you're thinking about how to get the next morsel into your mouth—no matter how unfit for consumption it is—you're not bored.

In March 2007, Yeonmi and her mother fled to China. Their flight was harrowing, but they made it. A Chinese "broker"—a smuggler or trafficker—decided that he would rape Yeonmi. Her mother said, "No, she's only 13." The broker said he didn't care. Girls younger than 13 were being raped, routinely. Yeonmi's mother said, "You will have to kill me. You're not going to have my daughter." The man threatened to call the police. Yeonmi and her mother were extremely vulnerable: If they were sent back to North Korea, they would be killed. Yeonmi's mother said, "Take me instead." The man did. He raped her, right in front of Yeonmi, 13 years old.

Yeonmi's father soon joined the family. (Yeonmi's sister was elsewhere—that is a separate drama.) They hid out in China, terrified of being discovered and sent back. Yeonmi's father died a terrible death in January

2008. Yeonmi helped bury him out in the mountains, at three in the morning. It was extremely cold. Yeonmi was afraid to cry and be discovered.

A year later, she and her mother made a run for Mongolia. In a group of five, they crossed the Gobi Desert. They walked for 24 hours. It was, again, extremely cold. The group had a compass, which broke. They followed the stars. They also had knives—with which to kill themselves, if they were caught. Among the dangers were wild animals, which they could hear, howling. Those animals were hungry, as the fugitives themselves were.

Yeonmi's main thought was to live. She had seen her father die "like an animal," she says: "It was not a human way to die. And I didn't want to die the same way." She had attempted suicide. But now she wanted to live. "I wanted to live for my mother, and she wanted to live for me." In the desert, Yeonmi developed a great respect for life, she says.

At the border with Mongolia, the guards said they could not pass. They would have to go back. Desperate, feeling they had no other choice, Yeonmi and her mother put their knives to their throats, threatening to kill themselves. The guards relented. The South Korean embassy offered asylum. By April 2009, Yeonmi was in Seoul, beginning a new life.

You would think that Yeonmi could face no more hardships, and, in a sense, she has not. Yet it was difficult to adjust to life in South Korea. For one thing, she wasn't sure of her identity: *What country am I from? Am I North Korean, South Korean, or just Korean?* The acceptance or non-acceptance of North Koreans by South Koreans is a story unto itself (and one frequently told, true). I ask Yeonmi whether South Koreans desire reunification. Her answer, in short, is, Absolutely not.

Rather than embrace North Koreans as persecuted brothers and sisters, many South Koreans shun them or shudder at them. These Koreans, says Yeonmi, consider North Koreans barbarians or subhuman. One of the most common questions she gets is, "Have you ever eaten human flesh?" The question is not asked sympathetically. I ask Yeonmi whether North Koreans do, in fact, eat human flesh. "Yeah," she says, quietly. I do not ask her—I can't bring myself to—whether *she* ever did.

Even while a free woman in South Korea, she did not feel completely free in her mind: To a degree, she still felt under the spell of the dictatorship under which she was raised. But in 2011, she read an extraordinary book: *Animal Farm*, by George Orwell. The book seemed to be about North Korea, she says. She cried all night as she read it. "*Animal Farm* set me free from brainwashing," she says.

Later, she read *Nineteen Eighty-four*, Orwell's magnum opus. This book too, she felt, was about North Korea. "A lot of people think it's just a novel, just fiction, but it tells the truth. It is the real story." Yeonmi is amazed at Orwell's capacity to understand. "He's a genius."

In Seoul, Yeonmi began to appear on a television show, a kind of variety show. Other North Korean girls are on it as well. I ask Yeonmi, "Are you famous? Are you recognized on the street?" Yes, she says. "Is it nice? Do you enjoy it?" Yeonmi doesn't answer for a long time. She gathers her thoughts, then she says, "I started to get attention in South Korea because I was young and pretty. Our show is a beauty show, so we wear lots of makeup and short shorts. We act cute and sexy." She figures it is worth it if they can get their message out: their message about the reality of North Korea. And they do get the message out, through the froth and glitz.

Also, says Yeonmi, this show proves to South Koreans that North Koreans are normal people, not merely beasts that scrounge for food, although they are forced to do that, as South Koreans and anybody else would in the same circumstances.

Her television fame provides her main platform, but she has also worked for a refugee newspaper. She uses every outlet she can find. She campaigns continually against the Kim dictatorship. For her troubles, she has received death threats from the regime. A South Korean official urged her to lie low and change her name. Yeonmi would not hear of either. "I have already experienced freedom," she tells me, "and I am satisfied." I take this to mean that she does not fear death. She also says she wants to use her time—however much time it is—to help her fellow North Koreans. As for her name, she says, "It is my legacy from my father, the only one he left me, and I am very proud of it." She will not give it up.

Yeonmi is now a student at Dongguk University in Seoul, studying criminal justice. She would like to study international relations in the United States. She reads widely, soaking everything up. In a sense, she is making up for lost time. She is interested in Bastiat, the classical-liberal economist. At the other end of the spectrum, she is interested in *The Communist Manifesto*. She is mainly interested in the freedom to read and think whatever she pleases. Among the "classics" she has enjoyed, she says, is *Wuthering Heights*.

I ask her whether she expects the North Korean dictatorship to fall. Yes, she says. "Nothing can last forever. That's one thing I have learned from history: Nothing is forever." After 70 years, for example, the Soviet Union fell. Also, "a lie does not have power. They lied to me for more than a decade, and they lied to my mother for four decades. And when you see the truth, the lie's all gone. The brainwashing stops. No more lie."

Yeonmi sees two possibilities for North Korea. In the first scenario, the regime falls, just as the Soviet Union did. Presumably, reunification would follow, with all of its challenges (to put it mildly). In the second scenario, the regime adjusts, as the Chinese Communists and the Vietnamese Communists have done. That would allow the North Korean Communists to hang on for untold years longer. "My dream is reunification," says Yeonmi.

Toward the end of our conversation, I ask a standard question: "Is there anything in particular you would like people to know?" She thinks for a while. Then she says, with an air of apology, "I know there are lots of problems in this world." She mentions the Dalits, the untouchables, in India, specifically. So, why should people care about North Korea? It's just one country. But "this is so urgent," she says. I tell her she should not feel apologetic. She is not being selfish. North Koreans have the unwanted distinction of suffering under the worst dictatorship there is.

It occurs to me that Yeonmi must be a hard person to complain to. I say to her, "How can anyone complain to you, or other North Koreans? You must be amazed when people say to you, 'Oh, my feet hurt,' or, 'Oh, I ate too much.' Your problem was never eating too much, was it?" She smiles. And she relates a conversation she had with an Egyptian, about the severe problems in that country. For one thing, said the Egyptian, people cannot get meat regularly. They have to make do with fruit, vegetables, bread, and so on. To Yeonmi, when she was hunting for dragonflies, such meals would have been unthinkably great.

She tells me about the time she and her father ate frozen potatoes, "black in color." They could not find any wood for fire. There was nothing to burn (and there was of course no electricity). So, they ate the black potatoes with snow. "That's how I lived," says Yeonmi. And she and her father felt lucky to have those potatoes. Lots of people were starving to death at the time. "If I could have eaten those black potatoes forever," she says, "I would never have made that journey to China. I would have stayed in North Korea." But she could not count on the luck of black potatoes, which could not be cooked.

At the beginning of this article, I mentioned that, when I met Kang Chol-hwan, I felt I was meeting someone from a different planet. I could not believe I was shaking hands with a North Korean (an escapee from the gulag—a concentration camp). I am now faintly surprised to be seeing Yeonmi, and she is faintly surprised to be seeing me. "When I was crossing the Gobi Desert, trying to stay alive," she says, "I never expected to be having this conversation, in English, in Norway."

Yeonmi Park is cute and bright and personable and adorable. Naturally, she is a hit on television, and on the human-rights circuit. What she mainly is, though, is brave. Unbelievably, unfathomably brave.

—November 17, 2014

Prima Ballerina

Julie Kent hangs up her slippers

When Julie Kent made her entrance as Juliet the other night, the applause for her was long and loud. And she seemed more girlish than ever, as she frolicked around the Nurse. Why was she retiring?

But retiring she was. Julie Kent is one of the outstanding ballerinas of our time. She was with the American Ballet Theatre for almost 30 years: 1986 to just the other night. She is a senior citizen, in ballet terms: age 45. Kent is, indeed, the longest-serving dancer in ABT history.

She has danced many roles, but it was fitting she bade farewell as Juliet. It has long been an especially touching role for this especially touching dancer. A few years ago, I heard something I don't think I had ever heard before in a theater of any kind: sobbing. Sobbing in the seats. It was at the end of *Romeo and Juliet.* Prokofiev and Shakespeare get most of the credit, I think. But some of the credit goes to that night's ballerina, Julie Kent.

I sat down with her some weeks before her retirement. We met at ABT HQ here in New York. Kent was in an oversize sweater, which is almost stereotypical ballerina-wear. She was thoughtful, gracious, articulate, and sweet. Wonderful smile, wonderful laugh. Her speech was just slightly southern, or mid-Atlantic, let's say.

Without question, she can enchant people onstage and off.

She grew up in Potomac, Md., outside Washington, D.C. Her mother was a ballet teacher; her father was an officer in the U.S. Public Health Service. He participated in Operation Deep Freeze, a series of missions to Antarctica. He is buried in Arlington National Cemetery—"just across the way from my husband's father," says Kent. "They are literally like ten feet from each other."

Her husband's father, Kent explains, was a decorated World War II vet. I make a remark about "the Greatest Generation." "Oh, yeah, they were," says Kent. Then, referring to her family members, she says, "Well, anyway, God bless them both." There are tears in her eyes.

She was just 16 when she joined the American Ballet Theatre. Soon, she was cast in a movie: *Dancers*, with Mikhail Baryshnikov, the great dancer who was then artistic director of ABT. Baryshnikov said, "I was absolutely mesmerized by her looks. She has really an extraordinary face, a classic face." One writer once referred to Kent's "Botticellian beauty."

She was born Julie Cox, not Julie Kent—but her family always figured she would change her name for the stage (or screen). Her father wanted "Julie Adams." Why? Her name would likely appear first on a roster! "That's such a dad thing," Kent tells me, laughingly. An assistant to Baryshnikov, Charles France, hit on "Kent." That, she accepted: Like Cox, it was short, English, and started with a "K" sound.

In 2000, by this time an established star of 30, she appeared in another film, *Center Stage*. The two films made a big difference in her career, she says. You can reach masses of people, and you are, in a sense, immortal—forever 16 or 30 or whatever. Many girls and young women have come up to Kent saying, "*Center Stage* is my favorite movie. I watched it a million times. *Thank you so much.*"

Screen immortality aside, I ask Kent about her longevity—her dancing longevity. She cites physical and mental health, among other factors. One of those other factors is her children: She had them when her career was well along. "I think they gave me strength and energy—a push." Some people might regard having children as a career-killer; for Julie Kent, it was a boost.

Her husband is Victor Barbee, a former dancer who is now the associate artistic director of ABT. Their children are William, eleven, and Josephine, six. I tell Julie they must get a kick out of seeing her dance.

They do, she says—"but it's really not a big deal to them. At the end of the day, I'm their mom. They understand that as much as I've been committed to my work, it's nothing compared with my commitment to them."

What she will do in retirement, she's not entirely sure. She will let it unfold. But she intends to "share my voice as an American artist, a woman, and a mother," and to be "an ambassador for dance" and "an advocate for the arts and arts education."

Will she attend the ballet? Or does one simply have to be on the stage? Laughing, she remembers a moment when "Natasha said, 'It's a whole lot more enjoyable to dance this than to watch it.'" By "Natasha," she means Natalia Makarova, the famed Russian ballerina. But "I love ballet," says Kent, "and I do love to watch it."

Nevertheless, "watching is a completely different experience from dancing." Here Kent takes a long, long, reflective pause. "I don't think you can even compare them."

On the stage, she has always been known for her classic lines, her elegance of line. Among other gifts, she has the body for it. The instrument. Which makes a difference, right? I mean, not just any body type can succeed in ballet. True, confirms Kent. "Not everybody can be Derek Jeter either." (This is the recently retired New York Yankee great.) "That's the reality. Otherwise, we all *would* be."

I bring up the issue of eating disorders among ballet dancers. Kent says that this issue, while important, is overblown. She herself is thin, and always has been. And "nobody would ever think that I have a normal diet"—but she does. Her mother always made sure that Julie had steak, potato, and salad. Other girls, says Julie, have nothing for dinner but a big salad with fat-free dressing on it. 'Round midnight, they're starving, and scarf a pint of Häagen-Dazs.

In the course of our discussion, I say that, for me, ballet is about the women. Sure, the men have their moments, but mainly they should frame the women. And stay out of the way. Kent laughs and laughs. "Honestly," I say, "who goes to the ballet for the men?" "A *lot* of people," she protests. Persisting, I say, "Is there a starring role for them?" She laughs and says, "Um . . ." Then she laughs some more.

"Do they have a title role?" I say. I concede there's *Le Corsaire*. Yes, says Kent, but that story is really about the women. "As well it should be," I say.

"Well," says Kent, "you and Balanchine are on the same page with that one." Then she laughs, heartily.

Continuing my shtick, or half shtick, I quote Lincoln Kirstein, the late ballet impresario. He said—or is said to have said—"Modern dance exists for people who can't do ballet." "Ooooh," says Kent, laughing. "*Ouch.*" "But it's kind of true, isn't it?" I say. Kent denies it, strongly. "I don't think Isadora Duncan had aspirations to be a ballerina," she says, and "I don't think Martha Graham had any desire to create *Sleeping Beauty*." Fair enough. But I still think Kirstein's (alleged) remark is kind of true.

"People don't say things like that anymore," observes Kent. "That's a reflection of another time." "Maybe," I say, "but I still love the political incorrectness of it." Kent is amused but, ever diplomatic and gracious, noncommittal.

Years ago, I read that Fred Astaire didn't like to dance socially—at parties and so on. Is that true of Kent? It is, for the most part. "I love to watch it, but I'm definitely a chair dancer. I'm far too shy to put myself out there like that." I ask what a chair dancer is. The answer is, someone who dances while remaining seated in his chair. Kent demonstrates a little of it—really elegantly.

In these twilight days, Kent has been talking about something she never spoke of before: a note given to her by Makarova, just before Kent appeared in Makarova's production of *La Bayadère*. The note said approximately this: "Dear Julie: Someone once said, 'Beauty can save the world.' What a great responsibility you have on your shoulders."

Here at ABT HQ, Kent says, "This note meant a lot to me, in many different ways over the years. I've interpreted it in different ways. It's inspired me in different ways. It's motivated me in different ways. And I feel now it's—well, it's true." She believes that beauty, in various forms, is a human need and balm.

From her girlhood, she wanted to be a ballet dancer. She had a little tape recorder and would go to sleep listening to ballet scores by Tchaikovsky, Prokofiev, et al. She saw in her head how she would dance to the music. Is there anything she has left undone?

She cites this and that, but she is "in no position to complain," as she says: She has had the longest career possible, and has had "such a really blessed experience" in essentially the entire classical repertoire.

Years ago, a pianist (Jerome Rose) taught me a saying: "You play who you are." I think of this when listening to Kent talk about Nina Ananiashvili, the Georgian ballerina who retired from ABT in 2009. She is one of my personal favorites. Kent says, "She's a very lovely, warm person, and one of the reasons she was so adored was that you could see that in her work." A similar statement might be made about Kent.

Romeo and Juliet is tough to take under normal circumstances, so tragic is it. At Julie Kent's farewell, it was triply hard to take. There must have been few dry eyes in the house. The ovation went on for almost a half hour, as the retiree's colleagues honored her with flowers, embraces, and whispered words.

Last to emerge from the wings were the family: Victor Barbee and the two children. Tears flowed freely from the boy. Julie took him to the front of the stage and curtsied to him. He smiled a bit. The house swooned.

Like a great many others, I can say this: I'm sorry she's gone, but I'm glad to have seen her.

—July 20, 2015

An American Original

'50 years of creating happiness'

New Market, Va.

Clive A. Babkirk is a Yankee in the South. He and his wife, Lois, are Mainers who live in the Shenandoah Valley of Virginia. Each has a marvelous Down East accent—the kind you hardly hear anymore in New England, to say nothing of Virginia.

It so happens, Clive is one of the most eloquent people I know. Also one of the most likeable. I tell him I want to come down and see him. He says, "When are you coming? As they say down here, I'll get a hold of a woodchuck, and we'll have woodchuck stew."

Clive is a designer and maker of furniture. He also designs and makes smaller things. He can create virtually anything out of wood, and has. His business card says, "50 years of creating happiness." I'll tell you a little of his story.

He was born in Berlin, N.H., in 1928. His father was from Maine, but was working in that town at a paper mill. The baby's mother had a couple of reasons to call her newborn "Clive." First, there was a movie star, Clive Brook. Second, there was "Clive of India," the British general and statesman in the 18th century.

Clive goes by both Clive and "Kirk," his nickname. As the "Kirk" part tells you, he's Scottish. He's also Swedish, French, and Irish. Whenever he talks about saving money, he says it's the Scotch coming out.

In the teeth of the Depression, the mill in New Hampshire went bust. Clive was three at the time. His father took the family back up to Maine—to the very top, Stockholm, Maine, in Aroostook County. This was potato-growing country. In all, the family had four children. At least they wouldn't starve to death.

Times were lean, though. "We had rolled oats for breakfast," says Clive, "and then Mum would fry 'em in a little bacon fat for lunch."

An uncle had a shortwave radio. It got Germany. Clive heard someone yelling on it—Hitler. Whenever there was a pause, Clive asked, "What's he doing?" The uncle would answer, "He's getting a mouthful of sauerkraut."

Several years before he learned to drive a car, Clive learned to fly a plane. He was taught by a trapper—Freddie Anderson, the Flying Trapper.

Clive's mother was born Ellen Nordica Norton. That peculiar middle name came from her great-aunt, Madame Lillian Nordica. Madame Nordica was born Lillian Allen Norton in Farmington, Maine. A soprano, she became the first American opera singer to achieve world renown. She was known as "the Yankee Diva" (as Joyce DiDonato, a mezzo-soprano from Kansas, is today).

According to Clive, his mother could sing, too. She would sing when she was down on her hands and knees, scrubbing the floor. When he was a boy, Clive heard this every day.

Madame Nordica was one of the first celebrity endorsers of Coca-Cola. In fact, she was featured in the first national magazine ad that Coke ever ran—the year was 1905. Today, Clive and Lois have a commemorative item on their wall: Aunt Lillian, advertising Coke.

A clever boy, Clive graduated from high school when he was 15. He had one teacher he thought was nothing but "a lousy old maid." Her name was Vera Peterson, and when Clive got older, he realized that she had taught him a great deal. She was the best teacher he ever had. Clive never went to college, but he went far.

When he was about 17, he was working down in the lower part of the state. A friend was dating a girl named Ruth. One night, they were going to the movies. Would Clive like to go along, with Ruth's younger sister, Lois? Sure, said Clive. And they have been together ever since.

Unfortunately, neither Clive nor Lois can remember what the movie was. That datum has been lost to history. Lois does remember, however, that they had brownies and strawberry ice cream afterward.

They were married in 1947, when Clive was 19 and Lois was 21. Clive likes to remind his wife that she's older than he. But he does this with great affection. "I've always liked older women," he says.

Lois is not related to an opera star, but she *is* related to a literary star: Ralph Waldo Emerson. Also the Winchesters, of rifle fame. She wonders, humorously, why no money made it down to her.

With work unavailable in Maine, Clive and Lois moved down to New Hartford, Conn. Clive had job after job, as a tool-and-die maker. But he really liked to fiddle with wood. I ask him whether his father had this talent. "No," says Clive, "he couldn't saw a straight line on a board." But Clive had the talent, and so do his children.

Clive and Lois had five children. One of them, Dale, died at the age of 20. He was killed in a car accident. He was a very talented woodworker, as the things he made prove.

When Clive was fiddling around, he made bookends, pipe racks, cribbage boards, and other such objects. They caught the notice of a buyer for G. Fox & Co., the department store in Hartford. He took them to a trade show in Chicago. Soon after, Clive heard from the chief buyer at Neiman-Marcus, in Dallas—who wanted as much as Clive could make. This led to orders from Marshall Field's, I. Magnin, and the rest of the big stores.

In the mid-1960s, Clive decided to leave tool-and-die–making behind and go full time into woodworking and furniture. The family decamped to New Hampshire, settling in Epsom. There, Clive presided over a village: a village of craftsmen. There were blacksmiths, potters, and more. Clive accepted a lot of hippies into his village. When they came to him, "you could hardly see 'em for hair." He told them to clean up and fly right—which, says Clive, they did.

His operation was known as the House of Kirk. He and his crew made everything from tables to pipe organs, from beekeeper's benches to armoires. They sold to ordinary people and to the country's most prominent families—including the Firestones, du Ponts, and Mellons.

"Which pieces are you proudest of?" I ask Clive. He thinks of a series of rolltop desks he made.

In 1985, he and Lois moved down here to Virginia. Why? "For the wood," says Clive—it was diverse and plentiful in this region. Also, he and Lois had gotten to love the Shenandoah Valley, on various trips.

They came to New Market and bought a building that was intended to be a warehouse. Then it was a rollerskating rink. Then it was Clive's shop and factory. The facility sits on a Civil War battlefield. Eight Confederate soldiers were killed on the very spot, says Clive. And there are three ghosts in the place. They didn't like the new occupants, the "damn Yankees." But ghosts and Yankees have made their peace, says Clive. They are living harmoniously together.

The shop is loaded with furniture-making machinery, and patterns, and wood. There are also antiques—including two streetlights from Boston, complete with their stanchions. These are exceedingly rare. Virtually all the other streetlights and stanchions were melted down during World War II. Everything was needed for the war effort.

Clive figures these things are worth quite a lot. "Mother and I could live good off them."

In addition to working with wood, he works with plants and trees, as a hobby. He has tended one ponytail palm for 50 years. (It has a name, "Palmie.") There is also a banana tree and a night-blooming cereus.

Clive stopped making furniture about five years ago, and is now making smaller pieces—"gift items," as he says. This is the way he started out, back in Connecticut. He has lazy Susans and flying geese and whatnot. His latest project is an ornament—not a Christmas ornament. He has done those in the past. This is a "forever ornament," as he says, and it has the word "Hope" on it. You might give one to "someone that's hurting," says Clive.

He is a believer in God, and goes to Him in prayer. He is also a man of tremendous compassion toward others.

He also knows a thing or two about hard work, and business success. Back in New Hampshire, Clive knew several politicians, including Meldrim Thomson, the governor during the 1970s. Thomson was a rock-ribbed conservative. He inscribed a copy of his memoir, *Live Free or Die*, to Clive: "a great American who is an outstanding proponent of the free-enterprise system."

I ask Clive whether he's optimistic about the country. No. Among the young, there is too much "disrespect," even "hate." And "it's hurting our country, terribly." Too many young people, says Clive, "have no allegiance to what we're all about, where we come from."

It could be that Americans in every generation have thought this. Maybe it will be true, someday? Maybe it's true now?

But Clive is anything but a sourpuss. He has come through a number of hardships, and has coped with physical pain for a long time—yet he will not be talked into gloom. "I found out in life that you can smile and be cheerful or you can be down in the dumps. And when I get down in the dumps, it doesn't take long before I say, 'Come on, Kirk, this isn't going to get you anywhere.'" And then he's back to his cheerful self.

Anyone who visits him will feel a similar lift. I don't know if they broke the mold with Clive—an exemplary American—but there probably aren't many more of him than there are of those streetlights and stanchions.

—December 31, 2015

AMERICA—SOME SNAPSHOTS

The State of Maine

Not all lobster bibs and brisk swims

Portland, Maine

Arriving at the airport, you see a sign: "Portland, Maine. Yes. Life's good here." The state at large has a slogan: "Maine: The way life should be." Mainers are proud of their state. Indeed, they have an almost Texan state pride. At a hotel, the sign does not say "Have a Great Day." It says "Have a Great Maine Day."

Mainers have a couple of charming linguistic habits (more than a couple). They tend not to say "Maine" but "the State of Maine." "That's simply the way we do it here in the State of Maine." Even while they are talking with fellow Mainers, they will not say they come from Bethel or Brunswick. They'll say they come from "Bethel, Maine," or "Brunswick, Maine."

Yes, life is good here. Scrappy kids romp through blueberry patches, go for a swim, and scarf lobster. That sort of idyll really exists. But there are severe problems in Maine. Life is tough all over, true—but Maine has some special challenges that are miserable to meet.

It is an interesting state, demographically. There are just 1.3 million people in a very roomy state. Maine has the lowest population density east of the Mississippi. It is also the whitest state—with some 95 percent being Caucasian. It is also the oldest state—with a median age of almost 43.

Tucker Carlson, the journalist and entrepreneur, has long lived part time in this state. He says, "Maine is like Oregon: a poor, rural, conservative state, dominated by Portland."

Portland is a liberal city, filled with people who come from elsewhere. It is a classic (and beautiful) "latte town." On a busy street, there is a shop pushing "fair trade" coffee. Its slogan is "Changing the world through coffee . . . one cup at a time." That sums up the spirit.

Interrupting the idyll is a large and new Somalian population. I think, "They must be very grateful to be here." Today's Somalia is one of the worst places on earth, along with North Korea, Syria, and a few others.

No doubt, many Somalians are grateful to be here. But they brought with them some of the maladies of the Old World.

These include gang warfare and brutality toward women. The Somalians are stressing the police, the welfare system, and everything else. Anti-integrationist Somalians can make life hell for those Somalians who wish to integrate—who wish to become Americans. A friend in Portland tells me, "Racism in this town is being stirred up."

Another friend, Carlson, makes a sardonic observation: "Racial strife is the only problem we didn't have in Maine, so we had to import it."

The heart of Somalian Maine, so to speak, is northwest of Portland. As California has L.A., Maine has an L-A—Lewiston-Auburn, twin cities, divided by the Androscoggin River. Lewiston in particular is a "little Mogadishu." I will have a look at it in due course.

L-A is just 35 miles from Portland, but, for some Portlanders, it might as well be in another state. There is Portland, an anchor in the southeast, and then there's the rest of Maine. I ask a young woman in Portland, "Have you ever been to Bethel?" (which is 70 miles away). "No," she says, "I don't really go up to Maine." Then she catches herself and says, "I mean, to northern Maine."

In truth, Bethel is in the southwestern part of the state—but I know what the young lady means: Virtually no one lives above what you might call the 50-yard line of Maine.

There is more than one divide here. In addition to Portland-and-the-rest, you have coastal versus inland. Coastal Maine tends to be prosperous and postcard-worthy: "Vacationland," as the state's nickname has it. (Maine has two nicknames, actually. The other is "The Pine Tree State.") Inland Maine is grittier, more Appalachian.

Maine has always been a poor state. It has high levels of welfare dependence. It has also been a booze-soaked state. Why? Another Maine friend of mine says, "We're remote, cold, and dark." And that adds up to alcohol—as in Russia, Finland, the Upper Peninsula of Michigan, etc.

In recent years, Maine has been very hard hit by drugs. A headline in 2011 read, "Maine tops nation in prescription drug abuse." On the heels of prescription drugs are heroin and meth. Dealers from New York and other points south find a ready market here. People are overdosing in increasing numbers—dying.

Politicians and others speak of an "epidemic," and that is not an exaggeration. All the New England governors are devoting more and more time to this problem, this crisis. In fact, there was a gubernatorial summit on drugs in Waltham, Mass., a few weeks ago.

Traveling around Maine, and hearing about it, I think, "This is a textbook example of what Charles Murray is talking about." Two years ago, the famed political scientist wrote *Coming Apart: The State of White America, 1960–2010*. It is about economic and moral decline. Of course, there are textbook examples all over the country.

Earlier this year, I was in rural Michigan, visiting Hillsdale College. Someone told me that local stores have trouble getting and keeping help: Too many citizens are hooked on meth. A little later, I was in Nebraska, doing a story from a lovely farming community. My host pointed out all the meth houses.

When did America become a continental ghetto?

In his state-of-the-state address last February, Maine's governor spoke of the drug epidemic. "It is tearing at the social fabric of our communities," he said. "While some are spending all their time trying to expand welfare, we are losing the war on drugs." He went on to say that "927 drug-addicted babies were born last year in Maine. That's more than 7 percent of all births."

The governor is Paul LePage, a conservative Republican. He is the most controversial, colorful, and quotable governor in America. His political incorrectness is spectacular. The liberal press doesn't know whether to be outraged or amused. *Politico* ran a story titled "How Did Mild-Mannered Maine Get America's Craziest Governor?"

A long way from crazy, LePage knows many things. Poverty, for one. He was born in Lewiston in 1948. The family was French-speaking, and Paul was the first of 18 children. His father was a mill worker and a drunk. He beat the hell out of Paul, who escaped home at age eleven. He lived on the streets for two years. With the help of some caring and responsible adults, he rose.

LePage has an advantage that few politicians do: You can't out-poor him. You can't lecture or guilt him on the subject of poverty. His tongue is amazingly free. In his state-of-the-state address, he said, "There is no excuse for able-bodied adults to spend a lifetime on welfare at the expense of hard-working, struggling Mainers." He is trying to crack down on welfare abusers.

I think of the Rockefellers, some of whom went to poor states to have their careers: Winthrop became governor of Arkansas; Jay became a U.S. senator from West Virginia. If a Rockefeller tries to reform welfare, the headline may well read, "Rockefeller Snatches Bread from Urchin's Mouth." Try that with LePage: He *is* the urchin.

What Lewiston looked like when LePage was a kid, I don't know. It's fairly sad now. This is not postcard Maine, not Camden (though Bates College is charmingly New England). Just about the only thing that enlivens one neighborhood is the garb of the East African women. It is gay and multicolored, contrasting with the general gray.

Outside a community center, Somalian boys are playing a rowdy game of basketball. They look pretty much like other American kids, enjoying an American game. Will they become Mainers? Downeasters? Are they already? A lot depends on the answer to that question. The nature of their lives, and the life of the society they inhabit, is at stake.

Maine is a state that young people leave in droves. They have pride, yes, but they also need opportunity. LePage wants to foster conditions that allow them to stay, if they want. He is doing his damnedest to make Maine business-friendlier, in the face of a social-democratic culture. Two years ago, I interviewed another governor, Susana Martinez of New Mexico. Like LePage, she is a conservative Republican. She said that New Mexico was a state that young people felt they had to leave, to get ahead. She wanted to change that.

True to the nickname, Maine is Vacationland. But I wonder whether that designation is insulting, or irksome, to the natives. It is Vacationland for others, but the place where *they* live. And it can be very hard.

—August 11, 2014

Decision at Pine Ridge

The ongoing, awful question of alcohol on the reservation

Pine Ridge, S.D.

In August, a potentially momentous vote took place—not momentous for the nation, but for the nation of the Oglala Sioux, or Oglala Lakota, as they're also called. Here on the Pine Ridge reservation, tribe members voted to lift the longstanding ban on alcohol: its sale, possession, and consumption. The vote was 1,843 to 1,683, or 52 percent to 48 percent. The issue has stirred passions on the reservation. And it's not quite over: Repeal is "not a done deal," as an official tells me. The Tribal Council must approve it.

Pine Ridge drifts in and out of the national consciousness, mainly out. In 1973, activists took over the village of Wounded Knee, creating a national drama. Pine Ridge is in the southwestern corner of South Dakota. It's larger than Delaware and Rhode Island combined—but smaller than Connecticut. Some 17,000 people live here. By contrast, Wyoming, the least populous state, has 576,000. Pine Ridge is a very poor place, the poorest of all the reservations.

One could cite many grim statistics, and tug at heartstrings. I will give a few facts, quickly. Infant mortality is sky high. Diabetes is sky high. So are any number of other illnesses, including depression. Suicide is sky high. It is virtually epidemic among teenagers. Life expectancy for men is 48; for women, it's 52. One hears that this is the worst life expectancy in the Western Hemisphere, except for Haiti.

Most people drop out of school, and most people don't work. Unemployment is over 80 percent. Most of those who do work are women, and they tend to work for one government entity or another. Homes are overcrowded. Often they have no water or electricity, and often they have a dangerous mold. Teen gangs have become a menace. To add insult to injury, the weather here is some of the most challenging in the country—a "weather of extremes," as they say. It's punishingly hot in the summer and punishingly cold in the winter. Severe winds blow at many times.

The reservation is, as most people know, alcohol-drenched. One reads that eight out of ten families are affected by alcohol. I talk to people who have no idea who the other two families are: They've lived here all their lives, and never knew a family unaffected by alcohol, and have barely known an individual unaffected. What are the effects of alcoholism? Robbery, rape, murder, poverty, family breakdown, disease, death—one could go on.

Like two-thirds of all Indian reservations in America, Pine Ridge has traditionally banned alcohol. Yet alcohol, of course, is rife. Tribe members can get it over the border, wherever the border is. They might get it in Martin, S.D., in the east. Most notoriously, they get it in Whiteclay, Neb., in the south. (Sometimes the name of this place is written "White Clay." It depends on the sign or map.) Whiteclay is just over the border from Pine Ridge—meaning the village of Pine Ridge, not the reservation at large. People in Whiteclay have been selling booze to the Sioux for over 100 years. There are four liquor stores in Whiteclay and only three times as many residents. Yes, Whiteclay has just a dozen people or so. The liquor stores do a booming business. They sell something like 4.5 million cans of beer a year, which comes out to more than 12,000 a day. Whiteclay has been a focus of tribal anger for a long time.

Last year, the tribe filed suit against the liquor stores in federal court. They also sued beer distributors and beer makers, including Anheuser-Busch, Miller, and Pabst. They claimed that alcohol was stocked and sold "far in excess" of what Nebraska law allows. The judge was sympathetic, saying, "There is, in fact, little question that alcohol sold in Whiteclay contributes significantly to tragic conditions on the Reservation." He also said that the case did not belong in federal court.

Less than a year later, the tribe held its referendum. For some, the victory of the repeal side had an air of, "If you can't beat 'em, join 'em." If you can't keep others from selling the stuff, sell it yourself. In all likelihood, the Tribal Council will not nullify the people's vote. But, again, it has a right to do so and may. Many leaders are against repeal, including the tribal president, Bryan Brewer. (Yes, his name is Brewer.) The police chief, Ron Duke, is on record as opposing repeal as well. By his own testimony, he drank until he was in his early 30s, and he has had two daughters killed in drunk-driving accidents.

To ban or not to ban is a very, very touchy issue on the reservation. Many people are reluctant to discuss it, certainly with a white stranger. But some open up. Three boys, hanging out together, are against repeal. They're also very nervous about it. They seem from 14 to 16 years old. If people have readier access to alcohol, they say, won't there be more alcoholism? "There's a lot of pressure on us kids," one boy says: pressure to drink, to give in to the general malaise. Would the lifting of the ban constitute some sort of abandonment of them? A surrender?

From the boys comes, not just nervousness, but also a sense of fear. Fear of alcohol is apparent in other people too. They talk about alcohol as if talking about a plague. Warnings against alcohol are in the air. Let me give an example. At the Prairie Wind casino—motto: "Feel the win!"—there are signs posted at the doors. They remind people, in strict terms, that alcohol is forbidden. What would Prairie Wind be like if booze were mixed in with the gambling? At the entrance of tribal offices in Pine Ridge—the village of Pine Ridge—a sign promises that anyone intoxicated will be evicted or arrested.

Naturally, a person will want to ask this question: How could alcohol be more plentiful, or prevalent, than it is now? Can't people just waltz over the border to Whiteclay? Those in the village of Pine Ridge can. And Pine Ridge is the largest of the villages, with 3,300 people. But the reservation is a very big place. It is also sparsely populated, and distances between communities are great. Many people live remotely, and relatively few have cars. Public transportation is almost nonexistent. People walk or hitchhike. Only once before have I seen so many people walking along highways: That was in India, where it was explained to me that the Jains, owing to their religious principles, don't drive.

On the reservation, there is the stereotype of the Indian car—the beater that can barely move. This stereotype exists for a reason. There is a bumper sticker that says "Official Indian Car." Not a few cars are missing half a windshield, and not a few are crunched up in the back. It's amazing they can stay on the road, or are allowed to do so. On the highways are signs warning against drunk driving. These signs include photos of cute kids, now dead.

In the parking lot of Big Bat's, I see a couple of young men on horseback. Later, down the street, they will playfully lasso each other. Big Bat's is the main hangout in the village of Pine Ridge—Sioux Central. It's a combination store, restaurant, and gas station. The manager on duty talks about the impending repeal: He's against it. On his face are bitterness and disgust. He does not believe that Big Bat's will sell alcohol, if repeal goes through. Why's that? He gestures behind him, in the direction of the Nebraska line. "Nobody wants Pine Ridge to look like Whiteclay."

Just before you get to Whiteclay, there's a mural that says, "Legalize alcohol on the rez." Downtown Whiteclay, so to speak, is a forlorn strip. On the other end of it is another mural, which says, "United we stand, divided we fall." In between is an Indian Bowery or skid row. Men sit or lie on the sidewalk, drunk. They are zombie-like, broken. Along the strip are the liquor stores. They are windowless, stark, brutish. They look closed. But they're not. The people come to them on foot or by car. In my observation, the cars tend to be driven by women, with male passengers. The women go in to buy the alcohol while the men wait in the cars. Transactions in the stores are mechanical and weary, with maybe a touch of shame about them.

There are grocery stores in Whiteclay too—two of them. You cannot get alcohol in them. "No, we wouldn't sell it," says a cashier. "Not every place in Whiteclay is for drinking, despite what you hear." What does she think of the Pine Ridge referendum and its result? (The cashier is white, by the way.) She says, brightly, "I think it's good. This has been going on for years"—and by "this" she means the drinking and the blaming. "It's their problem, let them deal with it." Unless I'm mistaken, her tone says, "Whiteclay has had enough of being the villain."

As I look at the Indians, lying on the sidewalks, I wonder, "What's the difference between them and the business executives who get sloshed in their offices or at home in their dens? What's the difference between them and alcohol-fueled writers, some of whom become immortal, such as Faulkner?" The answer, I suppose, is that some can cope and some can't.

The advocates of repeal make many arguments. They say that, with alcohol revenue, you can build detox centers and fund treatment programs. You may also have more money for the schools. Furthermore, repeal will cut down on drunk-driving accidents, as people will be able to go less far for alcohol. Police will not have to use their time investigating possession and smuggling and the like. The casinos will attract more visitors, because they'll be wet, not dry. And look: Prohibition has failed. It didn't work in America 80 or 90 years ago, and it's not working today on Pine Ridge. Time to try something else.

There is also, I believe, an element of pride on the repeal side—a sense that repeal will allow the Sioux to be masters of their own destiny, more than they are now. After the vote, a pro-repeal council member said, "I'm ecstatic. I'm so happy. Our tribe took the decision to move forward and make history." A pro-repeal writer described this step as a matter of "fighting back." Against whom? Against Whiteclay and outsiders in general, presumably.

The president, Bryan Brewer, recoils at the idea that alcohol revenue should fund alcohol treatment. "I consider this blood money," he has said. Many are skeptical that the detox centers and all the rest will appear if alcohol is legalized. Other reservations have promised the same and failed to deliver.

In my view, much of this debate turns on a single question: Could things on Pine Ridge be worse? Or not? Has Pine Ridge hit rock bottom? Or could it go down farther still? The anti-prohibitionists, by and large, say, "No, things could not be worse." Prohibitionists say, "Oh, yes, they could." The above-cited teenagers think so. The manager at Big Bat's thinks so. The same is true of a lady who describes the toll that alcohol has taken on the reservation. She goes through a whole litany, eloquently and emotionally. When she's through, I say, "Well, life is miserable already. Could it be worse?" Her face freezes for a moment. Then she fixes me with a look and says, "Yes, of course it could."

One big reason, she says, and others say, is that it is moderately difficult to get alcohol now. Not difficult enough, obviously—but moderately so. It takes something of an effort. If people could buy it at any of the general stores that dot the reservation, what then?

The cashier at the store in Kyle says she's against repeal. "It's better when people sneak it. You don't have to see it out in the open. I don't want my daughter to see drunk people." (The mother herself looks no more than 18.) But doesn't her daughter see drunk people now? "No. They're not out in the open. They sneak it in their homes." A convenience store in Martin, 35 miles to the southeast, sells alcohol. What does the cashier think of a Pine Ridge decision to do the same—to sell alcohol? "Listen," she says: "They might as well make money off it like everyone else."

One of the classic images in America is that of the wise old Indian—the tribal elder. At Pine Ridge, there aren't many old Indians. Marty Two Bulls says this wasn't always so. He is a journalist—a writer and cartoonist—born in 1962. When he was growing up, he knew not only grandparents but also great-uncles and great-aunts. "We used to see old people at weddings or funerals or sun dances. You don't see that anymore." Today, you might see an old person off by himself, or, more likely, herself. She has few peers. People used to die of natural causes, says Two Bulls. Now they are dying alcohol-related deaths.

There is a connection, he thinks, between an absence of old people and drinking. "When the old people left, it became okay to get drunk, in a way. You didn't *dare* drink around my grandfather." These days, who has a grandfather? Kids, says Two Bulls, grow up in the reservation equivalent of slums. The men around them may be in very bad shape: unable to care for themselves, much less others. Whom do the kids have to look up to? What hope is there for the future? Those who commit suicide have decided there is none.

Two Bulls is against the repeal of the alcohol ban. Like everyone else, he is loath to see the American Indian reduced to two vices, two signatures: drinking and gambling. He believes that repeal will exacerbate the former. But he has time and patience for the other side. A fellow journalist, Brandon Ecoffey, is a strong advocate of repeal. "Legalizing alcohol is not giving up," he writes. "It is punting in an attempt to flip the field. Those that drink will continue to drink and those of us who don't won't. The only difference now is that those with the desire to seek help will have local treatment facilities to access."

None of this would be an issue, as everyone says, if people simply resisted drink. But that is a lot to ask. The Oglala Sioux and other Indians, like individuals and groups all over the world, have been in the grip of a spiritual crisis, for a very long time. Alcoholism is but a symptom of it (though a terrible one). Would repeal of the ban make Pine Ridge worse? I suspect it would. But I also recognize, as others do, that the tribe can vote again, if repeal turns out to be a disaster—or a worsening of the present disaster. Democracy includes a spirit of pragmatism.

—October 14, 2013

N.B. The Tribal Council never approved the referendum of 2013. There were charges of electoral irregularities; the vote was deemed null and void. Repealers are still trying to schedule and win a referendum. The debate remains the same.

Booming North Dakota

What it's like, what it means

Bismarck, N.D.

For many years, North Dakota has been the least visited state in the Union. There are no real tourist attractions here; Mount Rushmore is in South Dakota. The late newsman Eric Sevareid, who was born in North Dakota, called his native state "a large, rectangular blank spot in the nation's mind." But reporters from all over the world have been coming here lately, because North Dakota boasts one of the most interesting and exciting stories in the country: an honest-to-goodness boom.

The state has the lowest unemployment rate in the country, at 3.1 percent. Some wonder who could be out of work, given all the "Help Wanted" signs. North Dakota is No. 1 in job growth and No. 1 in income growth. At the heart of this prosperity is the Bakken formation, located in the northwestern part of the state. It's a vast pot of oil. "Bakken," incidentally, rhymes with "rockin'." They have a bumper sticker here: "Rockin' the Bakken."

Oil was discovered in this area in 1951, but the trick was extracting it. Then, not long ago, came a marriage of two techniques—one older, one newer. The older one was "hydraulic fracturing," or "fracking," for short. This is the method by which oil or natural gas is forced from rock. The newer technique was horizontal drilling. A combination of the two proved a bonanza. Earlier this year, North Dakota passed California as the third-greatest oil-producing state. Before the year is out, they should pass Alaska, trailing only Texas.

People from the other 49 states are coming to North Dakota to participate in this boom. Entrepreneurs in and around the Bakken are having a field day. The common comparison is to the Gold Rush, and that comparison is apt. North Dakota's government is flush in money, and they are both investing in infrastructure and cutting taxes. Not every state has a Bakken, obviously—this goose laying golden eggs. Still, other states can learn from North Dakota, and so can Washington, D.C.

"There are 8 million stories in the naked city," goes an old movie line. There are almost as many in the Bakken. Gary Emineth, an entrepreneur and politico, is in the burrito business. For the Bakken, he had a special burrito made: big, manly, meal-like. He has done more business in 13 stores in the Bakken than in 450 stores elsewhere. In the town of Williston, the McDonald's had to close in the middle of a Wednesday afternoon. They had run out of food. The Williston Walmart does not really bother stocking the shelves anymore. First, who wants to work as a stockboy when you can make a bundle in the oil patch? Second, the goods would not stay on the shelves long. The store just sets the pallets in the aisles, and the customers grab the goods and go right to the register.

Someone says to me, "Do you mind if I tell you something blue?" I'm all ears. "From what I hear," he says, "the strippers are making more per night in Williston than they do in Las Vegas."

The best stories, of course, are those involving men and women whose lives have been renewed by work found in this state. The nation has been down and ailing. North Dakota has been a godsend for many thousands—maybe as many as 50,000, so far (and the state has fewer than 700,000). Next door in Minnesota, the *Star Tribune* ran an article that began, "There's no keeping up with North Dakota's surging economy, but at least they're hiring some of us to do chores." Hearing stories in North Dakota, I recall something I heard an Egyptian say at a Middle East conference. He was talking about unemployment in Egypt and other Arab countries. Young people were having to go to the Persian Gulf, in order to find work. He was sorry that they couldn't stay in their home countries. But "thank God there *is* a Gulf. It has served as a safety valve for the whole region."

In the Bakken, the greatest need is for truck drivers, to haul materials to and from drilling sites. They earn between $80,000 and $120,000 a year, with generous benefits. Dennis Lindahl, a councilman in Stanley, tells me about a family who lost their home in California. They came to the Bakken with one truck, which they ran 24 hours a day. Soon they had three trucks and five drivers, and bought a new home here—with cash. Many workers are paying off their mortgages back home, or buying land back home, or saving for a business they've always dreamed of. Many are simply sending cash back home, to family members who need it. If these workers get a per diem, they try to spend as little of it as possible. In a Mexican or Cuban context, we would use the word "remittances."

Not only are people coming to North Dakota, North Dakotans aren't leaving—as they have done for many years. For generations, North Dakotans who have wanted a chance in life have had to leave the state. Mom and Dad may have been left at home, but the kids were gone. North Dakota was a place you were from, not a place where you lived. Today, you probably don't have to leave, if you don't want to. And people who did leave are "coming back in droves," Lindahl says. (He himself is one of them.) Not a few North Dakotans, who have always lived modestly, are becoming rich overnight: because they have surface rights to sell, or, even better, mineral rights. Or they may have some land on which people can place RVs or trailer homes.

Ah, yes, housing—probably the biggest problem facing the Bakken. These sons of men have nowhere to lay their heads. You can sleep in your car or truck—and many do—but that can be dangerous in a North Dakota winter. (Fortunately, this last one has been mild.) Some people commute for hours. Throughout the oil patch are "man camps," also called "crew camps": modular housing occupied by thousands of men, some of whom sleep in shifts. These camps suddenly crop up in farmers' fields. They resemble military quarters in Iraq or Afghanistan. One camp outside Tioga has what may be the longest hallway I've ever seen. I ask one of the men in charge how long it is. He answers precisely: 1,008 feet.

With the blessings of boom, of course, have come problems: a strain on utilities, hospitals, and the like. There's a need for more teachers, more policemen—more of everything. At the high school in Stanley, they're holding class in the lunchroom, in the auditorium, and in the garage. They're about to have a $7 million expansion. Some don't like the changes that have occurred in this quiet, or once-quiet, part of the world. Before, they may have seen three to six cars a week. Now there are traffic jams. There's dust, noise, and other unpleasantness. There has been an uptick in crime, because there has been an uptick in everything. North Dakotans have long said, "Twenty-below keeps the riffraff away." I'm informed, "The riffraff is still about 5 percent. But now the population is bigger."

So, there are problems—but good problems to have, as many see it. These are problems that come from abundance rather than paucity. Ron Ness, president of the North Dakota Petroleum Council, grew up in Tolna, a tiny town in the eastern part of the state. He saw the town lose its school, its café, and its grocery store. He walked just 500 yards to high school. Kids after him were bused 45 miles each way. This is the kind of thing that happens when a state empties out. There are maybe worse things than boom.

As some North Dakota conservatives tell it—and they have a strong case—the current prosperity has its roots in conscientious policies of the past. It began with the election of a Republican governor in 1992, they say. He was Ed Schafer, later an agriculture secretary under George W. Bush. Scott Hennen, a radio host based in Fargo, describes Schafer as "the Ronald Reagan of North Dakota." (Hennen himself has been dubbed "the Rush Limbaugh of the Prairie" by the *Wall Street Journal.*) In the early '90s, North Dakota was flat on its back, without growth or opportunity. Morale was very low. What Schafer did, in a nutshell, was reform government and make North Dakota business-friendly.

He remembers when Harold Hamm came to visit him in the spring of 1993. Hamm, an Oklahoma oilman who ran Continental Resources, and still does, told him about horizontal drilling. Some in the industry thought horizontal drilling was a pipedream (so to speak). But Hamm thought he had something, and the Schafer government crafted policies to help Hamm and other oilmen see what they could do. They did well.

Long before the current boom, North Dakota was an energy-production and energy-minded state. They have many of the elements of "all of the above," as the politicians say. In other words, they have multiple sources of energy, including coal, hydropower, ethanol, biodiesel, and wind. (Being relatively flat and treeless, North Dakota has no shortage of wind. Sometimes, it's hard to stand up.) Politicians, regulators, and others here stress, "We're used to energy. It's part of who we are. We're not afraid of it, and we know how to deal with it."

While some refer to the current prosperity as "the North Dakota Miracle," others will have none of it. Ed Schafer is one of them: "It was more like a long, hard slog through the swamps. It took a lot of planning." Last month, the current governor, Jack Dalrymple, delivered the Republican response to President Obama's weekly radio address. Dalrymple said, "We have created a friendly business climate in North Dakota, where taxes and insurance rates are low, the regulatory environment is very reasonable, and we have the most responsive state government anywhere." It is true that other states with wonderful resources, including oil, have had different policies and different results. Until recently, New Mexico seemed determined not to produce or compete. California's hostility to energy production is legendary. Its unemployment rate is 10.9 percent, third worst in the country.

And yet, it doesn't hurt to have a Bakken formation. Kevin Cramer, a member of the Public Service Commission, and a Republican candidate for Congress, is grinningly aware of this. He recalls an old Steve Martin skit on *Saturday Night Live*: You can become a millionaire and never pay taxes! How? Well, first get a million dollars. "Let's be honest," says Cramer: "No politician invented the Bakken." He also points out that North Dakota is blessed with private lands, rather than state or federal ones: Almost all of the Bakken is in private hands. "So that made it easier right out of the chute," says Cramer. Companies could invest their capital and get a return on it.

Ron Ness, of the Petroleum Council, suggests that four factors made the Bakken boom: geology, technology, price, and business climate. And just about everybody can agree with Jason Stverak, a North Dakota–savvy journalist—or rather, with his mother: "My mother always said, 'Success is when opportunity meets preparation.'"

This state has more than energy going for it, as people here are keen to point out. Agriculture is still a mainstay. Microsoft's largest campus, apart from its headquarters in Redmond, Wash., is in Fargo. In his radio response to Obama, Governor Dalrymple said, "We have thousands of job openings in North Dakota today, but almost every day the national media asks me if it isn't all due to the oil boom in northwestern North Dakota. I enjoy telling them the county with the most job openings is not among western oil counties but is the county surrounding Fargo, our largest city and on the opposite side of the state." In that city, I meet Michael Chambers, a young man from Carrington, N.D. His parents, grandparents, and great-grandparents were beekeepers. He's a beekeeper too, but also a science whiz: His company, Aldevron, is the first biotech company in the state, and it employs 100 people.

For all the state's economic diversity, oil production is front and center now. "Drill, baby, drill," goes the cry, along with "Frack, baby, frack."

Fracking makes a lot of people nervous (though not in North Dakota). A few days before I came here, I was with some musicians back in Manhattan. They asked me whether I was traveling anytime soon. Yes, I said, to North Dakota. Why, they asked. To look into the oil boom, I said. One of them said, "Oh, yeah—fracking. Isn't that bad for the environment?"

Here in North Dakota, I put this question to all and sundry. And the answer, honestly, is no—not with intelligent regulations. Elsewhere in the country, there are concerns that fracking will contaminate the water. Not in North Dakota: The oil and the aquifers are two miles apart. Then there is the question of oil drilling in general. The footprint of such drilling is getting ever smaller. The environmental impacts are getting ever fewer. Derricks will be up for 20 to 30 days. Then they go away, leaving only simple, unobtrusive pumps (painted to blend in with the landscape). When the well is dry, the land will be back to normal, with no sign that any drilling ever took place. Contrast this with other ways in which we mess with the landscape: highways, railroads, telephone poles, telephone wires, wind turbines . . .

Over and over, North Dakotans tell me one thing: We love our land more than you do. More than musicians in Manhattan could. We have to live here. We are good stewards. We need this land. You don't have to worry that we'll rape and pillage our own backyard, for heaven's sake.

There tend not to be regulation wars in North Dakota: wars between government and industry, liberals and conservatives, crunchies and capitalists. (Pretty much everyone in North Dakota is a crunchy. And, increasingly, a capitalist.) People tend to solve problems together. There is a tradition of "North Dakota nice." Kevin Cramer says, "I tell companies, if you want to get along with me, get along with the people out where you're working. If you don't get along with them, you don't get along with me." The chief oil regulator is Lynn Helms, a man who roughnecked his way through college and worked just about every other job in the oil business, before landing in his present position. "I think it's important for a regulator to have a working knowledge of the regulated industry," he says. "For example, what does a rule mean to a roughneck or to a production engineer?" He says a regulator has to be able to go to a townhall meeting and take questions from all comers, all interests.

Some people consider Helms too tight with his regulations; others consider him too loose. The challenge is to find the sweet spot. "There are people in industry who will test the margins," he says. "That's why you have to have regulations. Then, at the other extreme, there are radicals who would write rules that make it impossible to operate or make money in the state."

Many North Dakotans were taken aback when the Obama Justice Department brought suit against Continental Resources and other oil companies last year. The charge: A handful of birds—between 25 and 30—had died in "reserve pits." The companies were prosecuted under the Migratory Bird Treaty Act. A district-court judge threw the suit out with little ado. In the bargain, he listed some of the ways in which birds die: including flying into wind turbines. That kills an estimated 33,000 a year. Why pick on oil? Why should wind be sacred and oil the bad guy?

Kathy Neset, a veteran oil consultant in Tioga, doesn't look like a bad guy. She is all femininity, and sweet reason. A native of New Jersey, she graduated from Brown University with a degree in geology. I say, "Do people ever say, 'What's a nice girl like you doing in a business like this?'" "Back East they do," she says. She decided to come out here in the late 1970s, shortly after graduating. A friend said to her, "You mean, people actually *live* in North Dakota?" Like Lynn Helms, she did practically every job in the oil business, including roughnecking. It was a different business back then, she says: dirtier, more dangerous. There were accidents. There was no drug testing. Guys would have six-packs in the truck. Today, she says, "it's a kinder, gentler oil business."

Channeling Barbara Walters, I ask Neset what the biggest misconception about the business is. She answers, "People don't know how technical it is. How much knowledge it takes, the huge amount of money behind it, the scientists working on it." In a recent article about Pennsylvania, my colleague Kevin D. Williamson noted "a strong whiff of chess club and Science Olympiad" in the oil patch. True. You encounter a mixture of Poindexters and hard hats. I ask Neset, "What do you say to people—outsiders like me—who think oil is no good? Who have swallowed the line since childhood?" She says, "Well, I can start by asking them how they got here. Whether it was by car, train, foot, or whatever, petroleum products had something to do with it."

Petroleum is an ingredient in sneakers, by the way. And in lipstick. And—how about this?—in wind turbines.

Kathy Neset has been through boom before, and boom is often followed by bust: During the boom periods, you have to guard against it, to the extent possible. There are negative stories to be written in North Dakota. A headline in the *New York Times* said, "Even Boom States Get the Blues." Another said, "A State with Plenty of Jobs but Few Places to Live." A headline in the *Los Angeles Times* said, "Despite jobs, not all is rosy in North Dakota." (Please point me to where all is rosy!) An article in the *Chronicle of Higher Education* worried about whether North Dakota's new wealth would find its way to colleges: "Dreams of lavish support are limited only by a persistent midwestern frugality." Yes, that midwestern frugality will screw you every time.

There are un-silver linings, sure. But the possibilities embodied by North Dakota are exciting. Many Americans dream of energy independence, a dream really within grasp. A headline in *The New Yorker* read, "Kuwait on the Prairie: Can North Dakota solve the energy problem?" A headline in *Maclean's* said, "Bye-Bye, Sheiks." While others talk about "energy independence," Kevin Cramer prefers to talk about "energy security." Like many another free-marketeer, he's happy to import cheap oil from abroad. But it never hurts to have some in your own back pocket, just in case. Even in the rockin' Bakken, oilmen are getting just a fraction of what's there: between 6 and 8 percent. With future technology, who knows what will be possible?

But there are those who would keep the Bakken from rockin', who would kill the goose laying the golden eggs. I ask several people what the biggest threat to them is, and they say, to a man or woman, "The EPA." (Some say price collapse, too.) If the Environmental Protection Agency decides to ban or stifle fracking, "we're out of business," as Cramer says. The Obama administration is clearly no fan of oil. Dalrymple said, "The federal government is killing energy development with overly burdensome regulations. The best example of this is the Keystone XL pipeline which the Obama administration will not allow to be built. . . . We cannot effectively market our crude oil domestically without a large North–South pipeline."

There are people who consider abundant American oil a mortal threat to their agenda: their agenda for "renewables." As John Kemp of Reuters wrote last year, many lobbyists "fear rising oil production would relieve upward pressure on prices and remove the threat of energy insecurity." He spoke of a "Manichean struggle," in which "leaders in Washington and state capitals across the United States are being pressed to decide between embracing the job and income gains that come with drilling" and curbing those gains, to "focus on clean technology investments and employment." President Obama has told Continental's Harold Hamm, personally, that he sees essentially no future for oil and gas. Hamm has signed on as an energy adviser to Republican Mitt Romney. The Obama campaign ran a TV ad saying that Romney stands with "Big Oil."

Okay, but is that bad, necessarily? Hamm's a bigshot, sure—one of the richest men in America. But he didn't start out that way. He was the son of a sharecropper, the last of 13 children. He knows what oil can do for people, in all sorts of ways.

"This is an upbeat story," says Kathy Neset. It is. North Dakota, certainly in its west, is throbbing with life. On the Fort Berthold Indian reservation, there was 40 percent unemployment and "no hope," as Lynn Helms says. Now there is virtually no unemployment and plenty of hope. People in North Dakota are feeling new pride. Someone tells me, "We were kind of the forgotten state on the prairie. Mount Rushmore's not in North Dakota, it's in South Dakota. But now we're showing the way in domestic oil. We're helping the whole country." Someone else says, "People always made fun of us. Now it's kind of cool to be from North Dakota, where all the action is."

Forgetting what the boom has done for North Dakota, think once more about what it has done for others: all those Americans who are newly employed. Some of them were out of work for *years*. Unemployment can have nasty side effects, including depression, alcoholism, and divorce. It's easy for the already employed to sniff at an oil boom. Men who have come to the Bakken are saying that, at long last, with work, they can look their children in the eye. That is really good news.

—April 30, 2012

Men with Plans

A look at an extraordinary prison in Texas

Houston, Texas

"Everyone he meets," says a friend of Brent Johnson's, "winds up going to prison." Johnson is a Houston businessman. And he volunteers in a prison. Those he meets, he encourages to volunteer as well. They often do, and they wind up enjoying it. There are some 1,200 volunteers in this particular prison—and only 300 prisoners. That is an astonishing ratio.

The prison is the Carol S. Vance Unit, in Richmond, outside of Houston. The prison is dedicated to the InnerChange Freedom Initiative, which is part of the Prison Fellowship started by Chuck Colson in 1976. IFI began in 1997. It started with 25 prisoners and five volunteers. In a biography of Colson, Jonathan Aitken, the British politician and ex-con, makes a large claim: IFI is the most successful prisoner-rehabilitation program in America. It may well be true. The program has many components, and one of them is a Business Plan Expo: Inmates present plans for businesses they'd like to start once they're on the outside. Pros like Brent Johnson serve as judges.

Colson got the idea for IFI when he visited a Christian-run prison, Humaitá, in Brazil. He thought there ought to be similar prisons in the United States. The governor of Texas, George W. Bush, accepted, and with alacrity. He ordered that such a prison be up and running in 90 days. It was. IFI is one of the "faith-based initiatives" associated with Bush.

This particular initiative, in the words of Prison Fellowship's website, "is a reentry program for prisoners based on the life and teachings of Jesus Christ." Inmates begin the program 18 to 24 months before their release date, and they stay in it for a year afterward. IFI offers "a prison like no other," says a brochure. Darrin Clifton, a "graduate" of the program, says it's true. "I got culture shock when I went in there." He had been in other prisons, but the atmosphere in this one was entirely different. Missing were the norms of prison life: deception, hostility, gambling, porn, and so on.

A big aim of IFI is to "break the cycle of criminality." Tommie Dorsett, the director at the Vance Unit, has a memory. (By the way, he is considered a hero by some in Texas, but he is not to be confused with another hero, Tony Dorsett, the ex–Cowboy running back. But confused with him, he has often been.) He once saw three generations huddled together in prison: grandfather, father, and grandson. All were inmates, and "they thought it was kind of cool, which broke my heart." The recidivism rate for IFI graduates is 10 percent. The rate for American prisoners in general is somewhere between 68 and 72 percent. There is one other IFI prison, located in Minnesota. There used to be one in Iowa, but it fell to its opponents: A group called Americans United for Separation of Church and State waged a political and legal battle against it.

The Carol S. Vance Unit, however, still stands, and tall. It is named for someone who was instrumental in the establishment of the prison. Though the first name may mislead, Carol Vance is a man, and a man and a half: In the 1960s and '70s, he was the district attorney in Harris County, i.e., Houston, and he has since devoted himself to prison reform. He was chairman of the board of directors of the Texas Department of Criminal Justice when Colson had his idea. He sold Vance on it. Vance figured he could sell Bush on it, which of course he did. In 1999, the prison was named after Vance himself. He still volunteers there, and in other prisons.

Inmates have to apply to IFI, from elsewhere in the Texas system. They do not have to be a Christian, or a believer, before they enter or after. Or during. But they have to want what the program has to offer, and they have to want a "spiritual or moral transformation," as the above-quoted brochure says. Many prisoners have no interest at all, says Dorsett.

They just want to do their time and not be bothered. The IFI prisoners want to be bothered. They are willing to give up some things—not just the obvious vices, but television and recreation, too.

A person might assume that IFI prisoners are the cream of the crop, relatively upstanding gentlemen who committed minor crimes and are ready to put on a suit and tie and go back to work. It's true that there are no sex offenders in the Vance Unit—Texas has a separate program for that. But everyone else is present, "from check-writers to murderers," as Dorsett says. The average sentence of IFI prisoners is 19 years. There is a range of ages, from 21 to 58. The goal is rehabilitation, but as Dru Bennett, a volunteer, says, some of these men have never been "habilitated" in the first place. (There are no women in the Vance Unit.) She's not really joking. They never had a foundation from which they could grow. Probably, they never knew a father, and if they had a mother, she might have been a drug addict or prostitute, or both.

They keep busy in the Vance Unit, engaged in the program from 6:30 in the morning till 9 at night. They study a variety of subjects. They learn to reconnect with their children, or connect with them for the first time. They hear from victims of crime, who explain how those crimes have affected their lives. In a steady stream, visitors, volunteers, mentors, come in from the outside. Darrin Clifton says that inmates in most prisons have little contact with "regular people," or people in the "free world." They may have forgotten how to relate to such people (or perhaps they never knew). It's important to have these contacts, so that reentry into the free world is less shocking. Experts from Toastmasters come into the Vance Unit, to prep inmates on how to speak in public. Capital One, the banking corporation, comes in to tutor inmates in their business plans.

"Business Leaders of Tomorrow," is how the annual expo is billed. The entrepreneurial talents of inmates are called forth. As Clifton says, many of these guys have been entrepreneurs their whole lives: dealing drugs, which takes a certain amount of planning and energy. Dru Bennett helps to coordinate the expo. She got into prison work when she pondered the

Biblical admonition to visit those in prison (as well as feed the hungry, clothe the naked, etc.). Her family is still not comfortable with her forays into prison, but she seems very comfortable. A financial officer in a company, she's a natural for the Business Expo.

For five to eight months, those inmates who choose—this is an "elective"—work on their business plans. These plans are meticulous, nearly exhaustive. The inmates have been coached by Capital One. In addition to mentors, Capital One provides loans, once the prisoners are out. This year, the expo was held on October 23. There were 44 participants and 30 judges. Capital One paid for the lunch—a Texas barbecue, naturally. The participants proposed businesses of many sorts: lawn service, a tattoo studio, commercial refrigeration, barber shops, a bakery, a car wash, a pizzeria . . . Ads for these businesses are already made up, as if the businesses already existed: "If you don't want to do it, call Snap 2 It!" (That's a painting company.) All the ads identify who the owner is: "Alan Parker—Owner." This suggests a certain pride or expectation. You can tell by the participants' names alone that there is a mixture in the Carol Vance population—a mixture of races and ethnicities: David Buckingham, Jonzz Re' Banks, Ernesto Aguilar, Success Nwosu, Nam Luong. (The last of these, in fine Vietnamese-American tradition, has proposed a nail salon.)

Judges come from the Houston business community. They fill out evaluations, ask questions of the presenters, and give them their advice. The judges are to be frank and honest. "They're not supposed to be cheerleaders," says Clifton. "The worst thing you can do to a con is lie to him. Don't spare a con's feelings." Tony Masraff has served as an expo judge. Some of the presenters are off base, he says. Others propose businesses that he himself would like to invest in. Dru Bennett says that IFI grads have succeeded in leatherworking, plumbing, and landscaping, among other endeavors. They might have to do some day-laboring at first—but some will get their businesses off the ground.

Arriving in town a little late, I visit the Carol Vance Unit a week after the expo. From the outside, the prison looks to me like a lot of other prisons. (I've been in a few.) But inside, it is much different. I'd heard the praise for this unit—the hype, if you will—but I may not have believed it if I hadn't come to see for myself. The prisoners are wearing white uniforms. Otherwise, as people have said, you might think you were in a Bible college. The prisoners do not have the usual demeanor: the shuffle, the swagger, the glower, the smirk. They look you in the eye, tell you their name, give you a firm handshake, and thank you for coming. I find it somewhat unnerving at first. Several of the inmates reprise their business-plan presentations for a group of us. They've already done it, but they welcome the practice. One or two seem nervous. All are eager to do their best. There seems to be no resentment of us outsiders, just genuine appreciation.

The presenters tend to be nicely theatrical, having a touch of showbiz about them. They say that they are "soon to be the owner-operator" of this or that business. Then they speak as if the businesses were already in operation: "We do this," "We do that"—and by "we," they may mean themselves alone. They think ambitiously.

One presenter is Benjamin Seawright, who proposes the Tejas Buckle Company—belt buckles depicting historical events and institutions in Texas. "Commemorating Texas History One Hand Made Buckle at a Time," is the motto. Seawright has been making these buckles for many years: for wardens, police officers, and others. One of his buckles honors the Texas Rangers, not the baseball team but the "iconic law enforcement organization that represents Texas heritage at its finest." (I'm quoting from his plan.) The Ranger buckle is on display in the Texas Ranger Museum. After his presentation, Seawright tells us that he has been in and out of prison since he was 17, and is now 55. Till now, he says, he has not been able to "shake the cycle"—the cycle of crime. But he is discovering that "you can teach an old dog new tricks." He says that IFI has shown him "more grace and mercy than I deserve."

While behind bars, and in IFI, Darrin Clifton learned about videography. (Incidentally, he was named after the character in *Bewitched*, the old sitcom.) He finds it amazing that he was able to "explore my passion," namely videography, while in prison. The offense that landed him there was aggravated assault with a deadly weapon, plus kidnapping. He says of IFI, "They prayed for me when I couldn't pray for myself." These days, he is getting some videography gigs. Tommie Dorsett tells me that an IFI grad recently got married. Another IFI grad was the best man. Clifton shot the wedding. Dorsett attended. Clifton's admiration of Dorsett is boundless, and this admiration is shared by everyone else, as far as I can tell. When I relate this to Dorsett, he will have none of it: "It's not me, it's God."

The day after my visit to the prison, I see Dorsett at an event in Houston. I ask him about eruptions of violence. How many times has he himself been attacked (and he has been at the prison since it opened, 16 years ago)? Not once, is the answer. There have been no attacks at all, on anyone. When I express surprise at this, Dorsett says it's the atmosphere: There is no need for a "game face," an attitude, machismo. This makes perfect sense: Just as there is pressure to conform to the bad, there is pressure to conform to the good. Later, I ask Dorsett about a dog not barking: I have heard not one word about race, in connection with the Carol Vance Unit or IFI. This is very unusual, not just for prison but for this country. Is race an issue at Carol Vance? Is there tension? Almost none, says Dorsett: "We make a big push for unity, and we support each other."

Not everyone is able to embrace a prisoner. One who can, literally, is George W. Bush. He attended the prison's opening ceremony 16 years ago. The men started to sing "Amazing Grace," and he joined in. He put his arm around one of them. As Dorsett tells me, someone muttered, "That guy will never get elected president. They'll call him soft on crime. The headlines will read 'Bush Hugs a Thug.' He just put his arm around a murderer." That murderer was George Mason, whom Bush later invited to the White House, three times. Mason would move in to hug the president; the Secret Service's eyes would get wide.

The first thing Tony Masraff ever did at Carol Vance was attend a Christmas party. The men, surrounded by their families, seemed so normal: friendly, articulate, poised. What could they have done? Brent Johnson assured him he could go ahead and ask. So Masraff asked the first guy, "What are you in for?" Murder. The man had killed a drug dealer. That was one thing—but Masraff asked the second guy, "What are you in for?" Murder again—but this man had killed a cop. Naturally, this gave the visitor pause. Masraff had always believed that if you took a man's life, you had to forfeit your own. His views have changed, though, in the course of his involvement with IFI.

Johnson has volunteered at Carol Vance for twelve years, and has had six "walkouts"—six opportunities to walk out of prison with an inmate on Release Day. These are exciting occasions, says Johnson: "to see them in their street clothes for the first time, to treat them to a meal of their choosing." Condemned prisoners get to choose a last meal, he points out; released prisoners should be able to choose a first meal, on the outside.

Personally, I am not dewy-eyed about prisoners and prison reform. I feel sure I have more sympathy for prisoners than do most people; but, like most people, I have yet more sympathy for their victims. I know full well that cons are good at conning—the cleverest of them could persuade the warden to drive the getaway car. I have long harbored skepticism about prison reform. Years ago, I heard a weary criminologist say that the only thing that cured a criminal was the passage of time—old age. But the wild card of religion is a wild and fascinating card indeed. IFI prisoners can cite such criminals as Moses (who killed a man, though the man was a slave-whipper), David (who committed assorted crimes), and Paul (ditto). There is no question that some, or many, IFI prisoners are transformed.

To borrow language from the first Bush, the InnerChange Freedom Initiative at the Carol S. Vance Unit is a "point of light." To borrow language from the second Bush, it is a prize example of "compassionate conservatism"—a term much derided, especially by conservatives, but one with obvious substance. People have come up with various euphemisms for prisons. We call them rehabilitation centers, but no one is ever rehabilitated. We call them correctional facilities, but no one is ever corrected. We call them penitentiaries, but no one is ever penitent. IFI is something rare and good under the sun. Frankly, I wouldn't mind investing in some of those proposed businesses myself.

—December 16, 2013

Blowing Up Barbie

The joy of explosives camp

Rolla, Mo.

There are many summer camps, something for everyone. But there's no other camp quite like this: an explosives camp. A hands-on explosives camp. Such a thing would seem impossible in modern America. These days, kids ride their trikes in protective gear. So, the very idea of explosives camp is thrilling.

Not to all, of course. Before I left the Upper West Side of Manhattan, I told a dear friend and neighbor where I was going. She could not get the look of horror off her face.

Explosives Camp is an offering of Missouri University of Science and Technology—formerly known as the University of Missouri–Rolla, formerly known as the Missouri School of Mines and Metallurgy. Rolla is midway between St. Louis and Springfield (Springfield, Mo., that is). On the main drag is The Lord's Library: "Your Full Service Christian Store."

An undergraduate at S&T can minor in explosives engineering. He can then go on to get his master's in it. Pretty soon, a doctoral program may be coming. Each year in this country, more than 6 billion pounds of explosives are used. Someone needs to know how to use them.

Explosives are used in mining, primarily. But they also figure in construction, for example—and demolition. It can be far safer to blow up a large building than to take it down bit by bit. Cheaper, too. Explosives are also used in agriculture, from time to time. A farmer may wish to clear boulders that way. In days gone by, he could go down to the general store and buy some dynamite. Those were more relaxed times.

Here in Rolla, the explosives guru is Dr. Paul N. Worsey. He is also a guru in the broader world. You could seat him and his true peers at one table, and you wouldn't need a very large table. And half the other people would be Worsey's onetime students. He has gained some celebrity, and so has his summer camp: When I arrive, cameras from a Canadian television show are just leaving. Worsey himself starred in a Discovery Channel program called *The Detonators*.

He is English-born, and so is his wife, Gillian, a civil engineer. They met at the University of Bristol. He earned his Ph.D. in Newcastle upon Tyne; she earned hers at Rolla. Barbara Robertson is an administrator, serving as a kind of den mother to the campers and university students. She is German-born. You hear some colorful accents in south-central Missouri.

Paul Worsey is a serious engineer—working in a very serious field—but he is free and easy. He laughs frequently. He wants his students to have fun, and he wants to have fun himself. He believes in straight talk, despising political correctness. He is scalding on the subject of government—particularly its regulators. He is not against regulations; he's just against silly and ignorant regulations.

Explosives Camp began in 2004, as a recruitment tool for the university. It had almost no advertising. But word spread. The camp takes just 20 students per session, and a session is a week long. There are two sessions this year. You have to be at least 16 to enroll, owing to the realities of insurance. The camp attracts mainly boys, as you would guess. But there are girls too—five in the session I drop in on, a full quarter of the bunch.

Most of the activities take place on the outskirts of town, at a site that features an experimental mine (established in 1913). The buildings are fairly rudimentary. Explosives Camp is not posh. This is not a country club. New facilities are in the works, but the camp has an old-style look, for now. Just up the road is Joe and Linda's Tater Patch. It's a favorite restaurant of the mining department.

During their week, campers get a "smorgasbord" of explosives engineering, as Worsey says. They learn about blasting—below ground and above ground. They learn about ordnance disposal. (This is a task our guys in Iraq had to perform, on roadside bombs.) They learn about pyrotechnics—a "wall of fire," for example. And they have more normal activities, such as cookouts and pool parties.

Again, this camp is hands-on. You learn first by instruction and then by doing. Worsey and his staff make an analogy to driving school: You would not give a person a license if he had never been behind the wheel. Simulators, books, and lectures can only do so much.

Needless to say, explosives are risky, and the camp stresses safety. There is a certain amount of bravado among explosives engineers, I find—a devil-may-care attitude—but beneath that is due awareness. Work with explosives was dangerous before Nobel, and dangerous after him.

Nobel? Alfred Nobel, the father of the prizes, and a pioneer in explosives engineering. This genius Swede had 355 patents to his name. His most famous invention, of course, is dynamite (1867). But his most important one, scientifically, is a blasting cap. Nobel's inventions made possible what today we call "infrastructure": tunnels, canals, railroads, and the like. The campers know about Nobel. In fact, Dyno Nobel—an international company born of companies founded by the inventor himself—sponsors an essay competition. This particular week, two of the campers have won, receiving a little scholarship money.

Among the staff, there is a marked spirit of independence. I think of a motto, "Don't Tread on Me." They believe that society has become too risk-averse, too confining. "Kids tend to be bubble-wrapped," says a staffer. She is an S&T undergrad from Cheyenne. She seems a typical westerner: open, confident, capable. I ask her what her family thinks of her studies in explosives. "My mom said, 'Be careful, and come home alive.'"

The Fourth of July is approaching, the big time of the year for pyrotechnicians. (A staffer from northeastern Missouri tells me, "People accord you more respect when you say, 'I'm the pyrotechnician.' They may not take you seriously enough if you say, 'I'm the fireworks guy.'") According to Paul Worsey, the big danger for pyrotechnicians on the Fourth of July is heatstroke. He has set up shows in 106-degree weather. The American revolutionaries should have declared independence on May 4 or June 4, he says.

On the second-to-last evening, the campers are taught to make three-inch shells—fireworks. Their instructor is wearing a shirt that says "Pyro Addiction." It occurs to me that he might be arrested in Massachusetts. As they sit at their tables, making their shells, the kids look like they're doing ordinary arts and crafts. But this is different. "Yes," says the young woman from Cheyenne: "arts and crafts with an edge."

One girl says to a fellow camper, "Did I get powder on my face again?" Indeed she did. The powder in question has nothing to do with pastries or cosmetics. It's black powder, the milk of explosives. Another girl tells me she has written "an evil laugh" on her shell. How do you write an evil laugh? Something like "Mwa-ha-ha."

She is a petite, brainy high-schooler from Houston. For a number of years, she has been involved in historical reenactment with her family: the Alamo, San Jacinto, and other trials of the "Texians." They fire muskets and cannons; they cast their own bullets. The girl's reading plans this summer include Conan Doyle, Dickens, and *Improvised Munitions*. She tells me about a favorite T-shirt: "Engineering: It's Like Math, but Louder."

When it gets dark, it's time to set off the shells. The campers troop out to the "shoot site," wearing their hard hats and safety glasses. They have made the shells, but staffers do the actual "shooting," this time. One girl expresses anxiety: "I just know mine's gonna be a dud." After one successful explosion, another girl says, "That was really pretty." A boy says, "That was cool." Some of the biggest cheers come when some fallout starts a little fire in the brush. A staffer quickly douses it with a fire extinguisher (of which there are many).

The next morning—the last one—campers look forward to the day's activities. These are to include the blowing up of a Barbie doll. She is riding a shark named Stanley. Why are they going to blow her up, or them up? I learn a stock response: "Because we can." First, though, there will be an underwater explosion, coming from a little pond. "Don't get a crick in your neck," Worsey quips to me. The spout goes way high, and I look way high—and can see what he means by "crick." The explosion also makes a little rain, which is welcome in a Missouri summer.

That evening, parents come to pick up their charges (no pun intended). One boy explains to his parents about a mortar. He does so with maturity and confidence. They look on a little wonderingly.

Then there is a barbecue dinner, followed by the grand finale: a fireworks show, which the kids have spent the afternoon setting up (in concert with staff). The local volunteer fire squad is on hand, just in case. But they have to go off, in response to a call. "Oh, well," says Dr. Worsey. "It'll be okay." And it is. There are plenty of personnel and fire extinguishers, regardless. The show is loud, hot, and exciting. At the end, the kids roar with pride and satisfaction. The adults roar too, though maybe more mildly.

Worsey knows he is doing something out of step—something incongruent with an Oprahfied age. He also knows he is doing something enviable. "My buddies used to come up to me and say, 'I admire what you're doing, but don't tell anyone I said so.'" They hung back, out of fear, or an excess of caution. Now they're more likely to flatter Worsey by imitating him. He has had an emboldening effect.

Explosives camp is not for everyone—nothing is. But it's a slice of America, part of our star-spangled diversity. And for the participants, and their well-wishers, it's a joy.

—July 15, 2013

ABROAD

'A Fragile State'
Impressions from Iraq

Baghdad

You hear certain things over and over, as you spend some time in Iraq. You hear them from Iraqis, Americans, and others. What you hear is: We've made great progress in 2008. Al-Qaeda, the militias, and the rest of those lovelies are on the run. But our progress is fragile and reversible. If the coalition leaves too soon—before Iraq can defend itself—there will be hell to pay. If we leave too soon, our work will be for nought.

You also hear, Iraqis don't want Americans and other foreigners in their country. (That includes foreign terrorists too, of course.) No one likes to be occupied. At the same time, Iraqis are very, very worried about the American departure: a departure that precedes stabilization. It's "Yankee, go home—but don't leave us at the mercy of the wolves. Go home at the right time."

One word you hear constantly is "normalcy." That is the great Iraqi desire: normalcy—a normal life, in which one can study, marry, have children, work, and pray, as countless people do elsewhere. Normalcy is not a modest goal, it is the shining ideal.

Four of us journalists are here in Iraq, invited by the State Department. The feeling at State, it seems, is that Americans have lost touch with Iraq. The war is off the front pages, and sometimes doesn't even make it to the inside pages. Is that because it's going better? Can Iraq be news when it's not a debacle?

The American embassy in Baghdad is one of Saddam's old palaces. Our GIs are swimming in his pool, an amazing fact. In the ballroom, missiles shoot upward—that is, they do so in a painting on the wall. The painting is as crude as Saddam's ideas and ambitions. In this ballroom are makeshift offices, and the sign on one of them catches my eye: "U.S. Department of Justice—Committee on Integrity." History is a remarkable thing.

We have a tour of the International Zone, or Green Zone, conducted by an Iraqi. He mentions the depravities of Saddam's regime, and you can almost hear the fear in his voice (a remembered fear). I'm reminded of the title of an invaluable book: "Republic of Fear" (Kanan Makiya). It seems to me that Westerners forget about Saddam's regime, or will themselves to: the "rape rooms," the children's prisons, the feeding of men into industrial shredders, the cutting out of tongues for dissent.

I often think, during my stay here, "It's good we got rid of Saddam. It's good that we overthrew him. No matter the difficulties that ensued—it was a good thing in the world."

We meet with an army of generals, led by Lt. Gen. Frank G. Helmick, who wears two hats: He's head of the "multinational security transition"—the handing over of responsibilities to Iraqi authorities; and he's head of the NATO mission. "A lot of people don't know NATO is here," he says. A lot of people don't know a lot of things about Iraq.

For two hours, the generals brief us about what is happening: about what the coalition is doing to stand Iraqis on their feet. In sum, the coalition is watching over every Iraqi sparrow. And I have a couple of main thoughts: One is, have foreigners ever done so much for a country? I think of another book title: "The Foreigner's Gift" (Fouad Ajami). Of course, you could say, "We broke it, we have to fix it"—but the country was broken before, badly. And we are changing it.

I also think, why aren't these guys on television? Why aren't they famous, explaining Iraq and our mission to the American public (and other publics), just as they're explaining it to us now? They are hardly Pollyannas or snowers; they are sober and realistic. And people could stand to hear from them. PR failings in this war have been pronounced.

Before we leave, Helmick, who likes football, quotes Coach Lou Holtz at Notre Dame: "We know we're not where we need to be. But we're glad we're not where we used to be."

Our journalistic group goes to a series of training centers, to see Iraqi forces being prepared to take over more of the fight. They practice going from house to house, and room to room, looking for terrorists. They learn to disable IEDs (improvised explosive devices). They show us how they protect dignitaries—cabinet members, judges, and the like. "Dignitary protection" is an extraordinarily important function.

From year to year, Iraqi officials come in for a lot of criticism, and criticism is no doubt deserved. (Saddam did not come in for much criticism, of the open kind.) But I try to remember: These guys risk a lot, when they assume their posts. They make themselves targets of terrorists, and they make their families, friends, and associates targets, too. How many of us would be willing to step up?

Where special forces are trained, we ask a man some basic questions. "Why did you join up?" "To defend my country." "Against whom?" "Terrorists." "Did your family suffer under Saddam Hussein?" "Yes, a lot of families did." "Are Americans occupying your country?" "'Occupation' has different meanings. Saddam Hussein occupied this country." Incidentally, this man's brother was killed not long ago, because terrorists learned that he—their victim—had a brother in the special forces. We hear a lot about sacrifices such as this.

An American who works with Iraqi special forces says, "They're all in. They're committed. This is their home. I can leave, but they have nowhere else to go. They have to stand and fight."

No one is more keen to stand and fight than Colonel Abbas, whom we talk to elsewhere. He says he was the first man to join the Iraqi army—the new Iraqi army, in July 2003. He calls you "my brother." No one is more grateful for American assistance than he. And he calls the enemies of Iraq—al-Qaeda, the militias, the Saddam remnant—"the bad people." That is his shorthand: "the bad people." To many, that would be simplistic, even laughable; but, to me, it sounds about right. Abbas has ample experience with the bad people: His infant daughter was killed when they attacked his house. And his father later died from the effects of that day.

Abbas wants one and all to realize what is at stake in Iraq. He says that, if the coalition pulled out—before its time—it would hand victory to al-Qaeda and Iran. And hand Iraq to those elements, too. "I wish I could talk to Obama, to tell him the reality of Iraq, instead of whatever is in his mind." About President Bush, he says, "He's a great man in the world. I want to see a monument to him in Baghdad. A man like him comes every

300 years." You don't hear this about Bush very often—at least at home. But Abbas is entitled to his opinion too, isn't he?

He has great faith in the American people, upcoming election or no upcoming election. In fact, I sense an almost naïve faith. And as our group walks to waiting helicopters, I think of Vietnam (as I do throughout this trip). There were lots and lots of Vietnamese like Abbas. The luckiest of them ended up in California. I think of April '75, one of the most shameful months in our history—all those people, desperately clinging to the helicopter skids. Could this happen to Iraq? Could we turn our backs on them, leaving them to be devoured?

In front of the "helos," Abbas embraces us and says, "God bless you." I say the same to him, and mean it, deeply.

On our schedule is a tour of a market called Doura, in Baghdad's Rashid district. As we make our way there, I meet a man named Walter Koenig, who works with a PRT, or Provincial Reconstruction Team. He calls himself a "State Department reservist." And I'll tell you his story, briefly.

A businessman, he worked in the Middle East for a number of years. He is now the CEO of a manufacturing company in Florida. He took a leave of absence from his company to come do this (after talking with his board and his family—not necessarily in that order). Why'd he do it? Why'd he come here? "I wanted to serve my country." Also, "it sort of makes up for not having been in the military." And "it's exciting to see things develop here"—to see Iraqi communities come back to life, or have a chance at life.

There is no doubt much cynicism in Iraq, and many Americans and other Westerners are surely tired. But I see a striking amount of idealism, too.

Rashid and Doura were once dead and deadly, but are now alive (more alive) and safe (more safe). We see a bridal shop and ask the owner, "How's business?" "Good, thank God." "How do you account for it?" "When people are more secure, they're more likely to marry." His best wedding gown rents for $60 a day.

Captain Daryl Carter knows this neighborhood like the back of his hand, and he leads our tour. He greets the kids, throws out bits of Arabic. He has coaxed many storeowners back to their stores, assuring them it is safe to return. That's the job of a captain? Yes, part of it. I'm often amazed, as I tour Iraq, at all the U.S. military does. This is really Erect-a-Nation.

And I note the easy interaction between American soldiers and Iraqi citizens, many of them. When doing so, I think of a German friend of mine. Earlier this year, he told me that his grandfather was a POW of the Americans, and always remembered the Americans fondly: because of their humanity. But such humanity is not being shown in Iraq, said my friend—at least as far as he could tell. What's happened to the American spirit and the American heart? No wonder the world has turned against America.

It's all baloney, of course: Bonds are being formed here as in WWII and other conflicts. But stories aren't getting out, that is true.

I walk through the market with General Robin Swan, and he notes a key distinction between Iraq now and Iraq then—Iraq post-surge and Iraq pre-surge. Terrorists can still perform spectacular bombings, for sure. But sectarian violence does not now follow those bombings. Life goes on. And the bombers are denounced.

He also answers a question of mine in an interesting way. Earlier, in a meeting, I asked, "Why are these terrorists so hard to beat? Why can't we subdue them, after all these years?" Swan points to a man browsing a stall and says, "Is he AQI?" (meaning Al Qaeda in Iraq). "How about this guy? And how about him? Are they AQI?" You can't tell. They don't wear uniforms. They melt into the population. All it takes, really, is one guy to wreak havoc. Say he rolls a grenade in a crowded place like this. It makes the news, and countless Americans say, "See? They don't want us there." What do you mean, "they"?

As we chopper from this district back to the Green Zone, Swan points below to an amusement park, recently reopened: "I really wanted to get that park open again. It's a return-to-normalcy issue." There are thousands of such issues in Iraq. And, to say once more, isn't it amazing what our military is doing—working to get people to reopen their amusement parks? Is that what the boys went to West Point for? This is, indeed, Erect-a-Nation—or "a full-service military," as Swan says, with a smile.

Ryan Crocker is the U.S. ambassador here, and he has been ambassador in many Middle Eastern countries—also in Pakistan. He gives us an extremely interesting and informative hour. And at the end, I ask one of the most clichéd questions (but often a useful question): "Is there anything else you'd like to say? Is there anything that people should know?" Yes, actually: "Iraq is really, really important. How things go here will transform the region and America's role in the region, one way or the other. . . . People are tired of Iraq. They say, 'Let's get it over and done with. We don't want to watch the Iraq movie anymore.' But the Iraq movie will go on for many more reels, with or without us. And it will have a big effect on us, whether we like it or not."

We visit the detention center at Camp Cropper—a place where they bring in jihadists, holding them for a spell. Must be a hellhole of torture and deprivation, huh? Not really. Detainees are treated to the best medical care, and to conscientious nutrition. To "life skills" classes, "Islamic discussion" sessions, and so on. They get regular visits with their families—"which is more than we get," comments a soldier. When they're released, they're given a choice of clothing—Western or Arab—and $25 to put in their pocket. Some mothers ask the center to keep their sons for longer.

Among the classes is a sewing class, and the instructor shows us the "graduation piece"—it is a stuffed camel, known as "the Cropper Camel." I'm thinking, "What does al-Qaeda teach the people *they* capture? What is *their* graduation piece?" But those are bitter thoughts, and one must not be bitter. It's hard to avoid, however, when thinking about Abu Ghraib: and how the world rejoices in identifying a few misdeeds with the entire American project in Iraq. [Abu Ghraib was a prison near Baghdad where American personnel committed various abuses, resulting in a huge worldwide scandal.]

Our group wends its way to the Faw Palace—one of Saddam's pleasure palaces. Hideous debauchery, and horrible crimes, took place here.

But now it is coalition headquarters. And the place is crawling with American soldiers, which does my heart good—just as it would have to see them crawl around Berchtesgaden.

Guarding the palace are marines from Tonga—yes, Tonga. And I see or hear about other foreign nationals working here in the coalition: Brits (of course), Aussies, Italians, Danes, Romanians, Bulgarians, Ukrainians, Ugandans, Peruvians, Salvadorans . . . I think about what Donald Rumsfeld once told me about the small countries, and the modest forces they send: "Yes, the countries may be small, and they may be contributing relatively few men." (I'm paraphrasing.) "But maybe it took political or personal courage to contribute even that number. And maybe those men constitute a significant percentage of their country's armed forces. Does anybody ever think of that?"

No.

In the Faw Palace, we sit down with Gen. Ray Odierno, who is "CG"—commanding general—of coalition forces in Iraq. He gives us an overview. And we question him hard. He has a knack for putting things plain. For example, "In 2006 Iraq was a failed state. Now it is a fragile state." We have not yet reached the point of Iraq's being a "stable state." But that is what we're driving toward. Gradually, we are turning matters over to the Iraqis, alone. "I want our forces to reduce their visibility yet maintain their effectiveness. I tell them I want everything." We have invested so much, over these five and a half years: "I hope we'll be able to finish this and do it right."

I chew over those words: "I hope we'll be able to finish this and do it right." Me too.

—November 3, 2008

HOMAGE TO MACEDONIA

Shaky times in a gutsy Balkan state

Skopje, Macedonia

When you say "Macedonia," you may have to clarify. Macedonia is both a region and a country. Regionally, it comprises parts of Greece and Bulgaria, and the whole of the country. That country, the Republic of Macedonia, is a former constituent of Yugoslavia.

The great hero in this part of the world is Alexander III of Macedon, a.k.a. Alexander the Great. He lived 2,300 years ago, but, to some people, it seems like yesterday.

Macedonia, the republic, is just north of Greece, and the size of Maryland. Its other neighbors are Bulgaria, Kosovo, Serbia, and Albania. A word to the wise: When you're in Greece, be careful about referring to the republic as "Macedonia."

In the Greek mind, Macedonia is Greek, period. The people in the former Yugoslavia have usurped the name and hijacked history. The Greeks fear, or say they fear, the republic's encroachment on them. A whipping up of greater Macedonian aspirations. So inflamed are they by the "name issue," as it's known, they have blocked the republic's accession to the EU and membership in NATO. In the mid-1990s, the Greeks went so far as to impose an economic embargo on the republic.

So, the Macedonians—the republicans—appeased them. They changed their flag, which had featured an ancient Macedonian symbol. It is now a splash of red and yellow, resembling the Arizona flag (and the Tibetan). Also, they reworded their constitution, making it clear that they had no designs on their big neighbor to the south.

The Greeks lifted the embargo, but, because of the name issue, still use their veto power to deny Macedonia its place in the EU and NATO. The American government has been calling Macedonia "Macedonia" since 2004. At the U.N., the country is known as the Former Yugoslav Republic of Macedonia, or FYROM.

As probably befits a Balkan state, the republic is Balkanized. Approximately 65 percent are ethnic Macedonians, who speak a Slavic tongue. Approximately 25 percent are Albanians (who speak Albanian). The rest are Turks, Roma, Vlachs, and so on.

Evidently, there is no intermarriage between ethnic Macedonians and Albanians. Such a thing is taboo, on both sides. I remark to a friend here, "Boys and girls tend to do what they do. Surely there are some Romeo and Juliet stories in this country." "Not really," he replies.

Near the Serbian border, there are Macedonian and Albanian villages cheek by jowl. In 2001, the people in these villages were killing each other. Before we enter an Albanian village, my friend says, "Once they find out you're an American, they'll probably slaughter a lamb in your honor." (In the 1998–99 Kosovo War, we Americans bombed Serbs, to protect Albanians.) The lambs are spared on this day.

Skopje is the Macedonian capital, and its airport is called "Alexander the Great." That is a middle finger to the Greeks. There is another middle finger downtown, a giant statue of Alexander. In recent years, Skopje has undergone a renaissance, at least architecturally. The government is erecting many neo-Classical buildings and monuments.

The capital could really use it. In decades past, Skopje was hit with twin disasters. One was an earthquake, which hit in 1963. It destroyed 80 percent of the city. The other disaster, of course, was Communism, with its preference for brutalist architecture. Little of pre-Communist Skopje remains.

Politically, there are two main parties, known by initials. The party in power is the VMRO-DPMNE (abbreviated to "VMRO"). This is a conservative party, led by Nikola Gruevski, the prime minister. The other party is the post-Communist party, the SDSM. They prefer to be known as social democrats now, and their leader is Zoran Zaev.

Both parties have different camps or strains. In VMRO, there are some gung-ho, Reagan-style, America-loving conservatives. They tend to be very knowledgeable about the United States. One politician asks me where I'm from. I tell him I live in New York but grew up in Ann Arbor, Mich. With a shocked expression, he says, "It's the *Soviet Union*!" (Ann Arbor is a university town.) While I'm laughing, he says, "Or northern Havana. Havana *del norte*!"

By and large, my VMRO friends are Euro-skeptics, and would not like to see Macedonia join the EU. At the same time, they're irked to be kept out by the Greeks. And they take bitter satisfaction in the following fact: Greece, which has blocked Macedonia, appears to be the first EU country to go down the tubes.

As I said, SDSM is the post-Communist party, but, in Eastern Europe, you often have to question the "post." Does redness linger? SDSM people are apt to call one another "comrade," and their party flag includes a traditional star and a clenched fist. But they are probably not Communists at heart. True-believing Communists are few and far between. SDSM-ers are more like opportunists, looking for power and control.

In April 2014, they lost their ninth straight election to VMRO. They have 31 seats in parliament to VMRO's dominant 61. Claiming electoral fraud, and not very credibly, SDSM has been boycotting parliament.

A very big name in Macedonia is George Soros. He is the Hungarian-born American billionaire who funds the political Left in America. He funds it in Macedonia too, which is a sore spot for conservatives, to put it mildly. Their view goes essentially like this:

In the early years after the collapse of Communism, Soros did many good things in Eastern Europe, with his Open Society Institute. He helped to liberalize and democratize. When the Greeks blockaded Macedonia, Soros loaned the new country money, a lifeline. In recent years, however, he has become a bald partisan, showering his millions on the Left and pushing for its agenda. He does this with an army of NGOs and activists—activists known, unflatteringly, as "Sorosoids."

One conservative remarks, "He came into Macedonia like a Trojan horse, and now he is an octopus."

For more than 20 years, the head of Soros's Open Society branch in Macedonia has been Vladimir Milcin. There is nothing more galling to conservatives. Milcin, they say, was proved by the country's lustration process to have been a police informant in Communist days. Not only conservatives are galled. A man of the democratic Left tells me, "Milcin does not belong at something called 'Open Society.' That is laughable." Milcin, for his part, has denied wrongdoing.

In America, Soros-funded groups have included MoveOn.org, Media

Matters, and the Center for American Progress. Macedonia has its rough equivalents. Consider an interesting tidbit: Open Society has translated Saul Alinsky's *Rules for Radicals*, that 1971 primer. It has guided Left activists for two or three generations now.

The U.S. taxpayer is involved in the following way: Our government, through USAID, gives money to the local Soros foundation. (Money to Soros may strike you as coals to Newcastle, but there you go.) Macedonian conservatives say that we have simply picked sides in the politics of their country: the SDSM or "post-Communist" side. Others say that the Right makes a bogeyman out of Soros, and that the U.S. acts as an honest broker, holding all sides to account.

In any event, conservatives are wounded—pained—by American relations with Macedonia in the Age of Obama. "We're the pro-American, pro-Western party," they say. Some add, "You're driving us into the arms of the Russians."

Moreover, it's the Soros people who inform the rest of the world about Macedonia. Conservatives say this, and it is almost certainly true. The "Sorosoids" are "well networked," in the words of one observer. And they portray a country governed by VMRO as sliding out of democracy and into authoritarianism.

Macedonia is now in the midst of a huge wiretapping scandal (not the first in its brief, 24-year history). The charges and countercharges are Byzantine, dizzying, but I will write a few lines about them.

According to SDSM, Prime Minister Gruevski wiretapped more than 20,000 people, a who's who of Macedonia. He did this in order to steal elections, undermine a free press, suborn the judiciary, and so on. SDSM's leader, Zaev, says that he was handed recordings by "patriots" within the UBK, the nation's secret police. They were appalled by the prime minister's undemocratic machinations, and wanted the recordings to see the light of day.

Nonsense, says VMRO. The UBK "patriots" are actually old Communists and "traitors," wanting to bring down a democratic government with their tried-and-true tricks. Zaev tried to blackmail Gruevski with these recordings, and Gruevski would not submit—instead exposing Zaev.

The crux of the matter, say conservatives, is that the "post-Communists" feel entitled to run the country, the way they or their forerunners did for so long. They are not used to having to compete for power, and, when they lose elections, they lash out or connive.

Smiling at all this are the Greeks, who say, "Told you these fake Macedonians were not fit for the EU and other international organizations" (as though Greece should talk).

May 1 is May Day, i.e., the Left's day. They are out on the streets of Skopje in force. There are public-sector unions, SDSM officials, professional protesters—the whole gang.

Red flags are everywhere, and they are plain, unadorned. They look a little forlorn without their hammers and sickles, or even a star. But soon I see one or two stamped with the image of Che Guevara.

The noise of the Left is deafening, as usual. People blow non-stop on whistles for no apparent reason—intimidation?—and bellow through bullhorns. The crowd is now chanting something. A friend says, "It's 'No justice, no peace.'" Makes me feel right at home.

A sign depicts Gruevski and says that he takes from the poor and gives to the rich. Virtually the whole Occupy tableau—with noise—is in place.

But this is a tableau that moves. They are marching on one side of a broad avenue. On the other, a smallish group is marching, in parallel, all by itself. Why? My friend explains, "They're feuding with another group. They think that the other group is corrupting the workers' movement, by accepting so much Soros money."

In September next year, the Republic of Macedonia will mark its 25th anniversary. The country is "not a perfect democracy," as the aforementioned man of the democratic Left says. "But you can't go to bed in a Communist country and wake up in Denmark. You have to cultivate roots and develop institutions." True, true—and may this country be given the time.

—June 1, 2015

Among the Progs

A peek at the conservatives and libertarians of Norway

Oslo, Norway

"We will be eating Israeli potatoes," announces our host, with mischievous, defiant glee. He is Kristian Norheim, "international secretary" of the Progress party, the Reaganite, Thatcherite party here in Norway. Seven of us are gathered for a festive meal. What's the big deal about Israeli potatoes? Ah, you need to get to know Norway. Israel is not the favorite country of this country. This is a country where Israeli products are typically boycotted and damned, not eaten. Norway's government was the first outside the Islamic world to recognize Hamas.

Put it this way: Norway's attitude toward Israel is approximately that of the Middle East Studies department of the University of Michigan.

But the Progress party is a group apart, on this as on virtually every other issue. The Progress party makes a point of serving Jaffa oranges—oranges from Israel—at its conferences. Its leader, Siv Jensen, visited Israel in February 2008. She and her delegation went to Sderot, a town on the border with Gaza. While they were there, the town came under rocket attack, from Hamas. The Norwegians, with others, made a run for the air-raid shelter. Israelis were killed that week, but not that day.

The next winter, Israel went into Gaza, to stop these rocket attacks. In Oslo, there were riots, as the Muslim community reacted. Jensen gave a speech outside the parliament building, in support of Israel, and in support of peace and coexistence in the Middle East. The mob—howling, armed, and violent—threatened her. (You can get a taste of this on YouTube.) But she carried through with the speech. She tells me, "That was the scariest thing I've ever done in my life. It was surreal"—Norway prides itself on being a peaceable country.

By the way, there are two items of particular interest in Jensen's office: a little Israeli flag and a bust of Reagan. It would be hard to convey how extraordinary these symbols are in the traditional Norwegian political culture. An American politician might be less scandalous for having kiddie porn in his office.

Back to our festive meal, at Kristian Norheim's place. Two of the guests are a couple from Taiwan—she works at the embassy. Taiwan, like Israel, is not one of Norway's most favored nations. The People's Republic of China has pride of place, naturally. But the Progress party is fond of Taiwan, this plucky democracy, with its free economy and free, independent spirit. Jensen led a delegation to Taiwan, too—this was earlier this year.

After we've eaten, Norheim takes our little group to the parliament building, the Storting. As we enter, I say, "Are you sure that a couple of Taiwanese and an American conservative are allowed in here?" Under Progress protection, sure.

Seven parties have seats in the Storting, and, with the exception of Progress, all of these parties are socialist, to varying degrees. The leader of the Conservative party—the party closest to Progress—attended the Democratic convention in Denver two years ago. (Siv Jensen attended the Republican convention.) The Socialist Left party is one of the three parties that form the current coalition government. (The others are Labor and the Center party.) The Socialist Left party, in its manifesto, declares that the United States is "the greatest threat to peace in the world today." There you go.

The Progress party was founded in 1973, to advance the principles of classical liberalism. The party declares that its philosophy "starts with the democratic assumption that the people are best placed to decide what is best for them." This is radical, almost revolutionary stuff here in Scandinavia. Progress's symbol is an apple: healthful, good for you. Norheim likes to crack, "An apple a day keeps the government away." The symbol of the party's youth branch is a thumbprint: a symbol of individualism. Everyone has a thumbprint, and everyone's is different, unique.

So, Progress must be a fringe party, right? Just a curiosity, in this strongly socialist culture. Not on your life. The country is getting less socialist. Progress is the second-largest party in the Storting (after Labor). It has 41 out of 169 seats; in the elections of 2009, it garnered 23 percent of the vote. I ask Siv Jensen, "Do you expect to be prime minister?" She says yes. I say, "When?" She says 2013—after the next elections. "In coalition with whom?" I ask. The Conservatives.

She will not get much help from the media—the Progress party never has. The media here are unremittingly hostile to the party and its philosophy. They are "very red," as Jensen says, "very red." To add insult to injury, they are state-funded—imagine a nation of NPRs (or worse)! The Progress party aims to change this. An American who has lived here twelve years, and is a news junkie, tells me, "I don't think I've ever seen a positive story about the Progress party. Not one. They're treated like the KKK or something." So, how does Progress make progress? Jensen says that the Internet has been a boon. It's a way around the official media. Televised debates have helped, too, as people can see Jensen and other Progs unfiltered.

"Progs"? Norheim has a friend at the Cato Institute in Washington who refers to Progress-party members as "Progs." It seems to suit them.

Hanging out with them for a few days, I find them, not only brainy, principled, and nervy, but fun—you might expect that. They tend to have a gonzo spirit, and an American spirit. They are unabashed in their America-love. The "special adviser on financial policy" for the party is the frontman of a group called Teddy Trigger and the Gatling Guns. They do rockabilly. Progs have been known to refer to Coke as "capitalist water." They revel in what others—so many others around them—condemn.

One of my habitual questions, for these conservatives and libertarians, is, "How did you get this way? How did you come to think as you do?" And they almost invariably respond, "I grew up in a socialist country!"—as if that were all the explanation needed. They felt stifled, and were bursting to break free into a new way of living.

Siv Jensen was such a Norwegian. She was born in 1969 to a couple who owned a shoe store, here in the capital. She soon found that she was a "liberalist," as she says. She argued with her staunchly, obediently socialist schoolmates—and she is arguing still. She does it extraordinarily well. I spend an hour with her, running the gamut of issues. I wonder, "If she's this articulate in English," a language she merely studied in school—she has never lived in an English-speaking country—"what can she be in Norwegian?"

She is one of the few politicians in Norway to stand up to radical Islam—and, in so doing, to stand up for Muslims here who want to integrate and live a free, Western-style life. There are women here who aren't allowed to leave the home. Who are forced into arranged marriages. Who are forced to undergo FGM, female genital mutilation. Jensen speaks up for these people, and she decries the country's political establishment for turning a blind eye.

It won't surprise you that the establishment routinely denounces her and Progress as racist, xenophobic, Islamophobic, blah, blah, blah. I hear it with my own ears. One Progress official, at least, is able to laugh off the denunciations fairly easily. He is Morten Hoeglund, the foreign-policy spokesman. He is married to a Muslim from Kazakhstan. And when he is called a hater of Muslims, he says, "May I introduce you to my wife?"

I ask Siv Jensen point-blank whether she regards Islamism—radical Islam—as a threat on a par with Nazism and Communism. She says, unblinkingly, yes. And, once more, it is a threat, not only to Western civilization (bad enough), but also to those Muslims who wish to live within that civilization: and who may have fled their homelands in order to escape the radicalism they now find choking them in places like Norway.

Chief among her political models are Reagan—he is sitting right behind her—and Thatcher. (In 2008, *Standpoint* magazine in London ran a feature about her titled "A Norwegian Thatcher?") And her writer of choice is Ayn Rand: "I have read her books over and over again. I just love them. They inspire me, they provoke me, they make me feel alive—they force you to reflect on a lot of issues in your society." Has any writer ever received a finer tribute? So, Jensen is a Randian, then? "No, not all the way through. Her ideas are a bit too radical for me. But, when I was younger, I got inspired by reading her, and I think everyone could benefit, because she forces you to think—and it's healthy to think, no matter what your ideology."

Follow me into Kristian Norheim's office, please—it must be the most politically incorrect room in Scandinavia. There are three posters of Churchill. There's Reagan, of course: "Viva the Reagan Revolution!" There's Barry Goldwater: "In your heart you know he's right." There's a

George Washington doll, and a George W. Bush doll. There's a picture of the Stealth bomber (!). There's a hat from the New York Fire Department. There's an Israeli flag, a GOP flag (with elephant), a Gadsden flag ("Don't Tread on Me"). And that's only a fraction of the inventory.

The pièce de résistance, perhaps, is a Pez dispenser shaped like a Wal-Mart truck. "This is so politically incorrect," Norheim explains. In Norway, Wal-Mart is the very symbol of gross American capitalism. In 2006, the Norwegian state divested its pension fund from Wal-Mart: The company's not unionized, you know. But Norheim thinks Wal-Mart's just fine. You know what else? "I was baptized on the Fourth of July."

—July 19, 2010

The View from Reagan Street

A centennial celebration in Prague

Prague, Czech Republic

"I never would have believed it," people keep saying. "If you had told me, in the 1980s, that one day we would have a street named after Ronald Reagan here in Prague, I would have said you were crazy." Prague will indeed name a street after Reagan. This year is the Reagan centennial, the late president having been born in 1911. They are commemorating him elsewhere on the Continent, too, and also over in Britain.

In Krakow, the cardinal said a special Mass, in honor of the relationship between Reagan and John Paul II. In Budapest, a Reagan statue went up in Freedom Square, the same square that features a monument to the Red Army. The Soviet-era monument is rather controversial in Hungary. And, on the Fourth of July—three days after the street renaming in Prague—another statue of Reagan will go up, this one in Grosvenor Square, London.

The base of that statue will quote Margaret Thatcher: "Ronald Reagan ended the Cold War without firing a single shot." That statement rests uneasily with some of us. So many shots were fired, in Central America, Africa, South Asia, and elsewhere. So many people died. But we all know what Lady T. means.

Prague is doing its part for Reagan, but there is another anniversary here, too. It has been 20 years since the end of the Warsaw Pact, 20 years since the last Soviet soldier left Czechoslovakian soil. He was a general named Vorobyov. In fact, Prague is having an entire Freedom Week. Organizers are commemorating the past, of course. But they are even more interested in the present.

There is an exhibition on Belarus—poor, battered Belarus, the last dictatorship in Europe. Czechs feel a kinship with the Belarusians. But this is not just a matter of (rough) geographical proximity. Czechs know what it is to suffer under a dictatorial lash, wherever it is wielded. There is another exhibition on Cuba, a long way off from this country. And there is another on North Korea. Pictures and reports from the North Korean gulag, or the Cuban gulag, or any, are not for the squeamish.

Along with exhibitions, there are discussions, panels. One is on democratic unrest in the Arab world. It's titled "Reagan's Grandchildren." I think how the title would upset many Americans: It would upset some conservatives who love Reagan but snort at any notion of an "Arab spring"; and it would upset some liberals, who are still smarting from Reagan but admire and root for the Arab protesters.

In Prague's Liechtenstein Palace, there is a dinner, sponsored by the Reagan Presidential Foundation, in California, and the Prague Security Studies Institute. A slew of dignitaries, Czech and American, are present. Condoleezza Rice is the personal representative of Nancy Reagan. The former secretary of state gives a toast both eloquent and personal. She recalls that her key professor in the field of international relations was a Czech exile, Josef Korbel. (She does not mention that he was the father of another future secretary of state: Madeleine Albright.)

The Czech ambassador to the U.S., Petr Gandalovič, recalls the intense propaganda he heard against Reagan in Communist Czechoslovakia. So great was this propaganda, "I figured there must be something to this fellow." The Czech prime minister, Petr Nečas, says, "In a symbolic sense, he was our president, too."

Over and over, Czechs say that Reagan's denunciation of the Soviet Union as an "evil empire" gave them hope and courage. And I think back to the time that he gave that particular speech. Our chattering class heaped derision on it. How could our president be such a simpleton, such a "fundamentalist," such a warmonger? Henry Steele Commager, the esteemed historian, said that Reagan had given "the worst presidential speech in American history," adding, "I've read them all." A couple of years ago, I had a talk with George Shultz (Reagan's main secretary of state). He remembered when Paul Nitze was testifying before a Senate committee. A leading Democrat said to this veteran and urbane diplomat, "How can you serve under a president who calls the Soviet Union an 'evil empire'?" Nitze answered, "Did you ever consider that it's true?"

Listening to former dissidents here, you realize how deeply Reagan's rhetoric penetrated. What might have seemed boilerplate or Mickey Mouse or bluster to us, meant a lot behind the Iron Curtain. In the Soviet Gulag, Anatoly Shcharansky heard, somehow, that Reagan had declared a particular year the "Year of the Bible." For a time, he was able to study the Bible with a fellow inmate, Volodya. They called their sessions "Reaganite readings."

In 2008, I heard President George W. Bush give a speech to an auditorium of Arab elites in Sharm El Sheikh, Egypt. They greeted his words (about democracy and freedom) with coldness and scorn. I thought, "This is the wrong audience. The men and women in prison cells would love it."

At the dinner in the Liechtenstein Palace, several Czechs say how thrilling it was to hear Reagan say he wanted to win the Cold War—not just manage or cope with it, but win it. It's possible to forget, today, just how radical and frightening Reagan's stance was judged in the West at the time. Détente, accommodation, coexistence was the name of the game. The Soviet Union and its empire were here to stay. Talk of winning, of bringing them down, was fanciful at best, dangerous at worst. The West German hero Willy Brandt had spoken for many, in his Nobel lecture: "Coexistence has become a question of the very existence of man." It was not merely "one of several acceptable possibilities, but the only chance of survival." Reagan was upsetting all this.

The morning after the dinner, there is a conference in Czernin Palace—in the very room where, 20 years ago to the day, Václav Havel announced the dissolution of the Warsaw Pact. The Czech foreign minister, Karel Schwarzenberg, gives a speech. He asks us to remember the great opposition Reagan had to overcome—not from the East, but in his own environment. He went against the foreign-policy establishment, "the dominant economic theorists," "the newspapers," and so on. "His example is one of courage." Schwarzenberg also says that statues and street signs are fine. But the best way to honor Reagan is to imitate him.

Roman Joch, a policy intellectual, tells a series of Reagan's favorite jokes. I thought I knew them all. But here's one I didn't: What's the difference between a democracy and a "people's democracy"? The difference between a jacket and a straitjacket. To end the morning, and the conference, Rice makes a speech, arguing for democracy against its many skeptics. She notes that people are always saying, "You can't impose democracy." Her retort is, you don't have to impose democracy. You have to impose tyranny.

In the late afternoon, Dr. Zikmund Winter Street—a portion of it—becomes Ronald Reagan Street. It runs in front of the U.S. ambassadorial residence. Our ambassador, Norman Eisen, presides over a ceremony. A stage has been erected right on the street. Eisen is an FOB, a Friend of Barack—a law-school classmate of the president. But all day long, he has been out-Reaganing us Reaganites. He hails a president "who looked evil in the face and dared to call it evil!" Wowser.

Off to the side, a sign is draped. It's obviously the new street sign. The drape is affixed to the top, but two young women hold the bottom of the drape, to keep the wind from blowing it up. They are in short black dresses and heels, and are wearing Miss America–style sashes, which say, "Praha 6." That is the particular municipal division we're in. And the look of these young women—these hostesses—is gloriously retro. Once all the speeches have been made, the drape comes off. From somewhere, we hear a few seconds of cheesy music: *Ta-dah!* And "Ronalda Reagana" Street is official. (The name looks feminine in the local rendering.)

Reagan is not the only president in town to be honored. The Czechs have long revered Woodrow Wilson, as so many Europeans do: for his insistence on national independence and self-determination. The railway station in Prague is named for Wilson. From 1928—the Fourth of July!—to December 1941, there was a statue of him in front of it. But after Pearl Harbor, Germany declared war on America, and the Nazis in Prague melted the thing down for bullets. A new statue will go up in its place, on October 5 of this year.

Back to Reagan, though: Would you say that most people are reconciled to that president and his achievements? Even Obama, who opposed him bitterly when Reagan was president, says nice things about him now. The passage of time is a remarkable animal. Throughout the 1980s, the Nobel peace committee handed out prizes to foes of Reagan: unilateral disarmers and the like. Committee members told Oscar Arias, in 1987, that they were giving him the prize to use as a weapon against Reagan. (Arias, the Costa Rican president, was against the Contra war versus the Sandinistas.) More than 20 years later, at Obama's Nobel ceremony, the committee chairman quoted Reagan, holding him up as a president who embodied universal values.

Again, my thoughts run to Bush 43. Throughout the 2000s, the Nobel committee gave prizes to his foes—Kofi Annan, Jimmy Carter, Mohamed ElBaradei, Al Gore . . . The Nobel chairman said that the prize to Carter, in particular, was meant as a rebuke to Bush. What will chairmen say in the future?

For two days here in Prague, I hear people, Czech and American, gush about Reagan. I too do some gushing. Which is only natural and right. Still, it can all be a bit much, even for a longstanding Reagan idolater like me. I am ready to give Reagan a rest. But I smile on remembering that wonderfully usable line from Robert Graves: "The thing about Shakespeare is, he really *is* good." So it is with our Gipper.

—August 1, 2011

Questions on Taiwan

The wonderfulness and anxiety of a little-known country

Taipei, Taiwan

Taiwan is one of the most admirable countries in the world, but that does not mean it is a well-known country. Say "Taiwan" to people, and they might well respond, "Thailand?" Taiwanese diplomats in the West hear this all the time. Their country, however, is a model. It left behind dictatorship to become a liberal democracy, with a free economy, flourishing. A Chinese dissident I know says Taiwan is his "favorite place." If Taiwan can have freedom of expression, freedom of assembly, freedom of worship, an independent judiciary, the rule of law, multiparty elections, rotation in office, human rights—why not China?

I have called Taiwan a "country," but this is a fighting word to some. It is definitely a fighting word to China's ruling Communists. To them, Taiwan is a Chinese island, a renegade province, to be brought to heel sooner or later, in some manner. Chen-Shen Yen, a Taiwanese political scientist, sometimes appears on Chinese television. When he refers to Taiwan's leader as "President Ma," the Chinese censor beeps out the word "President." This word carries the unfortunate connotation of Taiwanese sovereignty, or nationhood.

Most of the people I encounter, here in Taiwan, consider Taiwan a "country" or "nation." Some are startled that the question is even asked. Some will tell you that "Taiwan" is merely a geographical label—a word denoting an island. "The country is the Republic of China." Others like the idea of Taiwan, or Taiwanness—and they dream of a Republic of Taiwan, independent of the "People's Republic."

In her excellent book *Why Taiwan Matters*, Shelley Rigger, an American professor, reports an interesting story. There is a Web game called "ClickClickClick." You click on a button, and this action registers a click for your country. The country with the most clicks, in a set period, wins. In 2007, this game swept Taiwan—and Taiwan, an island with 23 million people, won. This suggests a certain hunger for nationhood, or international recognition, or something.

One of the commonest questions here is, "Do you feel Taiwanese, or Chinese, or both?" Journalists have asked it, and pollsters have asked it, for years. A person's answer depends on his family background, his own experience, his politics, his emotions—many things. One answer I hear a lot is, "I used to feel both Taiwanese and Chinese, but now I'm feeling more and more Taiwanese." Polls show that this is a national trend. Two decades ago, about a quarter of people considered themselves Chinese; now that number is maybe 5 percent. Thirty percent considered themselves Taiwanese; now that number is around 50. A Taiwanese consciousness is being shaped.

What almost everyone shares is resentment at being excluded from international organizations. The word "isolated," we might reflect, comes from "island." Taiwan is denied a seat at the U.N., of course. It cannot even get observer status, such as the PLO has. More amazingly, Taiwanese journalists can't get credentials to *cover* the U.N. China will not permit it—or, more accurately, the world's countries permit China not to permit it. Taiwan would like access to the most modest and uncontroversial of bodies, such as the International Civil Aviation Organization. But China and the world say no. Taiwan is allowed to compete in the Olympics under the awkward name "Chinese Taipei." Taiwanese womanhood is allowed to compete in beauty pageants under the same name. Otherwise . . . not much.

As Chong-Pin Lin, another political scientist here, says, China is bent on "the strangulation of our international space." The PRC wants Taiwan to be a nonentity—a non-person, so to speak—in the world. (By the way, Lin is a protégé of Jeane Kirkpatrick.) Diane Ying, the founder and publisher of *CommonWealth* magazine, says that Taiwanese businessmen may well have a better acquaintance of the world than do Taiwanese government officials. They have more contacts, more opportunities. They're apt to look down on government officials, whereas before it was the other way around.

I ask many Taiwanese what they would have America do for them. Almost uniformly, they answer, "Help us get into international organizations. Decrease our isolation in the world. Allow us to develop and participate like a normal country." (The other help they desire: advanced F-16 fighter jets.)

Though they may long for international recognition, and something like normality, Taiwanese do not necessarily long for independence. Or rather, they are unwilling to declare independence if it will mean a Chinese attack. "Status quo" is a byword on this island. People are content with the way things are, for the foreseeable future. Better to live in a kind of limbo—"What are we?"—than to risk losing the current freedom. We cannot predict the course of human events. There may come a day when the Taiwanese feel impelled to "assume among the powers of the earth" the "separate and equal station to which the Laws of Nature and of Nature's God entitle them." But that day is not at hand.

The terms "Left" and "Right" don't make much sense in Taiwanese politics. But "Blue" and "Green" do. The Blues are the Kuomintang (KMT), now in power, and the Greens are the Democratic Progressive Party (DPP). The former is more unification-minded—certainly more cautious, where China is concerned—and the latter is more independence-minded. Whoever is in power, "the government must walk a tightrope," as Mab Huang says. (He too is a political scientist, once a student of Leo Strauss and Friedrich Hayek.) The government must keep China at bay, clutch it close, assert Taiwan's rights, not be too loud about it, satisfy the United States—walk a tightrope while juggling guavas.

Since 2008, Taiwan and the PRC have signed 16 agreements with each other. These agreements concern such matters as trade and travel. In previous times, you couldn't fly directly from Taipei to, say, Shanghai. You had to go in a roundabout way—via Hong Kong, for example. But now you can fly directly, in about an hour and a half. There is a stream of Chinese tourists to Taiwan. The PRC places restrictions on who can come—not just any citizen of the People's Republic can up and visit Taiwan—but plenty do (more than a million last year).

By many accounts, the favorite activity of Chinese tourists here is TV-watching. They stay in their hotel rooms, glued to the political talk shows. They marvel at the robust, sometimes wild back-and-forth. They see the government criticized, examined, slammed. This is something alien to their experience. Visiting the Taiwanese capital's great skyscraper, Taipei 101, they see Falun Gong practitioners, protesting the PRC's persecution of their fellows. This, too, is alien.

Obviously, there are benefits to closer, warmer cross-strait relations. Taiwan can exercise its "soft power," as an official tells me. Chinese can get to know Taiwan, find out about a different way of life. Most important, the risk of war is reduced. But there is a negative side to closer, warmer relations. "Absorption" is another byword, or buzzword. Will the PRC absorb Taiwan? Lin notes that "buying Taiwan is cheaper than attacking it."

Take the case of A-mei, Taiwan's most popular singer. She sang the national anthem at the 2000 inauguration of President Chen Shui-bian, of the DPP. China banned her for more than a year. Coca-Cola, in the finest tradition of American capitalism, dropped her as a spokesman. Other entertainers in Taiwan got the message, loud and clear. Patriotism is well and good, but who wants to be stuck in Taiwan's market of 23 million, when there's China's market of a billion-plus?

A great many are concerned about the compromising of Taiwan's media. The independent media have been a jewel in Taiwan's crown, since the lifting of martial law in the late 1980s. But China throws its weight and money around, and both are considerable. Recently, a TV-station owner wanted to expand into China (or so the story goes). He fired one of his talk-show hosts, who was strongly critical of the PRC and in favor of Taiwanese independence. This was a gesture of goodwill to Beijing. There is also the danger of self-censorship. Say you're a Taiwanese news outlet, eyeing Chinese ad dollars. You think you might pull some punches?

One outlet that is not much for punch-pulling is the *Apple Daily*, in whose lobby sits a bust of Hayek. That lets you know where its sympathies lie. (Beneath the bust is a quotation from the great economist's Nobel lecture: "The recognition of the insuperable limits to his knowledge ought indeed to teach the student of society a lesson of humility which should guard him against becoming an accomplice in men's fatal striving to control society.") The paper's editor, Wei-Min Ma, confirms something I have already heard: As planes from Taiwan land in China, flight attendants warn passengers to leave their copies of the *Apple Daily* behind. PRC authorities would not be happy to see them.

In any case, Taiwan can set an example, a democratic example, for China. Professor Yen says that the more sophisticated Chinese tell him, "You need to remain outside China for a while, to push us for democratic reform. If you become part of China, like Hong Kong, there will be no incentive for us to reform." The above-mentioned Taiwanese official, who is involved in cross-strait relations, says, "We can show them three things: that democracy is possible in Chinese culture; that democratization and economic growth can go hand in hand; and that democracy need not mean chaos."

There was a time, says Yen, when many Taiwanese emigrated, leaving their homeland for the United States, Canada, Australia (all "Anglospheric" countries, interestingly enough). But emigration has greatly slowed. Why? One reason, says Yen, is that there is less fear of a military confrontation with China. People are breathing easier. I can't help thinking of what some Israelis say: If the Iranians acquire nuclear weapons, they don't really have to use them to wreck Israel. The psychological effect will be devastating. People will stop coming, and will leave.

Yen says that Taiwan is something like Georgia, the ex–Soviet republic: close to its adversary and far from its help. He jokes that Taiwan should trade places with Cuba: It would be cozy to the United States, and thousands of miles from the PRC. Plus, "we have similar weather, we both love baseball."

Taiwanese may fear war less, but the PRC still has 1,500 missiles pointed at them. That concentrates the mind, and hurts the heart. There are Taiwanese who are deeply resentful of those missiles pointed at them, by their "brother Chinese." The question of the United States and its support of Taiwan is a sensitive and important one here. For decades, the U.S. has followed a policy of "strategic ambiguity": "Will we or won't we?" Will the United States come to Taiwan's defense, in the event of a Chinese attack, or not? Early in his presidency—April 2001—George W.

Bush departed from this policy, saying that the U.S. would do "whatever it takes" to defend Taiwan. He later denied that he intended any change. I asked a White House national-security official, "Did the president simply slip, or was he trying to establish an American commitment?" The official gave me an amused look and, citing an old ad slogan, said, "Only his hairdresser knows for sure."

I ask many Taiwanese the terrible question: "If China attacks, do you think the U.S. will defend Taiwan? Will Washington lift a finger?" A few say, hopefully, "I don't know." A few say, "It depends"—for example, on whether Taiwan "provoked" the attack by declaring independence. A few say, "I doubt it," or, "Increasingly unlikely." Someone says, "You'll send us arms, but not men." Most say, flatly and somberly, "No." One woman says, "Particularly after Iraq and Afghanistan, I don't think you'll do anything." Almost everyone goes on to say that China could gobble Taiwan quickly, presenting the world with a fait accompli.

But the Taiwanese official involved in cross-strait relations says, "Don't forget that Taiwan is of some strategic value to the United States. Yes, we share political values, such as democracy, capitalism, and human rights. But Taiwan means something to the U.S. strategically too." The *Apple Daily*'s Ma says that Taiwanese have the feeling that their country is just a pawn, a pawn in a grand game of East Asian chess, played by others. But Americans might remember something, he says: "Taiwan is as pro-American a country as there is. We are your friends. Taiwan is a model for China, and if China becomes democratic, that will be a great benefit to the United States. So, for more than one reason: Don't abandon us."

Charles Krauthammer has said that Israel's survival depends on two things: the will of the people to live and the support of the United States. Some Taiwanese tell me that their own country's survival, as a liberal democracy, depends on the support of the United States. The Taiwanese certainly have a will to live: Taipei is one of the most vibrant cities you will ever see. There are important differences between Taiwan and Israel, not least in military standing: Israel is stronger against its (many) enemies than Taiwan is against China. But the similarities are worth pondering.

Both countries wish for normality in a world that won't give it to them. Both countries find themselves isolated in the "world community."

There are American scholars and analysts who say—not so bluntly, of course—"Let's throw Taiwan to the wolves, because our relationship with the PRC is so much more important. Why should this one little island disrupt relations with a coming superpower? The tail must not wag the dog." There are many who would be happy, or at least willing, to throw Israel to the wolves too—a tiny country in the vast Middle East, bringing on headache after headache.

Taiwan and Israel are small and vulnerable democracies, not able to count on other democracies to back them up. They are potential Czechoslovakias: feedable to the tiger, in the hope that the tiger will get full.

These are dark thoughts, but Taiwan is too booming, too boisterous, and too wonderful to allow dark thoughts for long. I will paraphrase that Taiwanese official: The ultimate disposition of Taiwan, or of the ROC–PRC relationship, is some distance into the future. Our children or grandchildren will have to handle the endgame. In the meantime, let us do all we can to achieve harmony across the Strait. Let us keep violence at bay, hang on, and keep going, until such time as the danger passes and we can get on with life.

—July 9, 2012

A Court in Cambodia

The struggle for justice in the wake of the Khmer Rouge

The court in Cambodia announced the death of Ieng Sary "with regret." Those words were puzzling: Did the court regret the passing of a human being, who may have meant a lot to his family? Or did the court regret that it had not yet completed its trial of him?

Ieng Sary was a Khmer Rouge leader, Brother Number 3, to be specific. Brother Number 1 was Pol Pot, who was Ieng Sary's brother-in-law. Ieng Sary was typical of the Khmer Rouge: a student in Paris; a member of the French Communist party; a professor of history back home; a forger of the new Red world that would smash inequality.

The Khmer Rouge took power on April 17, 1975. This was the launch of "Year Zero," as they had it. They ruled for three years, eight months, and 20 days—till January 7, 1979. Their rule was one of the most savage episodes in human history. They killed around 2 million people, which is to say, between a fifth and a quarter of the population. They had many apologists in the West, among intellectuals.

Ieng Sary was indicted for war crimes in the aforementioned court a long time after: on September 15, 2010. When he died last month, at the Khmer-Soviet Friendship Hospital in Phnom Penh, he was 87.

The court is known as the ECCC, which stands for Extraordinary Chambers in the Courts of Cambodia. To speak very formally, it is the Extraordinary Chambers in the Courts of Cambodia for the Prosecution of Crimes Committed during the Period of Democratic Kampuchea. That's what the Year Zero people called Cambodia: "Democratic Kampuchea."

It is a hybrid court, the ECCC: part Cambodian, part international, or U.N. But it is mainly Cambodian: A majority of the personnel are Cambodian. The court uses a mixture of Cambodian and international law.

Not until 2006 did the court begin its work. Not until 2009 did trials commence. What took so long, seeing as the Khmer Rouge fell in 1979? In brief, Cambodia was enmeshed in civil war, to one degree or another. And then there were protracted negotiations between the Cambodian government and the U.N.: What would the court look like? What would its powers be? In the government are plenty of former Khmer Rouge. This makes prosecution tricky.

The court is supposed to accomplish a number of things for Cambodia. It is supposed to expose the truth. It is supposed to enhance the rule of law. It is supposed to give survivors of the genocide a voice. (Survivors may participate in the trials either as complainants or as civil parties.) The court is supposed to punish the guilty, of course. And it is supposed to occasion some kind of catharsis. In a word, the court, like other courts, is supposed to achieve justice, however rough. This has proven elusive.

Ieng Sary was a defendant in the second and current trial of the ECCC—Case 002. He was one of four defendants. Now there are two: Nuon Chea and Khieu Samphan, i.e., Brother Number 2 and Brother Number 4. They are 86 and 81 years old. They are frail men who have suffered strokes. Brother Number 1, Pol Pot, died in 1998 at 72.

The Nazis were much younger during the Nuremberg trials—in their forties and fifties. Hitler himself had just turned 56 when he avoided capture and trial, shooting himself.

Ieng Sary's wife, Ieng Thirith, was a defendant in Case 002. When the Khmer Rouge ruled, she was social-affairs minister. Like her husband, she had been a student in Paris—majoring in Shakespeare at the Sorbonne. She was excused from the trial last September on grounds of dementia. This happened at Nuremberg too. Gustav Krupp was excused, and he died at his castle in Blühnbach, Austria. As it happens, I had lunch there last summer. The current proprietor is an American and an improvement, to say the very least.

Before Case 002 came Case 001—which had one defendant, Kaing Guek Eav. He is known as Duch, or Comrade Duch (pronounced "Doik"). What he did was preside over a prison called Tuol Sleng, also referred to as S-21. The prison was really a torture center: Some 16,000 people were tortured to death there. Seven people are known to have survived the place.

Duch gave the Nuremberg defense: He was merely following orders. He was convicted, and sentenced to 35 years in prison, reduced to 19. This sentence was appealed to a higher chamber within the ECCC: and that higher chamber upped the sentence to life. You never saw a sweeter-looking man than Duch. And, by the way, there is no death penalty in Cambodia. There isn't any in Israel either—but they made an exception for Eichmann.

So far, Duch is the only person to have been tried, in full, for Khmer Rouge crimes. Like Brother Number 3, Brothers 2 and 4 may not live until the end of their trial. They are in and out of the hospital, and are receiving the best of care. Think of what their victims, those millions, received.

The ECCC is a vast operation, with a cast of hundreds. These hundreds come from all over the world. They are judges, lawyers, administrators, staffers, and on and on. Ieng Sary had an international team of five lawyers. One of them was a pretty young woman from Indiana. As of now, the ECCC has spent $209 million. A lot of fuss has been made over a few old men, and one senile woman.

You can see pictures of them, all over the ECCC website. They are the stars of the show. You see them smiling, sitting serenely, exchanging confidences with their lawyers. You can almost forget they are genocidal monsters.

The trials have been marred by a number of things—prominent among them, the interference or lack of cooperation by the government. It seems clear that the government has pressured the court not to indict certain persons. And when the court has summoned government officials, merely to give testimony, those officials have felt free to ignore the summonses. Then there is good old-fashioned financial corruption.

Claudia Rosett, the American journalist, who is an authority on the U.N., makes a point about international bodies such as the ECCC: They can become gravy trains. They can start to exist mainly for the benefit of those who work for them. The ECCC may well limp on, doling out its salaries and per diems, until the last Khmer Rouge croaks.

It may have been better to have a truth commission: no prosecution, just lots of testimony, and amnesty for all. John Bolton, the American diplomat and lawyer, is of this view, and so are many Cambodians. The Khmer Rouge defendants, far from confessing and apologizing, are proclaiming their innocence. They have no incentive to sing. You have the spectacle of one of Brother Number 2's lawyers, a Dutchman, demanding that Henry Kissinger appear in the dock. It was the United States that made possible the rise of the Khmer Rouge, you see. "Without Kissinger, we would not be here today," said the lawyer.

The Khmer Rouge trials can seem a farce, and a cruel one at that. "Justice delayed is justice denied" is an expression often heard from the court's critics. If you look into the crimes of the Khmer Rouge, and then look into the seven-year history of the ECCC, you might ask, "Why bother?" I thought of an exclamation that rang through American politics earlier this year: "What difference, at this point, does it make?"

Ever since 1945, people have debated whether Nuremberg was worth it. The trials were tainted by the presence of the Soviets, of course, as judges and prosecutors. The Soviets were the Nazis' original partners in crime. Yet, as the historian David Pryce-Jones says, Nuremberg did this: It established a record. It taught us things about the Nazis and their conduct. Have the ECCC's trials—its trial and a half—served a similar purpose?

We have heard some interesting testimony, true. Some of it came from Vann Nath, one of that handful of survivors of the Tuol Sleng prison. He was so hungry, he almost ate into the corpses around him. He was spared execution because he was an artist who could paint portraits of Pol Pot. Chum Mey, another survivor, also gave testimony. Though almost tortured to death, he was spared when his jailers discovered that he could repair cars, typewriters, and other machines. (His wife and baby were killed.)

In court, Chum Mey was able to ask Duch why they insisted he say that he worked for the CIA. Duch gave a matter-of-fact answer: "The real CIA is different from people accused by the regime of being CIA. You were identified as someone who opposed the regime. That's why we called you CIA."

That is interesting. But in the past 35 years, we have learned a lot about the Khmer Rouge and its crimes, without benefit of the ECCC. For example, Vann Nath published a memoir in 1998. It must be said, though, that he greatly looked forward to the trials. "I could not sleep last night," he said as the first trial began. "I was waiting for the sunrise so that I could see Duch in the dock." (Vann Nath died in 2011.)

According to Sophal Ear, survivors of the genocide are split on the question of whether the court is worthwhile. He is a Cambodian-American political scientist in California, the author of a new book on foreign aid to Cambodia (harmful, he argues). Ear is a survivor himself; his father and brother were not. He says that the ECCC has almost no credibility now. Personally, he is not quite ready to give up on the court—but he is far from encouraged. He wonders whether the $209 million could have been spent in better ways in Cambodia.

So does Thida Mam, another survivor. (Her father, no.) She is a software engineer in Silicon Valley. At first, she had high hopes for the court. They have been dashed. She speaks of the ECCC with pain, frustration, and anger. She is dismayed at the corruption, the slow pace, the arrogance of the defendants, their proclamations of innocence, their self-justifications, the excusal of Ieng Thirith, the fact that Ieng Sary was given a grand and glorious funeral—the Ieng family is extremely rich, as leading Communists tend to be. She understands that the court must be civilized and humane, unlike the people it is trying. But must the defendants be so pampered? She finds she cannot follow the news from the ECCC any longer. Instead of helping her, it is tormenting her. "There's no justice. I was hoping for some justice, but forget it."

Sophal Ear points out that millions of Buddhists hold to the idea of karmic justice. His late mother trusted that, if there were no justice in this life, there would be in the next: The Khmer Rouge would come back as cockroaches.

—April 22, 2013

Freedom U

A unicorn of a university in Central America

Guatemala City

For years, people have said to me, "It's too good to be true. But it *is* true. It actually exists." These people are classical liberals, or Reagan conservatives, or in that general camp. And the thing they are talking about is Francisco Marroquín University, here in the Guatemalan capital. It is a classical-liberal university.

And it is virtually the only one in the entire world. A similar institution can be found in Montenegro, and it was inspired by UFM (to use the Guatemalan university's Spanish initials). But UFM stands pretty much alone.

UFM's mission statement, or mission sentence, is known by heart on this campus, at least by some: ". . . to teach and disseminate the ethical, legal, and economic principles of a society of free and responsible persons." (A teacher says to me, "Notice that 'ethical' comes first.")

On campus, you see Adam Smith Plaza. And the Ludwig von Mises Library. And the Friedrich Hayek Auditorium. And, for good measure, the Milton Friedman Auditorium. UFM has not forgotten Milton's better half: in the form of a Rose Friedman Terrace.

The university was founded in 1971 by Manuel Ayau and a group of like-minded partners. They were Guatemalan entrepreneurs, and they called themselves "rebel improvisers." They were fed up with the persistent socialism and poverty in their part of the world. They wanted to create at least an island of liberalism (for which Americans, with our peculiar vocabulary, can read "conservatism," or "Reaganism").

They named their university after Francisco Marroquín, who lived in the first half of the 16th century. He was the first bishop of Guatemala, and a pioneer in education. He was especially interested in the education of colonial girls and Indians. He was also interested in free trade and other elements of what would be known as classical liberalism.

Inaugurating the university, Ayau gave a simple, thoughtful, and profound address. At the end, he said, "May God help us and show us the road to the truth."

These were terrible times for Guatemala: civil-war times. One of the founders was kidnapped and murdered, by Communist guerrillas. So were other early participants in UFM. Evidently, the Communists did not appreciate diversity in education.

Today, UFM is flourishing, and true to its founding mission. There are nearly 3,000 students, and around 500 teachers (most of whom are part-time, and none of whom have tenure). Many of the teachers are alumni of the university.

UFM offers bachelor's degrees, master's degrees, and doctoral degrees. The subjects range from architecture to dentistry to psychology to law. A recent addition is a film program. But everyone takes fundamental courses, a core, in liberal economics and philosophy.

Workers on campus may take a colloquium in liberalism, free of charge. I'm talking about janitors, gardeners, everyone. They don't have to, because they are "free to choose" (in the Friedmans' phrase). But if they want to know what their employer is about, they may.

The place is beautiful—lush. Academic grove as tropical paradise. UFM is set in a ravine, and the buildings blend into the hills. I think of a statement by Frank Lloyd Wright: "A building should be a grace to its environment, not a disgrace."

Guatemala City has a reputation for crime, and I ask UFM's secretary-general, Ricardo Castillo, about the campus: Is it safe? Yes, he says, very. The biggest danger is that an avocado will fall from a tree and crack a windshield. It happened to a student recently, and she was quite upset.

The campus is dotted with art, including a sculpture of Atlas (as in "shrugged"). There is also a modern number called *Infinite Relationships*. It seems to me a bunch of coils or tubes. I'm told it represents the market.

Where the core courses are given is the Henry Hazlitt Center—named after the American journalist who wrote the iconic volume *Economics in One Lesson*. There is also a room named for Leonard Read, the American educator who wrote the iconic essay "I, Pencil." Next to one another, I see rooms named for Hannah Arendt, Lao-Tze, and Booker T. Washington.

Booker T. Washington? This especially warms my heart—for when I was growing up, he was often portrayed as a kind of Tom, an embarrassment, in contrast with the proud W. E. B. Du Bois.

Even the levels of the parking garage are named after worthies: specifically, members of the School of Salamanca (in 16th-century Spain). The idea is that car-driving students will eventually learn about these people, almost without trying.

Throughout campus—in virtually every corner—there are quotations and slogans. This bothers me a little at first, because I associate the ubiquity of quotations and slogans with the Left. But if you're going to have quotations and slogans—they might as well be true and salutary.

The rector, or president, of this university is Gabriel Calzada, an economist from Spain—from the Canary Islands, specifically. I ask him, "How did you become a liberal? Why are you not a socialist, as so many are?" In fact, I put this question to many of the faculty and administration. Everyone has a story, and it's interesting.

Calzada's is something like this: When he was in high school, he liked freedom—but he was on the left. He started a trade union of students. He read the usual: Hegel, Marx, Engels—even Bakunin. They didn't satisfy him.

When he got to college, he had a right-leaning (or liberal-leaning) professor. The young man argued with him in class. One day, the professor said, "Mr. Calzada, would you like to know more?" The young man said, "Yes, please give me more." The professor then invited him to come to his house weekly, for debate.

He gave young Calzada a variety of readings: left, right, and center. Calzada was drawn to the classical liberals. The first book that made a deep impression on him was by Jean-François Revel: *Useless Knowledge* (also known in English as *The Flight from Truth*). Then came Karl Popper, Hayek, others . . .

At UFM, there are plenty of left-leaning students, resisting and quarreling with the reigning ethos, of course. Students are exposed to a wide range of thought. They are free to explore, think, and argue as they will. Most of the time, they gravitate to classical liberalism—either before they graduate or after.

UFM has had an influence on Guatemala. This influence is seen in the liberalization of the telecommunications industry, for example. In the last presidential election, two of the three leading candidates mentioned Mises! (Including the eventual winner.)

Guy Wyld, the president of the university's board of trustees, tells me a somewhat touching story. Last year, he got a hold of an index of economic freedom worldwide. He looked from the middle of the list down, for Guatemala. He couldn't find it—for it was in the top-most quartile.

While other universities in Guatemala and the rest of the region may not like UFM, they have to respect it. UFM has been called "the Harvard of Central America." Not long ago, President Calzada was at a meeting of university officials and associated others. One of the university officials lit into him as a tool of Big Business, a defender of privilege, etc. Later, the official asked to speak to him privately.

"Listen," he said, "my son is approaching college age, and there is of course no other place for him to go but UFM. Do you think you can get him in? Also, how about a scholarship?"

One of the most sparkling personalities at UFM is Carla Hess, who, appropriately, leads a program called "Spark." It seeks to encourage the entrepreneurial spark in human beings. She herself grew up during the civil war and was taught by Maryknoll nuns. They preached Communist revolution to the girls in their charge. Most of these girls came from wealthy families. Some of them ran off with the rebels. But Carla did not. Why?

For one thing, her father had always impressed on her a respect for life: "Thou shalt not kill." Also a respect for private property: "Thou shalt not steal." You never take what's not yours—even a rubber band at school or work. This girl could not join the rebels.

She tells her students that they can be victims or achievers—their choice. They may say, "I was born in Guatemala, so how can I be or do anything in the world?" That is a mentality that UFM seeks to erase.

Carla Hess also leads rope courses and other physical activities up in the hills. They teach lessons such as, "What is the difference between central planning and spontaneous order?" In creative ways, students learn that one is a lot more effective than the other.

To speak personally: I like a campus without any intellectual or political slant. But if our universities—thousands and thousands of them—are going to be dominated by the Left, what's so bad about one classical-liberal university in all the world? Even ten or 20?

I realize I've sounded like a cheerleader in this article. But readers will forgive me because there's so much to cheer.

One of the things I notice at UFM is a strong, strong contrast with the trend of things in America. I notice no sense of entitlement. Quite the opposite. I notice eagerness, curiosity, and gratitude. At home, we have safe spaces and trigger warnings. These things would be laughable here—even incomprehensible. Last fall, I did a report from Brown University, where students had started a secret Facebook group so that they could discuss things freely. There is no such need at UFM. Everything is open and on the table.

I meet a student from rural Guatemala who won a scholarship here. In previous times, he picked beans on a coffee farm to support his family. A sense of entitlement would be utterly foreign to him.

A final thought: When I was growing up, I think I was led to believe that the capitalists, classical liberals, or free-marketeers were selfish, materialistic, greedy. They preached a gospel of dog-eat-dog. In due course, I realized that they were among the most caring people on earth. They want people to be prosperous, free, and well.

—March 28, 2016

Hung Up on Israel

An explanation for the sincere

At the recent Republican presidential debate, many of the candidates mentioned Israel. Jeb Bush, for example, said that we need to reestablish "our commitment to Israel, which has been altered by this administration." Carly Fiorina said that the first phone call she would make, from the Oval Office, would be to "my good friend Bibi Netanyahu." Its purpose would be "to reassure him we will stand with the State of Israel."

After the debate, some observers wondered, "Why so much attention to Israel? Are these people running for president of the United States or president of Israel?"

I myself have received similar questions over the years. People ask, sometimes with scorn, sometimes with sincere curiosity, "Why do you write so much about Israel? Why are you hung up on Israel?" I would think the answer were obvious. But if it were, people would not ask these questions. And honest questions deserve honest answers.

Israel is the only state whose very right to exist is called into question. (Ukraine, however, is beset with problems of its own. And Taiwan has well-founded anxieties.) Ever since it was born in 1948, people have tried to kill Israel. It is a tiny country amid enemies. Four wars of annihilation have been waged against it. There have been smaller conflicts as well, though still serious. Every day, Israel deals with Hezbollah, Hamas, and their like. And Iran has pledged to wipe it off the face of the earth.

I think Israel is a great and admirable state. I think Zionism is a great and admirable movement. The revival of Hebrew alone is one of the more astonishing developments of modern times. But Zionism aside, there is the fact that Israel was established a mere three years after the Holocaust. (Zionism began in the 19th century, remember.) Israel was established a mere three years after the ovens of Auschwitz and the rest stopped belching. Three years after two-thirds of European Jewry were murdered.

The Jews refused to disappear altogether. In Israel, they are living in sovereignty for the first time in 2,000 years. To begrudge the Jews their state, after the Holocaust, is particularly disgusting, I think.

People say that Israel has treated the Arabs badly. I disagree. Obviously, Israel has made mistakes, as people do. But that Israelis are more sinned against than sinning, I have no doubt. I also have no doubt that, as soon as the Palestinians and other Arabs are willing to coexist, there will be peace. I also know that Arabs serve in the Israeli parliament, heckling the prime minister. And that, when gays in the West Bank or Gaza are threatened with lynching, they flee to Israel.

You may not agree with me on the Israeli–Palestinian conflict, or Zionism, and that is perfectly understandable. But consider: Israel is the most condemned nation of all 200 in the world, virtually a pariah state. Why? Isn't this a little odd? A little out of order?

William F. Buckley Jr. observed that, within every person, there is a tank of indignation. A person's supply of indignation is not inexhaustible. What does he spend it on? Many people spend a shocking percentage of their tank on Israel. "To be anti-Israel is not to be anti-Jewish!" they protest. True. But I also think of what Paul Johnson says: "Scratch a person who is anti-Israel, and you won't have to dig very far until you reach the anti-Semite within."

Israel, encircled by enemies and threatened with destruction, should have *more* support than any other nation. Instead, it has the least.

The United Nations often seems to exist to oppose Israel. Since 2006, the U.N. Human Rights Council has condemned Israel 62 times. It has condemned the rest of the world a combined 59 times. (Syria is in second place, by the way, with twelve condemnations. North Korea has a paltry eight.)

There is a great BDS movement in the world—with "BDS" standing for "Boycott, Divestment, and Sanctions." This movement targets one country, and one country only: Israel. In 2013, Stephen Hawking accepted an invitation to attend a conference in Israel honoring Shimon Peres. Hawking is the British physicist, as you know. He is one of the most famous and most admired men in all the world. Peres is an Israeli statesman and dove. Under pressure, Hawking changed his mind about going to Israel, saying he needed to respect the BDS movement.

A glance at his travel record is illuminating. In 1973, Hawking went to the Soviet Union. In 2007, he went to Iran. The year before, he had gone to China, where, according to a state news agency, he was "treated to a Hollywood-style reception." Hawking said, "I like Chinese culture, Chinese food, and, above all, Chinese women. They are beautiful." Israeli women are pretty hot themselves. And they don't live in a one-party police state with a gulag. Nor does Israel imprison Nobel peace laureates, such as Shimon Peres. China does.

Travel now to Scotland, where the West Dunbartonshire Council forbids local libraries to carry Israeli books. More specifically, the libraries are forbidden to carry books printed in Israel. If they are by Israelis, but printed elsewhere, that's kosher. Not long ago, one of the libraries purchased *The Protocols of the Elders of Zion*, that infamous forgery, on grounds that people ought to read what they like.

Wherever they go in the world, Israeli athletes and musicians are hounded and harassed. In 2009, the Davis Cup was held in Sweden. (This is the annual tennis competition.) The Israelis had to play a match in an empty arena, because protests and other disruptions had been promised. For two years in a row, an Israeli female tennis player at the ASB Classic in New Zealand was screamed at. After one of the matches, the 22-year-old Shahar Peer said that the words had been hard to understand, "but I did hear my name all the time, which wasn't really nice."

In both London and Edinburgh, concerts of the Jerusalem Quartet have been disrupted. Prominent writers have defended those disruptions too, with one music critic saying that the quartet was "fair game for hecklers." A concert of the Israel Philharmonic Orchestra at the BBC Proms was disrupted. One of the critics present said that the hall "had the atmosphere of a riot."

In this general atmosphere, the Russian-born pianist Evgeny Kissin took out Israeli citizenship. He explained, "When Israel's enemies try to disrupt concerts of the Israel Philharmonic Orchestra or the Jerusalem Quartet, I want them to come and make trouble at my concerts, too—because Israel's case is my case, Israel's enemies are my enemies, and I do not want to be spared." Last summer, I did a public interview of Gianandrea Noseda, an Italian conductor. Among his posts is guest conductor of the Israel Phil. After the interview, I drew him aside and thanked him for going to Israel. To some people, it would have seemed strange to thank him. But he, for one, understood.

When the Alaska governor Sarah Palin became famous, some people thought it was strange that she had an Israeli flag in her office. I understood completely. She was obviously expressing solidarity with a gutsy country under siege. Later, she wore a lapel pin with the American and Israeli flags intertwined. In an article, I commended this. A reader wrote me to say, "I happen to be a Roman Catholic American of Irish descent. What would you think if, one day, Palin wore a pin with the American and Irish flags intertwined? Or the American and Vatican flags?" One thing I think is that, if Ireland were in Israel's position, a lot of us would plaster ourselves with shamrocks and fly the Irish flag.

If the world would leave Israel alone—simply let it be, let it live—I would probably think about Israel as much as I do, say, Uruguay. I don't mean to offend Uruguay. But Uruguay almost never crosses my mind.

I used to know a lot about South Africa, as many others did. This was during apartheid days, when South Africa was a focus of world attention. We knew the big players, Mandela and Tutu, of course, but also others, such as Steve Biko, and Joe Slovo, and Helen Suzman, and Chief Buthelezi. (I wish more people knew about an earlier chief and anti-apartheid leader, Albert Lutuli, who won the Nobel Peace Prize for 1960.) But after apartheid was overcome, South Africa hardly ever made the news. I would be hard pressed to tell you who was president today. Is it still Zuma?

There is a great civilizational divide in the world, with the likes of ISIS and the mullahs on one side, and their prey on the other. Israel's foes are our foes, or certainly my foes. If the world lets Israel go down, then the world is an ass, and a betrayer. Moreover, the prospects of civilization itself are in doubt. So, yes, I think and write a lot about Israel. I have been slammed as an "Israel Firster" (in imitation of the old, Lindberghian "America Firster"). I say again, leave Israel alone, and it will get the Uruguay treatment. Which it has longed for from the beginning.

I have a friend who says she wants to move to Israel when the crunch comes. She is not Jewish, but she has a conscience, probably formed in

World War II, when she was a girl. She and some family members had a narrow escape in that war. Not all of the family survived. And having seen one holocaust of the Jews, she can't stand the idea of another. "If the bombs are going to fall on them," she says, "I want them to fall on me, too." This is extreme, but I understand it.

Some years ago, I attended a conference in Jordan on the Dead Sea. One day, at twilight, I stood on the shore and looked over at Israel. I thought of the teeming hatred against Israel, the annihilationist hatred. And I wanted to throw my arms around that country, somehow, in protection. I feel sure you understand.

—October 19, 2015

Brushes through India

With special appearances by Henry Mancini and Area 51

"What's playing in India?" asked a friend of mine, before I took off. Oh, nothing in particular: just India itself, for two weeks of exploration. My friends and I begin in Bombay, or, as we're all supposed to say now, "Mumbai." I ask a local lady about this; she is a sharp and savvy schoolteacher. She says that "Mumbai" has been forced on everyone by a certain political crowd; she prefers, when speaking English, to say "Bombay"—and why not?

Bombay is a very, very populous city in this very, very populous country. People are everywhere, tucked into every nook and cranny. If traffic is moving—which is a very big if—they fly about on motorcycles, without helmets. There are children on those bikes, too, carefree, as well as helmet-free. You hear that India is a heavily regulated country. Yes, but it's interesting what they choose to regulate, and what not.

Here's a little political-economic note: I buy a packet of cracker-like things, and it says, "Less taxes = more biscuits." Oh, lower taxes mean a lot of good things, my friends.

Before I came here, several people who know the country told me one thing, independently. They said, "You've heard about the burgeoning middle class, and it is true. But bear in mind that India is still a very poor country—it may shock you." Poverty is a given, yes. The place is not all tech companies and call centers, to put it mildly. And animal transportation—camel-drawn carts, etc.—is utterly routine.

Children beg, saying "Hello, hello," while making eating gestures with their fingers. The adult beggars I see are very few: young mothers with infants; and old, wretched men. I see no able-bodied men beg—as I do where I live, in Manhattan, every day.

A morning walk in Bharuch—state of Gujarat—is enjoyable and instructive. Through the neighborhoods come vendors with handcarts. They sell fruit, or vegetables, or milk. They call out the names of their products as they go, leather-lunged. It occurs to me that this is an anti-Wal-Marter's dream. There is no one-stop shopping. Everyone pushes his own tiny line, earning pennies.

Girls are lovely in their saris. This is true of richer ones and poorer ones, spiffier ones and scruffier. Are girls here more attractive than elsewhere? You may think so; it's more likely that they're attractive because they're so feminine. They seem to enjoy being female, and carry themselves that way. They sort of sashay along. I doubt softball here is much good.

Generally speaking, men are almost as style-conscious as women. You might even say they are vain, matching their clothes, frequently combing their hair, Fonzie-style. Whether they have money or not, they want to cut a figure.

Down by the river in Bharuch, I see women washing clothes in mud pools, beating them with a paddle. I'm surprised that this is still going on. And I think of my Indian-American friends back home: super-educated, super-affluent, many of them. How many generations removed are they from this clothes-paddling? Not many. Human life can move fast. (In both directions?)

This country is famous for smells—good and bad—and I get plenty of whiffs on my walk. One whiff I get is of incense: and it flashes me back to boarding school. The kids used to burn incense, for two reasons: It was cool, because New Age; and they wanted to cover up the smell of their pot.

You hear that India is a polluted country, and I'm afraid it's so. You perhaps don't know pollution until you know Indian pollution, or Third World pollution in general. And once you experience it, you don't want to hear a word from an American environmentalist, about the American environment, again. The Kyoto Protocol? Oh, come on . . .

As I walk about Bharuch, my mind is a jumble of clichés. "Life and death are particularly stark in India. Everything is in bold relief." True. There is tremendous vibrancy, but also the odd dog carcass, just off the street. Life and death fill eyes, ears, and nostrils. "In India, the rich and poor live in very close proximity." True, so true. And then there are the famous contradictions: "India is alluring and repugnant, irresistible and abominable." True, true.

Everywhere, in villages, towns, and cities, you share the streets with animals. There are both Democrats and Republicans, both donkeys and elephants (although the former greatly outnumber the latter—just as at American universities). There are goats, monkeys, camels, boars, buffalo. In Bharuch, my hosts' garden is stuffed with peacocks. And, throughout India, it's a joy to see parrots: which are not meant only for the cages of little old ladies.

Cows, of course, are ubiquitous. Here, they all die of old age. An Indian-American friend tells me a funny story: Years ago, an Indian of her acquaintance came to America. He started eating hamburgers and steaks with abandon. Asked to explain himself, he said, "I figure only Indian cows are sacred." One of the most charming rationalizations I have ever heard.

It's a pleasure to hear Indian English, which is often musical. And it can be quite old-fashioned, even King Jamesian: Our guide in Jodhpur (home of the pants) says, "This maharajah had no male issue." I also like a sign, at the approach of a toll booth: "Dead Slow."

Even if you know the language, you may not. Return to Bombay with me, for a moment: I'm sitting in a restaurant with some old friends and new acquaintances—locals. In the course of the meal, I ask, "Does this restaurant seek out tourists, or does it exist mainly for natives?" Silence—unusual, for our talky group. Finally, a lady says, "What do you mean by 'natives'?" Uh-oh. I say, "Well, you know—'natives.' People born here, from here." More silence. I then say, "Is the word pejorative here?" Not in standard English, but here, yes: It was so under the British.

A foreign culture, even an accessible one, can be a minefield.

Here's something that takes some getting used to: the presence of the swastika, everywhere. It is a venerable Hindu symbol, twisted by the Nazis. You see it on the thresholds of homes. And, in Jaisalmer, I see the Hotel Swastika. I think, "Surely this must repel European tourists." I then have a darker thought: "Maybe it attracts some?"

You'll want a word on Indian toilets (won't you?). Some of them are terrifying—you'll hold it till kingdom come. Others of them are benign, even inviting. There is a great variety. An Udaipur restaurant presents two doors: One says "Indian Toilet," the other says "Western Toilet." You know the expression "When in Rome . . ."? I'm afraid I do not—do as the Romans.

This is a musical country, as you know, and you hear music everywhere: from TVs and radios, sure, but also from loudspeakers on trucks. And at marriage celebrations, which go on constantly, in this marriage-loving country. Oddly, I hear "Frère Jacques"—three times, in three separate Indian cities. Both played and sung. The singers need a little help with pronunciation.

And the variety of cellphone rings is dizzying, as it is the world over. Our guide in Udaipur has a phone that plays "Jingle Bells." Does he know it's a Christmas carol? He does now. And, in the little Gujarati village of Dantali, a cellphone breaks the still of the evening. What is it playing? I'll tell you, but first, a story.

Some months back, Paul Johnson, the British writer, wrote about Arthur Hugh Clough, the British poet who lived from 1819 to 1861. He wrote one poem that stuck: "Say not the struggle naught availeth." Johnson remembered hearing a car salesman in Perth recite this poem. And he, Johnson, thought, "That's fame."

Well, on this quiet Dantali evening, the cellphone plays the theme to *Love Story*, by Francis Lai (taken to great popular heights by Henry Mancini). And the thought immediately comes to me: "That's fame."

We have talked of variety, and what there's really a variety of is people. A *tremendous* variety of them. Seldom will you see a collection of people so diverse. You see men who look like they stepped out of antiquity: simple wrap, walking staff, painted face, wizened. And they're waiting for the same bus as people who look like Wall Streeters. Somewhere in Rajasthan, I see women with hoops through their noses carrying huge bundles of sticks on their heads. I think: "This is foreign travel—you ain't looking at Big Ben."

Race is a touchy subject here, maybe touchier than in most other places. In the *Hindustan Times*, I see brides advertised. Most of the ads say "fair and slim." I don't see any women advertised as dark and chunky. And the ads go on to give height and weight, as well as academic credentials ("MBA!") and other data. Talk about a meat market—although most of these ladies are advertised as vegetarian.

Great as the temples, palaces, forts, and other sites in India may be, most valuable are encounters with people. I could tell a hundred stories. Here's one:

One of my hosts in Bharuch is a distinguished intellectual—an educator and a novelist. He studied at Washington University (St. Louis) in the late 1950s and early 1960s. He ran out of money, and was on the point of leaving. But an American family—just middle-class, in his description—took him in. They expected nothing in return. The man marvels at their generosity, and at their egalitarian spirit: "Here they were, sharing a bathroom and a kitchen and everything with an Indian boy—just as though it was nothing."

Encounters with children are particularly delightful. There are masses and masses of them, everywhere. Front and center. Often they are in school uniforms, and shiny as pennies. No matter how filthy their surroundings—and they can be vile—these children are immaculate. And, as a rule, open, curious, fun-loving, and just plain loving. These kids have nothing, many of them. And yet they seem happier and better adjusted than our kids—in America.

I'll give you just one favorite kid story: We're in Gundi, another Gujarati village, like Dantali. Children are massed in a square. Seeing me, they see an opportunity to try out their English. They want to count to ten, and I test them. They know the numbers, well enough; but they're a little shaky on the order.

One boy specializes in the number seven. He likes to call out "Seven!" doggedly. I hold up six fingers: "Seven!" he exclaims. I have to shake my head. But then I hold up another finger, and it's his moment in the sun.

Not every child is in school, of course. The beggars aside, many kids work: Child labor is unshocking here, part of the furniture. Near the city of Bikaner, a boy checks the air in our tires. I think he's about ten—hard to tell, for in this country the kids, slight, look younger than they are.

And the adults? Like the children, they seem happy, content—amazingly so. A companion of mine comments, "There is no tension on faces." People smile, even beam. And, from a material point of view, they have nothing to beam about. Every day, I walk by people in New York who scowl, frown, sneer. And they have everything, by comparison. You hear that happiness is a state of mind. That may be a Hallmark sentiment—but not less true for that.

It goes without saying that Indians, being people, have their complaints. In Jaisalmer, I meet a group of young men who hawk products and services to tourists. They speak decent English, and have a tremendous curiosity about the world. Their faces shine, alive. One young man asks me about Area 51: What do I know about it? Not much, I have to tell him. I'm not sure he believes me—probably thinks I'm in on some conspiracy.

Another man in the group tells me about the obstacles they all face. If these obstacles had a name, it would be corruption. India is getting better, the man says—liberalizing. But fast enough and broadly enough? He and his friends do everything right, the man says: take the right classes, pass the right exams. But there comes a time to grease palms—and, being poor, they have no grease. So they feel stuck, stifled—denied the right to pursue their dreams and destinies.

What a waste.

Anyway, when they finish, I say, "Thank you. You have given me quite an education." They protest, "You're a lot more educated than we are." I say I'm not so sure. Then one young man—the Area 51 fellow—says, "You're more *experienced*." "That's right," I say. "I've had more experience, more opportunities. I was lucky to be born where I was." They agree enthusiastically.

But I am also lucky to have come here, and met them, and India.

—March 10, 2008

ISSUES AND ESSAYS

Hail to the Golfer-in-Chief

Barack Obama tees it up, no matter the winds

On Christmas break in his native Hawaii, President Obama played a lot of golf. He tends to do that: play golf. Through terror concerns and other matters of state, he played. The press noted that Obama has played more golf in his first year in office than George W. Bush did in his eight years. (More about that later.) This has rubbed some people the wrong way: Obama's love of, and indulgence in, golf. He loves and plays basketball, too. But he doesn't take any grief for that—only golf.

Michelle Cottle of *The New Republic* wrote a piece called "Bunker Mentality" (cute title). She said, "Golf is a dubious pastime for any decent, sane person, much less for this particular president. Why would a leader vowing to shake up Washington—to alter the very nature of politics—sell his soul to a leisure activity that screams stodgy, hyper-conventional Old Guard?" We can see that she doesn't like golf very much. She went on to list five possible explanations for Obama's "embrace of golf." One of them was, "Image control. Obama's enthusiastic adoption of this most corporate of pastimes reassures middle-Americans that their history-making black president isn't too urban, edgy, or cool." Here is something that was not among the five explanations: He really, you know—likes the game. Loves it.

One more quotation from Cottle, who said, "In the popular imagination, golf is the stuff of corporate deal-cutting, congressional junkets, and country club exclusivity." *In the popular imagination*. I see, once more, that my own imagination is unpopular.

I pretty much grew up in golf, on the munis of Ann Arbor, Mich. (A "muni," in golf-talk, is a municipal golf course.) I also worked at a couple of these courses. And golf was—is—a thoroughly democratic game. Everybody played. Young and old, male and female, wealthy and broke, respectable and scoundrelly. We had hippies and druggies, in tie-dyed shirts and sandals. We had grimy, tattooed union members. We had snotty left-wing professors from the University of Michigan. We had rednecks from the sticks. We had Korean immigrants who could barely speak English. And so on.

The whole world came by these golf courses, and all were united, a bit—not to get too sappy—by this game. Such a glorious game, and an equalizer. On the golf course, the only thing that matters is the game.

I might mention, too, that, on the courses of Greater Detroit, there was a whole, wonderful world of black hustling—I mean gambling and the like. I was lucky enough to be introduced to this world. It is very far from, say, Oakland Hills Country Club, the marquee course in the Detroit suburb of Bloomfield Hills. But it is certainly golf—a game that contains multitudes. Those who think that golf is a pastime for uptight WASPs should get out more. But uptight WASPs—as well as relaxed ones—are part of humanity too, remember. If you prick them, won't they bleed?

Plenty of political lefties play golf, but the Left in general has long had a bugaboo about the sport. I give you Hugo Chávez, the strongman down in Venezuela. Last summer, he ordered the closing of some of Venezuela's courses, and he denounced golf in the usual, asinine terms. He called it "bourgeois." (Has there ever been a dumber word?) He said, "I respect all sports. But there are sports and there are sports. Do you mean to tell me this is a people's sport? It is not." It is certainly more a people's sport than Chávez's government is a (genuine) people's government.

A democratic president, George W. Bush, had a touchy relationship with golf during his time in the White House. One early morning in August 2002, he went out for a round with his father and two others. It was his custom to talk with reporters before teeing off. And, on this occasion, he said he was "distressed to hear about the latest suicide bombers in Israel." He made a tough if standard statement, ending, "I call upon all nations to do everything they can to stop these terrorist killers." He then nodded grimly and, in perfect Bush fashion, said, "Thank you. Now watch this drive."

This was taken, by some, to be the height of insouciance, arrogance, and irresponsibility. Michael Moore used a video of this moment in his film *Fahrenheit 9/11*. Others of us found nothing to object to in how Bush performed. We even grinned, warmly, at the whole episode: "That's our boy." As usual, this president occasioned a wide range of reactions and emotions.

It was in August 2003 that Bush stopped playing golf. He didn't make a production out of it. He didn't even tell anyone. He simply—stopped. In 2008, he explained, "I remember when de Mello got killed in Baghdad." He meant Sérgio Vieira de Mello, the top U.N. official in Iraq, who was killed in a terrorist bombing along with 20 others. "I was playing golf—I think I was in central Texas—and they pulled me off the golf course, and I said, 'It's just not worth it anymore.' I didn't want some mom whose son may have recently died to see the commander-in-chief playing golf."

The president's motivation was perfectly honorable and understandable, obviously. But it was a shame that the weird stigma about golf had to be bowed to. Bush did not deny himself recreation altogether: He rode his mountain bike a lot, in those bright, huggy shorts. But golf, somehow, was too unseemly to be engaged in. Biking's okay, basketball's okay—golf is risky. Why? For no good reason, only because of the strange psychology with which some people are saddled.

In a column, I made a point about our boys at war: They have played golf for as long as anyone can remember. Golf at war is part and parcel of the American tradition. Our soldiers have played when and where they can, in makeshift fashion—we're not talking about teeing it up at Oakland Hills. At the USGA Museum in New Jersey—it used to be called Golf House—there is a World War II exhibit. Among the items are some homemade golf balls, from the hands of American POWs. I know for sure that our guys in Iraq are playing, on patches of desert here and there. One of them asked me to join him and his friends, when I visited the country in 2008. Wish the schedule had allowed.

Yes, yes: A president has to guard his image, even if it means bowing to prejudice or unreason. Bush's father, the 41st president, took some grief when he zipped around in his cigarette boat during the Gulf War. The elder Bush liked golf, too, a lot—and he liked to play fast. He developed something known in Bush circles as "speed golf." He boated fast, and he played fast.

President Clinton, not a country-clubber but the Man from Hope, played golf all the time. Absolutely craved the game. He once observed that he was probably the only president to leave office a better player than when he entered: because he had received many tips from the pros he played with. Of course, he was not known for scrupulous honesty on the golf course, as elsewhere. Bob Woodward tells a story in his book *Shadow*. One day in 1993, Clinton, President Ford, and Jack Nicklaus played 18 holes together. Afterward, Clinton claimed to have shot a score of 80 (far too low for him). Woodward writes, "Ford was shocked. Golf was a matter of honor, even for old duffers, and Clinton had repeatedly taken second shots, called mulligans. Nicklaus leaned over to Ford and whispered in disgust, 'Eighty with fifty floating mulligans.'"

Presidents since about Taft have played golf. Barack Obama joins a proud, happy tradition. And he is one of about 30 million Americans who play golf. Thirty million—not exactly an elite or exotic slice. Hell, people across the world have taken to golf ever since a shepherd boy, somewhere in Scotland hundreds of years ago, first swung at some dung with his crook. Golf is not for everybody, of course—just as certain types of music or food are not for everybody. But it's for some of us. We were kind of thrilled when Tiger Woods came to dominance, in the late 1990s. As Colin Montgomerie (the Scottish champion) put it, "We're fortunate to have the world's best athlete playing our game." Golf has been outright *cool* in the Age of Tiger. And now that he is a tabloid star—is it cooler yet?

But those who value this game don't care whether it is cool or uncool. We just want to play it, enjoy it, study it, agonize over it. As I once said to a co-worker, who was bad-mouthing golf in the harshest terms—this was a right-winger, by the way—"Good. Please stay away from the courses. It's hard enough to get a tee time as it is, and play is awfully slow."

Frankly, one of the best things I know about President Obama is that he plays golf. It probably gives him succor, solace, strength. On the golf course, as I have indicated, the rest of the world can sort of melt away. Also, a camaraderie, or brotherhood, can develop. The legendary teacher Harvey Penick once wrote a book with a memorable title: "And If You Play Golf, You're My Friend." I imagine that President Obama and Rush Limbaugh would enjoy a round of golf together. I'd like to make a third! And maybe the president could suggest a left-leaning fourth, so that our group is philosophically even? (Incidentally, Obama is a lefty on the golf course, same as he is off—he plays left-handed, I mean.)

He swatted that fly. He called that rapper—the one who disrupted the award ceremony—a "jackass." He has a serious jones for golf. Really, I could warm to our president.

—January 25, 2010

Books and Covers

On 'looking liberal' and 'looking conservative'

When we were in kindergarten—if not before—we were taught that you can't judge a book by its cover. Which is true. Or rather, you can't *necessarily* judge a book by its cover. Often, it is an error to do so. Related is an old expression, usually attributed to Oscar Wilde: "When you assume, you make an ass out of u and me."

Well and good. But I remember something I heard a writer say on television, many years ago. (It wasn't Oscar Wilde. It may have been Harlan Ellison.) He said, "If the cover shows a strapping woman amid the stars, wearing a metallic brassiere and brandishing a light saber, chances are the book is science fiction."

Which brings me to "Pajama Boy"—the young man pictured in a pre-Christmas ad touting ObamaCare. The ad said, "Wear pajamas. Drink hot chocolate. Talk about getting health insurance." That's what the young man was doing (we could assume). The ad came courtesy of Organizing for Action, a group dedicated to promoting President Obama's agenda.

By the way, leaving "action" aside, I have become allergic to the word "organizing." It's a fairly innocent word, but I remember what the actress Susan Sarandon said after Obama was elected: "He is a community organizer like Jesus was, and now we're a community and he can organize us."

It was said throughout the conservative universe that Pajama Boy "looked liberal." Others prefer the word "progressive" (including "progressives" themselves). George F. Will wrote a year-end column, saying,

"In 2013, the face of progressivism became Pajama Boy, the supercilious, semi-smirking, hot-chocolate-sipping faux-adult who embodies progressives' belief that life should be all politics all the time—come on, everybody, spend your holidays talking about health care. He is who progressives are."

The word "metrosexual" was used a lot. The editors of *Investor's Business Daily* spoke of the "hipster metrosexual cradling cocoa in his red onesie" (a kind of pajamas). Friends of the model felt obliged to protest his robust heterosexuality.

There was another issue, too—sort of in the shadows. In the first hours of the general mockery, I was concerned that anti-Semitism might enter into it. Either the mockery would include some anti-Semitic stuff or the mockery would be interpreted, by someone, as anti-Semitic. Sure enough, the *Forward* published an article headed "Obamacare 'Pajama Boy' Controversy Wrapped in Anti-Semitism."

The writer, Jay Michaelson, said,

> Yes, Virginia, Pajama Boy is a member of the tribe. Look at him. Pale Ashkenazic skin, Jew-fro'd black curls, Woody Allen specs. Even the smart-ass expression on his face screams of the Wise Son from the Passover Seder.
>
> Parenthetically, the model himself is one Ethan Krupp, an Organizing for America [actually, Action] staffer who is, in fact, Jewish. But whether Krupp himself is circumcised or not, Pajama Boy is semiotically Jewish, even stereotypically so.

I couldn't help thinking of a strange fact: The model/staffer shares a name with the famous, and infamous, arms-manufacturing family in Germany. Hitler once told the lads at Nuremberg, "In our eyes, the German boy of the future must be slim and slender, fast as a greyhound, tough as leather, and hard as Krupp steel."

At the very moment America was contemplating Pajama Boy, we were also contemplating Duck Man, i.e., Phil Robertson, the star of the *Duck Dynasty* reality series. He had made controversial remarks about homosexuality in a magazine interview. He could not be more unlike Pajama Boy in his appearance. He looks like a combination of prophet and backwoodsman, with long hair, bandana, and long gray beard. He looks like the homespun Christian conservative he is—unless he looks like a member of Willie Nelson's entourage, not unfamiliar with marijuana. And I could easily see him manning a booth at the Ann Arbor Art Fair (whose official atmosphere, come to think of it, is marijuana).

Ann Arbor, Mich., is the town I grew up in. I occasionally tease it in my writings, usually describing it as "a small citadel of the Left." When Pajama Boy splashed all over the media, a colleague of mine asked me, "Is that what the people in Ann Arbor looked like?" Yes and no. When I was growing up, the Left was scruffier, grungier, dirtier. They would not have wanted to be clean-cut, looking like a Boy Scout, churchgoer, or Republican.

Confronted by hippie hecklers, ol' George Wallace said, "They know a lot of four-letter words—but there are some they don't know. Like W-O-R-K and S-O-A-P." Campaigning for Eugene McCarthy in 1968, the countercultural types did not want to scare the Middle American types. So they shaved and showered, adhering to the slogan "Get clean for Gene."

The Left is very clean today, I find—scrubbed, slicked, and affluent. I was back in Ann Arbor over Christmas, and saw a store with the (typically) pretentious name of My Urban Toddler. That's the spirit now.

Is it possible to "look liberal" or "look conservative"? "At 50," George Orwell wrote, "everyone has the face he deserves." I don't know about that. And I know that looks can be deceiving, including in a political sense. There are some who "look conservative" but aren't, and vice versa. Let me remind you of Richard Armitage, the deputy secretary of state under Colin Powell (and George W. Bush). He looked like a right-winger, a bruiser, a bull of a man. But he consistently took unconservative, or Powellesque, positions.

William Safire, the late columnist, who liked to have fun, had fun with Armitage's appearance. One time, he wrote, "The heavyset, bullet-headed Armitage is known for having a good head on his shoulders. (That is primarily because he has no neck, but as they say on the seventh floor of Foggy Bottom, better neckless than feckless.)"

I'll occasionally see pictures or videos of Ed Schultz, the MSNBC host. If he were an actor, he could be cast as a right-wing blowhard: stocky, slightly sweating (maybe). Instead, he is a left-wing blowhard. But, according to Wikipedia, he used to be a conservative, so maybe his looks are left over from that period? Very different in appearance is Schultz's MSNBC colleague Rachel Maddow. She has the same views, but her looks are more classically liberal. (I hasten to say that classical liberalism, as represented by Locke et al., has nothing to do with MSNBC or its hosts.)

To me, Mussolini looks like the ultimate fascist thug. He is almost a cartoon. Do I think this because I know he was, in fact, a fascist thug? Stalin looks like a genocidal monster, with that menacing black crop of hair, and those "yellow tiger's eyes," as David Pryce-Jones says. But I imagine some of his victims looked like him, too, especially in Georgia. Mao probably looked like a number of his victims as well—although they would have been thinner, having to live, or not live, under Mao's policies.

When I look at Lincoln, I think I am looking at the soul of moral leadership. The visage matches the man. But could a bank robber have looked like that? Probably so. (And there are Americans even now who look at Lincoln and see a war criminal and tyrant.)

In the Reagan '80s, some Republicans made sport of Tip O'Neill, the Democratic speaker of the House. They said he looked like the liberal welfare state: bloated, boozy, creaky, past it. Our guy, Reagan, was one year older, but he looked more like the brighter, healthier future. Plenty of bloated and boozy types, however, were on our side.

All through the 2004 presidential campaign, James Taranto of the *Wall Street Journal* referred to John Kerry, the Democrats' nominee, as "haughty" and "French-looking." This was an effective taunt. One of my favorite politicians looks like a French aristocrat, and why not? He is Pete du Pont, or Pierre S. du Pont IV. When they were running for the 1988 Republican presidential nomination, George Bush—George Herbert Walker Bush, no peon—made use of du Pont's pedigree.

William F. Buckley Jr. was hosting the first debate of the season. Du Pont was jabbing at Bush for a lack of specifics on arms control. "We're waiting for details," he said, "and we're hearing generalities." Bush said, none too nicely, "Pierre, let me help you." Du Pont has never been known as "Pierre," only "Pete"—but Bush played the French card (underhandedly, I think). Later, David Broder, the "dean of the Washington press corps," wrote that the "night belonged to Bush—the man who dared to call a Pierre a Pierre."

In the 2008 Republican primaries, Mike Huckabee got a lot of mileage out of saying that Mitt Romney "looks like the guy who laid you off." I thought this was cheap populist nonsense. To me, Romney looked like a guy who could make an economy hum, and create jobs for the sadly unentrepreneurial like me. During his years in the national spotlight, Romney was a kind of Rorschach test: heartless capitalist to some, model citizen and leader to others.

To ask it again, is it possible to look conservative or look liberal? I think it is—but I could not give hard-and-fast descriptions. I'm a little like Justice Stewart and pornography ("I know it when I see it," he said). Are conservatives white and fat? Some are, sure, but so is Michael Moore, the leftist documentary-maker. Are there people who look like Pajama Boy in liberalism? Yes, lots of them, but they exist in conservative think tanks, too, and on the staffs of conservative congressmen. Thank heaven.

Years ago, I found out that an acquaintance of mine was conservative, or conservative-friendly, and you could have blown me down. An art critic with a ponytail and a dozen other liberal giveaways—except those "giveaways" were misleading. What a glorious discovery. More often than kindergarten teachers would like to admit, or should admit, you can judge a book by its cover. The glorious discoveries make life more interesting (and so, by the same token, do the inglorious ones).

—January 27, 2014

Many Boots, Many Faces

The problem of moral selectivity in human rights

Oslo, Norway

Virtually every cause under the sun gets a hearing at the Oslo Freedom Forum, sooner or later. The Freedom Forum is an annual human-rights conference, held here in the Norwegian capital. It is distinguished by its ecumenism. Its only slant, it seems, is toward freedom.

This year, we hear from a West Papuan tribal chief, outfitted in a spectacular headdress. He talks about the horrors visited upon him and his people by the Indonesian overlords. We hear from three former slaves, out of Cambodia, Haiti, and Nepal. They tell of their ordeals, and how they are trying to help others trapped in the same. We hear from a Zimbabwean about Mugabe. From South Americans about Chávez and his littler imitators.

There is even a drug legalizer from the United States, laying into our drug laws. He is immediately followed at the podium by a Syrian dissident, detailing the slaughter of his fellow citizens in the streets. Something for everybody.

When I was coming of age, human rights meant three things, basically: Pinochet in Chile; Marcos in the Philippines; and, above all, the apartheid government in South Africa. Not much was made of human-rights abuses behind the Iron Curtain. If you brought them up, you were lectured about the need to coexist with the Soviet Union. *Don't rock the boat, don't provoke war. Understand the Soviets.* There was hardly anything less cool than anti-Communism: It was almost a mental disorder, evidenced by McCarthyites, businessmen, and Babbitts in general.

Which is why I rub my eyes a little to see Tomas van Houtryve at the podium. He is very cool—an international photojournalist. He has put together a book called *Behind the Curtains of 21st Century Communism.* We all know, he says, that Communism collapsed many years ago. We all saw that wall come down. And yet, for many millions of people, Communism is all too uncollapsed.

We see photos from, and hear stories about, China, Cuba, North Korea, Vietnam, Laos, Nepal. They are not pretty pictures, or happy stories. The sheer brutality of man is flabbergasting—his sadistic imagination. "We should never forget the consequences of totalitarian power," says Houtryve. He cites 85 million dead, along with "a legacy of famines, purges, and gulags." He also notes the many "intellectuals, artists, and normal people who have cheered on the Communist party: from Pablo Picasso and Charlie Chaplin to Jean-Paul Sartre and Ernest Hemingway."

He ends with pictures of the Hmong, hunted and butchered by the Lao People's Army. "It would never cross their minds to tell you that Communism is dead."

The world can be fickle in its concern for human rights. Mysterious too. For the last ten years, there has been no hotter human-rights issue than genocide in Darfur. Yet, before that, there was another genocide in Sudan: in the south of that country. It went on for a full 20 years. Elie Wiesel called it a "slow-motion genocide." And the world yawned, except for some evangelical-Christian groups in the U.S.

In the weeks and months before the Beijing Olympics in 2008, there was much criticism of the ruling Chinese Communists: but for what they were doing to Tibetans, not so much for what they were doing to their fellow Chinese. Tibet has long been a popular cause. In the last couple of years, the cause of Chinese democracy and human rights has picked up a little. This may have to do with the 2010 Nobel Peace Prize to Liu Xiaobo, a political prisoner. And with the drama of Chen Guangcheng, the blind legal activist who escaped his confinement in April, fleeing to the American embassy.

The one cause the world at large embraced was the anti-apartheid cause. Speakers at the Oslo Freedom Forum mention it a lot. You sometimes get the impression that activists sort of miss the anti-apartheid cause: a pure one, involving the oppression of a black majority by a white minority. Consider what happened to South Africa in the realm of sports alone.

From 1964 to 1992, South Africa was banned from the Olympics. Also, athletes from other countries paid a penalty if they competed in South Africa. The United Nations kept a list of athletes who traveled to that country, called the U.N. Register of Sports Contacts with South Africa. This was meant to shame and correct the straying athletes.

We might debate whether individual citizens, such as athletes, should be punished for the policies of the governments that rule them. We might also debate whether any country should be off-limits to athletes or others. But what about the fact that, from 1964 to 1992, athletes governed by other beastly regimes were allowed to compete in the Olympics? These include athletes from Hoxha's Albania and Kim Il-sung's North Korea. In 1980, you remember, the Games were held in the Soviet Union.

When speakers here in Oslo list the great dissidents and human-rights symbols—when they call the roll—they always begin with Nelson Mandela. Often, Sakharov, Sharansky, and Aung San Suu Kyi are on the list, though the Burmese heroine's name is hard to pronounce. (Desmond Tutu once joked that he got the Nobel Peace Prize "because I have an easy surname. What if it were Waokaokao?") But Mandela is always on the list, and heads it.

Repeatedly, he is referred to as a "prisoner of conscience." But he was not. "Prisoner of conscience" is a term coined by Amnesty International to refer to someone who has been jailed for his opinions. Mandela was jailed for his engagement in an armed struggle. Therefore, Amnesty could not classify him as a prisoner of conscience (though the organization supported him nonetheless).

Mandela is a great man, whose presidency was key: It launched a democracy after decades of nasty undemocratic rule. But his admirers tend to look away from aspects of his record. When it came to human rights, his advocacy was less than universal. "This is an hard saying; who can hear it?"

Throughout his imprisonment, he was supported by some of the worst dictators and regimes: Castro, Qaddafi, the Soviets. They did not support him because they were kindhearted democrats, but because they were warring with the West, broadly speaking. It was only natural for Mandela to be appreciative of support, wherever it came from and whatever the motivation. But it also should have been natural for him to recognize, especially after his release, that dictators who were kind to him were monstrous to people under their control.

Mandela evinced no such recognition. He praised Qaddafi's "commitment to the fight for peace and human rights in the world." About Castro's Cuba, he said, "There's one thing where that country stands out head and shoulders above the rest. That is in its love for human rights and liberty." The Cuban people surely love those things; their rulers for 50-plus years, no. Mandela was the most revered statesman in the world, and one word from him would have done a world of good for political prisoners in Libya, Cuba, and elsewhere. But Mandela kept mum. Worse than keeping mum, he lent his moral authority to the jailers and persecutors.

One Libyan prisoner, he did visit: That was Abdelbaset Megrahi, the state agent convicted in the Lockerbie bombing (which killed 270 people). In 2002, Mandela went to Glasgow to see Megrahi in his prison cell. He pleaded for better conditions for this prisoner. "He says he is being treated well by the officials, but when he takes exercise he has been harassed by a number of prisoners. He cannot identify them because they shout at him from their cells through the windows and sometimes it is difficult even for the officials to know from which quarter the shouting occurs."

During this same period, Qaddafi and Libya were imprisoning five Bulgarian nurses and one Palestinian doctor, whom they had falsely accused of infecting children with AIDS. The prisoners were not shouted at through windows as they took exercise. They were tortured beyond human description, with rape, dogs, electricity, and more. One of the nurses, in her desperation, tried to kill herself by chewing the veins in her wrist. She had no other recourse.

Moral selectivity is a fault of most human beings, probably. Rare is the person who has equal concern for all. Almost no one keeps an eye on every falling sparrow. William F. Buckley Jr. once wrote that everyone has within him a tank of indignation. It is only so big. What do you spend your fuel on? You can't go around being indignant about everything all the time.

Politics can get in the way of equal concern. If you like the Castros' anti-Americanism and socialism, you will want to look away from what goes on in Combinado del Este Prison. If you don't like confrontation with Iran, you may avert your eyes from Evin Prison. If you hated the 2003 invasion of Iraq, you may not want to hear about Saddam Hussein's atrocities (the "children's prisons," the "rape rooms," the cutting out of tongues for dissent, the chemical gassings).

Probably the group of people that the world is most interested in is the Palestinians. Sometimes it seems that the entire United Nations is organized around them. But the world is interested only if Israel can be interpreted as abusing them. The world has next to no interest in the abuses of Palestinians by Palestinian bosses, in the West Bank and Gaza. It is a glaring blind spot.

Orwell wrote of "a boot stamping on a human face." Does it matter what color the boot is—black or red, fascist or Communist or something else? Does it matter what color the face is? It certainly does not. And those who know this, and prove their knowledge of it, are some of the most valuable people we have.

—June 11, 2012

The Even-Steven Temptation

Adventures in moral equivalence

When I was growing up, the worst thing you could be was a racist. (And racism was often defined with grotesque, malicious looseness.) The second-worst thing you could be, probably, was a jingoist. An "ethnocentrist." A flag-waver. Even simple patriotism was suspect, a sign of naivety and boobishness.

You were not to think yourself anything special as an American. You were not to be too big for your britches. Everything had to be equal, balanced, even-steven. The Soviet Union tossed poets into prisons? Yeah, well what about the Hollywood Ten?

At the time, there was a best-selling book called *I'm OK—You're OK*. It was by Thomas A. Harris, M.D. One of the original self-help books, it sold more than 15 million copies. Its title expresses the principle I'm talking about: "I'm okay, you're okay," or, maybe more accurately, "I'm not okay, you're not okay."

If I raised concerns about what the Chinese Communists were doing to the Tibetans, it would fall to you to say, "Well, what did *we* do to the Indians?" That wouldn't help the Tibetans at all. But it would obey "even-steven." If I said it wasn't nice to shoot people as they scaled the Berlin Wall, you would say, "It wasn't nice to lynch blacks in the South, was it?"

"GULAG," said one guy. "Japanese internment," said another (meaning the internment of Japanese Americans). "Nazi war machine," said one guy. "Dresden," said another (referring to the American and British bombing of that city). "Imperial Japan." "Hiroshima and Nagasaki!" Etc.

We were afraid of committing the sin of national pride, a pride that might suggest a sense of national superiority. No one wanted to come off as an Archie Bunker. (He was the main character, bigoted though somewhat lovable, in *All in the Family*, the popular sitcom.) We kind of policed ourselves. If you criticized something relating to a foreign land, you had to criticize something relating to home in the next breath.

The Communist East and the democratic West? They both had their strengths and weaknesses. We Westerners were keen on "political rights," such as freedom of speech and freedom of assembly. In the East, they were keen on "social rights," especially the rights to food, shelter, and health care. (It was a lie, but it was widely taught and believed.)

Interestingly, the even-steven principle applied only if you were talking about governments hostile to the United States. You could criticize apartheid South Africa, or Pinochet's Chile, or Marcos's Philippines, without a complementary criticism of America or the West. No one said, "Who are we to knock Pretoria? Reagan just reduced food stamps." But when it came to hostiles, equivalence was the name of the game.

I must say, I smiled a bit when I read about President Obama at the National Prayer Breakfast in February. He said we were not to "get on our high horse" about violent jihad. "Remember that during the Crusades and the Inquisition, people committed terrible deeds in the name of Christ. In our home country, slavery and Jim Crow all too often were justified in the name of Christ." That is a clear example of even-steven at work.

In 1978, the Soviet Union was putting dissidents through show trials. Our ambassador to the United Nations, Andrew Young, gave an interview to a French newspaper, saying, "In our prisons, too, there are hundreds, perhaps thousands, of people whom I would describe as political prisoners." He was obeying even-steven. He was not on his high horse. He probably thought he was being polite as well.

At a press conference, President Carter said, "I know that Andy regrets having made that statement, which was embarrassing to me." He kept him on in his job (for a while).

Some years later, I was in college and starting to read *National Review* and other subversive literature. In a social-theory class, we were studying Marx, and I dared approach the professor after class: What should we think of the terrible human-rights violations by Marxist governments all over the world? He was irked at me and said that Marx should not be held responsible for what others might do in his name. "Should we blame Thomas Jefferson for the sins of Richard Nixon?" (Say what you will about Nixon, but he didn't own slaves.)

Back to the Obama administration—which in 2010 participated in a "human-rights dialogue" with the Chinese government. Afterward, our representative, Assistant Secretary of State Michael H. Posner, held a press conference at Foggy Bottom. A reporter asked, "Did the recently passed Arizona immigration law come up? And, if so, did *they* bring it up or did *you* bring it up?" This law was an attempt to curb illegal immigration, and a mild one at that—but some portrayed it as onerous.

Our man said, "We brought it up early and often. It was mentioned in the first session, and as a troubling trend in our society and an indication that we have to deal with issues of discrimination or potential discrimination, and that these are issues very much being debated in our own society."

The reporter had a follow-up question: "Did they," meaning the Chinese officials, "discuss anything about their concerns about Chinese visiting in Arizona?" Posner said no.

Bear in mind that China is a one-party dictatorship with a gulag (*laogai*). Bear in mind that this is a government that imprisons a Nobel peace laureate (Liu Xiaobo), among thousands of other democrats and dissidents. Bear in mind that this is a government all too credibly accused of organ harvesting (the murder of human beings, such as Falun Gong practitioners, for the extraction of organs).

What must Liu and other political prisoners think—what must Falun Gong practitioners and other hunted people think—that we Americans would talk this way? That we would wonder whether Chinese are afraid to visit Arizona? Do they think we are mad?

In 2011 and 2012, our vice president, Joe Biden, spent time with Xi Jinping, who was then his counterpart in China. Now Xi is boss of the Communist party (and therefore of the country). Recently, Biden told Evan Osnos of *The New Yorker* that Xi had asked him why the United States put "so much emphasis on human rights." (I haven't noticed this in the last six years, but be that as it may.) Biden told Xi, "No president of the United States could represent the United States were he not committed to human rights. If you don't understand this, you can't deal with us. President Barack Obama would not be able to stay in power if he did not speak of it. So look at it as a political imperative. It doesn't make us better or worse."

No? I doubt that Joe Biden learned the even-steven principle when he was growing up in the 1940s and '50s in Pennsylvania and Delaware. But he learned it later.

Move with me now to the concert hall—to Avery Fisher Hall at New York's Lincoln Center, in the last week of March. A new piece was being premiered by the New York Philharmonic. It was *Scheherazade.2*, by John Adams. A markedly different man from our second president, this John Adams is probably America's most famous and important (classical) composer. Before the downbeat, Adams talked to the audience about how his piece came about. He said he wanted to respond, musically, to brutality toward women. He had been reading about such brutality in Egypt, Afghanistan, Iran, and elsewhere.

But we were not to be too big for our britches. We were not to get on our high horse. Because we have brutality toward women right here at home, Adams said. You can "find it on Rush Limbaugh."

At this, the audience responded with robust and sustained applause. I thought it was like the "Two Minutes Hate" found in Orwell's *1984*. My guess is, Adams did not want to be seen as picking on the "Other"—the Taliban, the Muslim Brotherhood, the theocrats in Iran. So did he pick on himself, or his friends? No, no, they never do. He decided to defame

Rush Limbaugh. And he must have known that the audience would delight in this defamation.

Let me say a couple of kind words for even-steven (believe it or not). The impulse behind it may be admirable. It's good to avoid judgmentalism. It's good to be self-aware, self-critical—on guard against hypocrisy. It's good to consider the beams in our own eyes while, or before, considering the motes in others' eyes. It is also good to keep history in mind.

When despairing of barbarism in the Arab world, I sometimes think, "You know, two seconds ago, Germans and their allies, on European soil, were carrying out a holocaust."

Furthermore, a mindless patriotism is unattractive. But then, so is a mindless national self-flagellation. Bernard Lewis, the great Middle East historian, recently observed that Americans once said, "My country, right or wrong." Now we're apt to say, "My country, wrong."

The even-steven principle—or moral equivalence or not getting on your high horse—can be taken to absurd extremes. It can be logically and morally perverse. It does no one any good to pretend that America has political prisoners or that Arizona is a police state. And what I heard in Avery Fisher Hall the other week was one of the most disgusting things I have ever heard in my life. (I'm not talking about the music, which was pretty good.)

—May 4, 2015

A Job Like No Other

On policing

The problem with some issues is that everything is true. Both sides of the question have merit. Which truths do you emphasize? Which truths seem most important in a given year or on a given day?

I sometimes think that everything people say about immigration is true. Hawks (like me) are right; so are doves, or immigration liberals, to a degree. Lately, policing has been in the news. This is because an officer shot and killed an unarmed young man in Ferguson, Mo. The officer is white; the victim was black. That's why we know about the case.

The police have come in for a very hard time on left and right. Are there police abuses? Of course. Do the police need to be policed, night and day? Of course. Does a badge make a person a lord or a god? Of course not. Should every government agency, be it ever so humble, have a SWAT team? No.

To speak personally for a moment, I have had family members on the wrong side of the law. I have not had a family member who has worn a badge. I know about police abuses, and, even more, about fear of such abuses. I don't think I need any lectures. Me good civil libertarian.

But: I sympathize with the police. I am grateful for them. And I try to slip into their shoes, or those of their families.

The police have a difficult, sometimes impossible job. They have to act defensively most of the time. (This "action" can be more like inaction.) They have to engage in rope-a-dope. Do you remember this boxing technique? It was popularized by Muhammad Ali. A fighter sticks to the ropes, letting his opponent punch him, absorbing the blows, hoping the opponent will tire and slip up.

"The best defense is a good offense," goes an old saying. As I understand it, this option is seldom available to the police. They must wait to be struck.

And they have to wait till the last possible second—certainly before pulling the trigger. Once they've done so, there will always be people who say, "It wasn't the last possible second. The cop didn't need to pull the trigger." For PR purposes, the cop may be better off dead. He can say from beyond the grave, "See, I *told* you I was in danger!"

I once had the experience of umping a baseball game—calling balls and strikes. It was miserable. I had always played baseball, and watched baseball, and I knew the game exceptionally well (if I say so myself). But I'd had no idea umping was so hard. From then on, I had greater sympathy for umps and refs. I thought that athletes, and maybe fans, should have to ump or ref a bit. That would make them less judgmental.

And I'm just talking about games! What about life-and-death situations out on the streets? Maybe we should all police, for an hour or two. And not in some cute Mayberry but in explosive communities. Anyone can theorize about policing—but, as in war, theory can go out the window when real life is confronted.

Speaking of war: "Demilitarize the police!" is the *cri du jour*. Fine. Demilitarize the police. But when a military or quasi-military posture is called for, don't let the police stand there, demilitarized. Don't sacrifice them to suit a more traditional view of policing. Call in the actual military.

It could be we want the police to be like the bobby in *Mary Poppins*. "The constable's responstable." I think that would be lovely. The police could concentrate on truancy and a little shoplifting. But America is a terribly violent place, and our lives are made worse by the racialization of everything. We ask our policemen to put their necks on the line, for us all.

The truth is, I think, we want the police to appear when we want them to appear, applying exactly the amount of force we deem necessary. We want them to be invisible, until we are threatened, when we want them to swoop in out of nowhere to save the day. We want them to be perfect—according to our own views of perfection. In this sense, a policeman's job is thankless.

I think of an oft-quoted verse from Kipling, about Tommy, the soldier who is despised until he is desperately needed. "...it's Tommy this, an' Tommy that, an' 'Chuck him out, the brute!' / But it's 'Saviour of 'is country' when the guns begin to shoot."

In recent weeks, I have heard people snort about the uniforms policemen wear: Our cops, suffering from warrior envy, or delusions of grandeur, think they're Rambo or something. I myself don't think police should strut around like special-ops specimens. But I also think of another verse from that same Kipling poem: "Yes, makin' mock o' uniforms that guard you while you sleep / Is cheaper than them uniforms, an' they're starvation cheap."

Above, I (sardonically) mentioned the PR advantages of dying. There is scarcely anything more moving than a police funeral. The men march somberly in their dress blues, to the wailing of the bagpipes. Who can fail to tear up? "Our finest! Our finest!" we say. Sure. But sometimes our finest have to scramble to stay alive, and protect our behinds. They have to make snap decisions in harrowing circumstances.

But it's their job, you can say. True. But what a job. *Well, they didn't have to sign up for it. They could work in a hardware store.* Again, true. But thank heaven someone is willing to do this work (and I wouldn't sign up for it).

The police face two criticisms, it seems to me. The first is, they're agents of a police state. Anybody who believes that America is a police state, or anything remotely like it, should be sentenced to live in a police state, for at least a day. The second criticism is that the police are lazy doughnut-scarfers, like the cops in *The Simpsons*. There are no doubt such cops, and power-crazed brutes, too.

But let me introduce you to a non-theoretical cop: a *National Review* reader in a major Midwestern city, and an occasional correspondent of mine. In the midst of the debate about policing occasioned by the Ferguson affair, he wrote to tell me about his day.

"We went to serve a drug and gun warrant. The house had surveillance cameras and reinforced doors. Which means they had plenty of warning that we were coming. As the TAC team makes entry, a suspect peeks out the window, sees the cover team standing outside, and fires a round at us. Lucky for us, he's a bad shot. The TAC team soon takes all four occupants into custody without further incident."

A TAC team, as I understand it, is a paramilitary unit similar to a SWAT team.

"Two guns and cocaine were recovered from the house. The house was notable only for the abundance of human feces on the floor and the dead mice everywhere. . . . The neighbors lived in fear because of this house, but didn't call the police. Similar scenes play out across the country countless times a day."

Giving vent to some frustration, my correspondent continued, "I keep hearing that the police are the problem, that our paramilitary dress agitates sensitivities. If we simply wore friendlier uniforms and had a lighter touch, problems would disappear." Chastising some conservatives, he said, "The same people who mock the Left for demanding an assault-weapons ban based solely on the aesthetics of a firearm are now demanding that we conform policing to aesthetics. If only we turned in our M-4s for wooden nightsticks, America would revert to some Tocquevillean ideal, and we could all live in a Norman Rockwell painting."

He said that police were seeing the effects of deep social problems. And "until we deal with why someone would so casually shoot at the police, I'll take my military-style tactics and equipment and I'll go home at the end of the day, whether my appearance has offended political sensitivities or not."

This is what I want for the police: that they be able to go home at the end of the day, to their families. I want them to have lopsided advantages over the criminal element. I don't want a fair fight, I want an unfair fight: in favor of the cops. I realize that some of them will "fall" in the "line of duty." ("Fall" can be an annoying euphemism.) But I want them to have every chance of standing. And if they are stripped of necessary tools, I want them to quit, rather than be sitting ducks.

My correspondent said to me, "This was my day today," and then explained that he was shot at. I reflected on what was my biggest problem that day. I was at the Salzburg Festival, doing some annual jobs. What was my biggest problem? That I was too hot in the world's most beautiful concert hall, the Grosser Saal of the Mozarteum, listening to a Schubertiade? Or that I had consumed one or two sweets too many?

When it comes to policing, as to other issues, many things are true. Post-Ferguson, when the police are being hammered, I feel more appreciative than ever.

—September 22, 2014

A Long Way from Harlan County

One man's reflections on labor unions in our time

In May, the Oslo Freedom Forum takes place. It is the premier human-rights conference, held in the Norwegian capital. This year, it was canceled, or postponed. The reason: a hotel-workers strike. Conference organizers could not find a way around it. Hundreds of people from all over the world were set to fly to Oslo. But, at the eleventh hour, they were called off.

They had something important to do. Many of them are former political prisoners or otherwise victims of gross persecution. They were going to give their testimonies to an international audience, including the press. But the hotel workers, in a sense, decided that the conference would not take place. So it didn't.

I thought, "We all have grievances at work, from time to time. But most of us, on account of our grievances, don't stop life for others."

I further thought back to October, and the opening night of Carnegie Hall in New York. Actually, Opening Night did not come off. There was to be a concert by the Philadelphia Orchestra. But the stagehands union had a grievance. And they decided that Opening Night would not take place. So it didn't.

The orchestra had no say. The conductor and soloists had no say. Neither did the thousands of ticket-buyers or anyone else. Only the five guys who belong to the union. They were like an emperor who can give thumbs up or thumbs down. They could stop life for others, and did.

These are not horny-handed sons of toil: The head guy makes $530,000 a year. The other four make over 400. There are millions of long-term unemployed in our country. I imagine some of them would be willing to put out chairs and stands for a mere $350K. Some of them might be willing to go as low as 295.

I once wanted to be a supporter of labor unions and their efforts, but I found that, in my time and place, it was impossible. When I was quite young, I got the idea that unions were noble, standing up for the rights of people who were relatively powerless. They were little people, being exploited by big people. To be on the side of the unions was to be on the side of the angels, or certainly of humanity.

In my part of the country—southeastern Michigan—we learned about Walter Reuther and the Battle of the Overpass. This was the day in 1937 when the United Auto Workers took a stand, and were smashed by the goons of Ford Motor. They rose again, however, stronger than before. There was something romantic about the Battle of the Overpass, and about unionism generally.

Countless TV shows and movies had businessmen as the villain and labor as the hero. In 1976, when I was twelve, there was a celebrated documentary about the Harlan County coalminers: black-lunged sufferers who merely wanted their simple rights. Three years after that, there was a big Hollywood movie, *Norma Rae*, about textile workers. Adorable Sally Field held up a sign that said "Union." Hearts and consciences swooned.

That same year, 1979, there was a truckers strike. I was 15 and becoming ever more interested in politics. The striking truckers were shooting at scabs (or "replacement workers," to use the hated euphemism). I mean, shooting bullets at them. They killed a driver, in Alabama. (His name was Robert Tate.) This shook me up a little: Strikers weren't supposed to be black hats. They weren't supposed to be murderers.

In my town, Ann Arbor, the teachers went on strike from time to time. They weren't murderers (well, one was), but it sure seemed they were working fewer and fewer hours, at greater and greater pay and benefits. There was a time when teachers were almost like missionaries. They took virtual vows of poverty, to serve the community. In the summer, they had to take odd jobs, such as painting houses, to make ends meet until September. I wouldn't have wanted a return to that. But weren't current demands a little excessive?

We had a neighbor, Mr. Southwick, who took walks around the block. One day, I asked him what he thought of the teachers strike, then under way. He said, "Well, first, I don't think professional people should strike." I was shocked at the answer. It wasn't that I disagreed with it. It's that I never knew anyone had that opinion.

In 1981, when I was going into my senior year, the new president, Reagan, fired the air-traffic controllers. ("I didn't fire them, they quit," he would say—because they broke a law that he was merely enforcing.) I heard a family friend say to his brother, "Say what you will about Reagan, but at least someone stood up to labor." These words were so foreign and interesting to me: Labor was something to stand up to? But didn't they exist to do the standing up? Like, to the Man? Was labor the Man?

A union, or union movement, I could admire without reservation was Solidarity in Poland. They were led by Lech Walesa, the stirring electrician. Solidarity was standing up to the Man of dictatorship. The movement was strongly supported by President Reagan, and also by the president of the AFL-CIO, Lane Kirkland—who was a dedicated anti-Communist. (He and the founder of *National Review*, William F. Buckley Jr., had a warm, teasing relationship. WFB would greet him with, "How's socialism?" Kirkland would answer, "How's Wall Street?")

I could pause at many points along the way—the Hormel meatpacking strike in 1985, for example—but let's go to Wisconsin, in 2011. The scenes there were among the most sickening I have ever seen in America. Teachers and other public employees descended on the capitol, to protest reforms by Governor Scott Walker. Fine. But how did they protest? By screaming, beating drums, littering, equating Walker with Hitler, etc.

These are people we want teaching children?

Worse, they and other public employees went to the homes of lawmakers they opposed, to rally on their lawns and intimidate families inside. There was a whiff of *actos de repudio* about this. These "acts of repudiation" are routine in Cuba, where Communist mobs go to the homes of dissenters for the purpose of screaming, denouncing, and cowing. There is physical violence, too, of course.

By the way, Fidel Castro holds the key to the City of Madison (the Wisconsin capital). It was given to him by Mayor Paul Soglin in the 1970s. That man, Soglin, is mayor today. And his friend Castro is still boss of a one-party dictatorship with a gulag.

I long ago reached the point where I can barely stand to read about unions and their tactics. Harry Bennett (Ford Motor's notorious head of security in the time of the Battle of the Overpass) had nothing on them. At the end of 2012, my *NR* colleague Jillian Kay Melchior had a piece called "Unions Defend the Worst of the Worst." It began with a report of nursing-home workers in Connecticut, who had a grievance. Before they walked off the job, they sabotaged their workplaces, endangering the health of their patients. For instance, they monkeyed with equipment.

Jillian talked to a man whose wife lives in one of the homes (or at least did at the time). He refused to have his name disclosed, though, because union members had threatened him, and her. "I don't want to get involved," he told Jillian. "My wife is helpless."

The nursing-home workers belong to the Service Employees International Union, famous for their purple T-shirts. In fact, the union boasts of forming a "purple ocean," in order to get their way. When I see these shirts, and the mob mentality that goes with them, I can't help thinking they seem a little brown.

On the sidewalks of New York, there is often a huge inflatable rat parked in front of a building, blocking your way. A union has put it there, to shame the people within. They are non-union. It is not a cute, cuddly rat, but a giant nasty one. Non-union workers are supposed to be "rats," you see. Didn't Nazis equate their opponents with vile animals? Last October, before the opening night that never occurred, the stagehands placed this rat in front of Carnegie Hall. That tells you even more about their character.

I hate this rat. I hate the word "scab." I hate the idea that you can't cross a picket line—some holy cordon. I hate the whole bullying, ugly, greedy, undemocratic nature of unions.

To a degree, I am stunned and abashed to be anti-union and pro-management. I would not have planned or wished it. Jeane Kirkpatrick, Reagan's first U.N. ambassador, became a Republican at age 59. She had always been a Democrat, and not just any Democrat, but a member of Hubert Humphrey's inner circle. When she switched her registration, she said, "I would rather be a liberal."

I know just what she means. But you have to adapt to the atmosphere and politics around you. And what have American unions been in my lifetime? From the Harlan County coalminers to the purple-shirted saboteurs, or the plutocrats of Carnegie Hall, it's a "fur piece," to use Faulkner language. It is a long way. Underdogs have become appalling overdogs. David is Goliath.

The Universal Declaration of Human Rights says, "Everyone has the right to form and to join trade unions for the protection of his interests." I believe that (I guess). But I also believe in temperance. With every passing year, I see that a bane of our existence is extremism—extremism of Right or Left. The taking of something good and pushing it too far, into destructiveness. One definition of conservatism, I suppose, is anti-extremism.

In the previous issue of *NR*, I ended a piece with the admonition attributed to Talleyrand, and often quoted by Bill Buckley: *Surtout pas trop de zèle*. Above all, not too much zeal. This maxim may be square or boring, but it's not unwise.

—June 23, 2014

Aren't They Cute?

America and some special criminals

According to news reports, George Wright is entertaining book and movie deals. He's a star, practically—yet another glam criminal out of reach of the law. Safe abroad, smirking at justice, holding forth on the iniquities of America. Wright and his comrades often spelled this word with a "k." Sometimes three of them.

He has an exciting story to tell, it's true. It has been all too exciting for those on the wrong end of his guns. In 1962, the day after Thanksgiving, he and some buddies went on a crime spree. This was at home in New Jersey. One of the people they robbed was Walter Patterson, a gas-station owner. With panty hose shoved over their faces, they shot him dead. Off they went with $70.

Patterson, 42 years old, was a member of what someone would call the Greatest Generation. He came home from the war with a Bronze Star, earned when he drove his truck into a hail of German bullets, in order to save some men. Patterson survived the Nazis, but not the two-bit thugs who came to his gas station.

George Wright, apprehended, was sentenced to 15 to 30 years. He served seven of them. In 1970, he escaped from his minimum-security prison, which was nothing but a dairy farm, really. He and a buddy hot-wired the warden's car. They got to Detroit, where they joined the "Black Liberation Army."

In 1972, they and three others hijacked a plane. Wright, dressed as a priest, pulled a gun from a hollowed-out Bible and held it to a stewardess's throat. The hijackers demanded a million-dollar ransom. Wright said, "If that money's not here by 2 o'clock, I'm going to start throwing a dead body out the door every minute." The U.S. government paid.

The gang forced the plane to Algeria, which was a haven for self-styled revolutionaries (in reality, robbers, rapists, and murderers who had learned a little black-power talk). When they landed, something funny happened: The Algerians confiscated the money. The gang was ticked. In a statement, they said, "We are shocked and bewildered to be branded as criminals for our revolutionary activities."

After a sojourn in their new "homeland," as they called it, they moved to another homeland: France. Eventually, they were arrested by French authorities—all but Wright, who escaped down into Portugal. From there, he went to Guinea-Bissau, a former Portuguese colony in West Africa. It was run by people much like Wright, and they were happy to give him a new identity: José Luís Jorge dos Santos. After acquiring a wife and two children, he went back to Portugal, to live a pleasant life by the sea.

U.S. law did not quite forget him. They tracked him down last September—49 years after the murder of Patterson, 41 years after Wright's prison escape, and 39 years after the hijacking. Wright commented, "Knowing the Americans, I always feared that they had their antennas up." He need not have feared too much: The Portuguese refused to extradite him. The case is now regarded as closed. Wright, who is 69, said, "I want to relax now, and spend time with my family and friends." Yes, don't we all?

Walter Patterson, too, had a family: a wife and two daughters. His wife died a year and three months after his murder, of a heart condition. When Wright was finally tracked down, Patterson's daughter Ann said, "He needs to come back here and pay his debt to society." She was 14 when her father was murdered. Wright "has had a good life for the past

40 years," she said, "but he took away about half of my father's life."

Wright and his fellow hijackers have been celebrated in at least two documentary films. These films portray them as strugglers against oppression, racism, and imperialism. They were virtually civil-rights heroes, you see—maybe a little overzealous. Maybe too impatient. Wright recently said that he hijacked the plane "to support the hopes of black people." One of the films borrows a title from James Baldwin: "Nobody Knows My Name."

The Black Liberation Army was part of a "family" of groups—that's what the criminal radicals called themselves, "The Family." (Rather bourgeois, when you think about it.) The groups included the Weather Underground, the Red Guerrilla Resistance, the Republic of New Afrika, and the May 19th Communist Organization. Why May 19th? The birthday of Malcolm X and, as a bonus, Ho Chi Minh. Now and then, Family members indulged in what they called "non-political murder"—the offing of a prostitute, for example. But mainly they liked to kill policemen ("pigs"), which, for them, was "political murder," or "revolution."

Several of the cops they killed were black, including two men named Waverly: Waverly Jones and Waverly Brown. The first belonged to the NYPD, the second to the force in Nyack, N.Y. Brown was an *actual* civil-rights pioneer: the first black man to join that force.

Like George Wright, many of the killers fled abroad, and mainly they fled to Cuba—Castro was happy to receive them and show them off. Something like 70 American fugitives are in Cuba. One of them is Charlie Hill, who, after killing a cop in New Mexico, hijacked a plane. But probably the most famous of them is Joanne Chesimard, a.k.a. Assata Shakur. She killed her cop in 1973. (His name was Werner Foerster; Hill's was Robert Rosenbloom.) In 1979, she escaped from prison, whereupon she found her way to Castro.

Oh, the press she enjoys! In 1997, *Essence* magazine published an interview with her: "Prisoner in Paradise." ("Paradise" would be totalitarian Cuba.) She said things like "I represent someone who has dedicated her life to the liberation of my people." Two years later, the *New York Times* published an article by a Princeton theologian, defending her. He called her an "activist"—which is one way of putting it. He also said she was "vibrant" and "articulate," which no doubt she is. More vibrant and articulate than a dead cop.

She has been the subject of many songs, poems, and other tributes. One of them is by a rapper called Common: "A Song for Assata." One line goes, "All this sh** so we could be free, so dig it, y'all." A year ago, Common was invited to perform in an "Evening of Poetry" at the White House. Law-enforcement associations and other squares objected, but they were easily brushed off. In the White House, President Obama made sure to give Common a big hug.

Undeniably, the radical fugitives make good copy. It's hard for journalists to resist. How it works is this: You go to Tanzania, let's say, and interview Pete O'Neal. You paint a picture of him in the old days: "He blazed with purpose: End racism and class inequality, fast." You describe his flight and wanderings: "Sweden . . . Algeria . . . Tanzania, whose socialist government welcomed left-wing militants." You note that he's gray and paunchy now, and gentler. But then you quote him defiant: "They will never convince me in my life that what I was doing wasn't right."

Undeniable, too, is that we Americans have always romanticized criminals. We sing of Bonnie & Clyde, Jesse James, Butch Cassidy & the Sundance Kid. Speaking of "Kids": André Previn composed a song cycle about Billy the Kid, in 1994. The George Wrights and Assata Shakurs are particularly ripe for romanticization, given our fraught relationship with race. But, as William Rosenau writes, "Historical amnesia about groups like the BLA [Black Liberation Army] is unfortunate." Rosenau is a scholar, and writes with fine scholarly understatement.

Few Americans knew or cared about President Clinton's granting of clemency to Susan Rosenberg and Linda Sue Evans, in the very last hours of his presidency. But his actions shocked and sickened people in law enforcement, and people who remember the Weather Underground, accurately: the bombings, the murders—the plan to wipe out NCOs as they danced with their dates at Fort Dix.

Why is it that so many liberals are so tender toward Rosenberg, Evans, et al.? Why do these terrorists, who are generally unrepentant, receive such sympathetic treatment from the *Times*, *The New Yorker*, *60 Minutes*, etc.? Is it because liberals, some of them, "hold their manhoods cheap" for not being part of the "struggle" themselves? Do they feel guilt over "preserving their viability within the system" (to paraphrase Clinton)? Do they regard The Family as "liberals in a hurry"? Rosa Parkses with itchy fingers?

Discussion of Bill Ayers and Bernardine Dohrn was essentially out of bounds during the 2008 presidential campaign. Question Obama's friendship with them, and you were slammed as uncouth, at best. Ayers and Dohrn are considered almost quaint figures now—living mementos of a colorful past, of "crazy times." Lincoln Diaz-Balart, the Cuban-American politician, has said he doesn't know how Castro can seem cute after decades of torturing people. To many, Ayers and Dohrn seem cute, too.

Ayers once summed up his situation to David Horowitz in a memorable way: "Guilty as hell, free as a bird—America is a great country."

It is, yes. But not because of the Weather Underground or the Black Liberation Army. More because of people such as their victims. Who are those victims, by the way, those dead? Talk about Nobody Knows My Name! Plenty of people know the names of their murderers. Often, those murderers get two names: George Wright and José Luís Jorge dos Santos; Joanne Chesimard and Assata Shakur; Wesley Cook and Mumia Abu-Jamal; H. Rap Brown and Jamil Abdullah Al-Amin; Donald Weems and Kuwasi Balagoon. Their victims aren't celebrated in films and songs. Their names aren't known at all, except to those who loved them.

Here is a partial list of those names: Waverly Brown, Patrick Curran, Daniel Faulkner, Werner Foerster, Gregory Foster, Robert Fromhold, James Green, Waverly Jones, Joseph V. Kelly, Ricky Kinchen, Rocco Laurie, Edward O'Grady, Peter Paige, Walter Patterson, Joseph Piagentini, Robert Rosenbloom, Sidney Thompson, Frank Von Colln, John Victor Young . . .

—May 14, 2012

The Book in the Drawer

On the Gideon Bible and American culture

For as long as anyone can remember, the Gideon Bible has been a fixture in hotel rooms. The Gideons started putting them there in 1908. But there is a campaign going on to remove them from hotel rooms. They are still there, in abundance. But the handwriting is on the wall (to quote the Book of Daniel).

At the beginning of this year, the University of Wisconsin removed the Gideon Bibles from its guest rooms. Why? The university had received a letter saying that, in having the Bibles in its rooms, the university was violating the Constitution. Who said so? Who sent the letter? The Freedom from Religion Foundation, in the university's hometown of Madison.

On its website, FFRF says, "The history of Western civilization shows us that most social and moral progress has been brought about by persons free from religion." And that is how the group generally describes atheists: "persons free from religion." They also use the word "freethinkers," as in, "Come Out of the Closet, Freethinker!" On this business of social and moral progress: The abolitionists did their part, I think we can all agree, and they were a notoriously Bible-thumping bunch. Those trying to abolish slavery in places such as Sudan still are.

FFRF has a motto: "In Reason We Trust." They have even mocked up a coin with this motto, replacing "In God We Trust." The group has stickers to place on Gideon Bibles, if the book happens to be in your hotel room: "Warning! Literal belief in this book may endanger your health and life!" As a rule, the group spells "Bible" with a lower-case "b." Tricks like this are attractive to some people. Christopher Hitchens titled one of his books "god Is Not Great."

So, FFRF sent its letter to the local university, Wisconsin. And the university president, Ray Cross (suspicious name), sent a quick reply: "After carefully reviewing your concern, we have decided to remove the Gideon Bibles from all guest rooms. Thank you for making us aware of this concern." That was easy.

With one down, FFRF turned to Iowa State University, in Ames. Same letter: The presence of the Gideon Bibles violates the Constitution, which forbids the establishment of religion. Replying for the university was Richard Reynolds, director of ISU's Memorial Union. He said, "The concern you raised about the availability of Bibles in the guest rooms of the Memorial Union has been taken under advisement and, effective March 1, 2014, the Bibles will be removed from the hotel rooms." Again, easy. FFRF said that it had "scored another victory for secularism." The group was "delighted to see reason and the Constitution prevailing. We can all sleep easier knowing secularism is being honored at our public universities."

After warming up on the two universities, FFRF set its sights on bigger game: the U.S. Navy. Universities are easy prey for an outfit like FFRF; a branch of the military is something else. The Navy has something called NEXCOM, the Navy Exchange Service Command, which runs lodges all over the world. FFRF said to them, "No Bibles." NEXCOM said, "Okay." They saluted. The Bibles were to be removed from Navy rooms and sent to lost-and-found bins. But they won a reprieve—the Bibles, that is. After a backlash, Navy brass said they wanted to ponder Bible policy.

In September, FFRF claimed another victory: Penn State University. A university spokesman, Lisa Powers, made a statement of Toynbee-esque sweep: "In the past few decades, the world and its people have changed dramatically."

Leaving the world aside for the moment, I note the speed with which things can change in the United States. For more than a century, the Gideons have been placing Bibles in hotel rooms, without objection, or at least notable objection. Many people have been grateful for the Bibles; most people have been indifferent, probably. And all it takes is one letter, from one activist group in Wisconsin, to get an institution to crumble.

In April, a fraternity and a sorority at Dartmouth, Phi Delta Alpha and Alpha Phi, were planning their annual "Phiesta." This is, or was, a fundraiser for cardiac care. And a student complained. "There are various problematic structures and ideologies regarding a Cinco de Mayo-inspired event," she wrote. The student went on to say, "As a Mexican-born,

United-States-raised, first-generation woman of color, it was sadly unsurprising that a culturally-themed party was seen as a casual venture for such a privileged institution as Dartmouth." The young lady has certainly learned the lingo, if nothing else. Hearing from her, the two Greek houses canceled their Phiesta—immediately. A frat spokesman said, "We felt that the possibility of offending even one member of the Dartmouth community was not worth the potential benefits of having the fundraiser."

Is there anything under the sun that doesn't offend at least one member of a community? How would anything ever get done, by this rule of one?

Movements such as the campaign of the Freedom from Religion Foundation concerning Gideon Bibles can gather a certain momentum. When Penn State made its announcement, a reporter for the local paper had an idea. She called up a hotel in town and said, in effect, "Hey! The university is removing the Bibles from its hotel rooms, because they violate the Constitution and make people uncomfortable. How about you?" In her subsequent article, the reporter wrote,

> Maggie Biddle, general manager of the Atherton Hotel in downtown State College, said her 149 rooms still have Bibles, but that she appreciated the motivation behind Penn State's move.
>
> "That's something we might think about ourselves," she said.

Note the word "still": "her 149 rooms *still* have Bibles." Of course they do. Two seconds ago, no one said boo about the Bibles. "Still"? How fast was Maggie Biddle supposed to move? And imagine you're Maggie Biddle, minding your own business, managing your hotel. A reporter calls up and says, "What about those Gideon Bibles, huh?" This must catch you off guard. *A reporter is calling? Am I in trouble? Have I been entangled in controversy? Am I violating the U.S. Constitution? Am I making the Atherton's guests uncomfortable? The university is the big game in town, and it's full of wise and legally aware people. They're pulling their Gideons? Uh-oh.* You find yourself saying just what Maggie Biddle said: "That's something we might think about ourselves."

You bet it is. And that's how these things work. That's how activists get their way, with people who simply want to proceed with life, obey the law, and avoid hassle.

The Freedom from Religion Foundation is not waging its campaign unopposed. Its main opposition is the Alliance Defending Freedom, a Christian legal organization in Scottsdale, Ariz. When FFRF sends a letter, ADF sends a counter-letter. FFRF says why the institution is violating the Constitution; ADF says why the institution isn't. The ADF letters have many legal citations, many arguments. They argue the thing six ways to Sunday (a constitutionally permissible expression). "No court in the country has ever ruled that allowing Bibles to be placed in the guest rooms of government-run guest facilities violates the First Amendment." "Numerous courts across the country have affirmed the Gideons' right to distribute Bibles in schools"—blah, blah, blah.

When the Navy flinched on Bibles, a group of Christian leaders sent a letter to the secretary of defense and the secretary of the Navy, telling them to buck up. One of the things they pointed out is that FDR made sure that each serviceman had a Bible. In March 1941—nine months before Pearl Harbor—he penned an inscription for the flyleaf: "As Commander-in-Chief I take pleasure in commending the reading of the Bible to all who serve in the armed forces of the United States. Throughout the centuries men of many faiths and diverse origins have found in the Sacred Book words of wisdom, counsel and inspiration. It is a fountain of strength and now, as always, an aid in attaining the highest aspirations of the human soul."

These arguments from history seldom cut ice. People sense that America was once an overwhelmingly religious place—and now things are different. If someone cites history and tradition, someone else will say, "Oh, yeah, what about slavery? You wanna go back to that?" When the University of Wisconsin jettisoned its Gideon Bibles, a local pastor said, "It seems very sad when a city that is named for a president who declared a 'National Day of Prayer and Fasting' is so quick to remove

God and His word from its facilities." Good luck with that. Madison may have written the Constitution, but that was a long time ago in a galaxy far, far away. Besides, he owned slaves, didn't he?

I have no doubt that the Alliance Defending Freedom is right in all of its constitutional and legal arguments. I have no doubt that the Freedom from Religion Foundation is wrong. I also doubt that it matters. A person can tell which way the wind is blowing. The zeitgeist is fairly plain. "The wind bloweth where it listeth" (John 3:8).

Gideons International was founded in 1899 in Janesville, Wis. They named themselves for Gideon of the Book of Judges, who was willing to serve God, no matter what. As I've mentioned, they began distributing their Bibles in 1908 (the year Taft beat Bryan). Quite possibly, the last figure to describe America as a Christian nation was the governor of Mississippi, in 1992. It was at a Republican governors' conference. Kirk Fordice said, "The United States of America is a Christian nation." Another governor, Carroll Campbell of South Carolina, sensing the political danger, said, "The value base of this country comes from the Judeo-Christian heritage, and that is something we need to realize. I just wanted to add the 'Judeo' part." Fordice snapped back, "If I wanted to do that, I would have done it."

(He was later revealed to be having an affair with an old high-school flame. He divorced his wife of 40-plus years. He married the flame, and they too divorced. As he lay dying, in 2004, his first wife was at his side.)

Around the world, and also here at home, Americans are known as an arrogant, brash, overly confident bunch. We are heedless of the feelings and desires of others. That is true of some, as how could it not be? But one of the outstanding American traits is fear of giving offense. This is a leading observation and insight of Dinesh D'Souza, the conservative author (who grew up in Bombay and became an American citizen when he was about 30). In an interview with me last summer, he said, "What I resent most of all about the Left is that they exploit American decency." If you tell Americans they are wrong, he continued, they're apt to say, "I'm so sorry about that. How can I do better? How can I make it up to you?"

Over the last 25 years, Americans have been told that they can't have prayer at commencement exercises and football games. They have been told they can't sing Christmas carols at school concerts. They have been told that all these things are unconstitutional, and that Americans in previous generations were in blatant violation of their Constitution, whether they knew it or not. So, modern Americans simply stopped. Told not to sing carols, they stopped. Most people, I think, would rather quit than fight. Or they may want to pick their battles, and figure that "The First Noël" is not quite worth it. Whatever the case, the secularization of society is remorseless. The public square grows ever more naked.

I myself don't think that the Gideon Bibles are a battle worth picking. As Penn State and other institutions point out, the Bibles are being made available in hotel libraries and other common areas. They may not be in the rooms, but they are not kicked off the premises altogether. And why, really, should *my* holy book be privileged over *yours*? Or yours over mine? That is a hard question to answer. One possible answer is, "We have a common culture!" We certainly had one. Do we still? Does the Bible give us a common culture in 2014? Are we as linked by the Bible as we are by, say, the Kardashians, or whoever is reigning on television at the moment?

Furthermore, everyone can have a Bible, if he wants one. You can download a Bible on your phone as easily as you can porn. One of the motivations of the Gideons, in the early days, was to provide Bibles to people who could not afford one. In our affluent society, everyone can afford a Bible. Our poor have iPhones and air conditioning and cars. Elsewhere in the world, the Gideons are giving Bibles to people who lack the money to buy one. In America, the point is moot.

What's next? Progressivism never rests, because progress, or someone's idea of progress, can always be made. There is always a "next": a next cause, a next campaign. Lately, some of us have been asking, "What follows gay marriage?" (Gay divorce, ha ha ha.) The blink of an eye ago, gay marriage was unthinkable. To oppose it now is to be labeled a "homophobe," and worse. Today, there is something unthinkable that, tomorrow, will be orthodoxy. What is it? The German Ethics Council suggested an answer a few weeks ago when it called for the decriminalization of incest. Incestuous pairs, said the council, "feel their fundamental freedoms have been violated" and that they "are forced into secrecy or to deny their love."

If the Freedom from Religion Foundation succeeds in chasing the Gideon Bibles from our hotel rooms, what will be next? In the midst of the Navy debate, a conservative activist said, "A Bible in a hotel room is no more illegal than a chaplain in the military." Uh-oh. That may be the next cause: chaplains. There are almost 3,000 of them on active duty in our military right now. Are they unconstitutional? Of course not, but does it matter, if the wind is blowing that way, and no one cares to blow back? Getting rid of chaplains would be harder than getting rid of Gideon Bibles, and easier than getting rid of our national motto: "In God We Trust." It may seem, right now, that this motto is permanent, ineffaceable. It will be on our currency forever. But many things that seem permanent turn out to be effaceable after all.

A Gideon Bible in a nightstand drawer once seemed as natural and harmless as a towel over a rack. But I, for one, can see them disappearing—first in bastions of progressivism (the University of Wisconsin was a beautifully logical starting place), and, at the end of the line, where? The Holiday Inn in Boise?

The Gideons' first Bibles, in 1908, went to the Superior Hotel in Superior, Mont. Since then, the Gideons have distributed almost 2 billion more Bibles. They have distributed them to schools, hospitals, prisons, police stations, fire stations, and military bases, as well as hotels. Gideons International operates in some 190 countries, which is pretty much all the countries there are. This organization seems a Rock of Gibraltar, hardly vulnerable to a few letters out of Madison (40 miles north of the Gideons' founding city, Janesville).

And yet organizations, like people, come and go. In the middle of the last century, a group called Moral Re-Armament was a pretty big deal. Its founder and leader was an American evangelist named Frank Buchman. He was nominated for the Nobel Peace Prize 85 times. He may be the most nominated person never to have won the prize. Who remembers Buchman or Moral Re-Armament today?

I can certainly bring my own Bible to hotel rooms. And if I forget it, I can turn to my phone. I might even tramp down to some lounge or library. Once, though, I was very glad to have a Gideon Bible in my room. It was in Norway. In the front or back of the book—I forget which—there was a note saying, "If this Bible has been helpful to you, or you have any questions, please write us at" such-and-such an address. I e-mailed the Gideons, thanking them for having placed the Bible, and saying that I was pleased they were still about this activity, after all these years. Someone wrote me back, telling me that fewer hotels were now accepting the book, but that the Gideons would keep at it, as long as there was any receptivity at all.

Like you, probably, I am offended, or could be offended, by many things, all the day long: what's on television, what's on the radio, what's in print advertising. On the tops of New York taxis, there are quasi-pornographic ads. They aren't hidden away in some drawer, like a Gideon Bible. I am offended, or could be offended, from the moment I open my eyes till the moment I close them at night. And so what? It would never occur to me that I had a right not to be offended. In this world, you have to live and let live a little, or a lot. Couldn't those who object to the Gideon Bible—you know, suck it up a little? No, they can't, some of them. The impulse to destroy or reshape is too strong.

I don't say that Gideon Bibles are the hill to die on, for reasons I have outlined. And I think that a respect for other people's feelings (to say nothing of their rights) is part of decency. But there must be some hill to die on, or we may die from a thousand cuts by the perpetually offended and activist and litigious and mean.

—November 3, 2014

Scholars with Spine

Notes from the field of China Studies

Jerome A. Cohen may not be known to the public, but he is well known to Chinese democrats and their supporters. A law professor at New York University, and a veteran China scholar, he is the sponsor and, in a way, protector of Chen Guangcheng. Chen is the Chinese legal activist—"the blind peasant lawyer," as he has been called—who made a run for the U.S. embassy in Beijing earlier this year. This was after six years of imprisonment, house arrest, and physical assaults. Cohen played a key role in the negotiations that led to Chen's departure from the country. Chen is now at NYU, under Cohen's supervision. Not many are the China scholars in the West who are willing to stick their neck out for Chinese dissidents, democrats, and other "troublemakers."

Why is that? First, it is perfectly human, probably, to shrink from trouble. But we can be more specific in our reasons. Obviously, some number of scholars are simply sympathetic to the Chinese regime. But a greater number are wary of crossing that regime, because they need or wish to go to China, and must have visas. Also, there is a great deal of Chinese money in China Studies—and biting the hand that feeds you is problematic. In sum, there are plenty of reasons to steer clear of controversy. Plenty of reasons to avoid Beijing's bad side, and blacklist.

There are similarities between China Studies and Middle East Studies. Bernard Lewis, the eminent Middle East historian, discussed them with me in an interview four years ago. First, there's the money: As Chinese money affects China Studies, Middle Eastern money—particularly Gulf money—affects Middle East Studies. "Vast sums of money are pouring in from Arab governments, Arab princes," said Lewis. Second, there's the curse of political correctness, or academic orthodoxy. "It is difficult to make a career unless you conform," Lewis said. Around the same time, I interviewed Richard Pipes, the eminent historian of Russia. There was never much money in Sovietology, he said. But there was certainly political correctness, plus a desire—a natural desire—to visit the Soviet Union. One day, Pipes testified in the Senate about an arms treaty. He took a hard, or realistic, line. A much softer line was taken by a fellow academic. As they were leaving the room, this second academic said to Pipes, "I really agree with you, but if I talked as you do, they wouldn't give me a visa."

The Chinese Communists are much more subtle about visas than were the Soviet Communists. The Soviets denied visas left and right, and they kicked foreigners out "by the shovelful," as Jonathan Mirsky says. Mirsky is a China scholar and journalist of long experience. The Chinese, on the other hand, ban relatively few—although they seem to be banning more and more, says Perry Link, another experienced China scholar. Also, they tend not to tell you why they're banning you. They'll say, "You know. You know the reason. You have chosen this outcome yourself." And when one scholar is banned, all the others wonder, "What did Smith do? How can I avoid the same fate?" Then they are all the more cautious. As Link says, the Chinese are much better at "psychological engineering" than the Soviets ever managed to be.

There are certain topics about which Beijing is especially sensitive. Sarah Cook, an East Asia specialist with Freedom House, mentions "the three T's": Tibet, Taiwan, and Tiananmen. This last, as you know, refers to Tiananmen Square, main site of the 1989 student protests, which ended in a massacre by the government. Cook also notes that Beijing is somewhat more relaxed about Taiwan than about the other two T's. Then there are the Uighurs and Falun Gong, she says. The Uighurs are a Muslim minority, much persecuted; Falun Gong is a spiritual movement, also much persecuted.

Link has been on the blacklist since the mid-1990s. And one of the annoying things about being on the list, he says, is that students and young professors regularly ask him, "What can I say or do? How can I be sure to stay off the list?" They might say, "Can I accept an internship at Human Rights Watch?" "Can I mention Tiananmen?" Even, "Can I say I know you?" Link can cite example after example of caution, or, to be more severe about it, cowardice. Some of his colleagues counseled a student not to write about Chinese democracy. He should pick another subject for his dissertation—democracy wasn't worth the trouble. Another colleague had useful things to say about Falun Gong—but refused to go on television to say them. Link and other bold scholars can understand the concerns of their younger colleagues, particularly. They do not necessarily condemn them: A ban by China can cripple a career.

Still, scholars can go further than they think. They can say and do more than they imagine. They censor themselves. "You become your own policeman," as Link says. Jianli Yang has observed this phenomenon for years. He is a Chinese democracy leader, a former political prisoner, and a scholar: the holder of two Ph.D.'s from American universities, one in math from Berkeley, and the other in political economy from Harvard. People who are in perfectly secure situations, he says, behave as though they were in imminent danger. They can perform good—or simply tell the truth (which may amount to the same thing)—at virtually no risk. Yet they shrink from doing so. In 2007, Yang gave a speech at Harvard's Kennedy School of Government entitled "Overcome Fear."

After Tiananmen Square, says Yang, the Chinese government made the decision to co-opt intellectuals—intellectuals both at home and abroad. This is something the Soviets never really bothered to do. The Chinese provide money, programs, and perks, in exchange for . . . cooperation? Goodwill? Non-hostility? Western scholars who visit China are often treated like royalty, says Yang. At home, they are just another guy or gal in the grocery store. In China, they are wined and dined. Naturally, this is pleasant and seductive—not easy to give up. What's more, polite people don't offend their hosts, do they? Above all, there is the lure of access—access not just to archives, but to people. A professor can say, "Well, as it happens, I was talking to someone close to Vice Chairman Liu, and he said . . ."

Arthur Waldron, a China scholar at the University of Pennsylvania, is very familiar with all this. "Once you have a project in China," he says, "you become its hostage." And "there's tremendous pressure on China specialists to stay current"—to drop names and prove, or flaunt, insider knowledge. "If you're like Perry Link and open to dissidents, people can say, 'Well, Perry—great scholar and all, but he hasn't been to China for more than a decade, and no matter how good he is, he's bound to be out of touch. After all, China changes all the time.'" This has a sinister effect, says Waldron. There are many ways of "undermining" a person's "academic authority."

From my experience, Link is modest, but others are immodest in his behalf. A professor at the University of California, Riverside, and a professor emeritus at Princeton, he has stuck his neck out a long way. At the time of Tiananmen Square, he took Fang Lizhi and his wife, Li Shuxian, to the U.S. embassy. Fang was a famed dissident scientist, and No. 1 on the regime's Most Wanted list. Years later, Link edited *The Tiananmen Papers*, a trove of (formerly) secret Chinese-government documents about the protests and massacre. His co-editor was Andrew Nathan, a scholar at Columbia—who is also on the blacklist. "Andy and I are sort of old standbys on the list," says Link, "the ones held up as examples of going too far. We inadvertently have become tools of the regime: They use Andy and me to frighten the younger scholars." Waldron tells me that Link used to head Princeton's Chinese-language program in Beijing. When China banned Link, Princeton did what American universities characteristically do: nothing. But there was an alternative course, says Waldron. "They could have said, 'Professor Link is our director, and will remain our director. If you don't want him, fine. We'll move the program to Taiwan. It's up to you.'" But that is not the American way, where China is concerned. Waldron quotes the late James Lilley, an East Asia hand who ended his diplomatic career as U.S. ambassador to China: "You won't get anything from them unless you squeeze them." But Westerners—scholars, businessmen, government officials—are almost never willing to squeeze.

Waldron, too, has stuck his neck out—but has not been banned. The Chinese authorities have made things difficult for him, and are stingy with the number of days they allow him to be in the country. But he is not on the blacklist. As he explains, he is on a kind of "graylist" instead. Recently, NHK, the Japanese broadcasting corporation, asked him to speak on air about Confucius Institutes. These are language-and-culture centers set up by the Chinese government all over the world, including on American campuses. They are an expression of Beijing's "soft power," its attempt to spread its influence in benign, or benign-seeming, ways. In my view, these centers are a mixed blessing at best, corrupting and malign at worst. In any case, NHK was having trouble finding an American academic willing to speak on the subject, and Waldron agreed. By agreeing, he thought, he could be costing himself a visa. But "the way I look at it is this: If your university has gone to the trouble of building an endowment so that you don't have to fight in the marketplace for a living, but are guaranteed rice for life in return for what you think, you should say what you think. That's part of the deal." Waldron says he could not have lived with himself if he had turned down NHK.

He has suffered various professional bumps and bruises for stating such things as, "North Korea started the Korean War"—a simple fact to you and me, maybe, but a primitive, embarrassing notion to many academics. "Like a car, you get banged up," says Waldron. "But I've survived, I'm at a top university, and others are in prison or dead." (Here, of course, he is speaking of Chinese dissidents.)

Possibly the most maddening, and effective, aspect of China's approach to visas is its randomness, or seeming randomness: You never know when the boom will be lowered—on whom and why. The Chinese will allow a foreign scholar to criticize as he pleases, and come and go as he pleases, and then, one day: boom. "You know the reason. We don't have to tell you." In 2002, Perry Link wrote a well-known essay called "The Anaconda in the Chandelier." The Chinese state is not like a snarling tiger or fire-breathing dragon in your living room (although it certainly can be that, for Chen Guangcheng and other dissidents). It's more like "a giant anaconda coiled in an overhead chandelier. Normally the great snake doesn't move. It doesn't have to. It feels no need to be clear about its prohibitions. Its constant silent message is 'You yourself decide,' after which, more often than not, everyone in its shadow makes his or her large and small adjustments—all quite 'naturally.'"

Jonathan Mirsky worked in China, coming and going, for almost 20 years. He was one of the first Westerners in, in 1972. Because he wrote honestly, he figured he would be tossed out any day. But it took the Chinese until 1991 to do it. Why did they do it when they did it? Who knows? One fine day, Mirsky's minder of many years said to him, "We would like you to leave our China the day after tomorrow." Mirsky replied, "Really, Mr. Wang? You're serious? Thank you so much. You've made me the happiest of men." Wang was nonplussed. It was not the reaction he was used to. Mirsky explained, "You mean I'm not going to have to be in your mother-raping country anymore, and have my phone listened to, and be followed on the street, and be constantly warned to watch what I write? What a relief that will be!" There is a coda to this story. Some years later, Mirsky was starting a stint at Harvard, and bumped into none other than his old minder. "Mr. Mirsky," said Wang, "this is like a dream!" "No, Mr. Wang, a nightmare." They never saw each other again.

Andrew Nathan, the Columbia scholar, has had the honor of being banned, or blocked, on three separate occasions. The latest followed his work on *The Tiananmen Papers*. Audacious, he is affiliated with various human-rights organizations: Freedom House, Human Rights Watch, Human Rights in China, the National Endowment for Democracy. Virtually the whole array. Obviously, he regrets not being able to go to China, as any China scholar would. But he has not been all that harmed by his banning. First, he says, he has tenure. Second, his research does not depend on fieldwork in China. (One of his subjects is Chinese foreign policy, and that does not require your presence on Chinese soil. Anthropology, by contrast, does.) And third, "being banned is a kind of fieldwork of its own." You learn all sorts of interesting things from it: about how the Chinese government operates, about how your colleagues operate. The government doesn't necessarily send you a telegram saying, "Guess what? You're banned!" They may simply not respond, next time you request a visa. Or they may say, "It is not a convenient time." As for your colleagues, they may disinvite you from a conference here at home, because Chinese officials will be there, and you know how it is . . .

Western scholars who keep their head down, says Nathan, are not all "lily-livered liars and knaves." He suggests that there are three groups. There are scholars who hold "the perfectly respectable view" that the U.S.-China relationship is too important to be disturbed in any way. We must have a dialogue with the Chinese Communists, find out what makes them tick, and get along with them. Then there are young scholars who have careers to make and simply cannot do without access to China. And the third group? Well, "the lily-livered liars and knaves."

Perry Link, for his part, says he felt "liberated" after being banned. The anaconda had ruled, or affected, his behavior, in ways conscious and unconscious. "You avoid sensitive terms and sensitive topics. You try to be acceptable." The relief he felt after being banned was confirmation that the anaconda's sway was real. In his essay, he cites a Chinese proverb: "Dead pigs aren't afraid of hot water." Once he was "dead," i.e., banned, you could threaten him with boiling water, or pour it all over him, what did he care? Besides which, his main scholarly concern is literature, and he can do his work in beautiful California as well as he can anywhere else.

Known to every China scholar, surely, is a book published in 2004. This is *Xinjiang: China's Muslim Borderland.* (Xinjiang is the home of the Uighurs.) The book brings together contributions by 15 scholars, all of them Western, or in the West, apparently. Last year, Bloomberg News ran a fascinating article by Daniel Golden and Oliver Staley about the publication of the book and its aftermath. The book's editor, S. Frederick Starr—a well-known Sovietologist and Russianist, actually—chose not to include scholars of Chinese nationality: He did not want to get anyone in trouble with his government. Furthermore, he assured the Chinese embassy in Washington, before publishing the book, that the book would be scholarly and objective—nothing much to worry about. He took yet other steps to reassure the Chinese. You and I may wonder, "Why should a man in a free country bend over backward to soothe the sensibilities of a one-party dictatorship with a gulag?" But this behavior is perfectly normal and, to a degree, understandable.

Working with Starr to assemble the contributors was Justin Rudelson, a China scholar then at Dartmouth. The Bloomberg article quoted him as follows: "I remember people saying at the beginning, 'Do you think China will ban us?'" China did ban them—all 15. Said Rudelson, "I wound up doing the stupidest thing, bringing all of the experts in the field into one room and having the Chinese take us all out." According to Bloomberg, "Dartmouth almost fired Rudelson because he couldn't go to China." He now works elsewhere, evidently of his own accord. One of the 15 authors, Dru Gladney of Pomona College, said, "As a group, most of us have been very disappointed in the colleges' and universities' lack of sympathy and support." Institutions are "so eager to jump on the China bandwagon, they put financial interests ahead of academic freedom." Incidentally, I said that all 15 contributors were banned, but that's not true, or did not remain true for long: At least two of them wrote statements disavowing any support for Xinjiang's independence movement. That did the trick.

Jianli Yang says that he and other dissidents are not entirely comfortable at American universities. Link says that another prominent dissident recently told him the same thing. If you're a dissident, says Yang, people may regard you as radioactive, a bit untouchable—as though they might catch a disease from you. You are too "political." You could put a professor or a program or a university in an awkward spot. Dissidents sometimes hear, "Sorry, but this conference is for scholars, not dissidents." Yet, as Yang says, some of the dissidents are top-notch scholars. Fang Lizhi, the man Link took to the U.S. embassy, was a towering scientist, an astrophysicist. Yang himself knows a thing or two about math, political theory, economics, international relations, the Chinese penal system, poetry—lots of things.

I have a memory from the mid-1980s. Harvard invited Armando Valladares to give a talk. He had just emerged from 22 years in the Cuban gulag, and had written a memoir called *Against All Hope*. Some people called him "the Cuban Solzhenitsyn." The university would not let him speak on his own. They paired him with a professor, whose job was to give the pro-Castro point of view. Every other day of the year, of course, the professor had the students to himself. Valladares, who knew something, was not allowed to appear for an hour by himself.

It is not the job of a scholar to help a dissident, you could say (although we might hope the scholar is not hostile). Scholars are not human-rights activists or heroes. But they should probably tell the truth, and the full truth, to the extent they can ascertain it. And we are constantly told how important China is to the world, and that this importance will only grow in the future. Shouldn't we, the "world," have solid and complete information? Even, or especially, on the verboten subjects? Also, when a Jerry Cohen runs interference for a Chen Guangcheng—we can applaud. This may not be the job, strictly speaking, of a scholar, but we can applaud. We can applaud even when an Arthur Waldron is willing to say we ought to think twice about Confucius Institutes. Some contend that Chinese authorities themselves have respect—highest respect—for those foreign scholars who challenge them. Whom they might even find it convenient to ban. If so, that's one thing we can give them credit for.

—August 27, 2012

Majoring in Anthro

A lament for a once-great—inherently great—discipline

Not long ago, Eric Owens of the *Daily Caller* wrote an article about the latest antics of the American Anthropological Association. (They were threatening to boycott Israel.) He described anthropology as "the most pathetic college major" whose name "doesn't end in the word 'studies.'" This made me grin and wince simultaneously (if such a thing is possible). I thought the remark was funny. I also thought it might be true, and this pained me—for I myself was an anthro major, and I once had great respect, even love, for the field. I still do, in a way. But I know that the field was long ago captured by the flaky Left, to use a shorthand.

By the way, I was interviewing Jeb Bush a few years ago and brought up the fact that he majored in Latin American Studies. I pointed out that this field is dominated by lefties. He said, "Well, most 'studies' are dominated by lefties, when you think about it." True.

What has happened to anthropology can't be separated from what has happened to academia as a whole. But anthro may have pride of place, when it comes to political correctness and the corruption of scholarship. Stanley Kurtz says, "I've always bragged that anthropology is the worst of all the disciplines, much worse than English, despite what some of our conservative friends think." Kurtz is a senior fellow at the Ethics and Public Policy Center in Washington, D.C., and an anthropologist, or former anthropologist: a Ph.D. from Harvard. He is, in a sense, a refugee from anthropology. There are others.

In 2008, the anthropologist Hugh Gusterson wrote, "Anthropology is, by many measures, the academy's most left-leaning discipline." (A fact of which he apparently approves wholeheartedly.) In 2004, a study was conducted on the political affiliations of American professors. Of all the disciplines, anthropology came out the most Democratic at 30 to 1. This is shocking to me: I would be surprised to find one Republican in a *hundred* anthropologists.

When I was in college—the mid-1980s—all of my anthro professors were Marxists, I believe. It would have been hard to be anything else. If you were an astronomer, you were a Copernican, if you were an anthropologist, you were a Marxist. But they were serious people, my professors. They were not flakes. Since that time, however, postmodernism and other such strains have flooded in. So has political activism (which, of course, has its place, though probably not in classrooms).

Anthropology is, simply, the "science of man," as we used to say in the bad old days, when you could use "man" in that sense. In the 1950s, the superb Mischa Titiev published a textbook called *The Science of Man*. One dictionary defines anthropology as "the science that deals with the origins, physical and cultural development, biological characteristics, and social customs and beliefs of humankind." Anthropology belongs to the sciences, the social sciences, and the humanities, all at once. It is a wonderful field for a generalist (like journalism, as it happens).

There are four main branches of anthropology: cultural (or social) anthropology; physical (or biological) anthropology; archeology; and linguistic anthropology. The cultural branch is the most populated, by far, and it is also the one most vulnerable to politics and fads. I will concentrate on this branch. Perhaps the Republicans, whatever their numbers, are to be found in the other branches?

I should not romanticize the past—a conservative vulnerability—but there were once giants: Lewis Henry Morgan, Franz Boas, Bronislaw Malinowski, E. E. Evans-Pritchard. They wrote famous books such as *Argonauts of the Western Pacific* (Malinowski) and *The Nuer* (Evans-Pritchard). I was assigned those two classics, and many others. As Peter Wood, an anthropologist who heads the National Association of Scholars, points out, I got in "just under the wire." I was exposed to serious work. I was also assigned a primatology textbook that was explicitly "feminist." Yes, there was feminist science, as distinct from scientific science, I suppose.

There came a time, says Wood, when "anthropology went off a cliff." Napoleon Chagnon uses similar language: "Anthropologists went nuts over new fads, and a lot of cultural anthropology went down the drain." Chagnon is possibly the most famous anthropologist in the world, as well as the most "controversial," as everyone says. He has made many enemies by insisting on a role for biological evolution in human behavior. His 1968 monograph, *The Yanomamö: The Fierce People*, is probably the most famous such book in the literature. It would be only natural for other anthropologists to resent this a bit.

In the 1970s and '80s, anthropologists began to regard their field's past as shameful. (I am taking the liberty of generalization, as throughout this piece.) Often heard was the bromide "Anthropology is the handmaiden of colonialism." The earlier heroes of the field were now painted as villains—as racists and exploiters. This was a gross defamation. These anthropologists cared enough about primitive peoples to study them, understand them, and in some cases make them famous. (A word of advice to the current anthro student: Better not say "primitive.")

Peter Wood cites two key dates in the downfall of anthropology: 1973 and 1984. In the first of those years, Clifford Geertz published his *Interpretation of Cultures*, hugely influential. According to Geertz, an anthropologist could interpret a culture the way a literary critic interprets a poem. Nothing was quite true; everything was subjective. In 1984, David M. Schneider came out with his *Critique of the Study of Kinship*. It essentially threw cold water on the very idea of kinship, saying it was just another instance of Western bias. Before, kinship had been fundamental to anthropology: a hard, exacting study. In a much-quoted remark, Robin Fox said, "Kinship is to anthropology what logic is to philosophy or the nude is to art." No more, however. Anthropologists were excused from this particular task, as from others.

Stanley Kurtz says, in effect, "Don't forget Edward Said." Said's book *Orientalism*, published in 1978, influenced anthropology the way it did many other fields. Said threw cold water on the very idea of *culture*, to say nothing of kinship. Napoleon Chagnon says, in effect, "Don't forget Derrida and Foucault." The postmodernism of these philosophers covered anthropology like a fog. Anthropologists began competing with one another, says Chagnon, to see who could find "the most arcane ways" of expressing simple things. "A lot of battles in anthropology were intellectually faddish battles between gurus and ayatollahs and rabbis and high priests." Respect for the scientific method went down, down.

The field proliferated into little anthropologies, such as "reflexive anthropology": You behold a culture and ponder your own relationship to it. Do you feel guilty to be a Westerner? (You ought to.) There is also "transpersonal anthropology"—something about altered states of consciousness. Then you have "public anthropology," which aims for political and social activism—as if anthropology didn't have enough of that already.

Anthropology came to resemble Victim Studies, or victimology, in which the central question is "Who is oppressing whom?" as Peter Wood puts it. Worse, it got to be so that you could call anything and everything "anthropology." Andy Warhol said, "Art is what you can get away with." Sadly, something like that maxim applies to anthropology.

Over the years, plenty of serious people have majored in anthropology. Saul Bellow did (and in sociology too). Rob Portman, the senator from

Ohio, did. Michael Crichton, the late writer, did. Today, however, anthro has a reputation as a major for basket-weavers, potheads, and slackers. The field seems not to attract the most talented or go-getting students. Practical considerations come into play, of course. In 2012, *Forbes* ranked anthropology the very worst major for post-graduation employment and earnings. A writer on the blog *Living Anthropologically* wore this ranking as a badge of honor. "We're #1!" he said. He also gloated, or sneered, "Anthropology is the worst major for being a corporate tool." He added, "Anthropology is the major most likely to change your life" (for the better, presumably).

The field was unhappy when Governor Rick Scott of Florida spoke in 2011 about his spending priorities for education. "If I'm going to take money from a citizen to put into education," said Scott, "then I'm going to take that money to create jobs. So I want that money to go to degrees where people can get jobs in this state. Is it a vital interest of the state to have more anthropologists? I don't think so." The president and the executive director of the American Anthropological Association wrote him a rebukeful but polite letter. It transpired that one of Scott's daughters had majored in anthropology—and gone on to business school.

Appreciation of capitalism is not a hallmark of the anthropological community. That same blogger at *Living Anthropologically* wrote, "A spectre is stalking Capitalism—the spectre of Anthropology. All the Powers of Capitalism have bound themselves in a crusade against this spectre," which powers include Governor Scott, *Forbes*, and Napoleon Chagnon (bizarrely). "Anthropology knows that what currently exists does not have to be. Anthropology knows more about capitalism than any other academic discipline." So, you see, anthropology is what will at last bring capitalism and the money-power down.

On its website, Princeton has a section on choosing majors. There are questions and answers, written by students. These are charming, and also helpful. One question on the page relevant to us is, "What are common misperceptions about anthropology majors?" The answer begins, "Some consider us 'fluffy humanities people.'" Another question is, "Why would anyone want to date an anthropology major?" Because "you can expect an anthropology student to have original and quirky opinions on everyday social phenomena." Frankly, given their "broad perspectives and experiences," you can think of anthro students as no less than "the most interesting people in the world."

I have no doubt that students of anthropology at Princeton are brilliant, fascinating, and datable. More generally, however, Peter Wood is surely right when he notes, with sorrow, that his field has become "flypaper for dimmer undergraduates," who need only have the approved attitudes, opinions, and commitments to win A's from their profs.

The American Anthropological Association has many task forces, and these tell us a fair amount. There is the Global Climate Change Task Force. The Race and Racism Task Force. The Task Force on AAA Engagement on Israel-Palestine. (This last one must bend over backward to be fair to Israel.) The AAA also has sub-associations, an alphabet soup of such associations, an array that would make the Balkans blush. You have the Association of Black Anthropologists, the Association for Feminist Anthropology, the Association of Latina and Latino Anthropologists, the Association for Queer Anthropology—"formerly the Society of Lesbian and Gay Anthropologists." (You can imagine the debate over that name change.)

A perusal of *Anthropology News*, the "official news source" of the AAA, is not much different from a perusal of *Mother Jones* or any other left-wing publication, except that there are extra helpings of self-importance and academic gobbledygook. A typical headline reads, "Capitalism vs. the Climate." There is, in fact, an "AAA Statement on Humanity and Climate Change." It contains such lines as "Anthropologists recognize that humanity's actions and cultures are now the most important causes of the dramatic environmental changes seen in the last 100 years. We consider this period the Anthropocene" (a geological epoch in which man wrecks the Earth).

There is a piece called "When Conversation Is Not Enough: Reflections on the Makings of the #AAA2014 Die-In." At the recent annual meeting of the AAA, hundreds of members lay down on the floor of the hotel lobby, pretending to be dead, in protest of what they regard as a police and broader national war on black Americans. A statement of the Association of Black Anthropologists begins, "The [ABA] condemns, in no uncertain terms, the ongoing terrorism waged against Black U.S. communities by the state, police, and White vigilantes." It goes on to say, "These are state-sponsored massacres of our people, massacres enabled by a long history of national and global anti-Blackness." In short, "we charge genocide."

The charge of genocide—the wholesale murder of a people—is one I heard on my campus in the 1980s. Protesters were incensed by the attempts of the Reagan administration to slow the rate of growth of social-welfare spending. They chanted, "Reagan, Bush, you can't hide, we charge you with genocide."

In one issue of *Anthropology News*, the editors published four pieces on the controversial death of Michael Brown in Ferguson, Mo., at the hands of a police officer. One anthropologist wrote of "a violence that is critical in maintaining the privilege that accompanies whiteness." There was a lot more where that came from. The four pieces prompted Peter Wood to write an essay for *Minding the Campus*: "Ferguson and the Decline in Anthropology." He said that the quartet of pieces published in *AN* showed what his field "has sunk to." He lamented "a profound misappropriation of an intellectual discipline." To its great credit, *AN* republished this piece—an act that kicked up a storm among the *AN* and AAA faithful.

It should go without saying—though I will say it—that there are anthropologists at our universities who do good and serious work, including good and serious teaching. They are scholars before they are political actors and indoctrinators. Napoleon Chagnon cites a number of departments where "researchers are not just cultural anthropologists but a new breed of people who have additional skills and training in evolutionary biology." Among these departments are those at Missouri, Arizona State, Michigan, Harvard, and Utah. Peter Wood has a tip for telling a real anthropologist from a fake one: If the guy talks about social structure, kinship, and other such concerns, rather than the political preoccupation du jour, he's apt to be the real McCoy.

I'm reminded of a friend of mine who said that the congregation in which he took part was mad at the rabbi. They suspected he was a conservative—because he never talked about politics. Instead, he talked about things like God, the Bible, and Judaism.

Academia is a minefield in which it is increasingly difficult to say anything without causing an explosion. Recently, a professor unburdened himself of his fears in a piece online, published anonymously, of course. "Personally, liberal students scare the sh** out of me." If a conservative student complained about him to administration or on social media, he could swat that student away like a fly. "The same cannot be said of liberal students. All it takes is one slip," and "that's it," you're finished. Anthropology is about human and cultural differences, as well as similarities. It is absolutely studded with mines. How the subject can still be taught at all is semi-miraculous. The pressures of political correctness are intense.

In that piece about Ferguson and decline, Wood writes,

> Anthropology, rightly understood, is an effort to understand human nature through systematic study of those qualities in us that vary in time and place—and those that don't. Anthropology looks at how we emerged as a species and how we have diversified into thousands of languages, tribes, and civilizations. The field became a "discipline" by sternly demanding of itself rigor in how it went about this inquiry. Mostly that rigor required a steadfast determination to stand outside the myths people tell themselves and, by standing outside, to see things as they really are.

That field sounds like very heaven to me—one I'd like to major in.

—April 20, 2015

IKE AS WEAPON

The use and abuse of Eisenhower's Farewell Address, with its warning about the 'military-industrial complex'

Suggest that the defense budget be increased, and you may well hear about Eisenhower's Farewell Address. Tsk tsk, people will say: the military-industrial complex. We must not forget Eisenhower's warning about that complex. A reminder of the 34th president is supposed to put a conservative Republican, in particular, in his place. People who otherwise have no use for Eisenhower or his brand of Republicanism—liberals, leftists, "paleocons," and libertarians—suddenly like Ike, when it comes to this military-industrial complex.

Recently, a video of a speech made by Rand Paul surfaced. The speech was given in 2009, the year before Paul was elected to the Senate. He was speaking to students at Western Kentucky University. He said, "Even Eisenhower, back in the '50s, said, you know, 'Beware of the military-industrial complex.'" The Farewell Address was given in January 1961, but that is immaterial. Paul continued, "We need to be fearful of companies that get so big that they can actually be directing policy." He then spoke of Halliburton—and Dick Cheney and the Iraq War. In the 1990s, Paul explained to the students, Cheney had opposed going into Iraq. But then he "goes to work for Halliburton. Makes hundreds of millions of dollars, their CEO. Next thing you know, he's back in government and it's a good idea to go into Iraq."

There have always been Americans who say that we went to war because big companies or financiers or their lackeys manipulated us into it. In World War I, J. P. Morgan was the villain. In the Vietnam War, it was Dow Chemical. In the Iraq War, Halliburton played the role of Dow Chemical. Last year, a columnist defended Rand Paul and his mindset, making the inevitable comparison: "In his farewell address, Eisenhower sounded a lot like Rand Paul."

Eisenhower had a long, distinguished career in war and peace, and just about the only thing people know about him is "military-industrial complex"—that and his generalship in World War II. And maybe his fondness for golf. Jimmy Carter did not have as long or distinguished a career, but he certainly rose to the presidency, meteorically. Today, he is remembered for two or three things—including a "malaise" speech in which he never uttered the word "malaise." He is also remembered for an interview he gave to *Playboy* when he was running for president: "I've looked on many women with lust. I've committed adultery in my heart many times. God knows I will do this and forgives me."

The other week, I reviewed a production of *La cenerentola*, the Rossini opera. At the end, the prince, with his bride, mounted a giant wedding cake. Looking at the (diminutive) tenor, I thought of Thomas E. Dewey—whom Alice Roosevelt Longworth indelibly labeled "the little man on the wedding cake." Dewey was governor of New York, in addition to a two-time presidential nominee. But all people know is the wedding-cake crack—and maybe the false headline "Dewey Defeats Truman."

"Military-industrial complex" is universally known, but the speech from which it comes is scarcely known at all. It is a "noble speech," as the historian Ted R. Bromund wrote three years ago, "and the mature reflection of a great national servant." In May 1959—a year and eight months before the end of the Eisenhower presidency—Malcolm "Mac" Moos, the chief speechwriter, wrote a memo for the record. The president was hoping that "the Congress might invite him to address them before he left office, at which time he would like to make a 10 minute farewell address to the Congress and the American people." Moos added, "I think this is a brilliant idea if it can be carried off with a minimum of fanfare and emotionalism." Those words, so foreign to our own times, are typical of the Eisenhower presidency.

A few days later, Eisenhower wrote to his brother Milton, the president of Johns Hopkins University. He said the purpose of a farewell address would be "to emphasize a few homely truths that apply to the responsibilities and duties of a government that must be responsive to the will of majorities, even when the decisions of those majorities create apparent paradoxes. A collateral purpose would be, of course, merely to say an official 'goodbye.'"

In April 1960, one Eisenhower aide, Frederic Fox, wrote a memo to another, Moos. He recommended the re-reading of Washington's Farewell Address. "It is a beautifully wise and modest piece by a faithful public servant who loved his country." Moreover, "I was struck by its relevance to our day: the call for Constitutional obedience; . . . the dangers of 'overgrown military establishments' but the necessity of maintaining 'a respectable defensive posture'; . . . the ungenerous habit of one generation to spend beyond its means and to throw 'upon posterity the burden which we ourselves ought to bear.'" Everyone involved in Eisenhower's Farewell Address had Washington's in mind.

In the end, Eisenhower did not go before Congress. He gave his address on television, on January 17, 1961, three days before his successor, John F. Kennedy, would be inaugurated. It is somewhat startling to watch a video of the speech now: Eisenhower is unpolished, and touchingly so, I think. He fumbles with papers, stumbles over words, mispronounces other words, and so on. No major politician could get away with such a performance today. *Saturday Night Live* might pronounce it beyond mockery. The speech itself, in any case, is "beautifully wise and modest," as Fox said about Washington's. It is also a minor classic of conservatism.

"Throughout America's adventure in free government," said Eisenhower, "our basic purposes have been to keep the peace; to foster progress in human achievement; and to enhance liberty, dignity, and integrity among peoples and among nations. To strive for less would be unworthy of a free and religious people."

He then spoke of "the conflict now engulfing the world," i.e., the Cold War. "It commands our whole attention, absorbs our very beings. We face a hostile ideology—global in scope, atheistic in character, ruthless in purpose, and insidious in method. Unhappily, the danger it poses promises to be of indefinite duration. To meet it successfully, there is called for, not so much the emotional and transitory sacrifices of crisis, but rather those which enable us to carry forward steadily, surely, and without complaint the burdens of a prolonged and complex struggle—with liberty the stake."

In this speech, Eisenhower laid stress on "balance": "the need to maintain balance in and among national programs." Five years later, in 1966, he wrote a letter about the speech. "Our struggle against world

Communism," he said, "involves military, economic and spiritual factors. Each is equally important and it is up to us to see that we maintain the necessary strength in each and the proper balance among the three."

Here is a line from the speech that is never quoted: "A vital element in keeping the peace is our military establishment. Our arms must be mighty, ready for instant action, so that no potential aggressor may be tempted to risk his own destruction." Goldwater and Reagan would have an encapsulating slogan, "Peace through strength." Eisenhower said, "Until the latest of our world conflicts, the United States had no armaments industry. American makers of plowshares could, with time and as required, make swords as well. But now we can no longer risk emergency improvisation of national defense; we have been compelled to create a permanent armaments industry of vast proportions." Note the word "compelled."

Said Eisenhower, "This conjunction of an immense military establishment and a large arms industry is new in the American experience." And here is another line that is never quoted: "We recognize the imperative need for this development." And here comes the "but," or the "yet": "Yet we must not fail to comprehend its grave implications." Finally, we get to the hallowed line: "In the councils of government, we must guard against the acquisition of unwarranted influence, whether sought or unsought, by the military-industrial complex. The potential for the disastrous rise of misplaced power exists and will persist."

Eisenhower also warned against a "scientific-technological elite": "Today, the solitary inventor, tinkering in his shop, has been overshadowed by task forces of scientists in laboratories and testing fields. In the same fashion, the free university, historically the fountainhead of free ideas and scientific discovery, has experienced a revolution in the conduct of research. Partly because of the huge costs involved, a government contract becomes virtually a substitute for intellectual curiosity. For every old blackboard there are now hundreds of new electronic computers." What must the ratio be now? Public policy, said Eisenhower, must not "become the captive of a scientific-technological elite."

Just as Washington counseled the payment of debt, and not "ungenerously throwing upon posterity the burden which we ourselves ought to bear," Eisenhower said, "As we peer into society's future, we—you and

I and our government—must avoid the impulse to live only for today, plundering for our own ease and convenience the precious resources of tomorrow. We cannot mortgage the material assets of our grandchildren without risking the loss also of their political and spiritual heritage. We want democracy to survive for all generations to come—not to become the insolvent phantom of tomorrow." Given our $17.5 trillion debt, people today might quote this line, as well as "military-industrial complex."

Fast-forward to 1985, the middle of the Reagan years. An old Eisenhower hand, Ralph E. Williams, is asked by the Eisenhower Library in Kansas about the Farewell Address, and in particular its one famous line. He says, "I have always been astonished at the attention that has been given to the 'military-industrial complex' portion of President Eisenhower's last speech, and agree with Pete Aurand [another Eisenhower hand] that its true significance has been distorted beyond recognition. I am sure that had it been uttered by anyone except a President who had also been the Army's five-star Chief of Staff it would long since have been forgotten. But as things were, it became red meat for the media, who have gleefully gnawed on it for twenty-five years."

Williams is sorry that "scientific-technological elite" did not catch on. It "is now about as well-remembered as Edward Everett's Gettysburg Address. (It no doubt would have fared better if Ike had been a Nobel Laureate in physics.)" Everett, recall, was the scholar and statesman who spoke for two hours at Gettysburg, before Lincoln gave his brief speech.

Ted Bromund gives a neat summation of what Eisenhower was doing in his warning about the military-industrial complex: "He was arguing that undemocratic direction from above, especially if directed by big and bureaucratic government, is dangerous. It was top-down control—not the possession and funding of armed forces that reflect the needs and threats of the day—that Eisenhower found threatening." Eisenhower's actions speak at least as loudly as his words (as men's actions usually do): When he handed over to Kennedy, we were spending about 10 percent of GDP on defense, and over 50 percent of the federal budget. For 2015, we are prepared to spend 3.4 percent of GDP and about 13 percent of the budget. It's always a tricky business to try to speak for the dead, or to claim to do so, but, given everything we know about Eisenhower, I believe he would be in the camp of those of us who say our defenses are dangerously low, inviting of aggression. National security is undoubtedly a federal responsibility, one that requires adequate funding. Our proper debate is over "adequate."

Anti-military types, or anti-hawks, love to quote Eisenhower on the "military-industrial complex" more than they love to quote, say, George McGovern: because Eisenhower was a general, war hero, and Republican, and that is supposed to put us in our place. "Military-industrial complex" is the one thing that liberals and others can bless Ike for. Remember what Rand Paul said: "Even Eisenhower . . ."—"even"! I am reminded of obits and commentary about the founder of *National Review*, William F. Buckley Jr., in 2008. You would think that all he had ever done, in his long, consequential, and conservative life, was advocate the legalization of marijuana. It was the one thing that the whole world, or much of the world, could bless him for.

WFB liked to quote a comment attributed to Talleyrand: "Surtout pas trop de zèle." Above all, not too much zeal. This was part of Eisenhower's speech and mind, and it is a major part of the conservative mind.

—May 29, 2014

An Unpretty Pass

What a song without words says about American life

In Mill Creek, Wash., there is a high school named after Scoop Jackson, the late senator and Cold War hero. Mill Creek is just outside Everett, which was the senator's hometown. And, in 2006, something curious happened at Jackson High—something that helps us know where we stand in American life.

The school had had a little tradition: Every year, the wind ensemble would choose a piece to play at graduation. In the previous three years, the group had picked *On a Hymnsong of Philip Bliss*, by David Holsinger. It is based on "It Is Well with My Soul." But in 2006, the group wanted to play a different piece, something they had played in a winter concert and loved: the *Ave Maria* of Franz Biebl. The 17 members of the group voted unanimously for the piece. And their music director duly put it on a list of pieces proposed for graduation, a list sent to the school principal.

He looked it over, and the words "Ave Maria" raised a red flag for him. He kicked the matter upstairs, where it eventually reached Carol Whitehead, superintendent of the Everett School District No. 2. The words raised a red flag for her, too. She later admitted she did not know what they meant, but she knew they related to religion—and that was enough for her to forbid the wind ensemble to play the piece. Winter concerts were one thing, graduation ceremonies another. She would not have Everett-area schools "endorsing" religion.

Mind you, the wind ensemble was not going to sing any words. They were wind players. They were just going to play the music, the notes. But that was still not allowed: The title of the piece, "Ave Maria," would have to be printed in the graduation program. And that was impermissible.

A student who played alto sax in the ensemble, Kathryn Nurre, sued. She claimed that her constitutional rights had been violated. Assisting her is the Rutherford Institute, a civil-liberties outfit based in Charlottesville, Va. Its president, John Whitehead—no relation to the superintendent—says this is the most extreme case he has ever seen. This is the end of the line, in a way: "It's gotten so weird—I don't know how to explain it. It goes very deep." If a school will not permit an instrumental version of an Ave Maria at graduation, hostility to religion is official and pretty much complete. And what, asks John Whitehead, will that do to culture at large? Leaving aside Bach, Michelangelo, and Tolstoy: What about "Stairway to Heaven"?

You can understand why the Everett school officials would have been nervous. In 2005—the year before the wind ensemble wanted to play Biebl's *Ave Maria*—a Jackson High chorus had sung a song at graduation: "Up Above My Head." The song makes reference to angels, heaven, and even God. This was too much for some in the audience, who complained to the school district and wrote letters to the Everett *Herald*. Therefore, school officials were on the alert: and something called "Ave Maria" was a no-go.

After Kathryn Nurre launched her suit, some letters were published in the *Seattle Times*. One lady wrote to "applaud" Superintendent Whitehead "for correctly insisting the wind ensemble play a more secular piece for commencement." Thinking of a different Ave Maria, no doubt, she continued, "That melody is very familiar to all of us, and when we hear the instruments play, the words are immediately heard in our brains." Now we are in the vicinity of thought-crime: We may not be singing about God, and we may not be hearing words about God, but the notes make us think of God, which is verboten at graduation.

The letter-writer went on to say, "If secular people of all stripes, whether atheist, agnostic, skeptic or freethinker, don't speak out about these abuses . . . we will be no better than the Islamic jihadists." She ended with a direct message to the student plaintiff: "Sorry, Kathryn Nurre, the majority doesn't always win in a true Democracy. You attend a tax-supported high school."

That is a near-perfect expression of "liberal" opinion in the United States today. And it is mean, ignorant, and illiberal.

The Ave Maria our letter-writer was thinking of was probably Schubert's—or the one Gounod fashioned out of a keyboard prelude by Bach. Franz Biebl's is less known. But, frankly, it is one of the most beautiful pieces of the 20th century. Biebl was a German who lived from 1906 to 2001. He wrote his Ave Maria in 1964, when a choir of firemen in Munich asked him to do so. (That was a different world.) It caught on in the United States mainly because Chanticleer, the *a cappella* group in San Francisco, made it a signature. Audiences are reluctant to let them end a concert without it.

Editorializing about the Nurre case, the newspaper in Tacoma asked, "Can music be religious without words?" Sure, in a way. You would be hard pressed to hear a Bruckner symphony without noticing the religious sensibility infusing it. Bruckner dedicated his final symphony to "my dear God." Bach was, is, equally God-soaked. At the end of many of his manuscripts, he placed the initials "S.D.G.," meaning, "Soli Deo Gloria," or "To God Alone the Glory." If you take religion out of music, or religious music out of the general repertoire, you will be left with a diet that is hardly worth eating.

In September 2007, the federal district court in Seattle ruled in *Nurre* v. *Whitehead*: against the student, for the superintendent and the schools. The case went to the Ninth Circuit Court of Appeals: where, in September 2009, a three-judge panel ruled as the district court had. The votes were 2 against 1. Nurre and her supporters are hoping that the Supreme Court will hear the case and rebuke the lower courts, giving clear guidelines.

Nurre is suing on three grounds: that Whitehead violated her free-speech rights, as granted in the First Amendment; that she acted hostilely toward religion, in violation of the First Amendment's Establishment Clause; and that she ran afoul of the Equal Protection Clause as given in the Fourteenth Amendment—previously, as you know, the Jackson High School wind ensemble had been allowed to play *On a Hymnsong of Philip Bliss*. Was the Class of 2006's desire so different?

Writing for the Ninth Circuit majority was Judge Richard C. Tallman. His is a thoughtful opinion, decently respectful of Nurre, religion, and music. Toward the end of it, he wrote, "We . . . wish to make clear that we do not hold that the performance of music, even 'Ave Maria,' would necessarily violate the Establishment Clause. We hold only that Whitehead's actions were reasonable in light of her past experience and her understanding of the law and did not violate Nurre's constitutional rights."

But Judge Milan D. Smith's dissent has won conservative hearts around the country. His was a partial dissent, finding that Superintendent Whitehead did, in fact, violate Nurre's free-speech rights. He wrote that "unnecessary measures by school administrators will only foster the increasingly sterile and hypersensitive way in which students may express themselves . . . and hasten the retrogression of our young into a nation of Philistines who have little or no understanding of our civic and cultural heritage." "The Hallelujah Chorus" would be out, of course—but also "The Battle Hymn of the Republic" and "When the Saints Go Marching In."

Will the Supreme Court take the same view as Smith, if that court hears *Nurre* v. *Whitehead*? The Ninth Circuit is a court overturned with reassuring frequency. Remember, these are the people who brought us the banning, for a time, of the Pledge of Allegiance, because of "under God."

But, whatever happens to *Nurre* v. *Whitehead*, we have reached a pretty pass when a school superintendent thinks she must ban an instrumental version of an Ave Maria on constitutional grounds. If she would rather avoid complaints from offended cranks, fine (sort of). And many of us are sympathetic to local control of education. But to say that an instrumental Ave Maria would violate the Bill of Rights? In acting as she did, Carol Whitehead herself might have been the violator.

We have reached a pass where, if we hear the word "God," or even "angels" and "heaven," we say, "Eek, a mouse!" American life has always been soaked in religion, from the Pilgrims to Abraham Lincoln to Martin Luther King and beyond. If American life, including graduation ceremonies, is purged of religion, American life is something new and twisted. Given the importance of religion to man in general, it is barely life itself.

The problem with Biebl's *Ave Maria*, in its wind-ensemble version, was the title alone. If the kids had told the principal that it was called "Against the Despoliation of the Environment," or "Ode to President Obama," that would have been fine, you can bet. No one in the audience would have been guilty of thought-crime. Many composers draw inspiration from God and religion when they put pen to paper, no matter what their titles. Should they tell Carol Whitehead when they have received such inspiration, just in case? Would she permit that Bach prelude—the one Gounod added to—alone, without words?

I know a singer who was asked to sing at a ceremony for a Christmas-tree lighting in a major American city—only they did not call it a "Christmas tree," of course: It was a "holiday tree." The singer was asked to sing "O Christmas Tree" and "Silent Night": but those in charge did not want her to sing them in English; she had to sing them in German, for fewer people would know that language—and words like "Christmas tree" and "Virgin" would not ring out over ears in the public square. We have reached a pretty pass, yes—in reality, a most unpretty pass.

—November 2, 2009

N.B. The Supreme Court decided not to hear Nurre v. Whitehead. *Dissenting from this decision—that is, wanting to hear the case—was Justice Samuel Alito, who wrote stirringly.*

Looking for Lefty

The problem of what, or whom, to read

About ten years ago, a friend of mine who works in public life made an announcement at lunch: "I've been reading newspapers and magazines since I was a kid. I'm very well informed. From now on, I'm not going to read anything I'm not going to agree with. At this stage, I'm entitled." I grinned at this, and was tempted to go my friend's way. I still am. But I know there must be fiber in our diets. We cannot just consume journalistic and political ice cream.

Being a conservative, I should seek out "progressive" opinion. But I have had a tough time of it. I have long tried to have a go-to lefty, someone who will give me the best arguments of the other side. The problem is, I keep running into simple invective and sneering.

For a while, I made it a point to read Michael Kinsley, the vaunted purveyor of "smart liberalism." Bill Buckley appreciated him, making him a regular on his television show, *Firing Line*. I appreciate him too, I guess—but he said such nutty and unfair things about George W. Bush during the Iraq War, I did not keep up with him. Possibly, I missed out.

I made it a point to read Richard Cohen, every column of his. But here again, the Iraq War was my Waterloo. It's not that I disagreed with Cohen, or with Kinsley. What's the point of reading the other side if you want to be agreed with? It's that they too often struck poses and sneered and played to their crowd (as I saw it). They would not take the other side, namely me and my allies, seriously. They made cartoons of us.

In a column of my own, I vented some frustration. "Richard Cohen," I said, "imagines conservatives who do not exist. He seems unwilling to debate, or consider, conservatives as we truly are. He is a caricaturist, and I'm looking for a columnist." I should pause here to say that I'm picking on Cohen for a reason: He's just about the best of them. If he were run-of-the-mill, I wouldn't bother.

At a conference abroad, I met Anthony Grayling, the British philosopher and journalist. This was in 2004 or 2005. Grayling assumed that I was on the left, like most everyone else (including him). When he found out I was not, he could not have been friendlier. We talked over the issues on that occasion and subsequent ones. Here was a man I could "do business with," to borrow Mrs. Thatcher's language about Gorbachev. I determined I would read Grayling, which the Internet makes easy to do. (The Internet makes it easy to read anyone.) I fell off the wagon, somehow. Maybe I should get back on.

Early in life, I read nearly everything under the sun, as young people should. I looked at *The Nation*, *Mother Jones*, and *In These Times* on the left, and *National Review*, *Commentary*, and *The American Spectator* on the right. I found myself drawn to one side, obviously. And gradually my reading narrowed. I didn't make a decision to give up certain publications. I just did, barely aware of it.

Actually, I can tell you when I gave up *The New Yorker*—it wasn't that long ago, relatively speaking. I can tell you almost like a reformed alcoholic who remembers the date of his last drink. It was in late 2002, when the magazine published a review of a movie called *8 Mile*. The star of this flick was Eminem, the rapper, and it was set in his hometown of Detroit. I myself grew up in the orbit of Detroit. I know this particular milieu fairly well.

A lot of conservatives objected to Eminem for his vulgarity, his depravity—you know, the usual. But *The New Yorker*'s critic wrote, "People who are convinced that Eminem is destroying America might want to consider the delicacy of the white-black friendships in *8 Mile*. (Perhaps the spectre of such friendships is what right-wingers actually hate most.)"

I was not the type to be easily stunned, and I am even less stunnable now. But I must say, those sentences stunned me. I thought, "Is that what they think of us? Do these *New Yorker* types know us so little? Have they ever met any of us? Do they ever get out?" And "if they won't bother with *us*, why should I bother with *them*?" It wasn't one lousy film review that repelled me; it was a pervasive attitude.

False accusations of racism, I think, are what is most repellent about the Left. They seem unable to stop throwing white sheets over us. Show me a lefty who won't tar his opponents with racism, and I'll show you a virtual hero! That man is my friend for life. Do conservatives have similar nasty habits? If so, they, we, should cut them out.

For about 20 years, starting when I was in college, I read the *New York Times* every day, from cover to cover (or the newspaper equivalent). I would no more have gone without reading the *Times* than I would have gone without dressing myself. It was automatic. Buckley once wrote that going without the *Times* would be "like going about without arms and legs." (He said this as a prelude to some complaint about the paper.)

In 2004, I wrote a piece called "Going *Times*less: Who dares give up the 'newspaper of record'?" The answer was: Plenty of people. And not just crotchety conservatives, but nice mainstreamers, too. I canvassed a number of writers and public figures. A veteran Washington reporter told me that bias and partisanship infected "every nook and cranny of that paper." Not just the news reports but "the arts pages and the food pages and the headlines and the photo selection and the captions"—everything.

At the end of that piece, I wrote that "some of us can't wean ourselves away" from the *Times*, "and may never." Yet wean myself I did. Though not really consciously: I just read less and less of it until I read almost nothing. I like to read the obits, however, via the *Times* app on my phone. I have this in common with the late Robert Bork—not the app, but he, too, gave up everything in the *Times* except the obits.

Don't think that conservatives who concentrate on the right-leaning press have lives of peace and quiet. Oh, no. You can spend 90 percent of your time stewing about the failings of other conservatives. Your own side can exasperate you more than the other side. Conservatives are very good at infighting and splintering. There are always people who present themselves as the One True Conservative, next to whom everyone else is a heretic.

Democrats, oddly enough, sometimes think that Republicans and conservatives are a monolith. At least they pretend to do so. We're all lined up like Rockettes, while they are gloriously independent. President Obama peddled this notion to a group of his donors in 2009: "Democrats are an opinionated bunch. You know, the other side, they just kinda sometimes do what they're told. Democrats, y'all thinkin' for yourselves." (The president, like most of us, enjoys slipping into the vernacular from time to time.) My experience of Republicans and Democrats has been completely different. We righties do an excellent impression of the Bolsheviks and Mensheviks, or the Trotskyites and Shachtmanites.

Everyone should have a balanced media diet, I suppose, but maybe not too balanced. Some narrowing down, some imbalance, is permissible, especially after ample experience. How long should you keep reading *Mother Jones* if a) you know what's in it and b) you think it's all bunk? (The same goes for *National Review* or other conservative publications.) Buckley would occasionally say, "The purpose of an open mind is to close it on some things." He was paraphrasing Chesterton, I'm sure: "The object of opening the mind, as of opening the mouth, is to shut it again on something solid."

We are always warned against "preaching to the choir." But, as I once heard Midge Decter say, preaching to the choir gets a bad rap: It is very, very important. The choir needs consolation, reminding, bolstering—the sense that they are not alone. I could not agree more, mainly as a choir member, but also as a sometime preacher.

I further make this contention: It's more important that lefties seek out right opinion than that righties seek out left opinion. "Liberalism"—though I choke on the corruption of that word—is in the air we breathe. We all go to school, and most people go to college, I think, and many of us go to grad school. We all go to the movies and watch television shows. Liberalism is almost the soundtrack of our lives. The conservative case often has to be sought out.

All this said, it's possible for a conservative to ghettoize himself, in the journalism he reads. I confess to being surprised by Mitt Romney's loss to Obama in the last election—certainly by the margin of that loss. And I was irked at being surprised. Was I in a conservative bubble? Did I need to get out more? I resolved to change my media diet: I would cut out some candy and add some fiber. This resolve lasted several weeks—until I fell back into old habits.

A new year is upon us, however, and one could make resolutions. For many years, I have been told by a British conservative friend that the *Guardian*, whatever its ideological coloration, is "the only serious newspaper in Britain." Maybe I should look at this famous left-wing daily online. But there is always a column by Thomas Sowell or Charles Moore or Mark Steyn to read—delicious, and nutritious, too.

—December 31, 2013

Symbols and Their Limits

A caution against the yellow-ribbon culture

After the latest terror attacks in Paris, a Twitter hashtag arose: "#PrayForParis." A symbol arose, too. Designed by Jean Jullien, a French illustrator, it was a peace sign with the Eiffel Tower in the middle. Like "#PrayForParis," it was tweeted around the world.

Symbols have their place, of course, and they can serve many purposes: to console, recall, stir, etc. But sometimes they can seem awfully weak, even escapist.

The peace sign—the original one—was designed in 1958 by Gerald Holtom, an Englishman who had been a conscientious objector in World War II. Using the flag-semaphore alphabet, he placed the letters "N" and "D" within a circle. Those stand for "nuclear disarmament." If you turn the peace sign upside down, you get the letters "U" and "D." Holtom came to prefer this variation, and said that the letters stood for "unilateral disarmament."

It so happens that the new leader of the British Labour party is a descendant of Holtom's, so to speak. Jeremy Corbyn favors the unilateral nuclear disarmament of Britain.

After the Paris attacks, a video shot round the world. It showed a French father talking to his little boy. The little boy notes that there are bad guys with guns. The father says, "It's okay: They might have guns, but we have flowers." The little boy says, "But flowers don't do anything." The father denies it.

I thought of one of the most famous news photos of the 1960s. A Vietnam War protester in America puts a flower in the barrel of a rifle carried by a National Guardsman. The Guardsman is sweet about it. Impassive. The thing about ISIS: They're not so sweet.

In the days following the Paris attacks, the "Marseillaise" was sung and played around the world—including at the Metropolitan Opera, before a performance of *Tosca*. Some people were miffed, however, remarking that the Lebanese national anthem was not being sung and played—and Lebanon, like France, had suffered a terror attack. Didn't this show a shameful pro-Western bias? Even racism?

These contentions aside, I had a memory: Last January, a conductor walked out of the Israeli Opera. Islamists had attacked Paris, killing people at a magazine (*Charlie Hebdo*), a kosher supermarket, and elsewhere. Maestro Frédéric Chaslin wanted to say a few words before a performance, and he wanted to perform the Israeli national anthem, "Hatikva." Management said no. In disgust, he walked.

I understand Chaslin real well: He's a Frenchman, a Jew, and the son of Holocaust survivors. I also understand management, real well. They said, in essence, We Jews are attacked and murdered all the time. If we paused and talked and played the national anthem every time this happened, we would do nothing but.

Twenty or more years ago, I coined a phrase for a side of America I didn't especially care for: the treacly, sentimental, touchy-feely side (which can also be morally preening). I spoke of "the yellow-ribbon culture." Yet this does a disservice to the original yellow ribbons, which came about during the Iranian hostage crisis.

Islamists in Tehran seized our embassy personnel in November 1979. Earlier in the decade, Tony Orlando and Dawn had a hit song: "Tie a Yellow Ribbon Round the Ole Oak Tree." The song had its origins in a folk tale about a convict coming home from years in prison. He didn't know whether his woman would want him back. If she did, she could tie a yellow ribbon round the oak tree. If she did not tie such a ribbon, he would keep on going, not bothering her at all.

The senior official in our embassy was Bruce Laingen. Back home, his wife, Penne (short for Penelope), tied a yellow ribbon around their oak tree—literally. Soon, people across the country were doing this, in solidarity with the American hostages and their families. Mrs. Laingen said, "One of these days, Bruce is going to untie that yellow ribbon"—her ribbon, the original one. "It's going to be out there until he does."

In 1991, she donated her ribbon to the Library of Congress.

A yellow ribbon became a symbol even as far away as the Philippines. Supporters of Benigno Aquino, the opposition leader exiled in America, tied yellow ribbons round their trees. When he returned home, he was murdered on the spot. His widow, Corazon, led a political movement, eventually becoming president. Yellow was her color, and sympathetic Americans wore yellow, in support of her.

We have ribbons for all sorts of causes, and these are called "awareness ribbons." Since the early '90s, a pink ribbon has been the symbol of the fight against breast cancer. Athletes are periodically asked to pin them to their jerseys.

Pink is a color for womanhood in general. Here in America, we have "Code Pink," the left-wing activists who are "Women for Peace." In Britain, during the most recent general-election campaign, Labour launched a pink minibus, for a "woman to woman" initiative. It was roundly mocked, and Labour was left a bit flush with embarrassment.

A Labour bête noire, Ronald Reagan, was not averse to symbolism, of the right kind. The old actor was certainly not averse to theater. In the second week of December 1981, the Communist dictatorship in Poland declared martial law. In Washington, the Polish ambassador defected to us. He asked President Reagan to light a candle in a White House window on Christmas Eve. This would show solidarity with the beleaguered Poles. Reagan agreed to do so, and, in a typically stirring address, he asked all Americans to place their own candles in their own windows.

Of course, Reagan was not a mere symbolist. He was working night and day to bring down the Soviet empire, by all means at his disposal—which included the symbolic and theatrical, as well as the military, economic, and so on.

Jump now to April of last year, when the Islamist terror group Boko Haram kidnapped hundreds of schoolgirls in Nigeria. There was a great hashtag campaign, "#BringBackOurGirls." The First Lady, Michelle Obama, got in on the act, frowning at a camera and holding up a sign with the hashtag. For their part, Boko Haram put out a video, mocking the campaign. Who can blame them, really? They are not the kind to be moved by a plaintive hashtag.

And yet I can't quite blame the hashtaggers either, who, in their impotence, wanted to do something, or say something—wanted not to be bystanders. This is an honorable impulse. Sometimes the hashtag or yellow ribbon is all we have. But I think of something my colleague Mona Charen said about Mrs. Obama. She said, essentially, Gee: If only the First Lady knew someone with guns and special forces or something . . .

More and more, I sympathize with the spirit of the Israeli Opera. Walking around Washington, D.C., or New York, I see flags at half staff all the time. We lower our flags at the drop of a hat. It's gotten to the point where I notice when they're flying high. Somebody, somewhere, is always doing something evil. Maybe we should reserve our flag-lowering for when an elderly statesman dies in bed?

In Canada, they lowered their flags every time a soldier of theirs was killed in Afghanistan. When he became prime minister in 2006, Stephen Harper stopped the practice. He reasoned as follows: There's a war on, and with war come casualties. The dead can be remembered on Remembrance Day. Otherwise, fight on, until victory.

How do you know a good and worthy symbol versus a treacly, escapist, or otherwise unworthy one? I'm not sure I can lay down rules. I think it's a matter of taste, of stomach. I, for one, am allergic to the COEXIST bumper sticker—the word "coexist" done up in religious and other symbols. Those who need the lesson or reminder don't see the sticker, or don't care about it. And the rest of us don't need to be preached to.

John Greenleaf Whittier wrote a Christmas poem, which includes the words "Keep while you need it, brothers mine, / With honest zeal your Christmas sign." By all means, keep your signs and symbols, for as long as you need them, and for as long as they have a scrap of potency. But let them not be substitutes for looking reality in the face and doing whatever can be done.

The little French boy said, "But flowers don't do anything"—a phrase that haunts.

—December 21, 2015

'Rhodes Must Fall'

The rights and wrongs of a movement

Cecil Rhodes had a rocky 2015. He died in 1902, at the age of 48. His last words, according to lore, were, "So little done; so much to do." He did a lot, in that relatively brief life. He made British colonialism boom in southern Africa. He also made a fortune in diamonds. And when he died, he left that fortune to a variety of public works.

He never married or had children. In this, he was like Alfred Nobel. And they wrote similar wills.

Rhodes was a racist, certainly in this sense: He believed that he and his fellow British were the superior race. He wanted to bring the whole world under its aegis. His ambition did not exclude the "recovery" of the United States, as he put it.

Back to his rocky 2015—or to his will, first. He left the University of Cape Town the land on which its main campus now sits. There is accordingly a statue of Rhodes on that land. Or was. For decades, people grumbled about the statue, and this very much included Afrikaners, who resented Rhodes as a symbol and leader of their enemy: the British.

In March 2015, students at the university decided that the statue of Rhodes at last had to go—or, as they put it in their hashtag, "#RhodesMustFall." Did they go about their protest in an orderly, logical, civilized way? Don't be silly. Students don't have the time or patience for that now.

First, they smeared excrement on the statue (human excrement). Then they occupied a university building, making numerous demands. And they revived an old radical slogan: "One settler, one bullet!"

Needless to say, they got their way. Within a month, the statue was felled, and the students had a new Black Studies program.

Eight months later, in December, the "Rhodes Must Fall" movement moved to Oxford. This was Rhodes's alma mater. He attended one of its colleges, Oriel, in the 1870s. On his death, he left the university a great deal of money—some of which was used for a building at Oriel, the

Rhodes Building. It has a modest statue of the donor. This is the Rhodes that "must fall."

There was also money for the scholarships, of course—the famous Rhodes Scholarships, which have now gone to almost 8,000 people. Rhodes wanted to help students who had, among other things, "moral force of character and instincts to lead." Our Bill Clinton was a recipient. He certainly had instincts to lead.

In addition, Rhodes wanted to promote harmony between nations and reduce the likelihood of war. So, of course, did his contemporary, Nobel.

At Oxford, the anti-Rhodes movement has been led by a law student from South Africa, Ntokozo Qwabe. He is a proud radical. He was disgusted by the widespread sympathy for France after Islamists attacked Paris in November, killing 130 people. "I do NOT stand with France," he wrote. "Not while it continues to terrorise and bomb Afrika & the Middle East for its imperial interests." (The young man makes a practice of spelling "Africa" with a "k." Why, I don't know.) He also called for the banning of the French flag on campuses such as Oxford's. He compared the tricolor to the Nazi swastika.

Interestingly, Qwabe is a Rhodes Scholar. Naturally, he has been accused of hypocrisy: benefiting from Rhodes's largesse while trying to tear him down. Qwabe will have none of it. "I'm no beneficiary of Rhodes," he wrote. "I'm a beneficiary of the resources and labour of MY people which Rhodes pillaged and enslaved." In his mind, all he is doing is "taking back crumbs of the colonial loot of Rhodes & his colonial cronies."

Hard as it may be to believe, Oriel College has not yet taken down the Rhodes statue. It says it will review the issue over a six-month period. From what we know about university administrators, especially when racial pressure is involved, I would not bet the ranch on the statue's retention.

Like you, I bet, I find some of Rhodes's views repulsive. Not all of them, but some. Yet I would be perfectly relaxed about him on a building. Would I think differently if I were a black African, or a black anything? Or if I were of Afrikaans descent, for that matter? There is a wise and old sentiment: It's remarkably easy to bear injuries done to others.

But if Rhodes must fall, what about other figures? Queen Victoria presided over the whole thing—the colonial and imperial enterprise, certainly in that era. Should Victoria Station be razed, or renamed? What about Victoria, British Columbia?

Every generation is appalled by the failings of previous generations. Every generation thinks, "How *could* they have?" and pats itself on the back for being infinitely better. Someone once said, "Will people in the future say, 'Can you believe that human beings once kept dogs on leashes and owned them as "pets"?'" That's far-fetched, though useful as a thought experiment.

I wonder, in all seriousness, how future generations will look on our policy of abortion-on-demand. Some of the best people I have known have been pro-abortion (or "pro-choice," they would probably say). I think they have a blind spot. What are my blind spots? I don't know.

If we subjected historical figures to our highest standards, few would 'scape whipping. I think of Gunnar and Alva Myrdal, those progressive heroes. Swedish, no less! He won the Nobel Memorial Prize in economics; she shared the Nobel Peace Prize, with a Mexican diplomat. No one would say they "must fall." But do their fans know about their early flirtation with eugenics? What they wrote in the 1930s might curl your hair. They said that society had to confront the problem of how to "root out all types of physical and mental inferiority within the population, both the mentally retarded and the mentally ill, the genetically defective and persons of bad character."

Bad character? Well, we can't all be Rhodes Scholars.

Reluctant as I am to whip erring figures of the past, I would not want to be too loosey-goosey. Not too relativistic. I'm practically the only person I know, left or right, who liked George W. Bush's second inaugural address—which was loaded with absolutes. "We will persistently clarify the choice before every ruler and every nation: the moral choice between oppression, which is always wrong, and freedom, which is eternally right."

Once, William F. Buckley Jr. and the Reverend William Sloane Coffin were arguing on the former's television show, *Firing Line*. Coffin didn't like WFB's moral stance (too firm). He quoted Goethe, to the effect that "I've never heard of a crime that I could not imagine myself committing."

WFB said (something like), "Oh? You can imagine yourself pushing them alive into ovens? Really?"

In brief, there is a line between judgment—proper judgment—and judgmentalism. It can be an effort to stay on the happy side of it.

Here at home, we have our own campus controversies. One of them has unfolded at Yale, where there is a residential college named after John C. Calhoun. He had an impressive résumé: House rep, senator, secretary of war, secretary of state, and vice president. He was also an alumnus of Yale, one of its brainy southerners.

There is a move to take his name off the college. I will quote the petition, which explains that Calhoun

> was respected during his time as an extraordinary American statesman. But he was also one of the most prolific defenders of slavery and white supremacy in American history. At a time when many of his southern colleagues viewed slavery as a necessary evil, Calhoun infamously defended the institution as "a positive good." His legacy is built on his vociferous defense of a state's right to enslave blacks.

So help me, I agree with them. And if I had a say or an interest at Yale, I would be in favor of striking Calhoun's name. Therefore, do I want to rename Washington, D.C.? Or raze the Jefferson Memorial? Or boycott Madison Square Garden? Let's not give in to extremes.

It consoles me about Jefferson that he said (concerning slavery), "I tremble for my country when I reflect that God is just." Calhoun never did any such trembling, so far as anyone's aware.

But again, where will it end? Elihu Yale—for whom the university at large is named—evidently had ties to the East Indian slave trade.

Not every college can be named for William Wilberforce, that great abolitionist from Britain, born in 1759, when slavery was a norm of human affairs (as it has been since human affairs began). We have a Wilberforce University in Ohio. Most of us would rather attend a Wilberforce than a Calhoun. And frankly, I would rather attend a Rhodes than an institution named after Ntokozo Qwabe, in his present, addled, ideologized state.

I have a friend who bought an apartment in Manhattan not long ago. (I'm not changing the subject.) He and his family liked the apartment a lot. But my friend didn't like the name of the building, at all: the Oliver Cromwell. Gritting his teeth, he bought anyway.

About ten blocks to the south is Lincoln Center, which has the David H. Koch Theater, named after a man who donated $100 million. Mr. Koch is a libertarian, and the people who work in the theater are generally . . . not. They tend to hate the name of the place, and some refuse to say it. But none has quit over the issue, I gather.

We all have to suck it up a little in life. In the future, no doubt, lots of things will be named after Barack Obama, our first black president, and a progressive hero. I won't like it, thinking Obama a disaster. When it looked like Iraq was going well, the comedian Jon Stewart said that he was worried his kids would have to attend George W. Bush High School. Unfortunately, he can rest easy.

Cecil Rhodes may not be resting too easy these days. Many people want to dig him up from the Matopos Hills of Zimbabwe—formerly Rhodesia—and ship him back to Britain, where he came from. Whole territories and countries were once named for him. Now he struggles to keep his mug on buildings that he paid for.

Next up for a name change? Rhodes University in Grahamstown, South Africa. He paid for that one, too. I don't say that people should have to live under names that they abhor (though surely donors have some right to be honored). I do say that we should strain to be as wise, and humble, as possible. And that the excrement-smearers and building-occupiers and slogan-chanters should be told to grow up or leave.

—January 25, 2016

An End to Borders

In which the topic is, not national frontiers, but book and music shops

"There's no crying in baseball!" says the manager in *A League of Their Own*, the 1992 movie about female baseball players. There's no crying in a free-market economy either. You either adapt or die. And Borders, apparently not adapting, has died. There will be no more Borders bookstores.

You're not supposed to cry, and I'm not, but I might have shed half a tear, when I heard the news. The reason is mainly personal and sentimental. The original Borders was in my hometown, Ann Arbor, Mich. The store was founded in 1971 by the Borders brothers, Tom and Louis, who were students at the University of Michigan. We all went into that store. The selection was enormous, even exciting, and they would let you read, as I recall.

The staff was renowned for its knowledge, although whether that renown was justified, I can't tell you. I think they were somewhat arrogant and snotty. I also think that most customers kind of liked it—the way people like waitresses in New England chowder houses who bark at you.

I was a little tickled—there's a Michigan word!—when the store went national. When it became a chain. Sometime in the mid-1990s, I went into a Borders in Washington, D.C., the city in which I was living. On the wall was a photo of the original Borders staff. I recognized most of them. Got a little pang.

I also remember reading that Borders had been acquired by Kmart. That, too, tickled me. The Borders people thought themselves so cool, and here they were being acquired by the uncoolest company in America—a company whose name was synonymous with downmarket. Made me laugh, I swear.

In any case, an Ann Arbor company had made good. "Can there any good thing come out of Nazareth?" Can a great business venture come out of Ann Arbor, one of the small citadels of the Left, a place not exactly friendly to enterprise? Oh, yes. Borders came out of Ann Arbor, and so did Domino's Pizza, which is still selling pizzas.

Now that I've gotten a little political on you, let me mention a piece that appeared in these pages in September 2004: "Little Suppressors: Dealing with the bookstore clerk who hates you." I should explain the title. While in Ann Arbor, I didn't work at Borders, but I worked, briefly, at a bookstore called The Little Professor. Our manager refused to put out some conservative magazines. (On the whole, he was a very nice guy.) My friend Eddie came up with a new name for the store: "The Little Suppressor."

Why did I write about this topic in September 2004? There was a book called *Unfit for Command*, by John O'Neill, a Vietnam vet. It attacked Senator John Kerry, who was the Democratic presidential nominee. There were stories around the country that bookstore clerks were refusing to display or sell the book. And Borders employees were telling their stories on their union website. This remark was typical: "We're 'finding' that most of the few copies we're getting are damaged and need to be sent back. So sad. Too bad, Bushies!"

You can say this about buying books over the Internet: You don't have to deal with a clerk who snarks at you about your politics. Did you ever have the experience of buying a conservative book or magazine and getting attitude from the clerk? It was no fun, really.

But let me return to the Ann Arbor of yore, and a particular record shop. I think it was a CD shop later. Do we still have CD shops? Not in my neighborhood (which I'll get to in a minute). I am thinking of Ann Arbor's Liberty Music, one of the great stores of its kind. It was famous all over the world. Like Borders, it had a vast selection and a knowledgeable—unquestionably knowledgeable—staff. Also a slightly quirky one, like all great staffs, right?

The shop had listening booths, so you could try things out, before buying. Say you had $5 (or whatever it was) for a Brahms Second. Would you get Klemperer, Walter, or Karajan, Bernstein, Solti, or Szell? You could stay in the booth for as long as you were unhassled. I was always a little nervous. Adding to the nervousness was this: You didn't want to scratch the record.

Liberty Music has gone by the wayside, needless to say. But, hang on, I see by the Internet that it still exists in a quaint form: It is a mail-order business, "centered on classical 78's."

I like progress as much as the next guy—making me a progressive, you see—but I've never been an "early adopter": someone who early adopts a new product or technology. I was one of the last to buy a CD player. In fact, I bought a CD before I bought a CD player. I spotted this particular CD in a store, and I thought I should snap it up, lest it become "nla"—no longer available. It was a historic reissue. And I knew I'd have a CD player sooner or later.

The disc, by the way, was a collection of duets sung by Elisabeth Schwarzkopf and Irmgard Seefried. As you might guess, you can go to the Internet right now and download it in about two seconds.

I was pretty much the last person to switch to a metal driver, too, and to other metal "woods." I thought they were cheating. So did Jack Nicklaus. But eventually he switched, and I did too. If Nicklaus was relenting, everyone had to. Would I have been late to switch from hickory shafts as well? I hope not, but I fear so.

Few things are easier or more pleasurable than buying books over the Internet. Click, click, click—bingo. Couple of months ago, I learned about memoirs written by Paul Gore-Booth, a British diplomat, in 1974. The book has long been out of print. But thanks to AbeBooks.com—one of the greatest things since the wheel—I had it in about a week.

Equally easy and pleasurable is the buying of CDs. Or the downloading of music that would be on CDs, if we needed CDs (or audiocassettes, or LPs). But to hell with buying: What about music that's *free*? Several weeks ago, I wrote a piece on the Russian composer Rodion Shchedrin. I asked his "people" to send me an assortment of CDs. These recordings did not reach me in time. But no problem: I found pretty much all the music I desired via YouTube—an invention so great, it dusts AbeBooks, and almost the wheel.

The Internet is great when you know what you want. But I must say I like shops—liked shops—for browsing. I'm told you can browse on the Internet, and I'm sure it's true. But I haven't quite learned how to do it. I do know this: You can click on a link to sample a CD before buying it. That's the modern equivalent of those listening booths. (No scratching.)

Earlier, I mentioned the neighborhood I live in: It's the lower Upper West Side of Manhattan, to use a term I believe I coined. Recently, we lost the gigantic Barnes & Noble that sat on the corner of 66th and Broadway. Some of my neighbors think it's the end of civilization. Of course, they thought it was the end of civilization when Barnes & Noble came to these parts in the 1980s. *Ewww, a chain!* It was threatening the beloved local establishment Shakespeare & Co.—an establishment not so beloved that the locals kept it in business.

A few years ago, we lost our gigantic Tower Records, which sat across Broadway from the recently defunct Barnes & Noble. These two stores constituted a browser's paradise. You could flit across the street, gorging yourself on books and music. People would spill out of a concert or opera at Lincoln Center, and go to Tower to buy a recording of music they had just heard. You met, or at least noticed, some interesting types in these stores. Now you bowl alone, so to speak: tapping and clicking at your computer.

And the Internet is not necessarily the Speed King. Ordering by computer is fast, of course. But you know how you can get your book or CD faster? By popping into the store and walking out with the thing. Say you need a gift, to take to your dinner hosts. If the Internet is your only option, you have to order well ahead.

Look, I'm not a nostalgist. Let me share with you an e-mail I received from my mother, about an hour ago. (She has no idea I'm writing about Borders, and I quote her without permission, of course.) She lives in the woods outside of Ann Arbor. She writes, "Quite annoyed at people mourning the demise of badly managed Borders." Mother is blunt. Once, she was asked why she didn't want to go to a particular restaurant, much praised. She said, "The food is bad, the carpet is dirty, and the waitresses are surly." Anyway, in her e-mail, she continues, "Our public libraries are *magnificent*. Even my hokey district one has latte, etc., and will find any book you want in a day or two."

No, I'm not a nostalgist. But neither am I a "Couéist," as Bill Buckley liked to say: someone who believes that things are getting better every day. Some things do, some things don't. There are young people—not all that young anymore, come to think of it—who have never held a newspaper or a magazine in their hands. They have read online. Pretty soon, there will be young people, and not-so-young people, who have never held a book: They have Kindled.

I think this new age for media is a bonanza, a multifaceted gift to mankind. But you'll understand, I bet, if I offer one cheer for bricks and mortar, and quirky staffs, and popping in and out. You'll understand, too, if I shed a tear—half a tear—for the dear old Borders Book Shop.

—August 15, 2011

Branded by Google

The problem of stigmas in our Internet age

In September, the *Washington Post* received an unusual request: Would it remove a music review from the Internet? The request came from Dejan Lazić, a Croatian-born pianist. Not hearing from the *Post*, he sent another request at the end of October, this time mentioning the "right to be forgotten." This is a concept, somewhat vague, that has taken hold in the European Union, where he lives. It has to do with information, misinformation, or opinions about oneself on the Internet. Does a person have to live with these things forever? What if they stigmatize him? Do we have any say at all over our "Google footprint"?

In 2010, Lazić received a mixed review from the *Post*'s music critic, Anne Midgette (a friend of mine, a lovely woman, and a superb critic). She liked some things, she didn't like some things—that's life in the big city. The pianist's point to the newspaper was that this review had dogged him for four years. The review was marring his "Google results" (i.e., what comes up when you Google his name). This was unfair.

The *Post* essentially laughed off his request, which one can well understand. Who will next want to expunge unflattering articles from the Internet? Nixon? Free speech, yay. Censorship, boo. And yet—the issue is not entirely black and white.

About ten years ago, I received a call from a friend of mine who works in the music business. She was the publicist for a violinist to whom I had given a sharply negative review. Somehow, this review was featured prominently on Amazon.com, meaning that when you entered the violinist's name, you saw my review. I was horrified. I had reviewed the violinist in a live recital, and he had had a terrible night. But he did not deserve to have that review, and that night, hung around his neck forever. It might have been different if I had reviewed a recording. It *would* have been different. But everyone has a lousy outing, now and then.

My publicist friend told me that the violinist in question was upset at the spoiling of his Amazon results. They were key to his career—his CD sales, his livelihood in general. Would I mind trying to remedy the problem? I was happy to do what I could. I meant to review one recital, not brand the guy forever.

Until the Internet, all music criticism was forgotten, instantly. There was a saying in the newspaper business: "It's fish wrap by Friday." (Alternatively, you lined your birdcage with it.) Only a few lines of music criticism have endured across the years. I will give you the two that spring to mind. Irving Kolodin put down the violin concerto by Erich Wolfgang Korngold as "more corn than gold." And James Huneker found Emma Eames's singing of Aida cold: "There was skating on the Nile last night."

Probably the most famous music review in American history was written by Paul Hume, one of Anne Midgette's predecessors at the *Washington Post*. In 1950, he reviewed a soprano named Margaret Truman—daughter of the president. He said, "Miss Truman is a unique American phenomenon with a pleasant voice of little size and fair quality. She is extremely attractive on stage." And yet the woman did not sing very well, as Hume made politely clear.

The soprano's father did not take the review very well. He sent the critic a letter, saying, "It seems to me that you are a frustrated old man who wishes he could have been successful." (Hume was 34, by the way.) Truman added, "Some day I hope to meet you. When that happens you'll need a new nose, a lot of beefsteak for black eyes, and perhaps a supporter below!" (I don't think the president meant the exclamation point in a friendly way.)

In the old days, if someone wrote something negative about you, that negative thing might have stung for a bit, but, again, it soon wrapped fish or lined birdcages. Or it was buried in libraries on something called "microfiche." These days, that thing can be called up, by everyone in the world, with a few flicks of the fingers. "Let's see, what is there to know about Joe Blow? Oh, he molests chickens?" So said an enemy of his, in 1997. Google and the Internet are wondrous, and they are also fearsome.

Early in the War on Terror, we had a debate in America about a national ID card. Had the time at last come for such a document? Conservatives like me had always opposed a national ID card, on the grounds that it was un-American, socialist, and creepy. It had a whiff of "Your papers, please" about it. But given the flow of modern life—with credit cards and the constant use of one's Social Security number and so on—I was softening on the subject. Would a national ID card really be so bad and Orwellian?

I raised the issue with a prominent libertarian. He was softening too. He said, "Do you know what the biggest threat to my privacy is?" I said, "What?" He said, "Google." I saw what he meant, and I see it even more now.

How Wikipedia entries get written, I'm not sure—but they get written. Someone or someones have written an entry about me. At conferences and before speeches, I have been introduced by people who recite that entry word for word. They must assume it is accurate. At one point, it had my birthplace wrong. I asked an Internet-savvy friend of mine to change it. (Everyone under 75 is more Internet-savvy than I am, I think.) I'm not sure how the Wikipedia entry reads today. I am somewhat nervous about checking.

But I have just Googled myself (sounds painful, I know). On the first page of my "results" is a scurrilous attack on me published at a left-wing website in 2010. This is unpleasant. It is also modern and normal. We are all supposed to live with it, unless we live in the EU and want to appeal to some court, I suppose. Americans are possibly the most litigious people on earth. I'm surprised we don't have a Google court already.

And, listen, no one has a right to complain around Rick Santorum, the Pennsylvania politician. Years ago, an activist objected to his views on homosexuality and same-sex marriage. He staged a contest to give the name "Santorum" a definition. The chosen entry is beyond vile. The activist and his supporters waged a campaign to spread their term and wreck Santorum's Google results. They triumphed completely. They were aided by powerful celebrities such as Jon Stewart, the TV host. The activist said he would cease and desist if Santorum gave $5 million to a gay-marriage group. Santorum asked Google to intervene for him, or for decency, and the company refused.

There is an old spiritual: "Scandalize My Name." I'm not sure anyone has had his name more scandalized than Rick Santorum has. In describing what happened to him, I reach for "the strongest of all epithets," as Norman Podhoretz says: evil. Santorum has borne this with more grace than most of us would.

When I was a kid, there was a slogan, a bumper sticker: "Herpes is forever." It was a play on "Love is forever," I think, and was a warning. Is an item on the Internet—whether it's benign or malignant, true or false—forever? "There are no second acts in American lives," said one of our writers. Yet there have always been second acts, and third acts, and fourth acts . . . Does the Internet make it harder for people, if they have experienced notoriety, to move on? I have used one of the most ubiquitous of modern phrases: "move on." Now I'll go Biblical on you: Does the Internet make it harder to put off the old man and put on the new? Sure.

Here is one more phrase, courtesy of Dejan Lazić, the aggrieved pianist: "A review can stick out there in cyberspace like a wart on one's chin."

Norman Podhoretz is not only a great writer, he is also a great editor. And he says that a writer, in an opinion piece, has to "pull the trigger." The writer has to declare his position, soon or late. I will pull the trigger: I would not tamper with the Internet, except in the most extreme circumstances. I would err on the side of letting it be, and gritting one's teeth. For one thing, a slippery slope beckons: Where would the removal of items end? I'm afraid the pianist and everyone else will just have to suck it up. The Soviets airbrushed, we don't. And yet, today's censors or would-be censors have a point. A very good one.

—December 8, 2014

'A PERPETUAL HISSING'

Notes on an unfavorite practice

A few nights ago, I had an interesting hissing experience. I was in a movie theater, and a preview for *W.* came on—this is the film about President Bush by Oliver Stone, the leftist director. The hissing was very strange: sort of tentative, unsure. It seemed to me that my neighbors were confused. They wanted to hiss the subject of the film, Bush, because they hate him. But they didn't want to hiss the film itself—which they were sure to like. They were kind of caught. So what came out of them was a half hissing, or trial hissing: *Should we hiss or not, gang?* Amusing, actually.

But there is nothing amusing about hissing in general, as far as I'm concerned. It is one of my least favorite practices, and it may well be one of yours. I have written on this subject in my column for *National Review Online* from time to time. Once I wrote, "I grew up with the sound of the Left hissing." That was a bit of an exaggeration, but not much of one. In my hometown of Ann Arbor, Mich.—a small citadel of the Left—hissing was de rigueur. They hissed at what they didn't like, and what they didn't like was usually conservative, or politically incorrect, or otherwise non-conforming. They especially hissed in movie theaters—not the ones out in the malls, but the ones on campus. (The University of Michigan.)

When I wrote specifically about Ann Arbor and hissing, I received an e-mail from Gilbert, Ariz. The man said, "I have heard hissing *only* in Ann Arbor. And it stands to reason that creepy ideological people should adopt this odious reptilian practice." He added that there was no hissing in Gilbert.

But there is definitely hissing beyond Ann Arbor! For example, it is common on Manhattan's Upper West Side, where I live, and where I saw the preview for *W.* Hissing, wherever it takes place, is always, or almost always, hateful. It is sinister, menacing, sneaky, insidious. (Note how those words sound like hissing itself.) It is sort of anonymous, hiding itself, rather than being out in the open. I like what another reader—not from Gilbert—wrote me: "Hissing is underhanded, and it expresses disapproval without accountability. People can hiss with their lips and jaws in a neutral position—and they can drown out that which is disapproved while obscuring the source."

When people hiss as a group, the specter of the mob is raised: bullying, united, dangerous. Group hissing is an expression of groupthink. Booing, certainly by individuals, is far better, I believe: It is more forthright. But best, of course, is neither booing nor hissing. If you can't stand what is being presented, you can leave (vote with your feet).

Hissing is almost surely as old as man—who may well have gotten it from snakes. There is plenty of hissing in the Hebrew Bible, for example in Jeremiah: where people have been caused to "make their land desolate, and a perpetual hissing." There is plenty of hissing in Shakespeare, too, where both snakes and people hiss—at speakers, at ideas, and so on. Caliban says, "Sometime am I all wound with adders who with cloven tongues do hiss me into madness." I know the feeling. And the hissing in Milton's *Paradise Lost* is horrible to ear, mind, and heart. Recall just one instance: when we hear "from innumerable tongues a dismal universal hiss, the sound of public scorn."

Now and then, hissing can be benign—as in vaudeville, when you hiss the villain, who has entered twirling his mustache. But how often do you watch vaudeville? In movie houses, my neighbors hiss anything and everything, starting with the ads for Coke. It's not just that they don't like ads in theaters, which is understandable; it's that they don't like all that Coke represents (or so I would wager). And, of course, they hiss anything they consider objectionable in the main feature itself. A man from Madison, Wis.—another small citadel of the Left—wrote me to say that he once tried rebuking his hissing neighbors. "Do you realize the actors can't hear you?" he said. "Or are you just advertising your virtue? Now that we know you're virtuous, can the rest of us enjoy the movie?"

One time, on the Upper West Side, there was no hissing—like the dog not barking. And it was so remarkable, I wrote about it in my *NRO* column, on June 24, 2002. An ad for the Marines came on before a movie. My stomach tightened: *Uh-oh*. And no one hissed. There was not so much as the beginning of an ess. I wrote that this showed something different about the culture, for surely they would have hissed pre-9/11. The non-hissing took place more than six years ago, of course. What would the Marines bring today?

I myself have been hissed a number of times—and not just when speaking about politics. I was hissed at the Salzburg Festival once! What happened was this: I was conducting a public interview of a famous singer, and I mentioned what had happened to song recitals: Everyone had to have a "theme" now, rather than a mixed program. "You know, you have songs to texts of Rilke, or songs about water, or songs by left-handed Hispanics." Most people laughed or chuckled—including the interviewee—but one woman (I think it was a woman, somehow) hissed. I have never forgotten that hiss: It cut through the general appreciation and good feeling like a knife.

It should give some comfort to know that even the best have been hissed. Do you know that Solzhenitsyn was hissed, when he gave his historic commencement address at Harvard? If you can hiss Solzhenitsyn—after his years in the Gulag, after what he struggled to bring to the world—you can hiss anybody. Of course, he faced a lot worse.

According to my e-mailers, Harvard—or more specifically, its law school—is, or was, a hotbed of hissing. (A snake's nest of hissing?) The *New York Times* has noted this, too. Last year, the paper published an article about Barack Obama at Harvard. And the article mentioned the ideological ardency of students, who would "boo and hiss one another in class." (Well, at least there was booing.)

A reader of mine recalled being at the law school in the mid-1980s: "one of a handful of conservatives speaking up against the party line in class." He was amazed to find that hissing was "a common tool used to drown out" disapproved opinion. "Things became so bad in our classes that the professors hosted a discussion of hissing, and, to their credit, discouraged the practice. It didn't help." But our reader had a nice story to share:

> During my first year of law school, Ronald Reagan was campaigning for his second term in the White House. He showed up in Boston for what was billed as his final campaign appearance (in his own behalf). So my buddies and I decided to skip out of contracts

class and attend. We did, and heard the great man at his best.

The next day in class, our (very liberal) professor announced that he had handed out an important assignment the day before, but that several students had been absent. He said there was a rumor that they had been in Boston attending a Reagan rally (much hissing). He then declared that if those students wanted a copy of the assignment, they would have to walk down to the front of the room (an auditorium-style lecture hall) and take one from his desk. He apparently thought we'd be too shamed to announce ourselves. We, of course, were proud of our views, and we all marched forward to get the assignment as our classmates hissed with great energy.

Not exactly heroic, but a great memory.

Well, if not exactly heroic—not exactly unheroic, either. Another reader wrote of her time as an undergrad at Stanford. She attended a Nader speech—and, before the great man came on, a local Green-party candidate warmed up the crowd. He took an informal poll of the audience's party affiliations: About 95 percent identified themselves as Democrats; most of the rest said they were Green or unaffiliated. And "approximately ten of us identified ourselves as Republicans and were soundly hissed." Said this reader, "I often think that the experience of sitting (nearly) alone, surrounded by leftists and angry, meaningless noise, beautifully represents my undergraduate experience."

Would you care for something lighter? I have an instance of what you might call preemptive hissing. A Yale alum wrote about his experience in a production of *Iolanthe.* (Gilbert & Sullivan—not Tchaikovsky's *Iolanta.*) A character, Lord Mountararat, says, "This comes of women interfering in politics." Our Yalie wrote, "We knew that the line would offend the audience—never mind that the line is ironic. The audience would simply have heard a sexist 19th-century white male. Our solution? As soon as Mountararat said the line, the women's chorus onstage hissed him. That got a big laugh—at least partly, I think, because the chorus looked and sounded exactly like the types we were worried about."

Finally, a different reader said, "At summer camp back in the '60s, the director prohibited hissing on the ground that the Nazis did that. (The camp was predominantly Jewish.) Have you ever heard anything like that?" I have not, no—but it's the kind of thing you like to think is true.

I must say, in all my years, I have never heard a conservative or conservatives hiss. Then again, I have probably hung around in the wrong places. And I was sort of touched by a note received from yet another reader not long ago—when I again addressed this subject in my column: "Every time you write about hissing, it makes me feel bad. We got to go see President Bush speak in Dallas, and when he would mention some awful Democrat, I would hiss. Now when you write about how distasteful it is, I wish I hadn't."

A few days from now, I will participate in a debate at Yale. Will there be hissing? Perhaps. But I'm done with the topic of the Left and hissing for now. Next up: the Left and Alger Hiss (a joke that, no doubt, deserves a hiss).

—November 17, 2008

Down with Eleven

On the overamplification of American life

It's not our biggest problem, or even in the top ten, or top 100. But it's still a problem, I think: the overamplification of American life. I have long held this view, but have been spurred to write about it by recent events.

I went to the New York Philharmonic to review a performance of *Sweeney Todd*, the Sondheim musical. (Every season or so, the Philharmonic will stage a musical, for variety's sake, I suppose, and maybe for the box office, too.) The cast was a mixture of classical and Broadway performers. In the title role was Bryn Terfel, the great Welsh bass-baritone. It was a shock to hear him sing into a microphone. The sound was unnatural—Terfel-like, but not quite Terfel. There is no hall anywhere that he can't fill, naturally. Was it really necessary to mike him? To gild that lily?

Soon, the entire company came in, and the hall shook, so great was the amplification. The crowd cheered, excited. It was a little vulgar.

But as amplification goes, the Philharmonic's *Sweeney* was tasteful. Certainly as compared with the next night—when I found myself in Minneapolis, at the Dakota Jazz Club & Restaurant. My friends and I enjoyed a nice dinner, then settled back for the show. Onstage were the musicians of Viva Brazil. They were good, and so was the music they played and sang. But the volume was absurd—painful, assaultive, and anti-musical. We had to leave, and quickly.

Why would someone have done that to music, and how could others have sat there? Why didn't it seem wrong to audience, management, and, maybe most important, the musicians themselves? They're musicians, right?

Complaining about the sound of music—not in the Julie Andrews sense—is a classic expression of fogeyism. But I can plead this: If I'm a fogey, I have always been. When I was in high school, a musician friend of mine asked me to go with him to hear Pat Metheny, a jazz guitarist. My friend said he was first-rate. That night, he may well have been—but the amplification was so great, I could hardly hear him. I could not really listen to the music. It was a question of enduring the sonic assault (which I could not do for long).

Much later, I went to a concert by Lyle Lovett. He has written and sings so many excellent songs. Why would he want to smother them in overamplification? Why would he want to drown them, and render them offensive? He did.

There is a place for loud in music, of course—a big and wonderful place. Richard Strauss was notorious for writing orchestrations so heavy, they drowned out the singers in his operas. The story is told that he attended a rehearsal of his *Elektra*, in which Ernestine Schumann-Heink had a part. He calls out to the conductor, "Louder, louder, I can still hear the Heink!"

Years ago, I interviewed Beverly Sills, and the subject of Birgit Nilsson came up. Sills was talking about her Elektra or Salome—one of those Strauss roles, I forget which. She said, "You wouldn't have believed the sheer volume of that voice. It was so *loud*. It simply blew your ears back." I said, "But her Salome [or Elektra]—was it musical?" Sills made a face: "It was cold." She quickly brightened again: "But that sound! It was so *loud*!"

The loudest music I ever heard in a concert hall or opera house—unamplified—was in Salzburg's Grosses Festspielhaus. The opera was *Das Rheingold*, the first installment in Wagner's *Ring*. The orchestra in the pit was the Berlin Philharmonic. When the giants (Fasolt and Fafner) came in, the ground shook, thrillingly. And when Wotan and Loge descended into Nibelheim, I thought the house would break apart. It was beyond thrilling—and entirely musical. Of course, these were just moments, not an entire evening.

There were no microphones on that night, as far as I know, but, more and more, microphones are creeping into the opera house. After one performance, a friend of mine said to a singer friend of his, "You sounded almost miked!" The singer admitted she had been. This is not merely a matter of "cheating"—a matter of using artificial means to do what your technique fails to do. Miking distorts, warps, or at least alters sound.

For a long time, Broadway musicals have been rock concerts—amplified to that extent. Singers prance around wearing headsets, with sticks at the side of their mouths. Even the plays are routinely and heavily miked. People seem to have forgotten how to speak—on Broadway and off.

Earlier this season, I was in a grand old church on Manhattan's Upper East Side, to review a choral concert. A priest came out to give introductory remarks. His microphone went dead. He stood there, silent, until another one was brought to him. I don't think it occurred to him to continue speaking, without a microphone. It's not done now. But for years, priests and others spoke in this church, without benefit of a microphone. Did they make themselves heard? I bet they did.

Above, I mentioned rock concerts, and those are another kettle of fish: Extreme amplification is part of the phenomenon. An aspect of the music. This is certainly true of heavy metal. There is a loved moment in *This Is Spinal Tap*, the 1984 satirical documentary, or "mockumentary," about the rock life. A guitarist explains that the knobs on his amplifier go up to eleven, rather than the standard ten. Why is eleven better than ten? Because it's "one louder."

At the Dakota club, with Viva Brazil on the stage, there was hardly any need for amplification at all. The space is not that big. But they had enough amplification for Yankee Stadium, and beyond. Everything was out of whack. The frustrating thing was that not everyone knew it. Or did they? One boy, who had come with his parents, had his fingers in his ears. That was the only visible sign of dissent. Everyone else . . . well, it was hard to read their feelings. Were they only pretending to think that everything was okay? Or did they really think it was?

Music is not a democracy, but I would have been interested to see a vote—by secret ballot. If the room could have voted on whether to turn down the volume, by a lot, what would the results have been?

William F. Buckley Jr.'s most famous essay was written in 1960 and has been anthologized many times. Its title: "Why Don't We Complain?" The author begins by describing a train trip of considerable discomfort. It is winter, yet the temperature inside the train is boiling. Everyone is sweating and miserable. Yet no one says anything to the conductor as he passes through. Writes Buckley,

> When the temperature outdoors is below freezing, it takes a positive act of will on somebody's part to set the temperature indoors at 85. Somewhere a valve was turned too far, a furnace overstoked, a thermostat maladjusted: something that could easily be remedied by turning off the heat and allowing the great outdoors to come indoors. All this is so obvious. What is not obvious is what has happened to the American people.

I had much these thoughts while sitting in the Dakota. For one thing, a "valve" was obviously "turned too far," a musical thermostat was "maladjusted." Later in his essay, Buckley talks of sitting in a movie, which is badly out of focus. Again, the people just take it. Toward the end of the essay, Buckley writes,

> I think the observable reluctance of the majority of Americans to

> assert themselves in minor matters is related to our increased sense of helplessness in an age of technology and centralized political and economic power. For generations, Americans who were too hot, or too cold, got up and did something about it. . . . With the technification of life goes our direct responsibility for our material environment, and we are conditioned to adopt a position of helplessness.

It could be that most people don't mind the amplification at ballgames, and at wedding receptions, and in restaurants, or elsewhere. Incidentally, that elsewhere includes movie theaters. The flicks are no longer out of focus. But have you noticed the volume? And that the previews are much louder than the movies? A friend of mine—it was Rich Lowry, *National Review*'s editor—recently said, "The previews are positively punishing. You can hear them through the soles of your feet." Maybe most people don't mind what I consider "overamplification." Perhaps they like it. But are we sure we would know for sure? That boy in the Dakota, with his fingers in his ears, has not yet learned to conform.

They say the unexamined life is not worth living; I say the overamplified life is nuts. Buckley asked, "Why don't we complain?" I am, Bill, in your magazine, and maybe someone will hear, over the awful din.

—April 7, 2014

Safe-Zone Violation!

Why sportswriters, and others, should be penalized

It's an old story, but one that deserves retelling now and then: I'm talking about the injection of politics—partisan politics—into sports columns. And into other areas where partisan politics have no place. More and more, there are no safe zones.

Take a recent column in the *New York Post*. (What would Henny Youngman say?) The writer, a sports guy, was talking about a local PGA tournament. He was complaining that Tiger Woods was not sufficiently open to the media. And he wrote, "It's not like we're trying to pull President Obama aside for a couple of questions while he's trying to save our country from itself."

Now, was that really necessary? Yes, it may have been, psychologically—for the columnist.

The spoiling of sports pages by politics is a flaming red sore point among conservatives of my acquaintance. (The liberals have less cause for soreness.) You'll often hear, "I always loved reading So-and-so"—Bill Simmons of ESPN.com, for example. "But finally I had to stop because he was constantly insulting my political views with little asides. Why do they have to do that? Why do they have to alienate half their audience, or at least some part of it?"

I could give you a thousand examples of safe-zone violations in sportswriting. So as to leave room for other topics in this issue of *National Review*, I will provide a relative few. I promise that they are more representative than aberrational.

A columnist for the *Boston Globe* was writing about hockey, and he said, "Bigger nets will likely bring, at most, a teeny-weeny uptick in scoring. Focusing on bigger nets, in many ways, is hockey's version of cutting taxes—eye-catching, but ineffective." You see, he knows about economics. And has college football's Bowl Championship Series ever reminded you of George W. Bush and Dick Cheney? No? You're weird.

In 2007, the *Washington Post*'s John Feinstein wrote, "The BCS Presidents are a lot like the current President of the United States. They think that if they keep repeating their lies and half-truths and remind people who they are enough times, people will buy into what they're selling. According to one poll, only 21 percent of the American people are buying what President Bush is selling, but it sure took a long time and lot of deaths to get there." The next year, Mike Celizic of NBCSports.com wrote, "Is Dick Cheney a member of the BCS? That's got to be the explanation for the latest load of nonsense to come out of the outfit that runs the system by which college football does not choose a legitimate champion."

Sarah Palin comes in for a lot of abuse, as you might expect—put-downs of her are a dime a dozen. But it's Cheney who seems most irresistible. This is particularly true at *Sports Illustrated*'s website. Perusing it, you may suppose that anti-Cheney remarks are required by *SI*. These remarks, these little jabs and asides, amount to a big, collective tic.

Here is a passage on a San Antonio Spur: "[He] remains as unpopular among non-Spurs as Dick Cheney is among Democrats, Independents, Americans with no political affiliation, a growing number of Republicans, the great majority of the world population as well as that poor guy he filled with buckshot." Here is a warning at the beginning of a column about David Beckham, the soccer star: "If you care about 'Goldenballs' about as much as Dick Cheney cares about Global Warming, feel free to click through somewhere else." Here is a columnist confessing error: "What could I possibly have been thinking when I picked the Knicks to finish sixth in the East? . . . Dick Cheney was more accurate in his prediction that we would be greeted as liberators."

Here is a line from a column on baseball: "The Red Sox even hired James, which is like Dick Cheney hiring a French chef." Here is a line from another column on baseball: "Watching Bonds talk to reporters is like watching Dick Cheney when he's asked to discuss his daughter's sexual preference."

Etc., etc. There are *many* more where those came from, from innocuous to rotten. These anti-Cheney blurts and smirks seem to be an open codeword, saying, "I'm cool, I'm with-it, I'm in the club." Sportswriting is as susceptible to groupthink as other fields.

As I said at the outset, this is not a new story: politics-in-sportswriting. Christopher Caldwell, who has just written a book about the Islamicization of Europe, once wrote a piece about the politicization of *SI*: "Sports Eliminated" (!). That was for the inaugural issue of *The Weekly Standard*, in September 1995. James Taranto, of OpinionJournal.com, has a series called "Wannabe Pundits," which includes political forays by sportswriters—I have quoted an example or two of his above. And I myself have banged this drum for a while.

The problem is worse than ever, I believe, and I also believe that we have a broader national problem: with political talk leaking over into almost everything. The "cable culture" is all around us, and safe zones—i.e., spheres free of partisan politics—are diminishing.

Why do sportswriters do it? Why do they bust out political? I have a theory, and it's an easy theory—maybe a too-easy one: Sports guys, some of them, may feel a touch embarrassed about being sportswriters. So they have to prove they're just as serious—just as liberal, virtuous, and "engaged" with the world—as their colleagues on the news and editorial desks. You can almost hear them saying, "I may cover the NFL, but hey! I hate Bush as much as you do, I swear."

It could be, too, that they simply have a platform and are exploiting it: "As long as I have your attention on Peyton Manning, let me tell you what I think of Bush."

Some sports guys are so political, they have simply crossed over. I mean, they have made honest men of themselves by being forthrightly political guys. Keith Olbermann of MSNBC is the most prominent such example. Other sports guys are just a blur: half sportswriter, half political pundit. The other week, Frank Fitzpatrick of the *Philadelphia Inquirer* devoted his column to mocking protests over health care. The sports fig leaf, I suppose, was that health-care policy was the latest "blood sport," reminiscent of "an Eagles-Jets game."

It's not only the sports sections of newspapers that are infected by politics—other ostensibly non-political sections may be unsafe zones. A correspondent of mine told me, "I stopped reading the *New York Times* in the '80s, when the cooking columns started saying things like, 'Just as Reagan should have known it was time to [do X], you must carefully monitor the exact time to [do Y].'" I have even heard complaints about chess columns.

And would you like to hear about another unsafe zone? Let's go on a city tour. Recently, a newlywed couple I know traveled to New York to spend a few special days. They took an open-air bus tour, and the guide peppered his commentary with anti-Republican jibes. For example, as the bus cruised up Sixth Avenue, he pointed out Fox News, calling it "the voice of evil." That certainly says to conservative-leaning couples, "Happy honeymoon!"

Of course, everyone has a right to an opinion, but people often confuse what you have a right to do with what's right to do. (I heard Bill Bennett say that, long ago.) I love opinions, heaven knows, including political opinions: but they have their place.

Last winter, wearing a music critic's hat, I covered a chamber concert in New York's Weill Recital Hall. A composer mounted the stage to give a talk about a piece of his, about to be played. Any talking at a concert is bad enough: but our guy duly inveighed against Bush and hailed the new president, Obama. I mentioned this, not in a concert review—which would have been perfectly within bounds, as the composer had injected politics into the evening—but on a political blog.

Our guy wrote me a profane e-mail saying (in essence), "Hey, no fair! You're supposed to be a music critic. Why don't you do your job?" I replied that the same question could be asked of him. To his credit, he took the point, and most graciously.

There are people who like walls of separation and those who don't. I like my sports, music, food, etc., politics-free. Others think that this is some sort of moral or civic negligence, or simply naivety. Laura Ingraham wrote a book about entertainers and politics called *Shut Up & Sing*. When I look at such publications as *Sports Illustrated*, I think of a variation: "Shut up and write about sports!"

Care for a final nugget? A football columnist at the *Philadelphia Daily News* wrote, "The [Eagles'] offensive numbers are poor, but if you really want a scary, my-daughter-married-a-Republican moment, take out the Detroit game and look at them again." I'm sure that Republican readers in Philly enjoyed that fleck of mud in their morning cereal.

As I keep saying, I could provide examples of these violations and intrusions till the cows come home. When I brought up the subject recently at *National Review Online*, I got an e-mail from a sportswriter at a major daily. He said, "Dear Sir: What the f*** [no asterisks] are you talking about? Love, The sportswriting community." Take an honest look at sportswriting in America today and you'll see. Love, Me.

—October 5, 2009

The Hills Are Alive

Augusta, for real

Augusta, Ga.

I would be embarrassed to admit how big a part the Masters has played in my life: in my mental life, and, to a degree, my writing life. I'm talking, of course, about the tournament held every April at the Augusta National Golf Club.

Over the years, on practice ranges far and wide, I have "played" holes at Augusta National. This relieves the tedium of practice. I take the clubs I believe will be necessary on each hole. For example, I'll take a 6-iron on 16 tee—aiming for the traditional Sunday pin position. And, at night, I compete in the Masters, as I'm drifting off to sleep. Often, I'm head to head with Tiger. Strangely, he loses.

I am not alone in this, by the way—this Masters fantasizing. In fact, it is a pretty common condition. I can introduce you to many others who suffer from it, or rather, enjoy it.

Like them, I have watched the Masters on television from an early age. I remember the tournaments more than I do Christmases, and probably as much as I do presidential elections. Seve slashing his way around the course. Mize chipping in on Norman. Lyle coming out of the bunker. Floyd hitting it into the water on 11. And, above all, Nicklaus winning the tournament in 1986, at the age of 46. (He was the oldest Masters champion ever.) I will never forget watching the final round unfold, as I sat in my dorm room. That was an afternoon of utter amazement and jubilation.

The next Sunday, in the same room, on the same television, I watched Horowitz return to Russia, for the first time in over 60 years. I was extremely nervous as he played—as I had been when Nicklaus played. But, like Jack, he triumphed. A couple weekends later, Willie Shoemaker was the winning jockey in the Kentucky Derby, at 54. That was a thrilling, odds-defying spring.

I have written about the Masters a lot—a whole lot: about its history, its politics, its aura. You could even speak of its spirituality. You can write drippily about the Masters, and I hope I have not done that. But it's hard not to drip at least a little. There are things about the Masters that irritate me, because there are things about virtually every institution that are irritating. For example, the Augusta brass insist that television commentators refer to the fans, not as fans, but as "patrons." Yeah, well, whatever. But we can live with some silliness and quirks.

From a lifetime of immersion, I feel like I know every blade of grass at Augusta National. In my mind, I have practically lived in the Eisenhower Cabin. And yet I have never been there—never been to Augusta. I'm like Ruth Benedict (if I may), who wrote her book about Japan, *The Chrysanthemum and the Sword*, without ever visiting there. (This was a wartime assignment.) Don't let anyone fool you: That's a very good book. Where Augusta is concerned, I even know what's supposed to surprise the first-time visitor: the hilliness of the course, for example. It's a lot hillier than you think.

I will soon find out for myself—because I'm going to Augusta National, to witness this year's Monday practice round. Will it spoil things for me, somehow? Will any harm come from setting foot on the course that has loomed so large in my imagination? Moreover, do I really *need* to go to Augusta National, given how much I know?

In any case, I am going. And I know that you can be surprised by things that you think you're already plenty familiar with. I was shocked by the pyramids—shocked by their size, their gargantuan, heaven-reaching size, and their mystery.

I fly into Augusta's little airport, here in east-central Georgia. The building looks like an old mansion, with its pillars. Inside is a cardboard mockup of 13 green. Once outside, I sniff the air, which smells marvelous. Or maybe it's just that I've come from Manhattan. Also, a huge American flag billows in the wind. A friend and I take the Bobby Jones Expressway to our hotel, and wait for the next day.

Monday dawns inclement, but everyone is eager, and the weather will soon clear anyway. Along Washington Road, a gas-station marquee reads "WELCOME PATRONS." So everyone's obedient, huh? People seeking tickets line the road, up and down. One man holds a sign that reads, simply, "HELP!" Our hotel shuttle van will not be able to enter Augusta National down the fabled Magnolia Lane. We are dropped near a Publix grocery store—but that's all right.

Though this is first thing Monday morning—three days before the competition begins—the place is jammed. Security lines are very long. Oddly, we did not have this at the Buick Open in Grand Blanc, Mich. (my home-state PGA tournament). As you approach security, you see a sign listing prohibited items: cellphones and the like. The last item is "Knives/Weapons." Really? Augusta is not as conservative a place as people think.

The workers could not be more polite, saying, "Welcome to the Masters." "Enjoy the Masters." "Have a great day." They give you a tournament booklet, as decreed by Bobby Jones, the founder. Inside the booklet is an essay by him on how to watch the tournament: "Spectator Suggestions." It holds up, beautifully.

On first sight of the course, my heart kicks a little. I'm reminded of my first visit, in childhood, to Tiger Stadium. These days, the sight of Detroit will make you weep for other reasons. I walk past the clubhouse and see a chef in a tall, tall toque. Beyond the clubhouse is Ike's Cabin—you can tell by the presidential eagle. And near it is the Butler Cabin, where you put on the green jacket. (Well, maybe *you* don't, but a select group of others do.)

Gary Player is practicing from the bunker. He was the best bunker player in the world, before every other pro got wise. Now they're all bunker virtuosos. As he practices, Player actually skulls one—which is kind of refreshing to see. It comforts the masses when a pro hits a mere-mortal shot.

Out on the course, you encounter the "pine cathedrals" of legend. And the azaleas "blaze." (That's the word every golf writer uses, writing about Augusta National and its azaleas.) Is anything surprising? Yes, some things. For example, I hadn't realized that No. 10 bends to the left like that. And I see that it's a considerable challenge not to hit it into the water on 11: Everything slopes that way. But, I have to tell you: I have heard so much about the hills of Augusta that the course is actually a bit less hilly than I expected.

There is no gouging at Augusta: oh, no. The sandwiches still cost

$1.50, and they're still wrapped in the light-green cellophane. At Amen Corner, I have a meal of a pimento-cheese sandwich, potato chips, a Diet Coke, and a moon pie. Total: $4.50. Life has tossed me in some pretty fancy and expensive restaurants. I have never had a more satisfying meal.

From time to time, I have said about Salzburg, Austria—where I am a frequent visitor—"Every place you rest your eye is a treat. At every turn there is beauty." The same is true of Augusta National. But speaking of Salzburg, I now have to go there, to work at the Easter Festival. And I will not be able to watch a shot of this Masters tournament—not a shot of the competition. Instead, I'll have to do what I do in the month of August, while working at the summer festival. During this time, the PGA Championship takes place.

There is no telecast in Austria. The webcasting doesn't work either, for some reason. So what I do is: go to the appropriate website and refresh the leaderboard, constantly. It's kind of fun, actually.

Oh, you'll want to know: Did I see him? Did I see Tiger at Augusta? No. I've written about him almost as much as I have about Bill Clinton, or George W. Bush. And I've never laid eyes on him. But I expect to someday—expect to interview him, too. And I imagine that will be an enhancement. As this visit to Augusta National has been. It is a good place—worth dreaming about.

—May 9, 2009

LANGUAGE

MERCI BEAUCOUP, BARACK

On the matter of Americans and foreign languages

Barack Obama was engaged in one of his favorite pastimes: lecturing Americans on their inadequacies. He said, "Instead of worrying about whether immigrants can learn English—they'll learn English—*you* need to make sure your child can speak Spanish. You should be thinking about, how can your child become bilingual? We should have every child speaking more than one language." He went on, "It's embarrassing when Europeans come over here. They all speak English—they speak French, they speak German. And then we go over to Europe. And all we can say is, 'Merci beaucoup.'"

It's embarrassing, says Senator Obama. There is a certain type of American who is always embarrassed, especially in front of Europeans. We've all seen them. "Oh, we're so fat, we're so loud, we're so unsophisticated. We use ketchup, we don't know what to do with a bidet, we have the death penalty!" And "we don't learn foreign languages!" Most of these Americans are young and callow, and grow out of these attitudes. But many do not—and Mr. and Mrs. Obama seem like unreformed college students, in so many ways.

This issue of foreign languages is one of many clubs with which to beat Americans. According to the Gallup organization, a quarter of Americans can speak a language other than English well enough to hold a conversation. That doesn't seem so bad to me, all things considered. But be that as it may.

Americans have long been jittery about their relationship with foreign languages. It is part of their self-examination, which, in a sickly form, is an inferiority complex. Earlier this decade, the U.S. Senate was moved to declare a year (2005) the "Year of Foreign Language Study." There was a time, about 15 years before that, when people were saying that Americans would have to learn Japanese. That was when Michael Dukakis was running political ads with an ominous rising sun. And I remember a football game, shown on television one Saturday afternoon.

During halftime, each university got to brag about itself with a video. Notre Dame, I believe, showed one of its students—an ordinary white kid—speaking Japanese. He narrated the video, and the rest of us got subtitles.

Soon, Japan went kaput (sort of), and Americans focused their worries elsewhere.

Some of us study foreign languages for the same reason others collect butterflies or play tennis: It's fun. Moreover, there are practical benefits, such as being strengthened in your home language. I believe I have studied five languages, formally—and maybe the same number informally. I hope to do more. But I reject the idea that Americans are especially guilty on the foreign-language front. There are differences between us and the Europeans: For us, the study of foreign languages is mainly a matter of choice; for them, it is something else.

America is a great big continental nation, stretching from the Atlantic to the Pacific. On our northern border, there is another vast continental nation, and it's almost entirely English-speaking. On our southern border, there is a Spanish-speaking country, plus the Gulf of Mexico. And guess what? Along our (short) border with Quebec, there is a fair amount of bilingualism—English and French. Along our (longer) border with Mexico, there's a fair amount of bilingualism—English and Spanish.

Exactly what you would expect. Because this is how these things work. If Europeans know foreign languages, it's not necessarily out of intellectual virtue; it's because the languages come naturally. A Swiss person—to take an easy example—lives in a small country with four official languages. A Nebraskan lives in a big state in the middle of a gigantic nation, and is a long, long way from other languages. But we should remember, too, that all the world's languages come to the United States—because all the world's people do.

Back to Europe for a moment: Eric Hobsbawm, the celebrated hard-Left British historian, was once praised for knowing foreign languages. One of his sharpest critics, David Pryce-Jones, pointed out that "Hobsbawm has mastered only some of the main European languages, a feat shared by lots of restaurant waiters, never mind academics." Furthermore, sometimes language is imposed, against the will of the people.

Many Eastern Europeans won't breathe a word of Russian, though they know it (and despite the fact that Russian is a great world language).

Consider this, too: For better or worse—and I say better—English is the world's lingua franca. And that bears on Americans and foreign languages. We are born into a language that virtually the entire world speaks or seeks to speak. For many, many of the world's people, it is a sine qua non. (Pardon my Latin.) The incentive to learn English is great, the incentive to learn other languages, not so great.

Incidentally, are you familiar with the old problem in Paris? You speak to them in French, and they answer you in English (however badly). You speak to them in English, and you'll get a stream of offended French from them. Sometimes, being an American means not being able to win.

I could tell 500 stories about the primacy of English in the world, but will tell you only this—my favorite. One afternoon, I was part of a small group of journalists who met with Álvaro Uribe, the president of Colombia. This was at the Annual Meeting of the World Economic Forum in Davos (Switzerland, as it happens). Before our session began, it became clear to me that I was the only non–Spanish speaker in the room. Not only that, I was the only non–*native* Spanish speaker in the room. I moved to leave. But Uribe insisted I stay—presidential order. And he, his cabinet members, the Latin American journalists, and I talked for an hour in English. No one batted an eye or so much as groped for a word. Amazing.

By the way, another charge against Americans is that they don't know geography—that *we* don't know geography. A couple of months ago, Omar Sharif, the Egyptian-born actor, was on Arab television. Chances are, he didn't think any American could hear him—but, thanks to the Middle East Media Research Institute and its translations, we did. Sharif, who made a fortune off America, said,

> [America] is a large and rich country, with great possibilities and everything, but they don't understand what's going on in the rest of the world. They just don't get it. I lived in America for a long time. Only 10 percent of Americans have a passport. In other words, 90 percent have never left America. . . . You show them an un-

> marked map of Europe and ask them where France is, and they don't know. Ask them were Italy is—okay, Italy they know, because it looks like a shoe. They don't know anything. They are ignorant.

First, Italy looks more like a boot than a shoe. Second, the United States—those 50—is itself kind of a geography quiz. Third, would Sharif like to put the general geographical knowledge of the average Egyptian or Arab up against that of the average American? How about simple literacy?

Not long after hearing about this Sharif interview, I was with some Lebanese in Long Island, N.Y. One said he had heard that Americans knew nothing about geography, but found this wasn't true. Another said, "That's because you're in New York. If you were in the Midwest . . ."—and she said "Midwest" as though she was describing the farthest reaches of the Sahara. I remarked that I was from the Midwest, and so was my sister (her friend). She just smiled, weakly.

Incidentally, not 10 percent, but about a third of Americans hold a passport. And that reminds me of one of the most depressing encounters I ever had. It was with a young U.S. Foreign Service officer in a European country. He maintained that Republicans, in particular, were ignorant of the world, and liked it that way. He said that GOP congressmen bragged about not having a passport. I said I doubted it.

At another point in the conversation, I mentioned a second Foreign Service officer, who was hoping to be posted back to the United States. The reason? His two sons, about ten and eight, had never lived in America, and he wanted them to know their country. My guy—the Republicans-and-passports guy—snorted, "Yeah—introduce 'em to the joys of Burger King." I said, "Do you really think that's all there is to American culture?" He said, "Well, there's jazz." "Anything else?" I asked. He said he couldn't think of anything.

He then said that all American children should be required to live abroad—all of them. I said, "How about the children of other countries? Should they, too, be required to live abroad?" He looked annoyed.

We are all familiar with the self-hating American (although, in my experience, these people aren't really self-hating, but rather supremely self-loving—they are just embarrassed to be American). But it is depressing indeed when they represent the U.S. abroad. Stupid college kids may put a Canadian maple leaf on their backpack, but American diplomats should be more mature. What's more, I believe that Americans who denigrate their country are less respected by foreigners than they think they are.

In the vice-presidential debate of 1984, the first Bush said something that has always stayed with me. "I'll be honest with you," he said. "It's a joy to serve with a president who does not apologize for the United States of America" (Reagan). I knew just what he meant. Would Barack Obama be such a president? We are to maintain "a decent respect [for] the opinions of mankind." But a little self-confidence—justified self-confidence—is nice, too.

Of course, Americans have plenty to be ashamed of. Right off the bat, I think of political correctness, foul popular music, neglect of the elderly, and abortion on demand. But on foreign languages, I believe, we are not guilty—and that includes Senator Obama, who, by his own admission, speaks no foreign language at all. That would not impair his ability to be president. Other things would.

—August 18, 2008

Entitled

The tricky business of addressing or referring to an unsavory foreign leader

In his recent address at the U.N., President Obama referred to Ali Khamenei, the head ayatollah in Iran. Each time, he referred to him as "the Supreme Leader." He did not even say his name: just "Supreme Leader." Was that really necessary, for the president of the United States? Those who control Iran may refer to Khamenei as "Supreme Leader"—but do democratic leaders, such as Obama, have to follow suit?

Two months after he became president, in 2009, Obama sent Nowruz greetings to Iran. (Nowruz is the Persian new year.) His predecessor, George W. Bush, had sent such greetings too. But Bush made clear that he was sending them to the people. Obama sent them to "the people and leaders" of Iran. He also referred to the country—twice—as "the Islamic Republic of Iran," as the mullahs style the country. Iranian democrats, many of whom are in jail, don't see it that way.

John Bolton, a U.S. ambassador to the U.N. under Bush, puts it plainly: You call Iran "the Islamic Republic" when you want to "kiss their posterior" (i.e., the rulers' posterior). There may come a time for such smooching. Otherwise, a simple "Iran" will do.

Little stylistic touches, which may seem nothing to us in the Free World, can mean a lot to those in unfree places. President Reagan declared 1983 the "Year of the Bible," which is the kind of thing that causes snickers in the West. But it was no laughing matter in the Gulag. Somehow, Natan Sharansky—or Anatoly Shcharansky, as he was then—heard about it. He studied the Bible with a fellow prisoner, for as long as authorities allowed. The two zeks (prisoners) called their sessions "Reaganite readings."

In 1984, the inimitable William F. Buckley Jr. began a column, "I want to know one very simple thing: Why do non-totalitarian leaders embrace totalitarian leaders?" He did not mean "embrace" in a metaphorical sense. He wrote, "I am staring at a picture of two men smiling at each other, their arms about each other, their noses not two inches separated. Any closer, and they'd have skirted sodomy." The picture showed Felipe González, the prime minister of Spain, greeting the Cuban dictator, Fidel Castro, at Madrid's airport.

As a rule, dictators crave the legitimacy that democratic statesmen can confer. They crave the mere rubbing of shoulders. At the U.N. in 2002, PLO chairman Yasser Arafat wanted to be up close and personal with President Bush. Elliott Abrams captures the moment in his recent memoir, *Tested by Zion*: The secretary of state, Colin Powell, "served as defensive tackle, literally pushing Arafat back when he tried to get into a photo with Bush as the president moved down a General Assembly corridor." At the latest U.N. gathering, President Obama was eager to meet Iran's "president," Hassan Rouhani. The Iranian snubbed him. But he later consented to a phone call with the American.

Referring to Rouhani, I have put "president" in quotation marks, because "president" is one of those titles that non-democrats, or anti-democrats, like to claim for themselves. It puts them on equal footing with, say, the president of the United States. For decades, two stylistic touches rankled Cubans: We in free countries called Castro "President Castro" (a designation he formally relinquished several years ago), and we called him, as we still do, "Fidel." This first-naming suggests a certain warmth or admiration. (True, the first-naming may be more justifiable now, seeing that the older brother has elevated the younger, Raúl, to prominence.)

In Iran, they have had just two Supreme Leaders since the Islamist revolution in 1979. Before Khamenei was Khomeini. President Carter addressed a letter to him "Dear Ayatollah Khomeini"—a respectful, unfawning salutation.

Moving back to Latin America, the late Hugo Chávez was a "president"—president of Venezuela—but he was more accurately described as a "presidential dictator," or a "strongman." When they met in 2009, Obama was all warmth to him. He gave Chávez a soul-brother handshake and called him "mi amigo," his friend. Afterward, Chávez was complimentary, saying of Obama, "He is a very intelligent man, young, and he is black."

In 1984—the same year Bill Buckley wrote his above-quoted column—ten Democrats in Congress sent a somewhat infamous letter to the head of the Nicaraguan junta, Daniel Ortega. "Dear Comandante," it began. Republicans hooted at this salutation. Challenged on a television show, Stephen Solarz, one of the Democrats, threw up his hands, grinned a little, and said, "But that's his title!" The phrase "Dear Comandante" entered the Republican lexicon, signifying an overly friendly overture to bad actors.

Just for the record, Ali Khamenei is not the only "Supreme Leader" in the world. The North Korean dictator, Kim Jong-un, has that title too. I don't believe that President Obama has referred to him that way. About Moammar Qaddafi, we used to joke that, after all his years as dictator, he was still known as "Colonel." When would he give himself a promotion? But he had other titles: "Brotherly Leader and Guide of the Revolution of Libya" was one; "Guide of the First of September Great Revolution of the Socialist People's Libyan Arab Jamahiriya" was another. (A little cumbersome.)

We have not had emperors for a while. Haile Selassie was one, ruling Ethiopia from 1930 to 1974. His complete mouthful was "His Imperial Majesty, Conquering Lion of the Tribe of Judah, King of Kings of Ethiopia, Elect of God." Toasting him in 1963, President Kennedy called him "Your Majesty." Jean-Bédel Bokassa set himself up as Emperor of Central Africa (quite a rise from army private). He was overthrown in 1979.

In addition to being the "Supreme Leader," Kim Jong-un is "First Secretary of the Workers' Party of Korea." Usually, we referred to the head of the Soviet Union as "general secretary"—the general secretary of the Communist party. In his last year on top, Gorbachev enjoyed the title "president." The late Robert D. Novak had an admirable practice: In his columns, he would refer to the Soviet No. 1 as "party boss"—as in "party boss Mikhail Gorbachev." That saw the situation clearly. Gorbachev (or Chernenko or Andropov or Brezhnev, etc.) was the boss of a party, and therefore he was boss of the country in a one-party dictatorship.

Like his Soviet counterparts, Pol Pot was the "general secretary" of his Communist party, in Cambodia. But his fellow Khmer Rouge, his fellow genocidalists, referred to him warmly as "Brother No. 1." (A man named Nuon Chea was Brother No. 2, and so on down the hierarchy.)

Sometimes, a U.S. president will withhold a title altogether—he may say "Mr." This is "a way to suggest criticism," says Marlin Fitzwater, who was press secretary to Presidents Reagan and Bush 41. Fitzwater adds that Lyndon Johnson would "misspell or mispronounce the names of leaders he didn't like." Bush 41 persistently pronounced Saddam Hussein's first name "Sodom," a pronunciation the Iraqi dictator apparently didn't appreciate. (Formally, Saddam Hussein, like so many other dictators, was "president.")

In Saudi Arabia, there are a great many princes. How many? I think of what a lady from Salzburg said when asked, "How many Habsburgs are there in Austria today?" She answered, "As many as there are gas stations in America." An official in a Republican White House decided he would not call these guys "Prince" or "Your Majesty," as his colleagues did. He did not want to endorse the Saudi system, so to speak. So, presented with the Saudis' foreign minister, for example, he'd say, "Hello, Mr. Minister, so good to see you." No one ever squawked or murmured.

More important than what to call a leader, sometimes, is what to call a country. Take "Burma" versus "Myanmar." When they seized power in the 1980s, the junta changed the name of the country to "Myanmar." The democratic opposition has clung to "Burma." It is the policy of the U.S. government to say "Burma," along with them. But on his visit to the country last year, Obama said "Myanmar," as a diplomatic courtesy. This is understandable (especially in light of Burma's nascent liberalization).

In the U.N., John Bolton points out, a government can call the country it represents whatever it wants. They'll get that name on the nameplate. But other governments don't have to play along. "I never said 'Myanmar,' only 'Burma,' just to tick them off, frankly." (This was in pre-liberalization days, when the Burmese government deserved no courtesy.)

The genocidalists of the Khmer Rouge renamed Cambodia "Democratic Kampuchea." East Germany, or Communist Germany, called itself "the German Democratic Republic." Many people, including Americans broadcasting the Olympic Games, were happy to play along. Others noted that "German Democratic Republic" was three lies in one: The eastern half of Germany was neither democratic nor a republic, and it was not strictly German, given rule from Moscow. The totalitarians in North Korea call that country "the Democratic People's Republic of Korea." These words may be considered tip-offs for dictatorship.

In October 1941, FDR wrote to Stalin. Three and a half months before, the Nazis had broken their pact with the Soviets, leaving Stalin in the unexpected position of Western ally. "My Dear Mr. Stalin," was Roosevelt's salutation. Most of the time, our president referred to Hitler as "Hitler," though sometimes he said "Herr Hitler." Churchill, too, would say "Herr Hitler." Once, he said, "Hitler, with his tattered lackey, Mussolini, at his tail . . ."

Diplomacy and statecraft require all sorts of nose-holding, flattery, and lies. In particular circumstances, it might be wise for a U.S. president to grant Ali Khamenei "Supreme Leader." If this gesture helps to prevent the Iranian regime's acquisition of nukes, well and good. But if it is merely gratuitous, it is offensive—grotesque. Remember, the Iranian regime is one that stones girls to death for the "crime" of having been gang-raped.

In his 1984 column, Bill Buckley proposed a plank for the Republican-party platform, mainly tongue in cheek: "No American President should embrace any world leader responsible for the death and/or torture and/or imprisonment of more than 0.01 per cent of his people." He said that, for short, we could call it "the Osculation Clause." ("Osculation," a Buckleyesque word, refers to kissing or "close contact.") No rule can be made for titles—for what to call tyrants, or frontmen for tyranny. Democratic statesmen ought to go with taste, nose, gut. But, again: Avoid the gratuitous. No flattering titles for free.

One winter in Davos, I had a memorable experience, where titles are concerned. A group of journalists were meeting with Ahmed Nazif, then the Egyptian prime minister. He was introduced as "His Excellency," and the journalists from the Middle East were addressing him as "Your Excellency." I thought this was a little curious, since the Egyptian government was very keen to be seen as democratic. Happy to be the brash Yank, I said to Nazif, "How did the prime minister of Egypt come to be called 'His Excellency'?" The Davos official overseeing the meeting looked at me with fiery hatred, as though he wanted to kill me.

But Nazif gave me sort of a grin and said, with a twinkle in his eye, "Well, 50 years ago it was 'Pasha.'"

—November 11, 2013

A World of Labels

'Moderate liberals' and other interesting creatures

The *New York Times* can be amazing in its language. After the Supreme Court voted to uphold ObamaCare, the paper said that Chief Justice Roberts had joined the Court's four "moderate liberals" to form a majority. Roberts and the other Republican justices were "conservatives," unqualified. That includes Justice Kennedy, who has long been a swing vote. But the Democratic justices—including President

Obama's picks, Sotomayor and Kagan, and Ginsburg, the former general counsel to the ACLU—were "moderate liberals."

Earlier in the year, the *Times* had described George Zimmerman as a "white Hispanic." He is the shooter in the Trayvon Martin case, Martin being the black teenager whose death is the subject of great and inflamed controversy. "White Hispanic" was a novelty. Bernard Goldberg and others asked, "If Zimmerman had done something heroic, would the *Times* have described him as a 'white Hispanic,' or a white anything?" And if he had been a victim?

Race is touchy in the Hispanic world, as it is most anywhere else. When Castro was hiding out in the Sierra Maestra, people in Spain referred to him as "the Great White Hope." Cuba's dictator, Batista, was mulatto. The next dictator would be of much paler hue.

By the way, why isn't Justice Sotomayor a "white Hispanic," in the *Times*' eyes? The paper describes her as a "Hispanic," plain and simple. Maybe there is some color chart at the *Times*, secret from the rest of us.

Most people, I imagine, like to think of themselves as "moderate," or certainly not immoderate. An exception would be Barry Goldwater—who famously declared at his convention, "Extremism in the defense of liberty is no vice," and "moderation in the pursuit of justice is no virtue." Goldwater was a conservative, the author of *The Conscience of a Conservative*, no less. But he was also a classical liberal: a free-marketeer, a constitutionalist, an anti-statist.

The *Times* allows for "moderate liberals," but the paper seems to have less room in its heart, and lexicon, for "moderate conservatives." Are there such creatures? In some liberal minds, the only good conservative is a dead conservative. Goldwater, Reagan, and William F. Buckley Jr. were all portrayed as right-wing monsters, to varying degrees, when they were alive and kicking. Since then, they have enjoyed a much better press.

And consider the case of the Bush family. People used to say of 41, "Why does he have to be such an awful right-winger, unlike his nice moderate father?" (Senator Prescott Bush of Connecticut). In the 1988 debates, Bush had to defend himself against the charge that his father would be ashamed of him. "I think my dad would be pretty proud of me." When 43 became president, people said, "Why does he have to be such an awful right-winger, unlike his nice moderate father?" And if one of 43's twin daughters becomes president? Will she face the same treatment?

"Liberal" has been a contentious word in America since the early 1930s. The New Dealers called themselves liberals, causing others to say, "Hey, wait a minute: Aren't you too keen on government expansion to be liberals?" In Europe, an older sense prevailed. The Nobel peace committee gave its prize to Cordell Hull, recently secretary of state, in 1945. The committee chairman, an economist of Norway's Liberal party, praised Hull as "representative of all that is best in liberalism." What he meant was that Hull was a lifelong foe of protectionism and friend of "free competition."

Americans applied the word "liberal" to all manner of left-of-center people, as the 20th century wore on. Some of these people were quite far to the left. I can tell you that serious leftists, among others, resented this: the equation of liberalism and leftism. One day, a Marxist professor of mine sneered that Christopher Hitchens was a "liberal," nothing more. That made an impression on me: the first time I had ever heard "liberal" as a pejorative from the left.

The memory of this professor (whom I loved) brings up another point: "Liberal" and "conservative" can be quite relative terms. She once chided a colleague of hers for being an arch-conservative. He said, "You have to remember, Barbara, that where I come from [a town in the South] they consider me a pinko."

In this country, we don't have Liberal and Conservative parties, nationally, although others countries do. Our neighbor to the north, Canada, has Liberals and Conservatives. Britain has Conservatives, but they no longer have Liberals. (They now have Liberal Democrats.) Churchill belonged to the Liberal party from 1904 to 1924. At the end of his long, illustrious, and Conservative life, in the 1960s, he made a curious statement: "I'm a Liberal. *Always have been.*"

Down in Australia, the conservative party—the Reaganite or Thatcherite party—is the Liberal party. During the Bush 43 years, the Aussie prime minister, John Howard, was denounced as a fellow warmonger and right-winger of our Texas cowboy. Howard was, of course, the leader of the Liberals. In Europe, they often denounce Reagan-Thatcher types as "neoliberals"—which throws Americans off. Here at home, neoliberalism was associated with a journalist named Charlie Peters and his magazine, *The Washington Monthly*. These people were moderate liberals, in my opinion. "Neoconservatism" used to mean something: but, in the last decade, unreason and malice rendered it meaningless.

Ed Koch, the fabled New Yorker, has always called himself "a liberal with sanity." This must bother liberals who are, by implication, without sanity. Bush 41 once declared, "I'm a conservative, but I'm not a nut about it." This bothered those of us who are nuts about it.

In the 1980s, conservatives had liberals on the run, and not many Democrats would embrace the designation "liberal." In Florida, Connie Mack III (No. 4 is now in the House) ran for the Senate against a congressman named Buddy McKay. He beat him with the simple ad line, "Hey, Buddy, you're a liberal." Liberals, meanwhile, made the term "conservative" as black as they could. In the last stage of the Cold War, American hawks—Peace through Strength types—were conservatives, of course. But so, in the liberals' language, were hard-line Communists in the Soviet Union. Either way, the bad guys were conservatives, see?

Not wanting to be a bad guy, Jack Kemp called himself a "progressive conservative." That did not catch on. Bush 43 called himself a "compassionate conservative"—which prompted Phil Gramm to remark, "Freedom *is* compassionate."

In recent years, left-leaning Democrats have called themselves "progressives," rather than "liberals." "Progressive" is an old American word. We used to have Progressive parties, and Theodore Roosevelt, Robert La Follette, and Henry Wallace ran under their banners. "Progressive" is a self-flattering word, too: Your opponents are regressives. "Realist," in foreign policy, is another self-flattering word: Your opponents are unrealists.

We have one socialist in the Senate—self-declared socialist—and that is Bernie Sanders of Vermont (who caucuses with the Democrats). Some have called Obama a socialist, which provokes a furious reaction, including, crazily enough, charges of racism. The president is probably more a social democrat, but consider: If he were a Frenchman or Italian, would he not be in the Socialist party? In America, the Socialist party is negligible.

A few years ago, Andrew Sullivan, who is sometimes described as a conservative, called me "an apparatchik of the far right." Understand, I am for equality under the law, equality of opportunity, colorblindness, *E pluribus unum*, civil liberties, human rights—all that good stuff. If I'm far-right, what language is left over to describe the actual far right?

I must say that, when I left the Left behind forever, sometime in college, I was not quite comfortable with the word "conservative." I choked on it. In my environment, "conservative" meant bigot, ignoramus, plutocrat, war-lover, and other nice things. Jeane Kirkpatrick had a very hard time leaving the Democrats for the Republicans. She did so at the ripe age of 59. (Reagan was 51.) "I'd rather be a liberal," she said.

"What are you?" I once asked Robert Conquest, in so many words. "I'm an anti-extremist," he said. "And I'm for a law-and-liberty culture. Those are Orwell's words: law and liberty." He continued, "I am strongly against the EU. I'm against regulationism and managerialism. I'm against activism of any sort." As for conservatism, he said, "I feel that, when other people and nations are veering from civilization, I would prefer to conserve." Me too. Although conservatives are obviously more than people who are against change. In my lifetime, the conservatives have been the reformers and the liberals have been the conservatives, so to speak: They have wanted to keep the New Deal and Great Society frozen.

Sometime in the mid-Nineties, I grumbled to Bill Kristol about being stuck with "conservative." He said, in essence, "Get over it. You have to accept labels as they are used and understood in your own time and place." In 1960, Hayek wrote an essay called "Why I Am Not a Conservative." Well, tough luck, Friedrich: Today you would for sure be a conservative or right-winger, whether you liked it or not. The world doesn't give you a choice.

Still, I have not entirely made peace with the standard terms. I especially balk at describing as "liberals" those who are plainly illiberal: supporters of speech codes, race preferences, abortion on demand . . .

The best thing Reagan ever did for me, I've long said, is give me something to call myself: a Reaganite. Neat, accurate, and, so far, understandable. I have sometimes described Obama as a "McGovernite"—but the meaning of that term fades in the national memory. A couple of years ago, some moderates founded a group they called "No Labels." Their slogan: "Not Left. Not Right. Forward." Not many people claim backwardness. In any event, labeling can be very useful, in part because normal conversation cries out for shorthands.

Before long, the *New York Times* may call Chief Justice Roberts a "moderate conservative," separating him from the villains who would have struck down ObamaCare: the unqualified conservatives, so to speak. Today, I saw a headline over an Associated Press report: "More nuanced view of Roberts after health care law." Ah, there you go.

—July 30, 2012

'Barack and I'

What's in a first name?

Joe Biden was goofy, sometimes alarming, before he became vice president, and he's goofy, sometimes alarming, now. He has said that he told Obama he would be his running mate on two conditions: I'm not going to wear any funny hats, and I'm not changing my brand." By "brand," he apparently means "style" or "persona." And, true to his word, he's not changing.

One curious thing about Biden is his habit of referring to the president by his first name—in public, I mean. Or quasi-public. He did this at a Democratic "issues conference" in June; and he did it at a fundraiser in July. The first time, he mentioned that "Barack and I sat in on" a particular meeting. The second time, he said, "Barack and I are realists"—about the economy, he meant. Let's hope so.

I don't know about you, but I have never heard a vice president refer to a president by his first name in public. Dick Cheney always spoke of George W. Bush as "the president" or "President Bush." Face to face, I believe, he called him "sir." In fact, some reporters pointed this out, when others were saying that Cheney, not Bush, was actually in charge: the top dog. I don't believe Bush's father ever referred to "Ron" or "Ronnie."

And did Nixon say "Ike"? Unthinkable. Did Garner, Wallace, or Truman say "Franklin"? How about "Frank"? Beyond unthinkable.

Someone once noted something about Reagan's White House staff. I don't remember who it was, or I would credit him. Talking together in private, they would refer to Reagan as "the president." They'd do this at the mess, out at a ballgame, wherever. And they would use an almost reverential tone. This was highly unusual, as political hands are a famously jaded, hard-boiled bunch. The reverence came in the first term; in the second, when Iran-Contra and other unpleasantness set in, things were a little different.

More than once, I saw Dave Powers, JFK's aide-de-camp, interviewed on television. Reminiscing about Election Night 1960, he'd say, ". . . and that was the last time I called him Jack." He also said, "I called him Jack for 14 years and Mr. President for two years, ten months, and two days."

The business of names, of course, can be a minefield. We have all stepped on a mine or two, as we try to navigate our way. To be safe, you might wait until someone asks you to call him by his first name. But even that can be tricky. For a while, I addressed an acquaintance of mine—about 70, the mother of a colleague—as "Mrs. Jones" (let's say). One day, she said to me, with annoyance, "Why don't you call me Alice?" (again, let's say). I myself was a little annoyed, inwardly: *Because you didn't ask me to, that's why.*

Should you go ahead and ask, without waiting to be asked? Anthony Daniels has made an interesting point, as he routinely does. He notes that "May I call you by your first name?" is not a neutral question. The person being asked is sort of trapped. If he says, "Actually, I would rather you called me Mr. Smith," he comes off as a total prig. Similarly, "Do you mind if I smoke?" is not a neutral question. If the other guy says, "In fact, I do mind"—again, total prig.

Once upon a time in America, people wanted to grow up real fast—to be considered adults. And that included "Mr." and other honorifics. Then, people wanted to grow up real slow, if at all: and be teenagers into their grayness. You called someone "Mr. Brown," and he might retort, "'Mr. Brown' is my father! I'm Toby." I admit that I myself have always had a problem with "Mr."—some discomfort at being called "Mr." I was a summer-camp counselor at the tender age of 18; the rules were, the kids couldn't call you by your first name. I rebelled at "Mr. Nordlinger"—so the compromise was "Mr. Jay," which was quite strange.

Bill Buckley spoke and wrote brilliantly about this first-name business. No surprise there, right? In a 1975 column on the subject, he lamented "the obsessive egalitarian familiarity which approaches a raid on one's privacy." A couple decades later, he said he hated it when he was in a doctor's waiting room and a nurse would call out, "William?" He was either "Bill" or "Mr. Buckley" (although one college classmate called him "Willie").

When I first met him, I called him "Mr. Buckley," of course. He said, "Call me Bill." I mistered him once more—I guess I just couldn't help it. And he said again, this time with vehemence, "Bill." And so it was, ever after. With some, however, Bill would not persist: If they could not bring themselves to call him Bill, he let them alone. Mary Tyler Moore, on her show, balked at calling her boss "Lou." To her, he had to be "Mr. Grant."

Bill had a show too, of course—and we might tell many stories about it. Here's one. Two of his guests one day were Jerry Falwell and Harriet Pilpel, an abortion-rights lawyer. Falwell was appearing by video hookup; Pilpel was in the studio. Beginning a point, Falwell said, "Now, Harriet, I don't know you . . . ," and Bill broke in, "Then why do you call her Harriet?" In front of my television, I winced hard for Falwell.

If names are a minefield at home, how about abroad? There, the mines multiply a hundredfold. And those mines include pronouns, not just names. *Vous* or *tu*? *Sie* or *du*? The formal *you* is not always the safe *you*, you know: That, too, can give offense (to those prepared to take offense, which is many people).

For years, I stayed at the same hotel in Salzburg, and knew the staff quite well. I could not get them—even the guys—to call me Jay. For a day or two, one of them tried: I was "Jay" to him, and he was "Klaus" to me. But I could see that it caused him almost physical pain to say my first name. So I let him off the hook—we went back to "Herr Mertel" and "Herr Nordlinger." (I will not first-name while others are "Herr"-ing.) The only one in the joint who easily called me Jay was the Indian-born head waiter.

I know a young German woman who works for a big German institution, where her boss is American-born. They work in both languages: German and English. When speaking in German, they are "Frau" to each other; when speaking in English, they call each other by their first names. They make the switch unconsciously; it is perfectly natural to them.

Class, among other things, can rear its head in the name business. When I was a teenager, I went into a pharmacy in Ypsilanti, Mich. A grandmotherly employee said to her manager—a man of about 40—"I'm going to go on break now, okay, Mr. Conner?" He said, "Okay, Mabel." I burned. I was ready to join the Communist party on the spot. Dignity comes into play in this business. I know a man whose grandfather, a pillar of the community, went into a nursing home. He had always been "Mr.," but now, enfeebled and helpless, he was "Mike" (or whatever) to the young women at the facility. This made the grandson nearly homicidal.

How do you know how to address people? What are the rules? I think you go by feel, as so often in life. You go by feel, judgment, sensitivity, stomach.

I don't know what Biden says to Obama face to face: I bet it's "Barack," and I think that's what Biden is signaling, in public. But I would not refer to Obama by his first name when out and about: when speaking to the public. It feels wrong to me. It puts a dissonance in my ear. Of course, we all have different ears.

Is Biden being condescending? Obama is a younger man than he, and Biden likes to consider himself a sage. In the general-election campaign of '08, he said, "I've forgotten more about foreign policy than most of my colleagues know." Yeah, sure, Joe (speaking of first names). When he says "Barack" in public, is he trying to convey intimacy (as I've already suggested)? *See how close I am to the president! We're a team, he and I. Incidentally, no way he'll dump me for '12.*

Then there is the awful question of race—an inescapable question in America, a question that taints everything. Shouldn't a vice president be especially careful not even to appear to condescend—to condescend to our first black president? During the '08 primary season, when he himself was running for president, Biden described Obama as "the first mainstream African American, who is articulate and bright and clean and a nice-looking guy." Al Sharpton protested, "I take a bath every day."

Um, what if a conservative Republican leader repeatedly referred to the president as "Barack" in public? Would everyone think that was fine? The Senate minority leader, Mitch McConnell, and the House minority leader, John Boehner, both know Obama—they served together in Congress, and they work together, sort of, now. If they said "Barack," would that be hunky-dory? Or honky-dory? Remember that some Democratic commentators even found Scott Brown's pickup truck, on the campaign trail in Massachusetts, racist.

I have no doubt that Biden is innocent in the "Barack" business—guilty only, perhaps, of bragging about his closeness to the president, and his own senior-statesman status. And Biden can be expected to be goofy: He maintains his "brand," remember. But he might want to rethink "Barack," if he thought in the first place.

—August 30, 2010

Adventures in Lexical Fashion

Today's progressive term may become tomorrow's slur

You may have noticed, as I have, that the word "homosexual" is becoming verboten. It is entering the territory of a slur. Last year, Maureen Dowd of the *New York Times* wrote a widely noticed column that began, "I'm worried about the Supreme Court." It continued, "I'm worried about how the justices can properly debate same-sex marriage when some don't even seem to realize that most Americans use the word 'gay' now instead of 'homosexual.'" Further down in the column, Dowd quoted a friend of hers, who said, "Scalia uses the word 'homosexual' the way George Wallace used the word 'Negro.' There's a tone to it. It's humiliating and hurtful."

GLAAD, the gay activist group, has a "Media Reference Guide," which includes "Offensive Terms to Avoid." "Homosexual" is at the top of the list. "Please use 'gay' or 'lesbian' to describe people attracted to members of the same sex. Because of the clinical history of the word 'homosexual,' it is aggressively used by anti-gay extremists to suggest that gay people are somehow diseased or psychologically/emotionally disordered." GLAAD goes on to say, "Please also avoid using 'homosexual' as a style variation simply to avoid repeated use of the word 'gay.'" That's vigilance. But, unlike most political language cops, they say "please."

"Homosexual" aside, I slightly regret the loss of the word "gay," in the older sense. I still use it, where I strongly feel it's the *mot juste*. But I often add, "in the older sense."

Shortly after Thanksgiving last year, I attended a ceremony on a village green. Nicely Rockwellesque. The village's Christmas tree was being lit. (The saga of the word "Christmas" is another essay.) A school choir sang carols. When they started "Deck the Halls," I thought, "Uh-oh: Will they say it?" Will they sing "Don we now our gay apparel"? They did not. They did not sing merely a replacement word, but a whole replacement lyric. Thus had a traditional carol been airbrushed, Bowdlerized.

Later, I wondered, "Will there be any dubbing of the *Flintstones* theme?" You remember the theme song of this '60s sitcom. It ends, "We'll have a gay ol' time!" They mean a happy, festive, fun time. And what about Zorro? Will he continue to be known as the "gay blade"? Gay Brewer, the late golf champion, was born in 1932. If he had been born in, say, 1982, his mother surely would have named him something else.

When I was a kid, I knew a man named Shirley—he was retired from the FBI. A genuinely tough guy. He said to me once, "Everything was just fine until that Shirley Temple came along." From then on, everyone took "Shirley" to be a girl's name, rather than one that swung both ways.

In the '60s—at the same time new episodes of *The Flintstones* were being aired—there was a progressive term for "homosexual": "homophile." In fact, there was a North American Conference of Homophile Organizations. There have always been insults and slurs, of course. And sometimes people "own" those slurs. That is, they adopt them, in part to take the sting out of them. The activist group Queer Nation was founded in 1990. Four years later, a gay activist ran for mayor of Washington, D.C., using the moniker "Luke Sissyfag."

The counterpart of "gay" is "straight." And often people speak of the "gay community" and the "straight community." This second term cracks me up a little: the "straight community," as if the vast majority of mankind lived in a neighborhood somewhere, with a church, a bar, a school, and an Elks lodge.

As GLAAD's instructions indicate, "lesbian" is still kosher, although lesbians are known as "gays" too. Those ubiquitous letters "LGBT" (sometimes the string is longer) make a split between "gay" and "lesbian." Spare a thought for the residents of Lesbos, all 100,000 of them. In 2008, some of them filed suit against a group on the mainland, the Gay and Lesbian Community of Greece (there's that word "community" again). They alleged that the term "lesbian," to mean a female homosexual, held them up to ridicule, and violated their human rights. Their suit went nowhere.

The term "same-sex marriage" is fashionable. (For instance, Maureen Dowd used it in her column.) This is interesting, because the word "gender" has largely replaced "sex," where male and female are concerned. My guess is, people like the alliteration of "same-sex," whether they're conscious of it or not. What's more, same-sex-marriage campaigners have hit on the term "marriage equality," to describe what they're after. That is a masterstroke, politically—but not quite as ingenious as "pro-choice," to describe support for legal abortion.

One day in 2004, the governor of New Jersey, Jim McGreevey, announced, "My truth is that I am a gay American." That is a very contemporary sentence—including the "my truth" part. Also, the phrase "gay American" has a civil-rightsy ring: "black American," "Japanese American." A few years ago, some people started to refer to illegal aliens as "undocumented Americans." To question these document-impaired individuals, you see, would be unpatriotic.

When it comes to race, we have gone through evolution upon evolution. "Colored" was once a progressive term. A remnant of it can be found in "NAACP"—the National Association for the Advancement of Colored People, established in 1909. The term "colored people" is now radioactive and ugly, but the term "people of color" is rather cool. In other languages, there would be no difference between the two terms (*gens de couleur*). We in America shave things very close.

"Negro" rode high for a while, and a remnant can be found in "United Negro College Fund," established in 1944. The last person I heard use the word "Negro" was Justice Thurgood Marshall, who proudly, defiantly used it until he died in 1993. Actually, the majority leader of the U.S. Senate used it far more recently—in 2008. Speaking privately, Harry Reid said that he had high hopes for Barack Obama's electoral success: because the candidate was "light-skinned" and had "no Negro dialect, unless he wanted to have one." When these words were reported, Obama gave his fellow Democrat a pass, saying, "I know what's in his heart."

"Afro-American" was a contender for a while. And then "black" reigned supreme. We had a slogan, "Black is beautiful." I suppose I thought "black" was here to stay. But it was supplanted, to a considerable degree, in the late 1980s, by "African American." One day (or so I remember), Jesse Jackson announced that, henceforward, black people would be known as "African Americans," and, lo, everyone complied. It was as rapid a social change as I've ever seen—even rapider than the stigmatization of smoking. I remember people around me—white people—turning on a dime, saying "African American" where they had always said "black." The term seemed awkward in their mouths, at first. All those syllables!

Plenty of people prefer "black," and one of them is Condoleezza Rice, as she told me in an interview years ago. One of her reasons was this: "Black" is parallel to "white." But some have seized on a parallel to "African American": "European American." Al Sharpton is one who uses that expression.

I find it a little amusing to hear "European American" as a stand-in for "white." I think of a friend of mine, an Italian American, who grew up in Kansas City. There were mothers who wouldn't let their daughters date him, because he wasn't "white." Now he lives in L.A. and is considered an "Anglo." He remarks, "I can't tell whether that's a demotion or a promotion."

"African American" can cause problems, as it did, hilariously, at the 2002 Winter Olympics. An American named Vonetta Flowers was part of a two-woman bobsled team. She and her partner won the gold, making Flowers the first black person ever to win a gold medal at the Winter

Games. But the poor NBC announcers had no way to report that fact—because they were forbidden, apparently, to say "black." So they wound up saying, "She's the first African American *from any country* to win a gold medal!"

Woe to anyone who enters the choppy waters between "Hispanic," "Latino," "Chicano," and related terms. There are people who feel strongly—hotly strongly—about those words. In 2012, the *New York Times* invented an expression for George Zimmerman, the shooter in the Trayvon Martin case: "white Hispanic." Evidently, the editors were trying to honkify the man who shot and killed a black teen.

There came a day—I can't give you a precise date, but I think it was in the mid-'90s—when "Oriental" was out and "Asian" was in. From this day forward, "Oriental" was a slur, except perhaps when used in reference to vases and rugs. I once used "Oriental" past its expiration date—in a totally innocent way—and a friend—a friend, mind you—berated me for it. I was shocked, frankly. By the way, the British use "Asian" to mean "South Asian," as in Pakistani, Indian, etc.

"Retarded" was once a progressive word—a wonderfully progressive word. It implied that the afflicted person was merely delayed. Long before that, there were "homes for idiots." The people who founded, ran, and staffed them were not hateful. On the contrary, they were among the most loving and humane people on earth—probably more loving and humane than you and I are. Eventually, "retarded" people became "developmentally disabled," "physically challenged," "differently able," "handicapable" . . . "Special" is a perennial—as in "Special Olympics," and "special needs."

Honestly, as I sit here today, I can't tell you what the respectable, approved word for "retarded" is. I just can't. Whatever it is today, it may change tomorrow.

Yes, today's progressive, ultra-correct word may become tomorrow's slur. "Gay," for example, is preferred now, even sacrosanct. But say it tomorrow, and you may be a bigot. As a rule, I think people ought to be called what they want to be called. But they should be maybe a little patient with people who aren't keeping pace. A little gentleness is called for—and that particular quality is not a hallmark of our age.

—May 5, 2014

Uncles, Fruits, and Nuts

A look at some American slurs

Writing for the website of CBS Sports, Mike Freeman blasted the nickname of the Washington, D.C., football team: the Redskins. He also blasted those who support or tolerate the name. He had a particular blast for one group of people. "Sure, there will be some Uncle Tom American Indians who will say 'Redskins' honors them," he wrote, "just like there were some Uncle Tom blacks who once didn't mind being called 'colored.'"

As a rule, we bow to the opinions of people belonging to minority groups, except when their opinions conflict with our own. I think of a case in a town I'm familiar with, Ypsilanti, Mich. There, the Eastern Michigan University teams were called the Hurons, after an Indian people. (There is also a Huron River, a Huron High School, etc.) Most of the real-live Hurons who could be found supported the nickname. But that was the "wrong" opinion, so the nickname had to go, and EMU became the Eagles.

Freeman's slur of choice was "Uncle Tom Indians," but there is a better slur, one he may not know: "Uncle Tomahawk." It was used by such militants as Russell Means and AIM (the American Indian Movement)—the kind of people who took over and trashed the Bureau of Indian Affairs in 1972. You still hear it today, mainly in Indian country. A guy who may want to leave the rez, immerse himself in the broader world, and get on with life could be called an "Uncle Tomahawk."

The term, obviously, derives from "Uncle Tom," one of the nastiest names in the whole, horrible American lexicon. Any conservative black is liable to be tagged with it. As luck would have it, two of the most prominent black conservatives have "Thomas" in their names: Clarence Thomas, the Supreme Court justice, and Thomas Sowell, the writer. Some who hate them can't resist. An especially nasty instance occurred in 1996, when a magazine called *Emerge* had a disgusting caricature of Justice Thomas on its cover, with the words "Uncle Thomas: Lawn Jockey for the Far Right."

Now and again, someone will protest that "Uncle Tom" ought not to be a putdown, because the character in Harriet Beecher Stowe's momentous novel of 1852 is noble. Fans of *The Jeffersons*, that clever and racially interesting sitcom, may remember an episode in which Louise's uncle Ward comes to visit. Ward works as a butler, and George couldn't be ruder to him. He calls him "Uncle Tom," to his face. Finally, Ward sits him down and gives him a lecture on Josiah Henson, sometimes thought to be the "real Uncle Tom." Ward's climactic lines are, "He was a brave man, a great leader. And I'll tell you something else, George: I'd never call you an 'Uncle Tom.'" The audience whoops.

Well, too late: Just as "decimate" can never mean one in ten, and "awful" can never mean "inspiring awe," "Uncle Tom" can never mean anything but a self-denigrating, toadying black.

Do you remember "Aunt Tom"? It was a term used by feminists to denote a woman who was reluctant or unwilling to go along with their program. Betty Friedan liked to use this term. In a debate with Phyllis Schlafly, her conservative nemesis, she said, "I'd like to burn you at the stake!" (Friedan can at least be credited with candor.) "I consider you a traitor to your sex. I consider you an Aunt Tom." There was an echo of this attitude in 2008, when Sarah Palin was the GOP vice-presidential nominee. A bumper sticker appeared that said, "She's not a woman, she's a Republican."

People use "Aunt Tom" in a racial way too—as the feminine (to be distinguished from "feminist") equivalent of "Uncle Tom." When Mia Love, the Utah Republican, spoke at the GOP convention last year, the Internet was stinking with such terms as "house nigger," "pickaninny," and, yes, "Aunt Tom."

Here is another slur that Mike Freeman and CBS Sports may like to add to their repertoires: "apple." An Indian you disapprove of—who's not "Indian" enough for you—is an apple. Red on the outside, white on the inside. Get it? They'll also want to know, and use, "coconut." That's the slur for a Hispanic deemed "brown on the outside, white on the inside." Linda Chavez, the conservative writer, has faced violence in her life: a dead cat left on her doorstep; a knife flicked in her face; death threats over the phone. She has also had coconuts thrown at her. In

Canada—and, to a degree, in the United States—people of South Asian origin are sometimes called "coconuts." Their sin is to integrate themselves into North American culture, or simply think for themselves.

Then you have "bananas"—the slur for people of East Asian origin who are deemed . . . well, you know. In Hong Kong, those who favored continued British rule, rather than rule by Beijing, were called "bananas." Here in America, the more "ethnically conscious" Asians deride and bully the more assimilated as "bananas." Those who are half Asian, half white have been known to question whether they are "bananas" or "eggs" (white on the outside . . .). Any chance they could be just people, or themselves?

There is one fruit that is neither racial nor ethnic but political and ideological: "watermelons." These are certain environmentalists who are "green on the outside, red on the inside." In my view, a political term of this type is far different from the racial and ethnic terms—far more benign. I also believe "RINO" is different from "LINO." More about those terms in just a second.

One of the more galling things about the racial-and-ethnic-slur business is this: Not just your own, but people outside your race or ethnicity may tar you as insufficiently loyal to your group. A few years ago, I asked Tom Sowell, "Who has treated you worse in your life? Other black people or white liberals?" He shook his head, chuckled, and said, "It's too close to call."

Which brings me to Aswini Anburajan, who recently called Ted Cruz a LINO. "LINO" is a takeoff from "RINO," which means "Republican in Name Only." "LINO" means "Latino in Name Only." Anburajan is a journalist who works for *BuzzFeed* and WNYC (the National Public Radio outlet in New York City). Cruz, as you know, is the new Republican senator from Texas. According to Señorita Anburajan, or so it seems, you have to be a left-winger in the mold of La Raza or MALDEF to qualify as a Latino. (I have named two prominent pressure groups.) Cruz is half Cuban, true. His father was a refugee. The senator makes no bones about this. In fact, he emphasizes it, when the occasion warrants. But he is also a conservative, and as American as apple pie—or as Texan as a steak. And this, the racialists can't stand.

Speaking of Cuban Americans, you may remember an affirmative-action case of a decade ago, *Grutter v. Bollinger*. It concerned the University of Michigan Law School. On that campus, the question arose, "Who qualifies as a Hispanic?" One professor said that Cuban Americans should be counted out, because they vote Republican.

To my knowledge, Wanda Sykes, the comedian, has cracked one good joke in her life. It was at the beginning of Barack Obama's presidency, in Obama's presence. "The first black president—proud to be able to say that," she began. "That's unless you screw up. And then it's going to be, 'What's up with the half-white guy, huh? Who voted for the mulatto, what the hell?'" The Obama presidency has revealed much racial strangeness in America—and revealed it redundantly, to be sure. Take merely the matter of golf.

Last summer, Bill Maher, another comedian, said that Obama was "too white" for some "progressives." For example, "he plays golf." A week and a half later, Lawrence O'Donnell, an MSNBC host, said that it was white racism to mention Obama's affinity for golf. Why? Because that is to associate the president with "the lifestyle of Tiger Woods." (O'Donnell was not alluding to a record-setting golf career, but to adultery.) A cigar may be a cigar, and golf may be golf—but not to the hard-bitten racialist.

"Sticks and stones may break my bones / But words will never hurt me." The problem with this pleasant ditty is that it isn't necessarily true. Words may hurt as much as sticks and stones, or more. It's hard enough to navigate through life without racial and ethnic pressure and condemnation. Without having to be "black" enough, "Hispanic" enough, or whatever. Furthermore, it's possible to make arguments without name-calling. When it comes to the Washington Redskins, I think I agree with Mike Freeman of CBS: The label, and logo, should probably go. (I believe "Redskins," as a name, is different in character from "Hurons," "Seminoles," and the like.) But when he says "Uncle Tom Indians," I want to stand up and sing the fight song, "Hail to the Redskins."

There is a name in America that covers a multitude of people—people of all types, biologically and mentally: "American." When Linda Chavez was a schoolgirl, a teacher asked her, "What nationality are you?" Later,

Linda told her mother about this. Her mother said, "I hope you said 'American.'" Linda, being Linda, had.

In 1997, Ward Connerly, the president of the American Civil Rights Institute, was interviewed by a *New York Times* reporter over the phone. The reporter said, "What are you?" Connerly said, "I am an American." The reporter said, "No, no, no! What are you?" Connerly said, "Yes, yes, yes! I am an American." The reporter continued, "That is not what I mean. I was told that you are African American. Are you ashamed to be African American?" "No," said Connerly, "I'm just proud to be an American."

Then there was the moment at the end of last year's presidential campaign, when Vice President Joe Biden said to a man in Sarasota, "Are you Indian?" The man responded, "American!" Oddly enough, that word can sound gloriously subversive.

—July 1, 2013

The E-Word

Thoughts on the use and abuse of 'establishment'

When we were schoolkids, we were taught that the longest word was "antidisestablishmentarianism." Lately, I've been thinking that the most *common* word is "establishment"—as in "establishment Republican." I read it every day, especially in the conservative press. I read it in virtually every article about politics, certainly in articles about the Republican party. And I find it nearly as empty and cheap as it is common.

At the end of October, a reporter for the Associated Press wrote, "The GOP is struggling to control tensions between its tea party and establishment wings and watching approval ratings sink to record lows." Further on in his article, he reached for different language, to describe the same division. He spoke of "business-oriented Republicans and the GOP's more ideological wing." None of these words will quite do.

"Establishment" really got going in the 1950s, when Henry Fairlie, the famed British journalist, employed it. He used it to mean "the whole matrix of official and social relations within which power is exercised." There have always been people eager to join the establishment (and if you want to make it seem really powerful and fixed, you use a capital E). They want to go to the right school, or work for the right firm, or belong to the right club. Dreaming on a grand scale, they may aspire to the Trilateral Commission or the Bilderberg Group.

On the flip side, there have always been people eager to oppose the establishment, or to give the impression of doing so—to stand up to the Man. "Hey, Johnny, what're you rebelling against?" asks the girl in *The Wild One*. "Whaddaya got?" answers Marlon Brando.

I'm not entirely sure what an establishment Republican is. Someone elected to office? Someone who has a position of serious responsibility? Someone who has been around for a while? Who doesn't huff and puff? Speaking of puffing, there used to be smoke-filled rooms, in which party bosses selected candidates. Now we have primaries—and voters, to a considerable degree, are the bosses.

The definition of "establishment Republican," I think, is partly emotional. The term is almost always used vituperatively. I don't think anyone has ever called himself an "establishment Republican." The term means something like, "I disagree with you, I think I'm to the right of you, I resent you, get out of the way." It is the latest form of derogation. A friend of mine said the other day—not in a light vein, but with genuine concern—"'Establishment' is the new 'neocon.'"

In December 2011, as the presidential primaries loomed, we at *National Review* published an editorial about those primaries. We counseled against nominating Newt Gingrich, among others. Shortly after, a colleague poked his head into my office and said, "They're calling us the E-word." Who was "they"? Certain conservative activists. What was the E-word? "Establishment." When I myself wrote critically of Gingrich, or Michele Bachmann, or Herman Cain, I too was called "establishment" (by angry e-mailers). That was kind of amusing. I held essentially the same views I'd held when I was working at a golf course for minimum wage.

I am in the position of many conservatives: blasted from the left for being Attila the Hun; blasted from the right for not being Attila the Hun. (Just to be clear: I am, indeed, Attila the Hun.)

The current poster boy for establishment Republicanism is Mitch McConnell—one of the smartest, ablest, most valuable conservatives in America. He has performed any number of services (such as standing athwart unconstitutional, or unwise, limits on campaign finance). We're lucky to have him in politics. But now he wears a scarlet E.

Probably, it's the position—McConnell is the Republican leader in the Senate. I have had occasion to recall something with my *NR* colleague Michael Potemra, who worked in the Senate for twelve years: When Howard Baker was Republican leader, a lot of us said, "We need to get rid of that moderate old compromiser and replace him with a real conservative, like Bob Dole." When Dole was leader, we said, "We need to get rid of that moderate old compromiser and replace him with a real conservative, like Trent Lott." When Lott was leader . . .

Baker went on to serve as chief of staff to that marshmallow President Reagan. And I find Dole a particularly interesting case: He was always known as a right-winger, a true-believing junkyard dog. President Ford had included him on the 1976 ticket, dumping the incumbent vice president, Nelson Rockefeller. In his debate against Walter Mondale that year, Dole inveighed against the "Democrat wars" of the 20th century: World War I, World War II, Korea, and Vietnam. (A sign of proper wingery is the use of "Democrat" as an adjective.) These days, some conservatives think of him as not much different from Rocky.

I was a Dole intern in 1984, the year he became Republican leader in the Senate. There was a mixture of Republicans in that body. We had true-blue, foursquare conservatives, such as the Idahoans, Jim McClure and Steve Symms. (McClure, in fact, ran for the leadership position that year, to the right of Dole. I think my feelings were slightly torn.) The Idahoans were the most conservative pairing—unless you count the North Carolinians, Jesse Helms and John East. (The wheelchair-bound East was known, usually affectionately, as Helms on Wheels.)

But there were also moderates and liberals: the Oregonians, Mark Hatfield and Bob Packwood; the Pennsylvanians, John Heinz and Arlen Specter. We also had Chuck Percy of Illinois, Mac Mathias of Maryland, John Chafee of Rhode Island, and Bill Cohen of Maine, among others. (Cohen ended up in a Clinton cabinet, as defense secretary.)

The most liberal Republican of all, probably, was Lowell Weicker. Plenty of us wanted him to up and leave the party. But "I'll always be the turd in the punchbowl," he said. Like other politicians, he broke his promise: He left the GOP in 1990, becoming governor of Connecticut under a third-party banner.

Today, there are no liberal Republicans in the Senate, and scarcely a moderate—maybe Susan Collins of Maine? There are no Rockefeller Republicans anywhere, so far as I'm aware. But, strangely enough, that term has come back into vogue: I know people who revere Ronald Reagan, and who worked for him, who have been tagged as "Rockefeller Republicans"—because they want to oppose ObamaCare in ways other than their critics want.

Reagan, too, was attacked from the right: He raised taxes, amnestied illegals, pursued arms control, racked up debt. Conservatives liked to quip, with a sigh, "None of this would be happening if Ronald Reagan were still alive."

Over in the House, though, there was genuine revolutionary, anti-establishment action: Newt and the boys were forming the Conservative Opportunity Society. This was after the 1982 elections, in which Republicans took a hit. They wanted to offer the public a positive agenda (rather than merely a blocking or temporizing one). And they wanted to reverse the minority mentality represented by our House leader, Bob Michel—a moderate and a swell guy. He played golf with Tip O'Neill, which, reasonably or not, bothered the hell out of us righties. Anyway, the Republicans triumphed at the polls in 1994, and Newt became speaker.

There is such a thing, no doubt, as a go-along, get-along mentality: a contentment with the status quo, a disinclination to fight. But there is not much of that in the Republican party today. Republicans have developed a healthy appetite for success. So, what is our division now? At the end of 1964, after the "Goldwater debacle," as it was called, Robert Novak published a book called *The Agony of the G.O.P.* It told of the warfare between the Goldwater wing and the Rockefeller wing (roughly speaking). That was a real division. And today?

Much of the turbulence, or "agony," I think, has to do with style. I repeatedly hear Mitt Romney described as a "moderate." Why? He is a free-marketeer, a traditionalist, and a hawk. But his manner is moderate—he's too polite or polished for some. I have noticed something curious over the years: If you espouse conservative positions in a moderate way, you may well be called a moderate. If you espouse moderate positions in an immoderate way, you may well be designated a "real conservative."

Obviously, governing is not for the pure, although we expect our officeholders to remember principle. Almost everyone who gets into a significant governing position is viewed by someone as a sell-out. Reagan certainly found this out (although he is now a conservative saint). By much of the Right, George W. Bush is seen as a moderate, an "establishment" type. But he was also the one who grabbed the "third rail," trying to reform Social Security, a national sacred cow. And he ran up against an immense force, which might be called "the establishment."

As of now, my friend Ted Cruz, the Texas senator, is the darling of the antiestablishmentarians. But if he becomes president, or even the GOP nominee, he'll disappoint many of them. And he will be the same sterling conservative, the same Reaganite, he was years ago, when he and I jawed and schemed at Earl Campbell's barbecue place in Austin.

No one who writes, no one who talks, can live without labels. We need our shorthands, generalizations, and crutches. In 2010, some people formed a group called "No Labels" (motto: "Stop fighting, start fixing"). But without labels, you're practically mute. I have often used "establishment media," instead of "mainstream media," to describe the *New York Times*, *60 Minutes*, the *Today* show—you know. But labels can also be lazy and misleading.

In early 2003, a bunch of us were sitting around, figuring out where we stood on the impending Iraq War. A colleague said, "I know what the *neoconservative* position is, but what's the *conservative* position?" In reality, there was no cupboard from which you could pluck conservative positions (or neoconservative ones). You had to think: "What's the right thing to do, or the least wrong thing to do? What is the wisest or most palatable of the options?"

It may be convenient to label something "tea party" or "establishment," "conservative" or "moderate," "hard-core" or "squishy." But it may be better to ask whether that thing is right or wrong, smart or dumb, promising or unpromising. I, for one, have had it with "establishment," which has been used with gross promiscuity. I have an E-word of my own: Enough.

—November 25, 2013

The Z-Word

When people say 'Zionist,' what do they mean?

A few weeks ago, a Labour MP in Britain, Paul Flynn, expressed displeasure with his country's ambassador to Israel. "I do not normally fall for conspiracy theories," he said, "but the ambassador has proclaimed himself to be a Zionist." What Britain needs in Israel, according to Flynn, is "someone with roots in the U.K." who "can't be accused of having Jewish loyalty."

Britain's ambassador to Israel, as you may have surmised, is a Jew, the first to serve in that capacity. He previously served in Pakistan and Iran (not Jewish states). As for Matthew Gould's "roots in the U.K.," they may not be as deep as Flynn's, but they are semi-respectable: On one side, his great-grandparents were immigrants, and on the other, his grandparents. Speaking of respectability, Gould is a graduate of St. Paul's School and Peterhouse, Cambridge. Not bad for a Semitic upstart.

In his widely publicized remarks, Flynn worried about "neocons and warmongers," now itching to invade Iran. "Warmongers" is a word we can easily understand. But what about two other words Flynn used, "neocons" and "Zionist"? These are very slippery terms. If you want to paralyze someone who denounces neocons, say, "What's a neocon?" If you want to paralyze someone who denounces Zionists, or even refers to them, say, "What's a Zionist?" People use these words cavalierly and ignorantly. And none too nicely, either.

We will concentrate on the older of the words, "Zionist." Though it may be older than "neocon," it is much, much newer than "Zion." We first encounter "Zion" in II Samuel, Chapter 5: "David took the strong hold of Zion: the same is the city of David." I am quoting King James's translators. In Psalm 48, we have one of the loveliest lines in the entire Bible: "Beautiful for situation, the joy of the whole earth, is mount Zion." Centuries later came a hymn that begins, "Glorious things of thee are spoken, Zion, city of our God!" Those words were written by the author of "Amazing Grace," John Newton.

"Zion" may refer to a hill in Jerusalem, or a section of Jerusalem, or Jerusalem itself, or all Israel. Or to the kingdom of God, period. It also may refer to the Jewish people or to all mankind. People in Illinois may know Zion as a city on the Wisconsin border.

"Zionism" arose in the late 19th century, and its believers and supporters were "Zionists." This was the movement to establish a Jewish state in ancient Israel—to *reestablish* that state, if you like. European Jews such as Theodor Herzl thought, or feared, that assimilation was a lost cause. The host countries would never allow it. The best answer was a return to Zion, to Israel. Other Jews held this return to be desirable in itself, regardless of whether assimilation in the broader world was possible.

Herzl wrote his pamphlet *The Jewish State* in 1896. The next year, he organized the first Zionist Congress, in Basel. Many Jews were Zionists, many were not. Those who were not, were free to stay where they were (as were those Jews who supported Zionism but did not wish to emigrate themselves). The ancient language, Hebrew, was revived. The movement gathered pace. After the Holocaust, and a war of independence, the Jews had their state. Zionism, i.e., Jewish nationalism, was fulfilled.

But the term hung on, particularly in the mouths of Israel's enemies. Indeed, many Arabs would not, and will not, say "Israel." They say "Zionist entity" or "Zionist presence." To say "Israel," apparently, would acknowledge statehood, which is unacknowledgeable, to some. The late Yasser Arafat was a frequent user of "Zionist aggressor," "Zionist conquest," and similar phrases.

One goal of Israel's enemies was to stigmatize "Zionism," and they had their greatest success in November 1975, when the United Nations passed its infamous Resolution 3379: Zionism equals racism. "Racism" was the severest term of the age, and it may well be that today, too. Vanessa Redgrave, a great supporter of Arafat and his PLO, said, "Zionism is a brutal, racist ideology." Other peoples could have their national expression, but not the Jews. Resolution 3379 was revoked in 1991, thanks chiefly to the work of the Bush 41 administration, and in particular to the work of one State Department official: John Bolton.

Over the years, people have denounced Zionism while proclaiming their great love of Jews. They're not anti-Jewish, you see, but merely anti-Zionist. They could just as well say "anti-Israel," but "Zionist" is somehow the word of choice.

Accepting an Academy Award in 1978, Redgrave congratulated her colleagues on standing up to "Zionist hoodlums," such as those picketing outside. Later in her remarks, she said, "I pledge to you that I will continue to fight against anti-Semitism and fascism." In 1980, Jesse Jackson called Zionism "a kind of poisonous weed that is choking Judaism." He was following the pattern of "Judaism good, Zionism bad." In 1992, he seemed to have a change of heart, hailing Zionism as a "liberation movement."

But old habits die hard, and Jackson is still liable to use "Zionism" or "Zionist" as a term of abuse. In October 2008, Amir Taheri, an exile journalist from Iran, recorded what Jackson said at a conference in France. An Obama administration was coming, he said, and this administration would diminish the "Zionists who have controlled American policy for decades." Whom did he mean, exactly? What do people ever mean when they say "Zionists"?

Louis Farrakhan talks about Zionists almost as much as Arafat did. An Associated Press report in 1984 said, "Farrakhan, who has been quoted as calling Judaism a 'gutter religion,' denied that he was against Jews. He has said that remark referred to Zionism, not Judaism." Here is an AP report from 1998: "Farrakhan suggested a Zionist plot was behind President Clinton's affair with Monica Lewinsky." Earlier this year, Farrakhan said that "Zionists dominate the government of the United States of America and her banking system." He added, "Some of you think that I'm just somebody who's got something out for the Jewish people. You're stupid. Do you think I would waste my time if I did not think it was important for you to know Satan? My job is to pull the cover off of Satan so that he will never deceive you and the people of the world again."

In Israel itself, the word "Zionist" is in bad odor, certainly on the left. Few academics, artists, and cool teens would want to be known as Zionists. This started "just after the 1967 war," says Zev Chafets, the veteran American-Israeli writer. "Zionist" came to mean superpatriot, flag-waver, jingo. The worldwide Left associates Zionism with colonialism, imperialism, and, of course, racism, and the Israeli Left does the same.

More than a few Israelis refer to themselves as "post-Zionists," which may mean any number of things. For instance, it may mean that they reject the old Zionist vision and instead welcome a "binational state," including the West Bank and Gaza and everyone in them. Jewish particularism is anathema to them. When they think "Zionist," they are apt to think "settler," and a settler, in their minds, is no good. Of course, not so long ago, just about every Israeli was a settler, and a Zionist, to boot.

There are still people who embrace the Z-word, no matter the opprobrium that comes with it. Paul Flynn, the British MP, said that Ambassador Gould "has proclaimed himself to be a Zionist." That is true. Gould has also said, "I thought long and hard about applying for the position" of ambassador to Israel. "I thought it might just be all too difficult. But then I thought to myself, 'Why should Jews rule themselves out of important positions?'" Gould has emphasized he is "the British ambassador to Israel, not the Jewish one."

Ten years ago, Gil Troy, a history professor at McGill University, wrote a book with a totally unabashed title: "Why I Am a Zionist: Israel, Jewish Identity and the Challenges of Today." There are also many millions of Americans who support Israel and are known as "Christian Zionists." Their critics utter this term with disdain or fear or both. I suspect that these Christians themselves have no problem with it.

To me, a Zionist has always been a person who supports the idea of a Jewish homeland, or state, in the Middle East. In ancient Israel. Therefore, being a Zionist is essentially the same as supporting the right of Israel to exist. When Farrakhan says that the U.S. government, the banks, and the media are "dominated by Zionists," I'm apt to say, "Sure:

Most Americans support Israel, both as idea and as reality." But I am being too clever, no doubt—because when people say "Zionist," they really mean . . .

Well, what *do* they mean? One clue comes from John J. Mearsheimer, the University of Chicago professor who, with Stephen M. Walt, wrote *The Israel Lobby and U.S. Foreign Policy*, a notorious book published in 2007. Mearsheimer has just written a blurb for a book by Gilad Atzmon, an ex-Israeli who hates Israel and hates himself, for that matter. He has described himself as a "proud self-hating Jew." In his blurb, Mearsheimer writes, "Panicked Jewish leaders, [Atzmon] argues, have turned to Zionism (blind loyalty to Israel) and scaremongering (the threat of another Holocaust) to keep the tribe united and distinct from the surrounding goyim."

So, there we have a definition of Zionism, from a professor of political science at one of our most distinguished universities: "blind loyalty to Israel." There is an old joke, told by Jews, that goes, "What's the definition of an anti-Semite? One who hates Jews more than is absolutely necessary." Is that what a Zionist is—someone who supports Israel more than is absolutely necessary? Someone who is too enthusiastic or unyielding in his support?

In my observation, people say "Zionist" when they don't want to say "Jew" or "Israeli." As Gil Troy wrote last year, "intellectuals have camouflaged modern anti-Semitism as anti-Zionism." There are certainly people who are anti-Zionist or anti-Israel—is there a difference?—without being anti-Jewish. Some of them are Jews. But, as Paul Johnson, the historian, once said to me in an interview, "Scratch the fellow who is anti-Israel, and you won't have to dig very far before you find the anti-Semite within." Another historian, Bernard Lewis, says that talk of Zionism "sometimes provides a useful cover": a cover to those who harbor the old, enduring hatred.

As you go about life, you may encounter someone who says "Zionism" or "Zionist," with an edge in his voice. Ask him what he means. The answer, or non-answer, you get is likely to be revealing.

—December 31, 2011

'The Right Side of History'
It's bunk

In politics, as in clothes, there is fashion. And that includes fashion in political language. About 15 years ago, everybody in Washington started to say "kabuki dance." I don't know why—they just did. Every process or procedure or exercise was a "kabuki dance." My impression is, that term is fading out a little. But it is still in frequent use. Last month, a writer for *The Atlantic* spoke of "the kabuki dance that is our justice system." The term has even crept into the sports pages: "NFL Talks Were a Kabuki Dance," read a headline, also from last month.

"Double down" is an expression very, very recent. Until about a year and a half ago, I don't think I had ever heard the expression in my life. It comes from gambling, from blackjack in particular. Suddenly, the expression was in every political conversation and every political article. President Obama and the Democrats, despite some setbacks, were "doubling down" on their health-care efforts. Anyone who was intensifying his activity, in any direction, was "doubling down." Seldom are people more herd-like than in matters of language.

Lately, "the right side of history" is everywhere. We have long had the phrase. But people are doubling down, or tripling down, on their use of it. A close cousin of this phrase is "the tide of history"—a tide not to be resisted. When Jody Williams won the Nobel Peace Prize in 1997 for her campaign to ban landmines, she said that President Clinton was "outside the tide of history"—because, under him, the United States refused to join the Mine Ban Treaty (chiefly because treaty organizers refused to make an exception for the demilitarized zone between the Koreas). The laureate also said that Clinton was "on the wrong side of humanity"—and a "weenie."

Back to "the right side of history." When they say it, what do people mean? They may mean "my side," or "the good side," or "the side that posterity will smile on." People may be alluding to the ultimate triumph of liberal democracy. Or they may be alluding to the ultimate triumph of socialism, or a stricter form of collectivism. For generations, the Left has assumed that history marches with them: Get out of the way, or be crushed.

Robert Conquest, the British historian, notes that "the right side of history" has a "Marxist twang." (He knows a thing or two about twangs, being married to a wonderful Texan.) Andrew Roberts, another British historian, says that "the right side of history" is "profoundly Marxian," although the phrase is used by people of varying political stripes. Yet another historian, the American Richard Pipes, says, bluntly, "The whole notion is nonsensical." History does not have sides, although historians do.

The recent upheavals in the Arab world have occasioned an outbreak of right-side-of-history-ism. Obama, defending his erratic posturings on Egypt, said, "History will end up recording that at every juncture . . . we were on the right side of history." Commenting on the Libyan drama, he said, "I believe that Qaddafi is on the wrong side of history." Speaking more broadly, he said, "I think that the region will be watching carefully to make sure we're on the right side of history, but also that we are doing so as a member of the world community." That means (if I may interpret), "George W. Bush was right about the power and necessity of freedom, but I'd rather swallow cyanide than say so."

At a White House press briefing, a reporter had a little fun with the presidential press secretary, Jay Carney: "You mentioned . . . that Mubarak [the ousted Egyptian leader] was on this 'wrong side of history.' Is the Bahraini monarchy also on the 'wrong side of history'?" (This monarchy is another American ally, embattled.) Faced with this, the press secretary had to do a little dancing.

Travel back to 1984, when Jesse Jackson was running for president. He said that the Sandinistas in Nicaragua, who were self-declared Marxist-Leninists, were "on the right side of history." He also had some thoughts on the Khmer Rouge in Cambodia. "Unfortunately," said the reverend, "sometimes the best of people lose their way." These particular best of people lost their way by murdering over 20 percent of the Cambodian population. Condoleezza Rice had, and has, a view of history much different from Jackson's. In a 2000 speech, she recalled her days in the White House of the first George Bush: "I was working very long hours, but I was working on the right side of history. And I started to wonder what it must be like to go to work every day in the Soviet Union, working on the wrong side of history."

When the subject is racial, or even vaguely racial, you can expect talk of history, and its "right" and "wrong" sides. In 1983, Chicago had a mayoral contest. Walter Mondale, gearing up to run for president, endorsed Richard M. Daley (as white as his father, Richard J., the late mayor). A group of black leaders, in which Jackson was prominent, was highly displeased. They were supporting Harold Washington, a black congressman (and the eventual winner). And they had a warning for Mondale: "It is imperative that you detach yourself from [the Daley] campaign at a minimum. At a maximum, you should reconsider and identify with the right side of history and support Congressman Harold Washington." Many years later, in 2007, Daley *fils* was mayor, as he had been for a long time: He was running for his sixth and final term. Illinois's junior senator, Barack Obama, endorsed him—which stung a black candidate challenging Daley. Obama, said this candidate, William "Dock" Walls III, had endorsed "the wrong side of history."

Over and over, Obama has made clear that he considers himself on the right side of history (if not history itself). During the 2008 presidential campaign, he said, "Listen, I respect John McCain for his half century of service to this country. But he is on the wrong side of history right now." In other words, the Republican nominee was in Obama's way. Some criticized the Democrat as too young and inexperienced to be president. Attacking this line of criticism, Bill Clinton said, "It didn't work in 1992, because we were on the right side of history"—he himself was a nominee, for the first time, then. "And it will not work in 2008, because Barack Obama is on the right side of history."

When it came time to effect their health-care transformation, Obama and the Democrats talked a lot about history. "This is history," congressmen would say. When their legislation passed, Obama said, "Tonight, we answered the call of history." Earlier, the *New York Times* columnist Nicholas D. Kristof wrote, "It's now broadly apparent that those who opposed Social Security in 1935 and Medicare in 1965 were wrong in their fears and tried to obstruct a historical tide"—there's that tide again. "This year, the fate of health care will come down to a handful of members of Congress. . . . If they flinch and health reform fails, they'll be letting down their country at a crucial juncture. They'll be on the wrong side of history." The Senate majority leader, Harry Reid, said, "Instead of joining us on the right side of history, all Republicans can come up with is this: 'Slow down, stop everything, let's start over.'" Reid had an analogy to make, just perfect for Republicans who opposed the Democrats' health-care vision: "When this country belatedly recognized the wrongs of slavery, there were those who dug in their heels and said, 'Slow down, it's too early, let's wait, things aren't bad enough.'"

In the midst of this health-care debate, Reid had an uncomfortable moment, when a book revealed what he had said about Obama's advantages as a candidate. Obama, mused Reid, was a "light-skinned" black "with no Negro dialect, unless he wanted to have one." Obama leapt to his defense, absolving his fellow Democrat by saying, "This is a good man who has always been on the right side of history."

Obama likes to talk, not only about the "right" and "wrong" "sides" of history, but about "the arc of history." For example, he praised the uprising in Egypt as having "bent the arc of history." In this, he is echoing Martin Luther King. Obama had a special rug made for the Oval Office, into which are woven quotations from U.S. presidents and MLK. King's quotation is, "The arc of the moral universe is long, but it bends towards justice." At the time the rug was unveiled, many pointed out that King was, in fact, echoing Theodore Parker, the abolitionist minister. But attribution was not of utmost importance here; there was no real need for a reweaving.

With every passing day, you hear something else about "the right side of history," or the "wrong side." Gay marriage is inevitable, people say: Better get on the right side of history. I say, gay marriage may be right or wrong, inevitable or evitable, but why drag history into it? The victorious side is not always the right one, is it? Remember what Whittaker Chambers said. After his break with Communism, he told the congressional committee, "I know that I am leaving the winning side for the losing side." He turned out to be wrong—although Cubans, North Koreans, and others are still being lashed by Communism. Che Guevara was part of the winning team in Cuba. That dictatorship is now over 50 years old. Guevara, a butcher and totalitarian, gazes out from a billion T-shirts. Is he on the right side of history?

The notion that history moves toward the light, says Andrew Roberts, should have died at Auschwitz. Human beings in any age are good at hurtling the world into the pit. Sometimes history, or the trend of affairs, deserves to be reversed, or at least opposed. William F. Buckley Jr. thought so, when he founded *National Review* in 1955. In a mission statement, he and his crew said that they would stand "athwart history, yelling Stop"—particularly because practically "no one" was "inclined to do so."

History may not be bunk, as Henry Ford said it was. But "the right side of history" is largely bunk. Its use may be benign and well-meaning; its use may be sinister and threatening. (We could do a whole essay, or book, on "social justice"!) In any case, we might ask whether we are on the right side of an issue, or a question, or a problem, leaving history—or worse, History—well out of it.

Like you, maybe, I favor a free-market approach to health care. I think it's better for all. But I don't pretend that history calls it forth.

—April 18, 2011

War of Words

Notes on a language cop and her struggle

"The Woman Who Stopped Us from Saying 'Stewardess,'" read a headline last month. The article was a celebration of Kate Swift, who had passed away. She is credited with rooting out sexism, or perceived sexism, in language. Credited by many, I should say, and blamed by a few. In addition to being a writer and editor, she was a gay-rights activist and a pro-choice activist. When I say "choice," you know I'm not talking about education.

With her partner, a woman named Casey Miller, Swift wrote an essay called "Desexing the English Language." That was for the inaugural issue of *Ms.* magazine, in 1972. That same year, they wrote "One Small Step for Genkind," for *The New York Times Magazine*. ("Genkind" was to replace "mankind.") They then produced a book, *Words and Women: New Language in New Times*.

I have written of Miller as Swift's "partner," and she was that, professionally and otherwise. (She died in 1997.) The word "partner" has had an interesting evolution. For decades, Rowland Evans and Robert Novak wrote a column together, and they considered themselves "partners." "My partner Bob Novak," Evans would say; "my partner Rowlie Evans," Novak would say. Toward the end, however, they started saying "writing partner." I'm sure it was because "partner" had taken on the connotation of "gay lover" (to use an antique phrase). Obituaries used to employ the euphemism "longtime companion"; now they regularly say "partner."

Back to "stewardess": Why do some words get stigmatized and other words not? It can be a mystery. I rather regret the loss of "stewardess," in part because I liked its companion, "steward." "Flight attendant" seems to me sort of mechanical: like something out of robotics or early sci-fi. We used to call Amelia Earhart an "aviatrix"—the only time we ever used "aviatrix." Wonderful old word. I see now that a dictionary has this usage note: "When relevant, sex is specified with the generic term: *Amelia Earhart was a pioneer woman aviator*." Too bad.

In music reviews, I like to use the word "concertmistress," when I can. It's a beautiful, flavorful old word. I do my tiny bit to keep it in circulation. I would never, however, refer to Emily Dickinson as a "poetess." Don't know exactly why. It sounds denigratory to me. Am I inconsistent? Oh, sure. These things are often felt, rather than reasoned out.

Miller & Swift did not like traditional pronouns, at all. They wanted you to say "tey," "ter," and "tem," for "he" or "she," "his" or "her," and "him" or "her." They lost that one. And yet people can be very touchy about pronouns. When I hear, or say, "To each his own," I don't think of sex—of a man, specifically. I think of a person, or people, generally. But others don't.

In Davos one year, I moderated a panel, and asked that each participant "say a few words about himself." It crossed my mind to add "or herself," but, in that split second, I thought, "No, everyone is grown up here. This is not Smith College. They know about English." I was wrong. The first panelist was a woman—an anthropology professor—who said, "To begin with, I am not a 'himself,' I am a person." The woman next to her—her partner, I believe—applauded, loudly, angrily, and alone. It was the sound of two hands clapping, so to speak. An incredibly awkward moment. And it taught me, or reaffirmed, that standard, or once-standard, English can be risky.

"To each their own" is ungrammatical. "To each his or her own" is uneuphonious. Pick your poison. Or stick to your guns.

Like "tey" and the rest, "genkind" has not caught on, thank goodness. "Humankind" is bad enough. Why did people ever begin to think that "mankind" referred, not to people in general, but to men only? Why did they begin to think that about "man"—as in "the rights of man"? Recently, I read an article that quoted a religious woman of the 19th century. The woman used the word "man," and the writer of the article felt the need to explain that, in the olden days, they said this, and meant nothing sex-specific by it. Has it come to that? Obviously so.

Swift & Miller did not want you to say "policeman," but "police officer." Not "mailman," or "postman," but "mail carrier." ("The Mail Carrier Always Rings Twice"?) Verboten, too, was "fireman," to be replaced by "firefighter." In the wake of 9/11, and the attendant rescue operations, many noted that people were saying "fireman," instead of the fussier "firefighter." This was no time for political correctness, was the feeling. Of course, "fireman" can refer to a worker on a train or ship too—so maybe "firefighter" saves you a little ambiguity. (But who stokes fires on steam locomotives these days?)

As I've mentioned in these pages before, I grew up in one of the most politically correct places in America, Ann Arbor, Mich.—and at a very, very politically correct time. This was a time when people were (seriously) saying "person-hole cover," instead of "manhole cover." We got to replacing "man" with "person" automatically. A friend and I would joke that Detroit's mayor was "Coleperson Young." Women, for some, became "womyn." You also heard the word "herstory," in rebuke of "history." Get it?

"Chairman" fell into disfavor, replaced by "chairperson" or simply "chair." Oddly, actresses, some of them, began to call themselves "actors." A woman introduced herself to me as an "actor" just the other week. But will the Oscars drop the Best Actress category and have just one, for men and women—Best Actor? Don't bet on it. Maybe "Best Actor, Male Division" and "Best Actor, Female Division"?

There came a time, certainly in "progressive" circles, when "husband" and "wife," especially the latter, acquired a stigma. You were supposed to say "spouse." When I was in graduate school, a young man came back to the dorm eager to tell us something: "I referred to Nancy Reagan today as 'the president's spouse,' without even thinking. It just came naturally to me to say 'spouse,' instead of 'wife.'" He was very pleased with himself—as though he had learned to love Big Brother, or Big Sister.

"Secretary" acquired an odor—not sure why. Don't know why "assistant" is any better, any nobler. Rather like "flight attendant," it seems to me more mechanical: A vacuum cleaner could be an "assistant," but never a "secretary." Incidentally, National Secretary's Day has now been replaced by Administrative Professionals Day. And have you heard the story—a legend—about the young woman seated next to Henry Kissinger in the mid-Seventies? "What do you do?" she says. "I'm secretary of state," he answers. "Oh, I'm a secretary too!" she responds.

Some colleges and universities have stricken the word "freshmen" in favor of "first years." "Sophomores," "juniors," and "seniors" are free of the dreaded "men." But "freshmen" needed fixing.

Even the word "girl" is frowned on by some—"girl" in all circumstances. Tell you a story. In the mid-Nineties, I was living in Washington, D.C., and paid a visit to Kramerbooks, on Dupont Circle. Two young men, a customer and a clerk, were having a conversation. They were speaking of a mutual friend who had just had a baby. "Boy or girl?" said the customer. The clerk gulped and said—swear—"She had a woman."

I personally am of two minds about "Ms.," which has achieved absolute acceptance, even dominance. On one hand, it was always a pain to dance around marital status: Was a woman "Miss" or "Mrs."? And it seemed slightly ridiculous to address an octogenarian as "Miss." On the other hand, "Ms." is so . . . so unattractive, kind of a non-word, don't you think? In any case, I credit Gloria Steinem with saying at least one charming thing in her life. When the *New York Times* acceded to "Ms." in 1986, she quipped, "Now I no longer have to be 'Miss Steinem of Ms. magazine.'"

The question of language and politics is an old and freighted one, and I'll just say a quick something about abortion. Years ago, on television, Kate Michelman, the famous pro-choice activist, was debating a pro-lifer, a woman whose name I forget. The pro-lifer spoke first, and, discussing pregnancy, referred to a "mother" and her "baby." When it was Michelman's turn, she said (as I recall), "First, let's get the language right: It's not a 'mother' and her 'baby,' it's a 'woman' and the 'fetus.'" I will say this, too: If "pro-choice" isn't the greatest, and most brazen, lexical triumph in the history of politics, I don't know what is.

Everyone accepts that language evolves, and most people accept that it ought to. There will always be "new language" for "new times," to borrow from Miller & Swift's subtitle. And yet I don't see why we should surrender to new language that's absurd, ugly, or merely PC. A tribute to Swift printed on *The Nation*'s website said, "A good memorial to Kate would be to let media outlets know when you see 'mankind' that it's not good English." Will the media outlets then have the nerve and sense to tell you to stuff it? I hope so, but I doubt it. Rarely are people so cowed as they are before language cops. ("Cowed and/or bulled"?)

According to the obituaries, Swift spent her last hours in a hospital called Middlesex. Given her struggle for "gender-neutral" language, that seems appropriate, almost poetic. During the George W. Bush years, she spelled the president's name with a lowercase "b": "bush." Like "genkind" and the pronouns, that didn't catch on. But "stewardess" is pretty much history, or herstory. Are we, is our society, the better for it? I don't think so, but, you know—win some, lose some.

—June 20, 2011

QUOTIN' OBAMA

A wire-service reporter opens a can of worms

When an MSNBC commentator accuses someone of racism, it's dog bites man. MSNBC is a Left-heavy channel; the Left can hardly talk without accusing others of racism. Last month, however, there was a whiff of man bites dog. An MSNBC commentator accused someone of racism, all right. But the accused was a reporter for the Associated Press—not an organization you would expect to come in for such condemnation. The AP is a member of the "mainstream media" in good standing (all too good).

Here's what happened: The AP's Mark S. Smith filed a report on a speech by President Obama to a Congressional Black Caucus dinner. He wrote,

> Obama said blacks know all too well from the civil rights struggle that the fight for what is right is never easy.
>
> "Take off your bedroom slippers. Put on your marching shoes," he said, his voice rising as applause and cheers mounted. "Shake it off. Stop complainin'. Stop grumblin'. Stop cryin'. We are going to press on. We have work to do."

Smith's offense, according to his accuser? He quoted Obama faithfully—"dropped g's" and all. His accuser, Karen Hunter, said this was "racist," and not just "racist" but "inherently racist." Hunter is a journalist and, depressingly, also a journalism professor. She once ghosted a book for Al Sharpton. She said that Smith should have standardized Obama's English: "complaining," "grumbling," etc.

I watched a video clip of Obama's speech. He went very, very southern in that speech. He slipped into preacher mode, strong on exhortation. Smith's report gave you an idea of what it was like to be in the room—which a report should do. "Complaining" and "grumbling" would have robbed the report of flavor, and also of some veracity. Actually, Obama said "marchin' shoes," rather than "marching shoes." Smith did not drop all the g's he could have.

This episode sparked a memory in me. In 1988, Jesse Jackson was running for president, as he had in 1984. Clark Clifford, the Democratic "wise man," said that Jackson was "bringing a new maturity to the American political scene." George Will, in a column, said, *Oh, yeah?* "Twenty years ago, Clifford was secretary of defense. Here is Jackson on defense policy: 'Don't nobody want no Midgetman missile for Christmas. They don't want no Star Wars for Christmas.'"

Will, naturally, was accused of racism, and some newspapers refused to run that particular column. The claim was that Will should have put Jackson's statements into conventional English. In other words, he should have misquoted him, in a way. But would that have opened Will to different charges of racism? You can hear it: "What's the matter with what the reverend said originally? You think he has to 'talk white'?" Shortly after Will's column appeared (or didn't appear), the *New York Times* ran a chin-stroking article headed "As Jackson Rises, Reporters Search for Proper Balance." The article asked, "How should Mr. Jackson be treated? As the first black to achieve such electoral success? As a liberal politician? Or simply as a contender for the Democratic Presidential nomination?"

The issue of quotation goes beyond skin color, of course. In the weeks before George W. Bush's second presidential inauguration, in 2005, I was asked to write a piece for an inaugural publication. I agreed. In my piece, I quoted something Bush repeatedly said in the 2000 campaign: "I'm runnin' for a reason." He usually said this when he was pushing Social Security reform. He didn't want to go to the White House and mark time. He wanted to do big things. "I'm runnin' for a reason."

An editor sent the piece back to me, with some changes he had made. In his version, Bush said, "I'm running for a reason." "No, no!" I replied. "That spoils the sentence, don't you see? It takes the music out of it. We must allow Bush his naturalness." The editor relented. Last month, during the AP brouhaha, a *Politico* blog noted an article that the *New York Times* had run in August. The article compared Bush and his successor as the governor of Texas, Rick Perry. It said the two share "a down-home way of speakin' that's heavy on the dropped g's." The paper offered an example: On the presidential campaign trail, Perry was warning against "over-taxin', over-regulatin', and over-litigatin'."

In the wake of Obama's Congressional Black Caucus appearance, some people criticized the president for his foray into preachin'. What was a guy brought up in Hawaii and Indonesia doing talking like that? Well, many people speak in different ways to different audiences, or different individuals, and that certainly includes politicians. There is nothing necessarily shameful or hypocritical about it.

When Jimmy Carter was the governor of Georgia, William F. Buckley Jr. had him as a guest on *Firing Line*. After the taping, the governor's aides told WFB that they were shocked at how their boss had sounded: He was far less southern than he was back home, among his constituents. Years later, in print, WFB teased Carter about his "*Firing Line* voice."

Sometimes a politician will take a different voice too far. Click on some Hillary Clinton videos from the 2008 Democratic primaries, and you may be shocked. To black audiences, she laid it on really, really thick—insultingly thick, to my ears. She might as well have been in blackface when she said the following to Al Sharpton's National Action Network: "When I walk into the Oval Office in January 2009, I'm afraid I'm gonna lift up the rug and I'm gonna see so much stuff under there. You know, what is it about us always havin' to clean up after people?" Thus did Hillary Rodham Clinton, of Wellesley, the White House, the Senate, and elsewhere, identify with the janitorial class.

When questioned about her "black voice," as some dubbed it, she answered quite gracefully: She had lived in several different places, including Arkansas, and "I think America is ready for a multilingual president."

Two years later, Barack Obama was in the White House, and his former pastor, Jeremiah Wright, had been estranged from him. A reporter asked Wright whether he had spoken to the president. No, said Wright: "Them Jews ain't going to let him talk to me." Apparently, he was alluding to Rahm Emanuel, then the presidential chief of staff and now the mayor of Chicago, and mysterious, insidious other Jews. When Wright talks that way, it's entirely by choice. He was raised in a bourgeois Philadelphia community by a father who was a distinguished minister and a mother who was a pioneering teacher and school administrator. I doubt Wright was ever allowed to say "Them Jews ain't . . ." in his house—for reasons of both style and content.

By the way, MSNBC played a tape of Wright's comment, and had the text on the screen. Viewers heard "Them Jews ain't" but saw "Them Jews aren't." That must have caused some disorientation. And whoever changed "ain't" to "aren't" neglected to change "Them" to "Those"—leaving it "Them Jews" instead of "Those Jews."

All of us who do reporting have to think about how to quote people. Do you do it absolutely verbatim? Not necessarily. You often tidy up the grammar of the speaker. The temptation is to tidy for those you like and leave in the raw those you don't like. More than once, I've quoted something Obama said about Wright: "He married Michelle and I." I shouldn't twit Obama like that, but sometimes I find his reputation for erudition annoying.

As a rule, I think written English ought to follow speech. I tend to write casually, and this is especially so in my online column. Once, I wrote "I'd've," as in, "If I'd known you were coming, I'd've baked a cake." An editor raised an eyebrow at my contractions. But "I'd have" was not quite right, and neither was "I would've." "I would have" would have been disastrous—it had to be "I'd've." Sometime later, inveighing against the moral indifference of my countrymen, I wrote, "The American people just want to get they freak on." An editor inquired, "Did you mean 'their'?" No, I didn't! If you're going to use a slang expression, go all the way. In for a penny, in for a pound.

When Karen Hunter accused Reporter Smith of racism, he defended himself ably. He said, among other things, that he was respecting Obama's "intent" in that Congressional Black Caucus speech: his rhythm, his cadence, his mode. True. I would have been tempted to respond to Hunter sharply: "If anything is 'racist,' it's shame at the way Americans speak."

Some 25 years ago, I heard a black congresswoman talking about the Martin Luther King holiday. She kept saying "birfday." I winced, thinking she would be subject to derision, that white racists somewhere might chuckle. Later on I learned that "f" instead of "th" is part of many southerners' speech, southerners white and black. (How southern English became the English of black Americans from Maine to California is "a whole 'nother subject," as we said in my family.) What's more, "th" into "f" comes from England, as English tends to. There's a reason Keith Richards, the Rolling Stone, is known as "Keef." There's a reason that the Health and Safety Executive—a pillar of the British nanny state—is known as "'Elf 'n' Safety."

Race is a minefield in America, and language can be a bit of a minefield too. When race and language mix, the minefields are doubly dangerous. How can we navigate them? I think of Abe Rosenthal, the late editor of the *New York Times*. Asked how he edited the paper, he answered, "With my stomach." I also think of a phrase from *A Midsummer Night's Dream*, a phrase made all the more famous by a Britten aria: "Be kind and courteous." Stomach, kindness, and courtesy should see you through. But they won't spare you being called a racist, because, in our environment, nothing will.

If it happens, you might reply with the words of a beloved old spiritual: "You can talk about me just as much as you please. I'm goin' talk about you when I git on my knees." Alternatively, "I been 'buked and I been scorned." But "I ain't never gonna lay my 'ligion down." That'll shake 'em up.

—October 31, 2011

Goodbye, McKinley

The rise and fall of names

With a stroke, President Obama changed the name of Mount McKinley to "Denali." "Denali" is an Indian name, or indigenous name. "McKinley," obviously, is not. No doubt, Obama thought he was "bending the arc of the moral universe toward justice." (He likes to use this phrase, borrowing from Martin Luther King, who borrowed it from Theodore Parker, an abolitionist pastor.)

White people have taken from the Indians a lot. It's true. I can understand how Obama was unable to resist a symbolic gesture. I can't help thinking, however, that these gestures are much, much easier than combating alcoholism, obesity, welfare dependence, a culture of perpetual grievance, and suicide.

Against "Denali," poor William McKinley had no chance. He is a dead white male, and a Republican, to boot. And yet, to my sense, there was something unseemly—something unsporting—about removing the name of a president who was murdered.

Lincoln was murdered, too, of course, and many things are named after him—but he was great, as well as murdered. Garfield was murdered, and there is next to nothing named after him. Schoolkids probably don't know about him. Everyone knows about John F. Kennedy, who, when murdered, was young and glamorous and fashionable. People used to call the international airport in New York "Idlewild" (after the golf course that the airport displaced). But since the assassination, it has been JFK.

Kennedy's brother Robert was murdered, too. A full 40 years after the fact, the Triborough Bridge in New York was renamed for him: Officially, it is the Robert F. Kennedy Bridge (though pretty much everybody still calls it "the Triborough"). I hope it's not unseemly or unsporting to ask, "For how many decades will we feel the need to rename things after JFK and RFK?" In 2011, two years before he died, the Queensboro Bridge was renamed for Ed Koch, the former mayor—but not entirely renamed: It is, officially, the Ed Koch Queensboro Bridge.

For years, I've teased a federal-judge friend of mine for working in the Daniel Patrick Moynihan United States Courthouse. (He and I are both Republicans; Moynihan was not.) "How's work going down at the Moynihan?" I'll say. One day, my friend said sternly, "You know what the best name for a U.S. courthouse is? 'U.S. Courthouse.'" That statement ought to be in Bartlett's.

Robert Byrd, the West Virginia Democrat, had no shame, and his fellow West Virginians may not have had much either. More than 50 buildings in that state are named for Byrd, or for his wife, Erma Ora. If you seek Byrd's monument, go to West Virginia and look about you.

Lest I seem an incorrigible partisan Republican—which I am—I'd like to record this: When the GOP Congress of the 1990s moved to rename Washington National Airport for Reagan, I opposed this move. I loved Reagan to an almost embarrassing extent. But I thought renaming the *national airport* for him was a finger in the eye to Democrats, roughly half the country. Besides which, what if *they* did something like that to *us*? How would I feel about *Bill Clinton* National Airport? (Bad.)

People tend to think that no one will ever get used to a new name. And then the world forgets the old name. When, in 2009, the Sears Tower became the Willis Tower, Chicagoans said, "We'll never say 'Willis.' It will always be 'Sears.'" Alternatively, they borrowed a famous line from a sitcom: "What you talkin' 'bout, Willis?" The truth is, "Sears" will sound as quaint as "Idlewild." I have a friend in Chicago who will always say "Sears." (In fact, he once worked in the tower.) His children, however, are bilingual: They say both "Sears" and "Willis," depending on the audience. *Their* children will *definitely* not say "Sears."

It was jarring to me in 1984 when the West African nation of Upper Volta became Burkina Faso. The new name sounded so . . . odd. Thirty years later, "Upper Volta" sounds not just dated but faintly racist or colonialist. There has been no "Siam" since about 1950; the country is Thailand. The old name lives only in the Rodgers & Hammerstein musical (though I very much like an American place-name: Siam, Ohio). "Formosa" may seem a condescending or insulting name for Taiwan—but, in Portuguese, the name means beautiful, which is no insult.

We are supposed to say "Mumbai," not "Bombay." Say "Bombay" to someone, and he may recoil, as though you had uttered a slur. In reality, there is a fierce debate among Indians about what to call that major city. A political and cultural debate. There are Indians, patriotic and proud, who would rather spit than say "Mumbai." I don't have a dog in this fight. But I have no patience for other palefaces who think they do.

Like you, maybe, I enjoy finding out about people whose names are on buildings, streets, or what have you. Those names are a link to the past. With his wife Liddie, the late historian Robert Conquest lived on Peter Coutts Circle near Stanford University. The first time I visited, I asked, "Who is or was Peter Coutts?" His face lighting up, Bob said, "You know, we've lived here for many years, and you're only the second person to ask that." I was flattered, I have to say. (The first to ask was an English-poet friend of the Conquests'. And "Peter Coutts" was the adopted name of a French financier who had some trouble after the Franco–Prussian War and found it convenient to flee his country.)

Last week, I was writing about wounded servicemen who are cared for at the Walter Reed center, outside Washington, D.C. I had forgotten, or never knew, who Walter Reed was. I looked him up: U.S. Army physician (1851–1902). Instrumental in combating yellow fever. His name has lasted on that institution for a long time (since 1909). Will it be removed one day, in favor of someone newer or in some respect more desirable?

Sometimes money is involved, of course. In the early 1970s, a man named Avery Fisher endowed the concert hall at New York's Lincoln Center. So for all this time it has been "Avery Fisher Hall." But the Lincoln Center people wanted to upgrade the place. To do that, they needed lots of money, and that meant an offer of "naming rights." The Fisher family pitched a fit, and threatened legal action: They figured Avery's name should be on the hall forever. Ultimately, they were paid off ($15 million), and Lincoln Center found a new donor: David Geffen, of Hollywood. He pledged $100 million, and, starting this season, the hall will be David Geffen Hall.

Across the plaza is the David H. Koch Theater, formerly the New York State Theater. In 2008, this Koch brother pledged—as Geffen would—$100 million. And he said that, after 50 years, his name could go. A half a century was enough. "A naming opportunity should be a defined length of time to allow the institution to regenerate itself with another round of major fundraising," Koch said. Geffen has a different view—and has said that his name must be on the concert hall forever.

His fellow Democrats have long held Jefferson-Jackson Day dinners. Those two men are the founders of the Democratic party. Recently, however, some Democratic groups have effaced the names of Jefferson and Jackson—because those men were slaveholders (and Jackson was also a brute to the Indians). The Republicans will obviously keep their Lincoln Day dinners.

"Washington, D.C." presents a double whammy, for those who keep historical score, in the current fashion. George Washington was another slaveholder. And the "C" in "D.C." relates to Christopher Columbus, the original sinner, according to the darkest view of America. What to do about President Obama's alma mater, Columbia?

I felt a pang for McKinley, when his name came off the mountain. But I also recognize that nearly everything crumbles. Not long ago, I visited the Temple of Artemis, or Diana, in Turkey. This was one of the Seven Wonders of the World. People traveled from far and wide to see it. The sight of it may have crowned a life. When *I* got there, it was a garbagey nothing, with a stork nesting on a lone column. Rarely has the ephemerality of things been so impressed on me.

There will be some, no doubt, who will continue to call the mountain in Alaska "Mount McKinley." (Politics, history, or culture aside, the alliteration is nice.) They will be a bit like Dartmouth alumni who continue to call their teams "the Indians" instead of the sanctioned "Big Green."

Speaking of mountains, Everest was named after a Welshman, Colonel Sir George Everest, who was Surveyor General of India from 1830 to 1843. He objected to the naming of the mountain after himself, in part because those who lived in the region could not pronounce "Everest." (Neither can we, in a sense: The colonel pronounced his name "Eve-rest," rather than as the world later would.)

Who knows what this tallest and mightiest of peaks will be called in generations to come? Nothing lasts, everything crumbles. Although our Supreme Court may still permit me to quote the Bible—Isaiah: "For the mountains shall depart, and the hills be removed; but my kindness shall not depart from thee."

—October 5, 2015

MUSIC

The Right Notes

Lee Hoiby, composer

"I'm just so grateful," said Lee Hoiby, in the last days of his life. "I'm grateful to have lived the life I've lived, to have written the music I've written, to have known the people I've known." He died at the end of March. I got to know him in 2004, something like that. And I thought I'd say a little about the friendship we shared. First, though, a bit of biography.

Hoiby was born in 1926, in Madison, Wis. He studied with two of the outstanding pianists and teachers of the age: Gunnar Johansen and Egon Petri. Johansen had studied with Petri, actually. And Petri had studied with Busoni (no less). Hoiby opted against becoming a pianist, but he played the piano all his life. He practiced every day, on Chopin études, specifically.

What he did was compose. His big teachers in composition were Gian Carlo Menotti, Darius Milhaud, and Samuel Barber. But he had other teachers, teachers he never met, in the flesh. "It was Schubert who taught me to write songs," he told me. And he said this of Richard Strauss: "He was the one, in *Capriccio* [an opera], who gave me the courage to write simple lyricism."

Why did he need courage? Hoiby grew up in a strange time for music. To put it briefly, tonality was out, atonality was in; beauty was out, severity was in; the idea of inspiration was out, formalism was in. And the enforcers of the new order were merciless. Hoiby often said, "I wanted to grow heirloom roses, but they allowed you nothing but cactuses." He paid a price for his nonconformity: a price in commissions, prizes, fame. But it was a price he gladly paid, for he felt free: free to write the music he wanted to write, the music that was in him. And plenty of people liked it, a lot.

A few years ago, a young composer referred to Hoiby as a "maverick." He got a kick out of this, Hoiby did.

He wrote all sorts of music, including sonatas, concertos, and quartets. But he is best known for music involving the voice: be it songs, oratorios, or operas. His most frequently performed operas are *Summer and Smoke*, based on the Tennessee Williams play, and *A Month in the Country*, based on the Turgenev. One day, Williams and Hoiby were walking down the street, and the playwright said, "Why don't you make an opera out of one of my plays?" Hoiby said, "Which one?" Williams replied, "Take your pick, sweetheart."

Not every composer has the ability to write an opera. Leonard Bernstein once said to Hoiby something quite gracious: "Maybe you'll teach me how to write an opera someday."

It was in songs, however, that Hoiby showed utmost skill. He wrote about a hundred of them. Many have entered the standard American repertory. Their greatest champion was Leontyne Price, the soprano who retired in the late '90s. One of the most popular Hoiby songs is "The Serpent," which sets a comical poem by Theodore Roethke. A voice coach once said, "If you throw a brick out the window on the Upper West Side [of Manhattan], you'll hit a soprano who has learned 'The Serpent.'"

In February 2005, I wrote a piece about Hoiby for *National Review*: "Singing His Own Song." He was grateful to have someone understand and appreciate him. Shortly after this piece appeared, I received a large envelope in the mail. Hoiby had sent me a new song—and it was dedicated to me. It's a very good song, too. Called "Winter Hubris," it is brief, shrewdly crafted, and moving. In my thank-you note to the composer, I referred to it as a "B-minor beauty." And that's how Lee would refer to the song, when speaking about it to me: "your B-minor beauty."

It sets a poem by a friend of his, who works for George Soros. Think of that: The text is by a lieutenant to Soros, great benefactor of the American and worldwide Left; the dedication is to an editor of a stalwart conservative magazine. Funny old world, and a fun one, too, sometimes.

In several ways, Lee and I were quite different. He was 1960s-ish, gay, and pot-smoking. ("Mary Jane has always been good to me," he said, as he lay in a medical facility toward the end. I'm not entirely sure about that.) Was he on the left? Presumably, but, you know? He never breathed a political word to me. Never. And I never breathed one to him, of course. I also think of this fact: He was damned as a "conservative"—a musical conservative—by his critics all his career.

We talked about religion once, and more than once. He said he had never really considered himself a religious person. "Spiritual," sure, but not religious. One day, he had an inspiration, as he was composing. Some compositional problem was solved for him. "And, much to my surprise, I found myself kneeling, in gratitude." He went on to say, "When it's really good, it doesn't come from you."

Far from Manhattan, where composers do their politicking, get their commissions, and keep their names and faces about, Hoiby lived in Long Eddy, N.Y. He lived with his partner and collaborator, the writer Mark Shulgasser. They lived on a ramshackle estate with a waterfall. (Lee, were he reading this, would chuckle over that word "estate.") I visited a few times. And we talked about everything: composers, composing, performers, performing, life experiences, good and bad. Everything, pretty much.

He would tell me what Petri said, about how to close a particular Schumann piece, for example. And he would tell me what Barber said. Here is one of those morsels: "When you learn a Beethoven sonata, you must play the notes on the page. Anything else is wrong. Writing music is the same. You have to find the right notes." Lee was always on the hunt for these "right notes."

One composer who came up in our discussions was Ned Rorem. He was, and is, not unlike Lee: American, tonal (to use the shortest of shorthands), a celebrated writer of art songs. They should have been allies and brothers; they were not. Lee recounted something terrible that Rorem had said about his music. I can see the look on Lee's face, full of disgust and pain. He then said that, years after the offending remark, Rorem wrote him a note, saying, in effect, "We're old now. Can we see each other and make up?" Lee never answered. I wish he had.

We did a lot of talking, yes. But the best thing about being at Lee's place was the music: going into his studio and singing through his songs. I would sing, and he would play. Or he would sing, or we would both sing. All the while, he would comment on his songs: how they were written, how they should be performed. You can't do that with, say, Schubert.

Lee sent me a steady stream of CDs, scores, and e-mails, with various observations and reports. Almost always, there was an eagerness, a kid-like excitement about his life and work. "On the homefront, great happenings!" one e-mail began. Another said, "I am quasi-trembling, on the verge of really digging into the next text I shall set, an Emerson plum, which Mark found after long searching. It's for the Vassar sesquicentennial commission."

One day, he might forward a spoof on Elliott Carter (the apostle of modernism—whom, by the way, I interviewed in 2008, just before his hundredth birthday. He's still going). Another day, he might write something like this: "Last night, probably owing to our recent exchanges about her, I got a little scotch under my belt, took a big breath, and called Leontyne." He and the great soprano had not communicated in a while. "To my delight, she was delighted."

Money was often tight—this despite a "Madame von Meck," as we referred to her, who helped him out from time to time. (Nadezhda von Meck was Tchaikovsky's patroness.) Lee wrote, for example, "Dreading extreme cold leading to extremely expensive heat." And, "Another day at the dentist, the bill rising another $800. They live well."

Mainly, he wrote in his e-mails about the joys and challenges of composing—with the emphasis on the joys. "Today I got one of those ideas that are immediate, which the French call *trouvailles* [findings, or discoveries]. (Doesn't sound very modest, but you know I never brag.)" He did—brag, that is. But usually in a charming and forgivable way.

Here was a note out of the blue, as so many of his were:

> Last night as I was drifting off to sleep, I had some thoughts about music which recur to me today. In tonality, the tonic is Home. You can leave, go many places, have many adventures, stray where you like, but you can always come home. Without tonality, you set out, you may have a lot of fun and do a lot of things, but you have no map, you can never come home. You are lost.

I can't tell you how grateful he was to be a composer. But he can: "I have this lovely awareness of having been possessed by one thing, all my life, and loving it." He also wrote, "Bach didn't grind out all those pages in the Gesellschaft just because it was his job. He couldn't help himself, just as I have to try, again and again, to write something, even if it's not a commission."

One of Hoiby's most beloved songs is "Where the Music Comes From," for which he wrote the lyrics, too. He wrote it at a quite down time of his life: when he was really searching. It's kind of a New Age hymn, a hippie hymn, or prayer. Many singers have sung it, including Price. But no one sang it as well as Lee. We did a Q&A once at the Cosmos Club in Washington. At the end, I asked him to play and sing "Where the Music Comes From." He needed no arm-twisting. He croaked it out in his wonderful old-man's voice. The performance was stunningly personal, and heartfelt, and moving. The room was kind of in suspension.

He always said he would live a very long time, coming from a long-lived family. An aunt of his died at 108. She bowled almost to the last. Lee died at 85. On meeting him, the pianist and accompanist Dalton Baldwin paid him this compliment: "Your songs are for the ages." I suspect that's true. Some of Lee Hoiby's songs are among my favorite songs—by anybody, in any age. I count him one of my favorite people, too.

—May 16, 2011

Carter at 100

The centenarian composer

Elliott Carter, the American composer, turns 100 this month—and the music world is duly celebrating. There are Carter-centered concerts, there are boxes of retrospective CDs. Carter is surely the senior composer in the world, and he is steadily working. But he is not the longest-lived composer we've had. That distinction probably goes to Leo Ornstein, who lived from 1893 to 2002—to the age of 108. The musicologist David Dubal once told me that Ornstein must be the only person to have written music in three different centuries.

When Carter was born in 1908, Theodore Roosevelt was president. Mahler and Debussy were still working. Rimsky-Korsakov had died a few months before. Richard Strauss was only in his mid-forties. Rachmaninoff was merely in his mid-thirties. As Carter himself points out, he has seen tremendous changes, in music and elsewhere.

Amid the celebrations, I pay him a visit. Carter is a native New Yorker, and still lives in the city: in Greenwich Village. He has occupied the same, gracious apartment since 1945. Among his neighbors were E. E. Cummings, Marianne Moore, and the composer Edgard Varèse. In conversation, Carter is quick and amusing, with a ready smile and a twinkle in his eye. He talks in a way that very, very few New Yorkers do now: New England-y. You encounter this type of speech, in Manhattan, only once in a while.

Carter's paternal grandfather, Eli, fought in the Civil War. He was at Gettysburg, in fact—and Carter knew him well. "Grandpa was a jolly old man, who had lots of fun, and was very shrewd. How he made the transition from fighting in the Civil War to becoming the leading lace-curtain importer in New York City, I cannot understand, but that is what he did." Eventually, the grandfather sold the business to the father (Elliott Sr.). He did so "at a considerable price, meaning we were quite poor for some time!"

Carter was already eight years old when America entered World War I. Living on 114th St. at Riverside Drive, he saw a little bit of this war: "The Hudson River was full of British warships, and I remember very distinctly British sailors wandering around on Riverside Drive." Radio was new then, and the young Carter toyed with them—homemade—on the roof of his building.

After the war, his father took him on several trips to Europe, and they saw the devastation that had occurred: "dreadful things." Hunger was acute. A later trip took them to Baden-Baden in 1923—and Carter remembers reading in a newspaper that President Harding had died.

Neither of Carter's parents was musical, and they would certainly not have chosen a composing career for their son. But Carter caught a break at the famed Horace Mann School (whose students included Eugene O'Neill's son, who became one of Carter's best friends). A teacher introduced the kids to Charles Ives, and the composer took an interest in

Carter. "Mr. Ives used to subscribe to a box in Carnegie Hall, and he'd occasionally invite me to sit with him." He also played the young man some of his own compositions—for instance, the Concord Sonata (in a version different from the one known by the public).

A pivotal moment came when Carter heard Stravinsky's *Rite of Spring*, a notorious departure in music. He figured, then, that he had to be a composer.

He went to Harvard College, in part to be near the Boston Symphony, which, under Serge Koussevitzky, was playing a lot of modern music. He did not enroll in the music department, however: "In those years, the department was entirely devoted to teaching church organists, and it was extremely conventional. I was interested in what was called advanced or avant-garde music," and they were not. He studied English, availing himself of such eminent scholars as Irving Babbitt and George Lyman Kittredge ("a tyrant!"). Another teacher was Alfred North Whitehead, the philosopher.

After college, Carter enrolled in the Harvard graduate school—in music. The atmosphere had rapidly grown more congenial. His two principal teachers were Walter Piston and Gustav Holst (composer of *The Planets*). Piston, says Carter, was a "fussy" man who "liked to turn everything into a rather disagreeable joke." But one could learn a great deal from him: particularly about the instruments of the orchestra and how to write for them. Holst, visiting from England, was "rather aged" and had poor eyesight. That meant that the students had to play him their pieces on the piano, rather than handing in manuscripts. "Whenever we wrote anything dissonant, he would say, 'You'd better learn to play the piano better'!"

By the way, Holst—whom Carter has described (correctly) as "rather aged"—died at 59, not long after he taught Carter. Carter, of course, is 41 years older.

After Harvard, Carter went to Paris to study with Nadia Boulanger, teacher of generations of Americans (in particular). Ives advised Carter against this move, thinking that he should remain on native grounds; Carter went anyway. And he has many interesting stories and memories about "Nadia." "Evidently, she had been told, when she was very young, that she would go blind," which indeed happened, but over decades. "So she made an enormous effort to memorize everything. And as a result, she had all these scores right in her head," enabling her to cite you something in an instant.

Carter himself would become a teacher: at Columbia, Yale, Juilliard, and other places. One of his earliest jobs was at St. John's College, the Great Books redoubt in Annapolis. It was Carter's mission to introduce music to the program. He taught Euclid's geometry and suchlike, finding out what the ancients had to say about music. Carter's scientific knowledge is considerable (even if he demurs from this assessment). Has it been a help in his music? "I don't think so. Scientific knowledge is above what I do in music. I'm concerned with a very practical field"—fitting music to performers and so on. "I don't care what the numerical relations of the notes are and all that." Time was, numerical relations were all the rage in composition. "I tried to write like that once, and it bored me, so I stopped."

Evolving as a composer, Carter made important investigations into rhythm. "I spent some time in Tunisia, and got very interested in the drumming patterns of Arabic music." Carter is liable to have two different speeds going at the same time. He is a pioneer in what is possible in tempo and rhythm. And "my music got started, I think, by listening to jazz. In jazz, as in almost all dance music, there's a regular beat in the background and, against that, improvisation. My music is all like that."

Some people think that melody is passé. Does Carter? No, he says—but one can mean many different things by melody. He writes melodies that may not be recognized as such by listeners. And Schubert, he says, could make a melody out of just a couple of notes. Moreover, "Nadia used to talk about 'Tea for Two'"—there is a real economy about that melody.

When Carter speaks of "the old music," he does not mean Monteverdi, Byrd, and Rameau—or only them. He means the sweep of music from those early composers up through Wagner or so. And the "old" composers did well in that "they dealt with the material available at the time and made it speak very strongly." But he regards this music as belonging to the past, and "no longer the most vivid thing that one can do." The old music may be "fantastically beautiful," but "it doesn't quite speak in the way that modern music does." (On that, many, of diverse opinions, can agree.)

What about the so-called Neo-Romantics such as Barber—can Carter respect them, even as he diverges from them? "Well, some of us felt that the kind of music Sam wrote had already been done, only done better than anybody could do it now. Therefore there was no reason to do it now." Grinning, Carter says, "What Sam did was deplorable," but his music, nonetheless, "is rather good."

Carter has known many composers well—including Stravinsky—but I ask him which composer from the past he would most like to meet and talk things over with. He names Debussy. Carter had plenty of talks with Stravinsky—"but he'd say, 'Oh, I forgot how I wrote that,' so you couldn't get anything out of it!"

Entering his eleventh decade, Carter feels he is still learning about music: "Each piece I write I consider an adventure. I've learned a lot by trying to be a composer." And does he think he has gotten better? "Of course I think I've gotten better—who wouldn't think that?"

Then there is the touchy question of whether he cares whether people like his music. "That depends on the degree of 'care' you mean. What I care about is having performers who like my music and want to play it and play it well." The public has a way of coming around. As to whether Carter believes that his music will last, "You tell me what the future's going to be, and I'll tell you the answer. God only knows the future. In my own lifetime, there has been such an enormous change in every conceivable way that it would be hard to predict the future"—even ten or fifteen years out.

He does not have a roster of pieces he feels he needs to write—he simply goes from one project or commission to the next. "I guess I'm just walking through life, where my music is concerned." But there are certain books he would like to read. He's reading through Shakespeare's plays now, and he would like to read more Balzac, Dostoevsky, and Proust. He does not think he will get to it, though.

And he does not listen to a lot of music on his stereo. "At my age, I'm extremely busy writing my music and keeping fatigue out of the way. Most of the music is in my head by now. I don't like to listen to recordings of my own music, either: because a) people don't play it right and b) I feel I didn't write the right thing. I think I should have changed something." Does he ever go back and revise? "Yes, but my experience is, having done that, I like it better the way it was the first time!"

Toward the end of our discussion, I ask whether the 100th-birthday celebrations are a bother to him, distracting from his work, or a pleasure. "They bother me," he says, "but I'd be disappointed if they didn't happen." Rising to leave, I say, "Well, we've covered a lot of ground." He says, "I didn't talk about my wife, but . . ." Is that not a lovely tribute from a husband to a wife?

We do indeed talk about her. She was Helen Jones Carter, a "sculptress," as her husband says. A year older than he, she died five years ago, aged 95. I gaze at an example of her work: a self-portrait. Striking, and beautiful.

—December 29, 2008

Right Song, Wrong Place

'Lift Ev'ry Voice and Sing' makes the news

"Lift Ev'ry Voice and Sing" is one of the best songs in the entire American treasury. It is part gospel song, part traditional hymn, and part anthem. It was written in 1900—and became known as the "Negro national hymn," or the "Negro national anthem." Today, of course, people refer to it as the "black national anthem," or possibly the "African-American national anthem." The last person to say "Negro" was Thurgood Marshall, who did it till the day he died, in 1993.

In any case, "Lift Ev'ry Voice and Sing" managed to make national news in early July. Here's what happened.

The mayor of Denver gives a "State of the City" speech. Apparently, they have a somewhat grand view of themselves in Denver. And they invited a local jazz singer and actress to sing the national anthem. Her name is Rene Marie.

Well, she pulled a switcheroonie on them—that is her own language: "I pulled a switcheroonie on them." Instead of singing the national anthem, she sang "Lift Ev'ry Voice and Sing." But not really: It was quite strange. She sang the words of "Lift Ev'ry Voice" to the tune of "The Star-Spangled Banner." She effected a melding of the two.

The audience must have been mighty confused. There they were, hands on hearts, listening to a familiar tune, but to unfamiliar words—unfamiliar, that is, to the white people present. Black people, most of them, probably figured out what was happening.

After the event, a ruckus took place. The mayor, John Hickenlooper, was piqued that he had been deceived, not to mention upstaged. (Everyone talked about the singing, not the speech.) "We all respect artistic license and support freedom of expression," he said. But, at the State of the City event, "making a personal substitution for the national anthem was not an option." Quite so.

Rene Marie, for her part, was unbowed. "I am an artist," she said. And, as such, she has a need to express herself artistically—she will not ask anyone's permission to do so. Moreover, she does not "feel like an American." And, at some point, she decided not to sing the national anthem again.

The lady is black, I should note. And, from the lengthy remarks on her website, she is an interesting and thoughtful woman. Full of herself, but interesting and thoughtful. Obviously, she is torn by age-old questions of race and identity.

The Denver affair quickly became part of the presidential campaign, with the Democratic nominee, Barack Obama, forced to declare, "We have only one national anthem."

That other anthem, "Lift Ev'ry Voice and Sing," was written by two brothers: James Weldon Johnson and J. Rosamond Johnson. The former wrote the words, the latter the music. They did so, these 108 years ago, for a Lincoln birthday celebration, in their hometown of Jacksonville, Fla. Here are the words to the first verse:

Lift ev'ry voice and sing,
'Til earth and heaven ring,
Ring with the harmonies of Liberty;
Let our rejoicing rise
High as the list'ning skies,
Let it resound loud as the rolling sea.

Sing a song full of the faith that the dark past has taught us,
Sing a song full of the hope that the present has brought us;
Facing the rising sun of our new day begun,
Let us march on 'til victory is won.

James Weldon Johnson was one of the most remarkable men in American history—and certainly one of the most versatile. He was a poet, a politician, a lawyer, an anthologist, a diplomat, an educator, a novelist, and, yes, more. He took part in the Harlem Renaissance and was himself a definition of "Renaissance man." He did more in his 67 years—1871 to 1938—than it seems possible to do.

Toward the end of his life, Johnson helped Ignatz Waghalter, a Jewish refugee, found the American Negro Orchestra. Johnson wanted black Americans to have the best of Western civilization, and to contribute to it. And there is no question that he regarded himself, and all blacks, as part and parcel of America. This fact is reflected in the titles of some of his books: *The Book of American Negro Poetry* (1922), *The Book of American Negro Spirituals* (1925), *Negro Americans, What Now?* (1934). Johnson was as American as anyone, and more than most.

His brother, J. Rosamond, was less dazzling than he, but impressive in his own right. In addition to composing, he sang: He appeared in the original *Porgy and Bess*. And he advanced spirituals by the arrangements he made of them. For example, Marian Anderson used to sing his arrangement of the spiritual about finding lost sheep.

Of all that the Johnson brothers did, it is one song, "Lift Ev'ry Voice and Sing," that has won them enduring fame. In 1935, James Weldon wrote, "The lines of this song repay me in elation, almost of exquisite anguish, whenever I hear them sung by Negro children." "Lift Ev'ry Voice" is sometimes jazzed up. It is best when it is stately, soulful, and majestic.

Leontyne Price, the soprano, made probably the finest recording of it. It is on her album of patriotic songs and hymns, *God Bless America*, recorded in 1982 (and still in print). "Lift Ev'ry Voice" follows "The Star-Spangled Banner"—an order you can be sure Miss Price intended. She is a fierce, One America patriot.

The second verse of the song goes,

Stony the road we trod,
Bitter the chast'ning rod,
Felt in the days when hope unborn had died;
Yet with a steady beat,
Have not our weary feet
Come to the place for which our fathers sighed?
We have come over a way that with tears has been watered,
We have come, treading our path through the blood of the slaughtered,
Out from the gloomy past,
'Til now we stand at last
Where the white gleam of our bright star is cast.

It is sometimes remarked that white Americans know little of Black America. And that is no doubt true. The country is in important ways segregated, although this might not be recognized by white Americans, because blacks are the minority and whites not. How often do white Americans listen to black talk radio? Black Americans know about the majority culture—that is unavoidable. But you can live your whole life without knowing about the minority culture.

White Americans have now been given a window into Black America, by a surprising means: the candidacy of Senator Obama. Why surprising? Because Obama's roots in Black America are fairly shallow, or so you might claim. His father was from Kenya, and his mother is white. But in this political year of 2008, white Americans are learning things, not all of them pleasant. Think of what the Reverend Jeremiah Wright, Obama's former pastor, taught the country.

Did it shock you to hear that the U.S. government invented AIDS for the purpose of decimating black people? This view is widely held among black Americans—not just by crazies and demagogues, but by respectable folk, too. Yet there is much that is golden to learn as well. And one might start with "Lift Ev'ry Voice and Sing."

Not to pat myself on my good liberal back, but I contributed a mite, years ago, when I was a teenager. I was a summer-camp counselor in Illinois. This was Camp Wa-ta-ga-mie, a.k.a. Camp Want My Mommy. Every day, we had a flag raising, accompanied by a patriotic song: the national anthem, “My Country, ’Tis of Thee,” “You’re a Grand Old Flag,” etc.

When it was my turn to lead the ceremony, I introduced “Lift Ev’ry Voice.” I didn’t pull a switcheroonie—the choice of song was the counselor’s (as I remember). And why did I make this choice? Well, social reasons aside—what a great song! It ought to be a staple in the general American repertory.

And this is where Rene Marie missed her chance. If she was going to usurp an event—which she did—she might have sung “Lift Ev’ry Voice” as written, music and words. One without the other is like Schiller without Beethoven (sort of).

Turn your thoughts to next January, for a moment. Presidential inaugurations always have music: the national anthem, of course, and other songs. Jessye Norman sang “Simple Gifts” at Reagan’s second. If disaster occurs and Obama is elected, why not have “Lift Ev’ry Voice” at the inauguration? But the new president might be nervous about hints of separatism. It would be even better to have the song at a McCain inauguration.

As a rule, “Lift Ev’ry Voice” might be treated like a state flag: flying under the national flag, the greater above the lesser, the lesser under the greater. “The Star-Spangled Banner” is our national anthem. But “Lift Ev’ry Voice” is a precious part of our patrimony.

And the third and final verse is the best:

God of our weary years,
God of our silent tears,
Thou who has brought us thus far on the way;
Thou who has by Thy might
Led us into the light,
Keep us forever in the path, we pray.
Lest our feet stray from the places, our God, where we met Thee,
Lest, our hearts drunk with the wine of the world, we forget Thee;
Shadowed beneath Thy hand,
May we forever stand,
True to our God,
True to our native land.

"True to our native land"? J. W. Johnson meant America, of course—no other place. This song is full of patriotism, as well as beauty and truth. "Black national anthem" it may be called; but it is an American anthem, and, more than that, a song for all the world. The best tend to be like that.

—*August 4, 2008*

The Twain, Meeting

On the Sinification of music

About ten, fifteen years ago, a phrase occurred to me: "the Sinification of music." This refers to the ever-growing influence of Chinese musicians on Western classical music. Has this influence been positive or negative? It's hard to think of it as anything but positive. Westerners are letting music go, some people say. If that's true, others are eagerly picking it up. In 2009, I interviewed Lorin Maazel, the veteran conductor, and asked him about the future of classical music. (A standard question, usually posed nervously.) The first words out of his mouth were, "Thank God for China."

Time was, Chinese or Chinese Americans were string players or pianists. The kid practicing the violin in the back room of his parents' laundry may be a stereotype—but it's perfectly true. I saw it with my own eyes, or heard it with my own ears. Asians and Asian Americans (if I may broaden our categories) are still string players (and pianists). About half the violinists in the New York Philharmonic—a not atypical American orchestra—are Asian. So are about half the cellists. Asian Americans face quotas at universities—ceilings. But the beauty of blind auditions, which are the rule in music, is that no one can be discriminated against, except musically.

Over time, Asians branched out from the piano and the string instruments—into the woodwinds, for example. The Philharmonic's principal oboe is Chinese (and its English-horn player is Japanese). I have not seen many Asians in brass sections, I must say. (Should I mention that the English horn, somewhat misleadingly, is a big oboe?) But I met a young woman a couple of weeks ago—Chinese-American, I believe—whose instrument is the trumpet.

There came a time—about ten years ago—when I was seeing Chinese sopranos. Not in Chinese opera, but in Handel, Mozart, Verdi, and the rest. This was something new under the sun. In 2007, I saw a Chinese Pamina at the Met. (Ying Huan sang the role of Pamina in Mozart's *Magic Flute* at the Metropolitan Opera.) Not long after, I saw a Chinese Tosca—Hui He. She was markedly Italianate, too. And Chinese conductors in the pit, or on the symphonic podium, are increasingly commonplace.

Most important, probably, are the composers: the Chinese and Chinese-American composers. For the last many years, the accent of much contemporary classical music has been Chinese. Typically, the Chinese-born American composer was born in the mid-1950s. He was an adolescent, or younger, when the Cultural Revolution hit. He was made to do hard labor. He was lucky to survive. When the schools reopened, he attended the conservatory in Beijing or Shanghai. Then, in the mid-1980s, he came to America, to complete his studies and have his career. Often the school he came to was Columbia University, where Chou Wen-chung taught. Chou, who is now in his early 90s, immigrated to the U.S. in the brief years after World War II and before Communism.

One of the most prominent Chinese-American composers is Tan Dun, who wrote the score to *Crouching Tiger, Hidden Dragon*. (And an opera for the Met: *The First Emperor*, which starred Plácido Domingo.) Another prominent composer has the wonderful name of Bright Sheng—he teaches at the University of Michigan. Then there is Chen Yi and her husband, Zhou Long.

Recently, Xuefei Yang played a piece by Chen in a New York recital. Yang is a guitarist, and therefore an honorary Spaniard—all guitarists are Spaniards, in a way, because Spanish music is the heart of their repertoire. In 2008, Yang made an album called *40 Degrees North*, a title that refers to the line of latitude connecting Madrid and Beijing. One of her life ambitions has been to forge a Chinese repertoire for the guitar. The piece she played in New York was commissioned for her, from Chen, by London's Wigmore Hall.

Many cities have Chinese New Year's concerts, and New York has one in store. The Philharmonic will present a program featuring a typical mix of East and West. The Chinese pieces have such titles as "Soaring Song of Miaoling" and "Flying Song of the Earth." (There seems to be a lot of airborne motion in China.) Then there are Western staples from Dvořák, Tchaikovsky, and Rachmaninoff. Among the soloists is Yuja Wang, the sensational young pianist, born in 1987. She attended the Central Conservatory in Beijing and then made her way to Philadelphia, where she studied with Gary Graffman at the Curtis Institute. That's exactly what Lang Lang did, a few years earlier. (He is another sensational pianist.)

At American conservatories, we see a pattern: a pattern of Jewish teachers and Asian students. The same pattern is evident in orchestras—in string sections, that is. Gray and white heads are apt to be Jewish, and black heads are apt to be Asian. It is a cliché to say that Asians are the "new Jews," but there is merit to the cliché. America became the center of the musical universe for a reason: The Jews were hunted out of Europe (if they were lucky enough to be hunted out rather than murdered). There are other reasons, but that is a big one.

In mid-December, Hao Jiang Tian gave a recital in a New York hall, Zankel (the downstairs venue in the building known generically as "Carnegie Hall"). Tian is a basso long associated with the Metropolitan Opera. Born in 1954, he was just about the first of the Chinese singers on Western stages. He has a one-man show, which was made into a television special: *From Mao to the Met*. This sort of alliteration is apparently irresistible. When Isaac Stern traveled to China in 1979, the resulting documentary was called *From Mao to Mozart*.

On December 17, 1983, Tian landed at JFK Airport with $35 in his pocket, a handful of English words, a guitar on his back, and two opera arias in his repertoire. He went right to the Met, where he bought a standing-room ticket for $8. The opera was *Ernani* (Verdi), starring Luciano Pavarotti. Tian was to make his Met debut in 1991.

His recital in Zankel Hall took place exactly 30 years after his landing in New York, December 17, 2013. The place was jam-packed, mainly with well-wishers, it seemed. The program notes were in both English and Chinese. The audience was that kind of blend—and included white parents with their adopted Chinese-born kids. As for the program that Tian sang, it must have been the strangest mélange I have ever encountered in a concert hall. Tian sang music that was meaningful to him, and it was beyond diverse.

He began with Chinese art songs, composed in the early part of the 20th century. These were written by composers under the influence of the West. Then he sang the two arias he arrived in America with: "Ella giammai m'amò," which is King Philip's monologue from *Don Carlo* (Verdi), and "Non più andrai," from Mozart's *Marriage of Figaro*. The latter aria, he knew half in Italian, half in Chinese, when he got here.

How did he sing, by the way? Throughout the evening, he was up and down, but he was always personable, professional, and completely sincere. He is the kind of performer you warm to and root for. In the Chinese music, he sounded completely idiomatic (so far as I could judge). And he made the following announcement, at one point in the proceedings: "Ladies and gentlemen, forgive me: I have laryngitis. I'll do my best. If one note is weak, the next note will be stronger."

He sang "revolutionary" songs—Party songs—and "unhealthy" songs. Those "unhealthy" songs were ones judged by the Party to be corrupting. They were love songs, mainly. Then Tian sang "Danny Boy"—yes, "Danny Boy," which he learned from an Irish friend in Colorado. Following that was "The Impossible Dream," from *Man of La Mancha*. Tian rose from the Beijing Boiler Factory, where he was a sheet-metal worker, to an international opera career—so he believes in impossible dreams.

In this song, he was surrounded by young people, singing with him. Where had they come from? They belong to a program called "I Sing Beijing." For a variety of songs, Tian had onstage with him members of this program. He is the artistic director of it. The program's aim, according to its literature, is to instill Mandarin as "a lyric language." It was somewhat startling to hear young white singers, and young black singers, sing in Chinese. When one of them started speaking to the audience, in Chinese, the audience broke into applause. Several of the students paid tribute to Tian's wife, Martha (as Tian himself did). She seems to be a kind of den mother to all of them. Seldom have I seen a concert hall filled with so much warmth, goodwill, and, indeed, love.

The final piece on the printed program was a weird one (in keeping with the evening at large): a combination of a Chinese folk song and the tenor aria from Puccini's *Turandot*, "Nessun dorma." (*Turandot*, note, is set in Beijing, or "Pechino.") I thought of a corny lyric from Cole Porter: "It's friendship, friendship / Just a perfect blendship." This Hao Jiang Tian evening was corny too—and also touching, moving.

It would get more so in the two encores. The first was "America the Beautiful." The second was "O Holy Night" (in this week or so before Christmas). Tian's appreciation for the United States is obvious. And of all the Christmas carols in the world—many of them having to do with Santa Claus, reindeer, and snowmen—why did he have to pick just about the Christ-iest?

The global influence of the Chinese government is not benign, to put it mildly. For 65 years, China has been ruled by a one-party dictatorship with a gulag (*laogai*). There is no end in sight, despite regular predictions of that end. But the influence of the Chinese people in music is something else. Regardless, it is a fact of life.

—February 10, 2014

Celebrating Horne

The great mezzo at 75

Publicists wrote me to say, "Marilyn Horne is about to celebrate her 75th birthday. And her foundation is about to celebrate its 15th. Would you like to interview her?" Let me give you a word of advice, dear readers: When you have a chance to talk with Marilyn Horne, don't pass it up. She is not only one of the greatest singers who ever lived (yes, who ever lived—since man first opened his mouth to make a sound). She is an extremely smart, interesting, and fun woman.

I had a couple of hours with her in her New York apartment, overlooking Central Park. Around the apartment are busts of Rossini, Schubert, and other gents with whom Horne has been friendly. There are also pictures of her grandchildren: the three of them. "Someone said that having a grandchild is like falling in love again," says Horne. "And it's so true."

She started out in Bradford, Pa., did this legendary mezzo-soprano—and I remember that she had some hard things to say about Bradford in her memoirs, published years ago. I ask whether she retains any ill feelings toward the town. No, she says: none. "I think I was disappointed, because when my father tried to get people to subsidize me in some way—to go to Europe or whatever—they declined." I ask whether Bradford claims her now. "Oh, yes! As a matter of fact, there's a bust of me in the new concert hall."

The amazing Horne girl finished her growing up in the L.A. area. And she speaks of "a gilded time in my life," from about age 17 to age 22. She rehearsed with Stravinsky in his home, she heard Aldous Huxley speak, she ran into Schoenberg, though "I never got to know him." (His widow, she knew very well.) And then there were the many Hollywood figures: such as Judy Garland, with whom she once sang during a party at Rock Hudson's.

She eventually married Henry Lewis, a double-bassist and conductor. He was the first black player in a major symphony orchestra, the first black conductor to lead a major orchestra: a pioneer. Horne speaks of him frequently during our conversation together. "He was quite something. We divorced, ultimately, but I miss him very greatly. He's been dead now for quite a while" (1996).

Naturally, we talk a fair amount about singing, and Horne says this: "A lot of us are born with voices that work—but you have to put an awful lot into it," with studying, practicing, being coached, and so on. "It's a very hard profession. I have argued with ballet dancers that it's the hardest there is—singing." And the challenge is as much mental as physical: actually, more. And a singer is, roughly speaking, as Horne says, "half artist, half athlete."

Like plenty of others, she is not too pleased about some shifts in opera today. For example, "you've got many lighter voices singing things that should be sung by heavier voices." Take the role of Mimì, in *La bohème*: "My Mimì, when I was coming along, was Renata Tebaldi, and she had probably the biggest voice I have ever heard. Renata had a *huuuuge* voice—I think it was even bigger than Birgit's." That would be Birgit Nilsson, the Swedish Wagnerian. "Birgit had a laser beam on hers, but Renata also had a laser beam," and more. "Now I'm hearing lyric sopranos—light lyrics—sing Mimì, and that's not for me."

Reviewing some singers of the past, I ask about Ebe Stignani, Horne's mezzo forebear. "Wow," she says. "I mean, that's a wow. She was absolutely great." She also has something highly, highly interesting to say about Marian Anderson, the beloved contralto: She was magnificent, of course. But she also had "technical deficiencies," as everyone knows. And, in truth, "she might have been a soprano"—a soprano who never developed in that direction.

And how about two great mezzos of Horne's own time, Christa Ludwig and Janet Baker? She has nothing but glowing things to say about each. In early days, "Christa and I sang madrigals of Gesualdo together, with Hindemith conducting, in Vienna." How about that? As for singers on the scene today, we spend some time on René Pape, the German bass: "Unbelievably great," says Horne. I concur, of course, but suggest that, in some Italian roles, he is not especially Italianate. Horne isn't really buying: "I just love him, in everything he does—and there just aren't voices like that around."

We turn to conductors, including Leonard Bernstein—who "had so much to give. One could learn so much from Lenny, just by having a meal with him." And she says something funny about George Solti. Solti would say to her, "You're flat, darling, you're flat!" (Think Hungarian accent.) Now, Horne's intonation was the envy of the music world. "I think George heard high," she says.

She is a great lover of popular music, which is to say first-class popular music: Gershwin, Porter, Arlen, and the like. She is also a wonderful exponent of such music: Anyone who heard her sing "In the Still of the Night" will never forget it. Horne has admired many a pop or jazz singer, but I ask who really did it for her: Ella, Sarah, Peggy? "Lena," she says—her fellow Horne. They became good friends, and Lena would tell her, "We're sistahs under the skin." Were they ever confused for each other? Yes, from time to time. "One of my closest friends went to a recital of mine, and the woman sitting behind her said, 'But I thought we were going to hear *Lena* Horne!'"

Speaking of recitals, this institution is not doing very well in America—the recital, I mean. And that is one of the problems that the Marilyn Horne Foundation seeks to address. The foundation trains, supports, and encourages young singers—and it dots the country with recitals. If the recital eventually dies, perish the thought, it will not be the fault of Marilyn Horne.

Does she ever sing for herself, alone in her room, for example? Not really, she says. But she teaches a lot, and she does a good amount of demonstrating in her teaching. Also, she'll listen to Sinatra CDs in her car—and sing along with them. "Now they're in the right keys for me," she notes. (The historic Horne instrument is getting lower.) And look: She does some demonstrating in this conversation of ours, too. For example, she sings a little of the aria from *Oedipus Rex*. She imitates Pavarotti at the end of "Pourquoi me réveiller." She even imitates Schwarzkopf singing "Danny Boy"! (And no, you can't listen to my tape—well, maybe we can talk about a fee.)

Horne had a phenomenal technique, being a virtuoso of the voice: "No one taught me to sing coloratura," she says. She just did. And she had a stunning range stretching two and a half octaves. That is a true accounting. Don't believe those who claim a bigger range, for themselves or others. Horne puts it this way: "I hear people talk about having three-octave ranges, and I say, 'Bullsh**!'" Quite right.

Our conversation turns to Gustav Mahler, who loved the mezzo voice, and wrote immortal music for it. Horne sang it all, including the solo part in the Second Symphony, known as the "Resurrection." (Actually, she sang the solo part for soprano, too.) She relates something extremely personal, and perfectly understandable, to me: Her brother was killed in a plane crash. And "I could not get over it, it was such a blow. I just walked the floor at night with the headphones on, listening to the 'Resurrection,' trying to find some peace. It took me about ten years to put that one on the backburner."

I ask whether there's any music she feels closer to now than she once did. She answers, "You know, I've become so partial to Brahms. I just love Brahms. He makes me feel good when I hear his music, when I sing it, when I teach it." She was one of the great singers of "Von ewiger

Liebe," an especially good Brahms song. "It has a little story in it," she says. "And that's one of the great things I learned from Lotte Lehmann: You make each song a story."

Before we part, Horne talks about her health, her family. She is overcoming pancreatic cancer—the disease from which Pavarotti died last year. They talked about it quite a bit toward the end of his life. And she speaks to me again about her much-loved grandchildren. Many singers—I could name you a few—never had children, and feel it keenly. Horne has a vivid memory of Tebaldi: "When she would see pictures of my grandchildren, lights would come into her eyes. 'Oh, you're so lucky to have these children,' she would say. I always tell my students, especially the women: 'Don't miss that, if you can help it. Having children is worth it—especially when you get old.'"

At her doorstep, I mention that I have already done two pieces on her for *National Review*. The second was a Horne-at-70 number. She exclaims, "And now we have Horne at 75—thank God!" She has a lot to be thankful for, yes, and so do those who have heard her—at La Scala, in her living room, wherever.

—December 1, 2008

His Own Drum

Composer Michael Hersch

Cleveland, Ohio

The story of Michael Hersch is one of the most amazing you'll ever hear—in music or out. He is an American composer, born in 1971. He is one of the most honored and lauded composers before the public today. He deserves this recognition too (say I, as a critic who has covered him for years). Why is his story so amazing? First, there is his extraordinary talent. Second, there is the fact that he started in music at a late age—and rapidly soared to something like the top.

Here in Cleveland, he is premiering two works. To put it differently, and maybe more accurately, the Cleveland Orchestra is premiering one of them, and he is premiering the other, as a pianist. Before the concert, there is a "pre-concert concert." Hersch takes the stage as he usually does: shyly, almost apologetically—as if to say, "Sorry to bother you, your applause is so embarrassing."

He sits down to play his massive and monumental piano work *The Vanishing Pavilions*, which he completed in 2005. It is apocalyptic, visionary, and staggering. And it takes approximately two and a half hours to play. Hersch does not play it all, in this pre-concert concert. He plays excerpts, a little suite. And he plays it with his prodigious technique, one that draws gasps. Apparently, his fingers can do whatever his brain commands.

Which brings us to another reason Hersch's story is amazing: He could have a big, big piano career, which would only boost his fame as a composer. But he eschews it—playing only his own music, and that very rarely.

After the excerpts from *The Vanishing Pavilions*, he premieres his *Two Lullabies*. These are not what you might call traditional lullabies, tunes to put baby to sleep. The first is marked "Tense, disquieted" (as well as "restrained"). Both are formidable piano pieces, not easy to play. But there is definitely a lullaby aspect to them. The composer wrote them, he has explained, in response to the death of his closest friend.

That is true of his *Night Pieces*, too, the work premiered by the Cleveland Orchestra. It is a kind of trumpet concerto (with the Cleveland's principal, Michael Sachs, doing the honors). The audience showers this work with applause. Hersch is willing to take a couple of bows, but he is eager to get off the stage. I know composers who could have milked that applause for a good five minutes more. A soprano worth her salt, ten more.

The next morning, I sit down with Hersch, for a long talk. He describes what a premiere feels like, to him: "The music is sort of safe in your mind. And then it's out there, naked." This gives a composer "a feeling of incredible vulnerability. That's why, for years, I didn't go to concerts of my music. George Rochberg once said, 'A composer needs an iron stomach.'" (Rochberg was an American composer, living from 1918 to 2005.)

Hersch grew up in Virginia. His family divided their time between Reston, on the outskirts of Washington, and a place deep in the mountains, on the West Virginia border. "Was this a weekend home?" I say. "More like a weekend tent," says Hersch. "What do you mean, 'tent'?" I say. He says, "I mean, a tent, with little stakes in the ground." The family had a tent on their farm for more than ten years. Finally, they built a house. Hersch says that his life in rural Virginia "shaped who I am. I carry that place with me all the time."

He has two younger brothers: Jamie and Eric. Their dad, Jay, once worked for the federal government, but then he went into the beef business. Their mom, Pat, is a writer. Michael remembers going around with his dad "in this refrigerated truck, and we'd stop by slaughterhouses—which was, you know, a little traumatic. We'd stop by grocery stores and try to sell our wares."

Hersch's parents weren't musical, and there was no piano in the house (either house, or tent). An uncle played the guitar; Jamie played the French horn. The family would listen to the radio on their frequent car trips: bluegrass, rock, Casey Kasem's *American Top 40*. Michael appreciated everything he heard. "I joined the KISS Army in 1978," he says. He would have been six or seven then. There were also bands like Bad Brains and Corrosion of Conformity.

Hersch is extremely reluctant to talk about his abilities, but Jamie has talked about them, publicly: If Michael heard a song, even once, he knew all the words, forever. And all the notes, forever. He could also draw things with photographic realism. Jamie was progressing on the French horn, and is, in fact, a professional today. He pestered his older brother to listen to some classical music, which he finally did—at age 18. It was Beethoven's Fifth Symphony, in a videotaped performance by Georg Solti and the Chicago Symphony Orchestra. Michael knew what his life would be.

Ordinarily, music is a child prodigy's game. Think for a second about what 18 means. Juan Crisóstomo Arriaga, "the Spanish Mozart," died at 19. Lili Boulanger died at 24. Schubert, greedy, had 31 years.

Hersch does not feel at all disadvantaged, having started when he did. "I didn't look at it as, 'I have so much to catch up on.' People sometimes say, 'You started so late, it must have been daunting.' But I wasn't thinking in terms of chronology or lost years. I was just overjoyed at my luck. I had found this world, and I had it all to explore." His parents, he says, have "caught a lot of flak from people who think, 'What if he had started at four or five?' Well, maybe I would have burned out."

He quickly learned to play the piano. He wrote his first composition at 19, a piano fantasy. (Mozart wrote all five of his violin concertos when he was 19.) As the music critic Tim Page wrote in 2005, "Hersch discovered, as geniuses will, that he somehow already knew what he was doing." Hersch himself will allow only this: "My mind works for music."

"Miraculously," he says, he was admitted to the Peabody Institute in Baltimore. He earned two degrees in composition there. He started teaching at Peabody in 2006, when he was 34; he became chairman of the department (the composition department) four years later. But we're getting too far ahead in our story.

After studying music just a few years, he started to win all the prizes: a Guggenheim Fellowship, the Rome Prize, the Berlin Prize, etc. Veteran and famed composers were agog at what he could do. Some of the top performers took up his cause, including Mariss Jansons, the conductor. In 2008, I did a public interview of Jansons in Salzburg. I asked him which living composers stood out for him. He first named three septuagenarians: Penderecki, Pärt, and Kancheli. And then he paused to make special mention of this young American, Hersch.

He has written music of virtually all types: symphonies, concertos, chamber music, songs. The only thing that's missing is opera, which will no doubt come. Much of his music is intense, as though communicating something urgently important. I've often said, "He writes as though his life depended on it." Few notes are wasted. Nothing is for show. The music is unyieldingly honest. "Uncompromising" is a word several of us have used. Also, we've said, "When you're at a Hersch premiere, you feel like you're at something historic. Like you're hearing, for the first time, something that will last."

Be aware of something else about Hersch's music: It can be practically unbearable. In person, Hersch is a sunny, pleasant, affable type. But his music tends to express pain and despair. Of one of his symphonies, a critic wrote, "Nearly unbearable, it spoke to the kind of injury from which one does not heal." Already in 1996, when Hersch was 24, Rochberg commented, "His music sounds the dark places of the human heart and soul."

When he was about 30, he decided he wanted to write some very big and long pieces, such as *The Vanishing Pavilions*. These would take years to write, each of them. No one commissioned them. He recalls that people said, "You're not doing yourself any favors, you know—writing these pieces that no one is going to program. That have no commercial appeal." He knew. But he could do no other, by his lights. When money got tight, he worked part-time for his father, selling beef. This was while he was teaching at Peabody, and had umpteen international prizes on his shelf. He would finish a lecture on Bruckner, then go to the phone to call federal penitentiaries, talking up beef.

A colleague said to him, "You're the most own-drummer person I know"—an excellent observation, and a high compliment.

Because of his own-drumness, he won't, as I've said, accept piano engagements. People have said, "Why don't you play a Brahms concerto on one half of a program and one of your own on the other half?" He will not. Curious, I ask whether he has to practice the piano (because I suspect he doesn't). Does he have to practice, like mortals, or can he play whatever he wants, whenever he wants, cold? He won't say. I browbeat him until he at last confesses: No, he doesn't have to practice. He can just play at will.

But what he wants to do is compose. A bout with cancer, in 2007, only increased his determination to release the pieces that are in him. He lives with the two girls he loves: his wife, Karen, a classicist; and their daughter, Abigail. Abby was born on January 27, 2006, the 250th anniversary of Mozart's birth. His favorite time to compose is at night, when they are asleep. "It's better than any artist's colony." Among his gifts is the need for very little sleep—about four hours. One can get a lot done, in 20 waking hours.

He does not struggle to compose, but he does need time. He cannot be rushed. He works on a piece in his head until it's ready. Then he writes it down, with no revision. It took almost a year to write down *The Vanishing Pavilions*, which runs more than 300 pages.

Toward the end of our conversation, I ask, "Do you care if they listen?" The allusion does not have to be explained to him: In the 1950s, there was a famous essay by Milton Babbitt called "Who Cares If You Listen?" Hersch, somewhat to my surprise, says he does care. "If people listen, and they connect with my music, it's deeply meaningful. And if they don't like it, it's hurtful. But I'm gonna write it anyway."

Shostakovich liked to quip, "I like all music, from Bach to Offenbach." Hersch is the same way—a man who devours music from Gregorian chant to this week. When I press him about favorite music, he says, "For me, late Schubert piano music is where it's at." He adds, "The thing about music is, you can go for years without listening to a given composer, and then suddenly have a need to hear him. The music is lying dormant, waiting for you. You can activate it anytime, simply by engaging with it."

Like most artists worth paying attention to, Hersch is grateful to be doing what he's doing. He considers himself incredibly lucky—lucky to have been exposed to music, even at a late date (or an untraditional date, let's say). And "it just anguishes me that there are so many people out there, possibly, who could have been like me, or are like me, who weren't fortunate enough to have a brother who would say, 'You need to sit down and listen to Beethoven.' What about all the people who are just as talented as I am, or more talented, and didn't have the opportunity?"

There you have some of Michael Hersch's greatness: not just a mind that "works for music," not just what people unblushingly call his "genius," but a humanity, evident in his music and in his life at large.

—May 28, 2012

Faking It and Making It

A few notes on lip-synching, etc.

At the recent inauguration of President Obama, Beyoncé, the one-named pop star, sang the national anthem. But not really. She lip-synched it. This was obvious from the first note, when lips and music were not in sync. Beyoncé and the Marine Band had recorded the anthem. When it was showtime, Beyoncé pretended to sing, the band pretended to play, and the conductor conducted—though there was no need to, except to keep up appearances.

The lip-synching made the news, and some of the more uptight among us murmured. Beyoncé was defensive, even defiant. It was too cold to sing, she said. There hadn't been a "proper sound check." And so on. "I did not feel comfortable taking a risk." Plus, singing along with a "pre-recorded track" is "very common in the music industry." It certainly is.

A pop singer at an inauguration is a relatively new phenomenon. Traditionally, we have had classical singers: Marian Anderson, Marilyn Horne, Jessye Norman, Susan Graham . . . And classical musicians have higher standards than pop musicians, right? They have greater integrity, and a purer sense of art. Right? Well, consider Obama's first inauguration, in 2009.

On that occasion, Senator Dianne Feinstein announced that the nation would be treated to "a unique musical performance." It was, actually. A quartet had been assembled: Gabriela Montero, piano; Itzhak Perlman, violin; Yo-Yo Ma, cello; and Anthony McGill, clarinet. (They made a near-perfect modern-American tableau. Diversity committees everywhere must have rejoiced.) The four played a piece by John Williams—but not really. They pretended to play. They had recorded the piece in the Marine Barracks two days before. At the inauguration itself, they "hand-synched."

They did a lot more than that—they went all out, in this charade. Perlman made his usual faces. (He bites his lip, à la Bill Clinton.) Ma made his usual faces. (Think silent movies.) The musicians pretended to coordinate with one another, as ensembles do. It was a brazen, shameless act.

Later, everyone explained that it was simply too cold to play. The instruments could not have taken it. "It would have been a disaster if we had done it any other way," said Perlman. "This occasion's got to be perfect. You can't have any slip-ups." Ma said, "A broken string was not an option. It was wicked cold."

Fair enough. But what would you have done, reader? Would you have gone through the charade, as these guys did? Or would you have said something like the following? "Play the recording, and announce why. Or make some other arrangement. I don't want to take part in a deception. I don't want to pretend I'm playing when I'm not."

The great Pavarotti lip-synched, on more than one occasion. In my opinion, it was the most disgraceful thing he ever did (in his professional life). He committed fraud, basically. In 1992, the BBC demanded its money back, because they had paid for broadcast rights to a live concert, not for lip-synching. And how about people who had bought tickets? If they wanted to listen to Pavarotti recordings, couldn't they have stayed home and saved themselves the expense?

The most famous instance of operatic lip-synching took place in 1916. It is a beautiful episode. The Metropolitan Opera was performing *La bohème* in Philadelphia. When it came time for the bass aria, "Vecchia zimarra," in Act IV, Andrés de Segurola had no voice. He whispered to the tenor onstage with him, "I can't sing." The tenor was Enrico Caruso—who said, "Don't worry. I'll turn my back to the audience and sing the aria for you. You stand there and mouth along"—which he did.

In 1952, there was an incident that shook a lot of people up. The EMI label made a recording of *Tristan und Isolde*, conducted by Wilhelm Furtwängler. Kirsten Flagstad was the Isolde. But she could not sing the high C's in Act II, so Elisabeth Schwarzkopf sang them for her. These notes were dubbed in. When the public found out, many were, as I said, shaken up. Scandalized. It was a trick, a fraud, a deception!

If you had been Flagstad—first of all, congratulations—what would you have done? Would you have allowed the notes to be dubbed? "What's important is that the music sound right," you might have said. Or would your position have been, "It is a matter of honor, and honesty. If I can't sing the notes, either I will not record the role, or I will sing some alternative to the high notes [as happens in live performances all the time]. But I won't let people think I'm singing them when I'm not."

In 1965, Vladimir Horowitz played a recital at Carnegie Hall—one of the most famous piano recitals ever played. Horowitz was performing in public for the first time in twelve years. The recital was recorded—and when the "live recording" came out, those who had attended the recital were shocked: because the wrong notes were missing. Correct ones had been substituted. The recording was not a faithful representation, was not really live.

Horowitz defended himself passionately. It had been hot in the hall, he said, and he was nervous, and he was sweating. The sweat got in his eyes, blinding him. He missed notes. It was not his fault. It was an "act of God." That was the line he clung to: "act of God." He was entitled to correct the notes, he said, because they were not really his fault in the first place. They did not have to do with his ability. And he had to think of posterity—what would future generations think? He was certainly not the type to miss notes, except when God was filling his eyes with sweat.

As the years rolled on, recordings got ever more doctored, ever more sterile, ever more scrubbed. They are, to a degree, unnatural. The critic and scholar Dennis Rooney told me a story about Miriam Fried, the violinist. She was recording the Bach sonatas and partitas, and, after a particular take, someone informed her that she had squeaked. "So?" she said. Violinists squeak. But thereafter, she became self-conscious about these occurrences, and this self-consciousness had an inhibiting effect. Rooney is one who decries the "cosmetic perfection" of modern recordings.

Listen to a recording of Josef Hofmann, or Alfred Cortot! (These are pianists who recorded in a pre-modern age.) You may hear some missed notes, but you will also hear a genuine article. Rare is the pianist who plays note-perfectly. I have heard Mikhail Pletnev play this way, and a handful of others—but not a large handful. In reviewing a concert, I'll often say, "Virtuosic as he is, he missed a few notes. But that only proved that it wasn't a studio recording, thank heaven." There's nothing like the realism—the wondrous, exciting, human realism—of live.

Let's return to a more popular world. Hollywood, land of make-believe, made people believe that such stars as Audrey Hepburn, Deborah

Kerr, and Natalie Wood were singing. Actually, Marni Nixon was singing, for those three. (The "Ghostess with the Mostest," she was called.) Marilyn Horne sang for Dorothy Dandridge in *Carmen Jones*. Was this a fraud, a deception? Will I get on my high horse about it? My answer is, it was Hollywood, the movies—and one would not want to take the show business out of show business.

The dawn of MTV, in 1981, must have been important. Everyone lip-synched then. You were supposed to. One of the network's taglines was, "You'll never look at music the same way again." So true.

Forget inaugurations, what about an even greater American rite, the Super Bowl? Whitney Houston lip-synched, Jennifer Hudson lip-synched, everyone has lip-synched. In 2009, music director Rickey Minor said, "There's too many variables to go live. I would never recommend any artist go live, because the slightest glitch would devastate the performance." What a sad commentary. Doing away with live is like doing away with life. Those "variables" are what makes it great!

Most have accepted the modern way, surely, but there are still murmurs, even the occasional shout. At an awards ceremony in 2004, Elton John ripped into Madonna, who had been nominated in a "live act" category. "Since when has lip-synching been live?" Sir Elton said. "Anyone who lip-synchs in public onstage, when you pay 75 pounds to see them, should be shot."

I think Beyoncé was sheepish about what she had done at this year's inauguration. Days later, she went down to New Orleans, to sing (or whatever) at the Super Bowl. At a press conference beforehand, she asked everybody to stand up. Then she sang the national anthem, for real—as though she had something to prove. "Any questions?" she said, with a laugh. She issued no apology for what happened at the inauguration. In fact, she said, "I am very proud of my performance." (That is very modern-American: to be very proud of oneself.)

But get this: "I will absolutely be singing live" at the Super Bowl. She said it again: "I will absolutely be singing live." Then she said, "This is what I was born to do, what I was born for."

What would *you* have done at the inauguration? Would you have lip-synched, sung live, or what? I don't think we can lay down hard-and-fast rules on these things. It's a matter of stomach, conscience, taste—circumstance. But I don't believe I myself could have pretended to be singing the national anthem, when I wasn't. Lip-synching isn't the worst thing in the world. It was not the worst thing at that inauguration. But it is problematic, at a minimum. And if people don't know you're doing it—if they don't expect it, and think otherwise—it's a lie. An artistic illusion, you might say. But still, a lie, of a kind. A swindle.

—February 25, 2013

Maestro Maazel

A conversation with a conductor

Lorin Maazel is in his office, wearing blue jeans, surrounded by musical scores—some of them written by himself. The conductor, born in 1930, is wrapping up his tenure as music director of the New York Philharmonic. He began in 2002—60 years after his debut with the Philharmonic. Yes, he was twelve, and he was a rare thing: a child prodigy who conducted. Almost all are instrumentalists; the Maazel case is nearly unique. His bio says, "Between ages 9 and 15 Lorin Maazel conducted most of the major American orchestras." What does *your* bio say?

Some musicians are not especially articulate, which is no shame: Their profession or art does not require speech. But Lorin Maazel is fabulously articulate, and we settle into a wide-ranging conversation. His speech is curious, interesting: somewhat rarefied, not from anywhere, really. His hometown is Pittsburgh, but his English, no.

I ask whether he likes music as much as ever, after these eight decades. He says yes: "Your appreciation grows. It deepens as one's life experience widens. One's perception of music deepens." And does he still enjoy even very familiar music—say, Tchaikovsky's Fifth Symphony? Is that still glorious and thrilling to him? Oh, "it's as glorious and thrilling as the day it was written. If you become jaded because of overexposure, the problem is yours, not the composer's."

Most people think that age is an advantage on the podium. Does Maazel think so? Surely he does. But he says, "Well, it depends on who's growing older. I've always tried to learn as I've moved forward in life, and I consider each performance to be a learning experience." That is not true of all conductors or other musicians, Maazel notes. Some of them "age complacently, and those folks don't improve, I'm afraid. It's a question of mindset."

Later on, we return to this question, and Maazel avers, "Youth is a mindset, not a physiological state. I know so many young people who were born old. If you have an enthusiasm and an inquisitive mind, are quick-witted and have good reflexes, it doesn't matter whether you're 10 or 100, you're going to function very well" as a conductor. "The music that you touch will have the impetus, drive, and vitality it needs." Incidentally, Maazel's father is 106.

Lorin was not just a conducting prodigy, but a violin prodigy. Might he have made an entire career of the violin? "I was thinking of it. I love the violin, and there was something called the Glazunov Contest, right here in New York, right after the Second World War. I decided I was going to win that contest, and fortunately for me I got double pneumonia two days before I was supposed to come to New York, and ended up in bed for weeks." Maazel figures he would have won—"I was playing amazingly well"—and then "I would have missed my whole career as a conductor, because I would have marched around the world" playing violin concertos. "I would have grown bored, I would have stopped practicing, and I would have ended up in some orchestra, probably."

We talk about two of the great violinists of mid-century: Heifetz and Milstein. Maazel played for Heifetz, who was "very critical of my playing, as he should have been." (Heifetz was critical—caustically critical—of everything.) Amazingly, Heifetz got hold of a cadenza that young Maazel had fashioned for a Mozart concerto, and taught it to his students. As for Milstein, "he was not the greatest fan of yours truly." Once, Maazel collaborated with him on the Beethoven Concerto, and Milstein got his nose all out of joint. He walked out of rehearsals. "I'm not quite sure why I rubbed him the wrong way, because he was a god to me, and I was not only deferential, I would have shined his shoes. But he was just in that mood." Eventually, Milstein came back, played the performances, "and actually talked to me at the end of the fourth concert, almost civilly."

We turn to the subject of composition, and Maazel's career, or sideline, as a composer. Has he achieved all he wanted? "I never set out to achieve anything." Rather, "I write because somebody asks me to write, and Rostropovich started me off on this." Rostropovich is the late, great cellist. And he heard "some stupid piece of mine"—a waltz, a *pièce d'occasion*—and said he had to have a concerto. Maazel agreed, but "with many misgivings. I had never written a major piece like this before, and all the music I had written up to that time, I had found uninteresting. I figured there was so much bad music being written every day, why add to it?" But Rostropovich's "conviction moved me to write a rather good piece, actually." And others (e.g., the flutist James Galway) asked him for more.

So, who are the composers of today worth listening to? Maazel has an immediate answer: "Penderecki." Then he says, "Um . . . well . . ." Long, long pause. "Mention some American composers I've conducted here," he says. I say, "I hesitate." He says, "Kernis? I think he's a very, very talented composer, a master of what he does." That is Aaron Jay Kernis. He also praises Rodion Shchedrin, the Russian, and "an important composer."

He says that the taboo on melody, harmony, and the like no longer exists—"That was 30 years ago," and it was always "for the birds." Maazel goes on to observe, "If you have something to say, the idiom in which you choose to say it is irrelevant." He mentions the great Alban Berg, who chose to write "tonal-sounding twelve-tone music," which "I find quite remarkable." We speak of his violin concerto, and also his two operas: *Wozzeck* and *Lulu*.

I say that I find *Wozzeck* "one of the great unwatchable operas," so horrible is the subject matter, so keen is the injustice, so devastating is the work the composer has produced. I say that I feel similarly about *Madama Butterfly* (Puccini). Whereupon Maazel comments, "When I conduct that opera, I can't look at the stage for the last five minutes—when she gets ready to disembowel herself. I can't bear it." And "the music is so powerful."

"Why do people sneer at Puccini and Tchaikovsky?" I ask. Maazel answers, dismissively, "Envy."

On to other composers, including Bruckner. A conductor once told me that he had a hard time conducting Bruckner, probably because he, the conductor, lacked religious belief. I say to Maazel, "Do you have to be a believer to conduct Bruckner?" He answers, "No, not at all. I'm certainly not, but I have a streak of spirituality. I think that every musician worth his salt simply must, and Bruckner's music has a breadth and depth and an innocent genius which I find absolutely unbelievable."

A discussion of conductors brings up Carlos Kleiber, of whom Maazel says, "I think he was the finest conductor of his generation." (Kleiber was born the same year as Maazel, 1930, and died in 2004.) Not that the two saw eye to eye. They were good friends, and had a revealing lunch once. Maazel said, "Carlos, I have never heard a note from you that I could possibly agree with." Kleiber said, "Lorin, I feel the same way about you." Maazel said, "How do you explain that I am one of your biggest fans, and think that you're in a class by yourself?" Kleiber said, "I feel the same way about you, Lorin!"

Many of us have observed, over the years, that Maazel is tinged with jazz—which comes out in remarkable ways, as he traverses the classical repertoire. The maestro says, "I used to play jazz piano," and, "like every American, I have rhythm." Technically, that should be "I got rhythm." Speaking of Gershwin, I say, "He is unquestionably great, right?" Maazel answers, "No doubt about it." With André Previn, Maazel is probably our foremost interpreter of Gershwin. He once recorded the complete *Porgy and Bess* with the Cleveland Orchestra (and associated forces).

Speaking of operas, we get on the subject of opera productions, and specifically "Euro-trash," to use an impolite term—Maazel's is "Euro-dreck." He thinks that this phenomenon "will gradually peter out, because audiences will have had enough." Let us hope—it's been a long time already. "The faddists are clever," says Maazel, "because they paint you into a corner." Their trick is to say, "If you object to us, you're a conservative, you're a fuddy-duddy, you're a living anachronism! What we do is *new*!" Maazel says, "It's not new. It's boring. It's not even vulgar. It's just . . . dull." The way Maazel says "dull" would wither any of these Euro-dreck directors.

And where does Maazel stand on the future of classical music, about which so many fret? He says, "Thank God for China." They are ravenous for music there. He also cites South America, in particular Venezuela, where a storied man named Abreu set up a system of youth orchestras. Maazel went down to conduct the main such orchestra, and found the experience "mind-blowing." All those kids, full of enthusiasm, "making the most fantastic sound I've ever heard." These were "youngsters who were pushing drugs the year before, or mugging people in the streets." And now they were "sitting there like angels and playing their hearts out."

Before we part, I ask a left-field question: Lorin Maazel is a real dancer on the podium, or can be. Does he dance off the stage, socially? He laughs: "I did go to dancing school, but I was the world's worst student." And he recalls a time in Spain, during "my wild youth, when I was sowing my oats." In a club, he asked a girl to dance. After a few minutes, she "stopped cold" and said, "I don't want to dance with you anymore." "What's the problem?" asked Maazel. "You have no rhythm," she said. Offering catnip, I say, "That woman probably went on to be a music critic." Maazel throws back his head and laughs again, hard.

—July 20, 2009

Prima Donna Assoluta

A tête-à-tête with La Gheorghiu in the Champagne Bar

Angela Gheorghiu waltzes down to the lobby of the Plaza Hotel in New York. We will have a tête-à-tête in the Champagne Bar. Who is Gheorghiu? In prosaic terms, she is a Romanian soprano born in 1965. In less prosaic terms, she is "the most glamorous and gifted opera singer of our time." I have quoted from her website. This is publicist's hyperbole, of course—but it is not far off.

Gheorghiu is not only an extraordinary singer and performer, she is great copy. There is often controversy swirling about her, as well as excitement. She has run-ins with opera administrators and stage directors.

She has marriages and romances. People love to gossip about her, snipe at her, hate her, adore her.

She is certainly a top-notch interviewee. In the Champagne Bar, she is amusing, frank, coquettish, catty, and smart as hell. She speaks in a flavorful English, mixing in French, Italian, and Romanian. It is an opera-world patois. And her name, by the way, is pronounced (something like) Ghee'or-GHEE'oo.

It is now the evening after a concert performance of *Adriana Lecouvreur* at Carnegie Hall. The title role was taken by Gheorghiu, of course, and she, Adriana, is an actress. So is Gheorghiu, very much. In fact, she tells me, the National Theatre in Bucharest has invited her to appear in a play, just straight, "*basta* with the music." She is looking forward to it.

We talk a bit about Ionesco, the late playwright, whose daughter she knows. ("Elle habite à Paris.") We also talk about Enescu, the composer. "Did he write any songs?" I ask. (I can't remember.) Oh, yes, she says. Gheorghiu has done recitals, and done them well. But she does not look with favor on, for example, an all-Schumann evening. "It's nice," she says, "but not nice enough. Something is missing. It's like a prelude to making love. I want more!"

What she is, principally, is an opera star, born to be. She is fully aware of this fact. "Shame on me!" she says. She has no problem whatsoever with being a prima donna. "I'm proud of it," she says. "I've always been proud of it. And I always knew it"—always knew she was one. When she was five years old, she sang with her sister in front of an audience. She saw the emotions in that audience. She saw similar emotions in Carnegie Hall, for her *Adriana*. "I have seen this reaction all my life."

Her sister, Elena, died several years ago in a car accident. When she mentions her death—maybe halfway through our conversation—she falls suddenly silent and somber.

Romania, when they were growing up, was one of the worst of the Communist dictatorships. There were not many opportunities for budding singers (or for anyone else). "Imagine me to be an American!" says Gheorghiu. Imagine if she had been an American. "Everything I did, I did only because of me—*moi*!" She worked and scrapped for everything she achieved.

She did have a teacher, of whom she speaks gratefully. Her name was Mia Barbu, and she taught Angela for some five years—from the time the girl was 14 until she was 18. "I did my *canto* lessons," says Gheorghiu, "pure *canto*. All the studies" (the Vaccai method and so on). But she did everything "very quick." What can take others years, she says, took her just a day. She remembers a particular occasion: Barbu said to her, "Breathe." Angela breathed. The teacher said, "That's it! Don't ever change that."

According to Gheorghiu, she has never had any teaching or coaching help since she was 18. There are two reasons for this, she says: "First, I really want to be original. Even if I make a mistake, it's me. Second, I understand *canto* very well, trust me. You can ask my colleagues."

Her first trip out of the Eastern bloc was to Vienna, where she was agog at the beauty and the abundance. She couldn't understand why people weren't celebrating in the streets. They were walking around as though such beauty and abundance were normal. She stared at the meat, the fruit, the flowers. I mention to her that René Pape—the Dresden-born bass—had the same reaction when he first went to Austria. She says, "The shops in Romania—not like in Germany, excuse me—were *completely empty*. Just white. Just white."

In 1994, she had a big breakthrough, singing *La traviata* with Georg Solti in London. As she reminds me, the conductor was then 82, and cried when hearing the young soprano sing "Addio del passato" in a rehearsal room. Overcome, he had to leave that room. He made a much-circulated statement, to wit, "The girl is wonderful. She can do anything."

Two years later, having ditched her husband (whose name she retains), she married Roberto Alagna, the Italian-French tenor. The ceremony took place during a performance of *La bohème* on the stage of the Metropolitan Opera, Mayor Rudolph Giuliani presiding. In the years that followed, the legend of Gheorghiu grew and grew. She walked away from productions, and was dismissed from them. She made incendiary and delicious statements to the press—e.g., "If directors want to do something new with operas, why not do something beautiful?" She canceled performances on what seemed like whims.

They are never whims, says Gheorghiu in the Champagne Bar. If she feels she cannot do her best, why should she suffer, and why should the audience suffer? Callas did the same, she says. "She said, 'I'm not good enough tonight—*ciao, ragazzi*.'" That is what a prima donna worth the name should do, says Gheorghiu.

Her latest album, by the way, is called *Homage to Maria Callas—Favourite Opera Arias* (EMI). In conjunction with this album, she has made a video that takes advantage of some technical wizardry: She appears to sing a duet with Callas herself. "Why not?" says Gheorghiu. "She's with EMI. She's my colleague."

For her conflicts with directors, Gheorghiu makes no apologies. She feels she must stand up to those who would undermine composers, librettists, and their operas. In her mind, she is defending art against the barbarians. Take the current *Faust* at the Met (please). She was to appear in it but withdrew because she could not abide the production. It transplants *Faust* into the nuclear age (etc.). This production was a "fiasco" at the English National Opera, Gheorghiu says, and it is a fiasco here in New York. Moreover, why should she and other experienced singers be good boys and girls and obey a "Mr. Nobody" (i.e., the director)?

I can assure readers that many, many singers wish they could take the stands that Gheorghiu takes. But they lack the status and independence. Frankly, they may lack the guts as well.

In a Met *Traviata* two seasons ago, Gheorghiu clashed with Leonard Slatkin, the conductor. He did not return after the opening night. Slatkin has admitted that he was ill-prepared for the opera, but has also claimed that the diva was intolerable to him (not hard to believe). I ask her, "Do you have any regrets about the *Traviata* with Slatkin?" She does not recognize the name, or affects not to do so. After a few moments, she says, "Ah, the conductor. He left. This happened." Okay, but *why* did he leave? Gheorghiu makes the general point that people often use her as a scapegoat. "My name helps, you know what I mean?" If a person is having problems, he can blame the raven-haired terror from Transylvania. "I don't care. Use my name, but use it well: Ghee'or-GHEE'oo!"

There are books of opera anecdotes, and I suggest to this soprano that books in the future will have whole chapters devoted to her. Yes, she says, "and I'm not finished yet!" I ask her about one of my favorite stories: Did she really demand hair and makeup for a radio interview? No, she says: There was a photo-shoot the same day as the radio interview. Too bad, I say, it's such a good story. Yes, she says, "but I have lots of others."

Unquestionably, she is the target of some envy, jealousy, and overall resentment. She lets me in on a secret: It's worse from men than from women. "Really?" I ask. "Yes," she says. I ask whether she can explain this. She hesitates (which is unusual for her). I hazard, "Is it because men desire you and, when they can't have you, get angry?" She gives me a look that says, *Bingo*. That is a major reason, yes. "Thank you for helping me," she says.

Gheorghiu provokes big emotions, in colleagues and audiences alike, in a field of big emotions. She is an especially operatic personality in a field (naturally) filled with them. And an opera role takes a lot out of her, she says. "I'm not just making a sound. I am *living* that sound. I am *living* the *personnage*. And it costs me." She cites her latest outing in *Adriana*. "After the monologue, I thought I was going to faint."

Singing cannot go on forever, and I ask Gheorghiu a delicate question: Does she fear retirement? Not at all, she says. She has thought about it for a long time. And an idea has come to her strongly in just the last month: She will direct. I say, "Then *you* will be the boss." "No!" she protests. In opera, there can be no boss, as it is a collaborative process. Everyone has a part to play, and each part is connected to another. Once, she relates, a conductor was trying to boss her around. "*I'm* doing the *personnage*," she told him. He retorted, "I'm not [merely] accompanying you." She answered, "Oh, you're not accompanying me? Then change your job, dear. Of *course* you are accompanying me. Excuse me?"

Gheorghiu loves being famous, as she readily confirms. But she says there is a big downside to having the kind of career she has. You are "everywhere and nowhere," and are "alone almost all of the time." There is always a post-performance *tristesse*, "a little emptiness." You go back to your hotel room, talk on the phone, click through YouTube. The roar and adulation of the crowd are gone. And "I want it back!" says Gheorghiu. "All that love, I want it back! It's never enough for me." But then there is another performance, more roars, more adulation—"a *rinascimento*" (rebirth).

After we say goodbye, she goes off with companions to a concert by

Sting. She has a nickname for him: "Stingo" (rhymes with Ringo). "He's such a nice artist," she says. Gheorghiu herself is an artist and a half: a great opera singer, an immortal. And whatever else you may say about her—and you could say plenty—she is just about the fizziest guest the Champagne Bar will ever see.

—January 23, 2012

A Composer's Hour

Appreciating Rodion Shchedrin

Every now and then, I'll interview a musician, and I'll often ask, "Who are the living composers you admire or respect? Is there anyone worth listening to today?" Usually, the musician will smile at the cheeky way the question is phrased. Almost never will he protest, "What do you mean? There are many, many fine composers among us." Chances are, he'll say, "Well . . ."—then give me two or three names. One of those names is likely to be that of a Russian composer, Rodion Shchedrin.

In the last 15 years, he has grown ever more popular, championed by some of our best musicians. These include three major conductors: Valery Gergiev, Lorin Maazel, and Mariss Jansons. One of his biggest boosters was Mstislav Rostropovich, the great cellist and conductor who died in 2007. When you had "Slava" in your corner, you were the beneficiary of an almost superhuman force.

The Lincoln Center Festival, here in New York, will feature Shchedrin this month, when the Mariinsky Ballet, from St. Petersburg, comes to town. Gergiev will conduct, and such luminaries as Diana Vishneva will dance. Two of Shchedrin's ballets will be performed: *The Little Humpbacked Horse* (1955–56), based on the fairytale poem by Yershov, and *Anna Karenina* (1971), based on you-know-what. The Mariinsky will also perform Shchedrin's *Carmen Suite*—i.e., his arrangement of Bizet's score. Maya Plisetskaya, one of the greatest dancers of all time, premiered this ballet with the Bolshoi in 1967.

Shchedrin has a great affinity for ballet in general, and for Plisetskaya in particular: They were married in 1958. They are still an attractive, even a glamorous couple, she in her mid-eighties, he in his late seventies. Also, you could argue that they are the most talented couple in the world. Seriously. Of course, you might put in a bid for Andre Agassi and Steffi Graf, too.

Rodion Shchedrin was born on December 16, 1932. (There was another composer born on December 16: Beethoven.) His father was a composer and music teacher. Many, many composers have been sons of composers, or of professional musicians: Bach, Mozart, and Beethoven, to begin with. Shchedrin's first name is an old-fashioned Russian one, shared by Raskolnikov in *Crime and Punishment*. The last name looks fearsome in its spelling, but is easy to pronounce, or approximate: Shed-REEN.

He studied with two top musicians at the Moscow Conservatory: Yuri Shaporin and Yakov Flier. The former was his composition teacher, the latter his piano teacher. Flier was little-known in the West, unlike some other pianists from the Soviet Union. But he was magnificent. Shchedrin has said he was the best he ever heard, after Vladimir Horowitz. That's a powerful statement, even allowing for a student's natural loyalty.

With respect to composition, Shchedrin came of age in "a rather lean time," as he put it in an interview earlier this year. Even the Impressionists —Debussy, Ravel—were scorned as tune-happy squares. Abstraction and devotion to method were the rule of the day. "For 35 years, there was a dictatorship of the avant-garde," Shchedrin said in another interview, "and I was never a part of it." He lays great stress on what he calls "intuition." Especially in earlier years, he wrote his share of abstract, or semi-abstract, music. But he insists that "music should touch the heart and soul." And he has referred to himself as "a post-avant-garde composer."

Once, he was asked what he was prepared to listen to, right that second. He replied that he was always prepared to listen to Tchaikovsky's *Nutcracker*—"because each and every section of the score is a masterpiece." That is a very rare declaration for a modern composer to make. Even those who believe it—who know it's true—would shrink from saying it.

Shchedrin is one of those people with a huge appetite for music, music of every period, and of every type. And his own music reflects an awareness, and absorption, of the past. He is not trying to invent the wheel; he knows he stands on shoulders. Shostakovich liked to say, "I love everything from Bach to Offenbach." Incidentally, Shchedrin knew Shostakovich, and knew him well. And, as Shostakovich wrote a tremendous variety of music—from elephant walks to unbearably painful string quartets and symphonies—so has Shchedrin. He'll give you an atonal piano concerto, an Orthodox liturgy, or a quadrille.

In his catalogue are five operas and five ballets. And, for these and other works, he has drawn on a library of Russian writers: Pushkin, Gogol, Chekhov, Mandelstam, Nabokov . . . (One of his operas is *Lolita*.) Shchedrin is devoted to all things Russian, drinking deep from his culture, and extending it. You can see this in the titles of his works. For example, his Concerto for Orchestra No. 3 is subtitled "Old Russian Circus Music." And his Op. 94 is, get this, *The House of Ice: Russian Fairytale for Marimbaphone*.

His regard for music at large can be seen in yet more titles: such as *Hommage à Chopin* and *In the Style of Albéniz*. And no one is more important to him than Bach. "The highest point of music," he has said. In common with Shostakovich, Shchedrin has written 24 preludes and fugues—for such composers, it is almost a duty, a happy duty.

One summer, the Shchedrins and the Shostakoviches were vacationing together in Armenia. Shostakovich asked Shchedrin, out of the blue, "If you could take one score with you to a desert island, what would it be? And you have ten seconds to decide." Shchedrin named Bach's *Art of the Fugue*. Shostakovich—surprisingly, you may well think—named Mahler's *Song of the Earth*.

Be assured that Shchedrin cares if you listen. (In 1958, the American composer Milton Babbitt wrote a notorious essay called "Who Cares If You Listen?" The title came from an editor, not him, and he always bemoaned it.) Shchedrin doesn't mind pleasing his audience, while remaining true to artistic standards, and he especially doesn't mind pleasing those who perform his music, who are the first audience, so to speak. He regards it as a mortal sin to be boring.

Often in his pictures, you see Shchedrin with a twinkle in his eye. He loves humor, as Shostakovich did. (Shostakovich did not have much to twinkle about.) The subtitle of Shchedrin's Concerto for Orchestra No. 1 is "Naughty Limericks." Later, he wrote *Three Funny Pieces*, for piano trio. (They are, too.) And his *Humoresque* is one of his most popular pieces—ingeniously funny, almost laugh-out-loud. Of course, the humor in Shchedrin's catalogue can be of the dark or ironic kind. For 40 years, he composed in the Soviet Union, after all.

Since the demise of that country, or entity, or empire, he and Plisetskaya have divided their time between Moscow and Munich. And Shchedrin has written a lot of music, a gusher of music. The end of Communism, he has said, freed his mind, his body, his spirit, and his pen. More than a third of his overall output has been written since the Soviet Union expired in 1991, when he was 59.

A delicate subject, Soviet times. Since 1991, there have been many arguments and recriminations concerning Shchedrin and others. Who did what? Who was honorable and who was dishonorable? What can be given a pass and what must be atoned for? Shchedrin has spoken of awful compromises: "In a totalitarian system, relations between the artist and the regime are always extremely complex and contradictory. If the artist sets himself against the system, he is put behind bars or simply killed."

I will not don judicial robes or put Shchedrin in the dock. I will record just a few facts. He wrote an oratorio, *Lenin Is Among Us*, for the centenary of the founding tyrant in 1970. Of course, others, including Prokofiev and Shostakovich, wrote such music too. He was head of a composers union—like Shostakovich. Perhaps worst of all, he signed a letter denouncing Andrei Sakharov, the great physicist and greater dissident and man. So did Shostakovich, Khachaturian, others.

Shchedrin, in various venues, points out that he never joined the Communist party, and that, in 1968, he refused to sign a letter supporting the invasion of Czechoslovakia. Here is something else: Plisetskaya's father was executed by the state; her mother was sent to the Gulag, but survived. In 1964, Plisetskaya accepted the Lenin Prize. Her husband accepted it 20 years later. The Soviet Union, as you know, was a strange place, as well as a vicious, evil one.

Prokofiev died the same day as Stalin; Shostakovich, who was eleven when the Communists seized power, died 16 years before they fell. Shchedrin has pointed out the ways in which he himself has been lucky: He was 20, just starting out, when Stalin died. He got to compose in relative—and let me stress "relative"—freedom. And when the Soviet Union ended, he still had some time left: and is having a hell of an Indian summer, as Haydn, Verdi, and Saint-Saëns, to name three, did. (Schubert died at 31.)

Will some of his music last? That is always a hard thing to predict, but I myself think so, yes. There will be audiences who want to hear it, musicians who want to play or sing it—dancers who want to dance to it. Type the name Shchedrin into YouTube. See the happy faces, and engaged faces, and moved faces. Shchedrin reaches people. By enriching musical life, he has enriched life in general. Right this second, I'm going to listen to his little *Troika* for piano again. After that, maybe the Amoroso from the *Chamber Suite*—a sweet, sad caress.

—July 18, 2011

There They Go A-Caroling

A century-plus of Christmas albums

There has been Christmas music ever since there has been Christmas. And there have been Christmas albums ever since there have been albums. Before albums, of course, there were single cuts. In 1916, Caruso recorded "Cantique de Noël," which we Anglos know as "O Holy Night." The great Italian sang it in French. But we can go back farther than 1916. Olive Fremstad, the Swedish-American soprano, recorded "Silent Night"—actually, "Stille Nacht"—in 1911. And Charles Gilibert, the French baritone, recorded "La Vierge à la crèche" (Périlhou, not Franck) in 1907. You can find both of these cuts on a Masterworks Heritage disc, *The Christmas Album*. Gilibert comes through with amazing vibrancy.

One thing about Christmas albums, they almost always sell well. Otherwise, they wouldn't continue to be made. A few years ago, I said to a well-known soprano, "Why haven't you made a Christmas album? I think you should." She said, "A record exec once told me that you know a singer is on her way out when she makes a Christmas album. It's a last stop, a last gasp." Well, sometimes it is, sometimes it isn't.

Let's run through a few Christmas albums, including a new one. I will be far from exhaustive. I will leave out many of your favorites, and some of mine. And I think we'll stick to classical artists. Jimmy Durante singing "Frosty the Snowman," Eartha Kitt singing "Santa Baby," Mel Tormé singing his "Christmas Song"—all wonderful. I appreciate Mariah Carey singing "All I Want for Christmas Is You," too. I admit, though, that I've never seen the point of Bruce Springsteen shouting "Santa Claus Is Comin' to Town."

And before we leave the popular world, let us bow our heads to Bing Crosby and "White Christmas"—the best-selling Christmas song penned by a Russian-born Jew, Irving Berlin. It appeared in the 1942 movie *Holiday Inn*. (The motel chain later named itself after the movie.) Many a classical singer has recorded "White Christmas"—and not just baritones, and not just men, either. Do you know the verse of this song (as opposed to the chorus, which we all know)? It's seldom done. And it tells you why the person is dreaming of a white Christmas. I first heard the verse from Marilyn Horne, the great American mezzo-soprano. It goes,

The sun is shining, the grass is green,
The orange and palm trees sway.
There's never been such a day
In Beverly Hills, L.A.

But it's December the 24th
And I'm longing to be up north . . .

I have a feeling that one of the reasons Horne sings the verse is that she did much of her growing up in Southern California.

She made her Christmas album in 1983, just before she turned 50. She did so with the Mormon Tabernacle Choir, no less. So this is a grand album, with all the bells and whistles, or many of them. It is not schlocky or absurd, however. Horne has too much taste, and too much musicality, for that. The noble power with which she sings "The First Nowell" is thrilling. And there is also on this album a rarity: a homely little carol called "The Bethlehem Babe," which she learned in grade school. Just about no one else had ever heard it. And Horne has given it a certain immortality. She sang this carol, by the way, in Carnegie Hall two Christmases ago. At 74, she still sounded like Horne.

Tebaldi was a little past it when she made her Christmas album in 1971. She wasn't old: only 49, the same age Horne was when she made *her* Christmas album. But she was wearing out. Still, she was Tebaldi—and such carols as "Mille cherubini in coro" have charm and allure. ("Mille cherubini . . ." is practically the Italian national carol. It is fashioned after a Schubert song, "Wiegenlied," or "Lullaby.") Another great soprano, Schwarzkopf, made her Christmas album in 1957, when she was 41. I doubt there is a better Christmas album, recorded by a lone classical singer. Schwarzkopf is all fervency, style, and devotion. Astonishing what can be done with "I Saw Three Ships (Come Sailing In)." A third great soprano, Leontyne Price, was a mere 34 when she made her Christmas album, or rather, her first one. The year was 1961. She was accompanied by a ritzy band, the Vienna Philharmonic, conducted by Karajan. The album has always been a brisk seller, and probably always will be: It captures Price at the zenith of her youthful purity.

In the late 1990s, the Swedish mezzo Anne Sofie von Otter made *Home for Christmas*—one of the best-loved Christmas albums of recent years. Von Otter is an erudite, cosmopolitan, musicianly musician, and this album shows it. She followed it up with *Noël* in 2006. It is an eclectic and warming album, like the first. Another recording of recent years is *The Gifts of Christmas*, with Heidi Grant Murphy, the soprano from Washington State, accompanied by her pianist husband Kevin. "HGM," as she's known in the business, is "radiant," "angelic," "soul-filled." These are all clichés about her; but they're true. The Murphys' album is marked by simplicity (in the best sense), sincerity, and high musical values. I must tell you, on the principle of full disclosure, that I am a friend of the couple. But may I say I was a fan first?

Bergonzi—whom I have never met—made his Christmas album in 1982, at the ripe age (for a singer) of 58. Being an Italian, the famed tenor sings "Mille cherubini in coro." He also sings, in magnificent Italian English, "White Christmas." Can you think of another Italian tenor? Maybe Pavarotti? He frequently recorded Christmas music, with that incomparable instrument. Sometimes his singing is too trumpet-like—without enough bend or lilt. Sometimes it is perfect. Domingo made a recording with the Vienna Choir Boys back in the 1970s. They pipe innocently; he pours forth Latin virility. "Adeste Fideles"—"A Dusty Fiddle," in my house—is a ringing anthem, loaded with testosterone.

Sticking with tenors, Roberto Alagna, the Frenchman of Sicilian parentage, made one of the weirdest Christmas albums ever in 2000. It is a mixture of the corny, the vulgar, the touching, and the brilliant. It begins with a carol that Alagna himself wrote: "Gentil Père Noël." This is a pleasant, bubblegum-ish, catchy number. He also sings a song, "Guardian Angels," co-written by the distinguished harpist Harpo Marx. (I understand he also worked with his brothers in comedy.) And the disc ends with a freaky-deaky, Hawaiian (yes) "White Christmas."

The bins—symbolically speaking, these days—are filled with choral albums: choral albums for Christmas. I will mention just a few. Is there anything wrong with *A Robert Shaw Christmas—Angels on High*? No. "O magnum mysterium," by the contemporary American composer Morten Lauridsen, is a stunning track on that disc. If you feel like Christmas *à la russe*, try *Russian Christmas*, with the St. Petersburg Chamber Choir, led by Nikolai Korniev. The Russians know how to do Christmas. So, for sure, does John Rutter, who with his Cambridge Singers made an album called *Christmas Star*. Rutter is the English composer, arranger, and conductor. He has written plenty of Christmas music that, I believe, will last. Some of his fellow composers like to mock him, as too "traditional" and all. I believe they mock him because they have half his talent and a fiftieth of his success. One thing in favor of *Christmas Star* is that it avoids an overall grimness. You know the English and Christmas: Sometimes the midwinter can be all too bleak.

Sometimes "mystery" turns into undue solemnity, even a melancholy.

This perhaps gives me an opening to do my annual grumping about *Messiah* performances nowadays. Everyone is eager to be musicologically correct, which is certainly not the same thing as musically correct. So we get itty-bitty *Messiah*s, with itty-bitty orchestras and choruses, making itty-bitty, scratchy, airless, hooty sounds. Handel, I believe, would be appalled. Most distressing is that so many performances are joyless. I always say, "If you're singing 'For unto us a child is born,' can't you at least *pretend* to be happy about it?" There is a middle ground between swollen, 19th-century-style *Messiah*s and the wheat germ we are often served today. I value Colin Davis's recording with the London Symphony Orchestra and Chorus from 1966. It is a tremendous experience, musically and spiritually. And if you feel like indulging in Sir Thomas Beecham's grandiose, illegitimate *Messiah* from 1959—go ahead. Everyone needs a hot-fudge sundae now and then, to go with his wheat germ. And Sir Thomas was incapable of being other than musical.

Back to choral albums, of carols and whatnot: The King's Singers are the six-man a cappella group from England; Chanticleer is the twelve-man a cappella group from San Francisco. They have both made many Christmas albums, and they both do a very good Christmas. I think some of Chanticleer's arrangements are unfortunate—smacking too much of the cocktail lounge. But others are right on the money.

I said I would discuss a new album, and so I will. It comes from Bryn Terfel, the Welsh bass-baritone. Over the years, I have called him the most likable man in music, and he is not getting any less likable. On the cover of his new album—*Carols & Christmas Songs*—he is wearing a scarf. There is a time-honored tradition of scarf-wearing on Christmas-album covers. Domingo wore one, on an album years ago. Alagna has a scarf. Terfel is even hugging himself, as though shivering. Nice try, Bryn.

His album is two albums, actually. One disc is mainly in English, and the other is all in Welsh. The record label, Deutsche Grammophon (which is not Welsh), calls this a "bonus disc." On both discs, Terfel sings a range of songs, most of them traditional: "O Come, All Ye Faithful," "In the Bleak Midwinter" (!), and so on. On the first disc, he sings "White Christmas." This is not a solo version: It's a duet with—who else?—Bing Crosby. Technology makes this possible. We are in an era when you can perform with just about anybody. Recently, Joshua Bell, the Hoosier violinist born in 1967, recorded a Grieg sonata with Sergei Rachmaninoff, the Russian pianist-composer who died in 1943 (in Beverly Hills, L.A., as it happens—where they dream of a white Christmas). How this works, I'm not really sure. I just know it does, pretty much.

In all of his carols and songs, Terfel sings with his usual immediacy of communication, and also with one of the most beautiful voices in creation. I think some of the arrangements are hard to stomach—too soupy, too cutesy, too cocktail-lounge. In many cases, straighter and more classical would be better. But Terfel and his team apparently like what they like.

What are your three favorite Christmas tracks, all-time? I will spit out three, just as a parlor exercise. I will name 1) Leontyne Price, on that 1961 album, singing "O Holy Night." "Holy" is the word. 2) Heidi Grant Murphy and Kevin Murphy performing the "Shepherd's Pipe Carol," by Rutter. Lilting, sinuous, a little bluesy—irresistible. And 3) Chanticleer singing a spiritual, "Jerusalem in the Morning," which comes on their 2001 disc *Christmas with Chanticleer*. It brings you hootin' and hollerin' tidings of great joy. Every year, I wear the grooves off—or what would be grooves, if this were a record from the Great Caruso's time.

—December 20, 2010

Pots and Pans, Glubs and Glurps

A brief listen to contemporary (classical) music

Some years ago, I was covering a concert at Carnegie Hall, whose program included a new work. A world premiere. When it had ended, I leaned over to the critic across the aisle from me and said, "I'm so sick of that piece." He threw back his head and laughed. He knew exactly what I meant.

We had never heard this specific piece, of course—but we certainly knew the type. It was the "perpetual-motion piece," as I sometimes call it, or the "frenetic piece." Busy busy busy. There are other standard types, too.

There's the sci-fi piece, with glubs and glurps and other such sounds. Relatedly, you have the spooky-jungle piece, with hoots and growls and so on. Then there's the end-of-the-world piece—very popular. The post-apocalypse piece, the "bleakscape," as I have termed it. You also have the cinematic, Disneyesque piece, filled with swells and tinkles.

All of these pieces tend to be loaded with percussion. Music historians of the future might label our age "The Age of Percussion." I often say, "Today's music has more pots and pans than Williams-Sonoma."

A herd mentality exists in classical music, as in other fields. Composers are loath to stray too far from their fellows. People say that all Vivaldi concertos sound alike. That's not true, but if it were, they'd have the excuse of having been written by one person.

There are other types I could mention, including the environmental piece, the global-warming piece: I call them "greenpieces."

Let me not be too dismissive or snotty: There is good music about. But we may be in something of a drought, greatness-wise. Who was the last great composer? Shostakovich, who died in 1975? You will also get votes for Britten (d. 1976), Bernstein (d. 1990), and others.

"You can never tell who's great or durable in your own age!" people exclaim, sometimes anxiously or angrily. The answer is: Sometimes you can, sometimes you can't.

Arvo Pärt is a figure to be reckoned with, the genuine article. Someone once said to me, "Who's a good composer today, and don't say Arvo Pärt!" I think my questioner meant that too many say Pärt. Well, I do too. Pärt is one of the holy minimalists, i.e., practitioners of compositional minimalism who are inspired by religion. The grandees of regular old minimalism are still around, chiefly Philip Glass and Steve Reich. A few years ago, Glass composed his Violin Concerto No. 2, subtitled "The American Four Seasons." It is intelligent and ultimately very moving.

Say this for the minimalists, if nothing else: During the second half of the 20th century, they helped keep tonality alive, while it was under assault. The serialists ruled the roost. (Practitioners of musical serialism.) Ned Rorem labeled them the "serial killers." Some of them were talented and commendable. But Pierre Boulez, Elliott Carter, Roger Sessions (all of them talented and commendable): Will anyone listen to their music in the future? I have my doubts.

There is a lot of intellectualism in music today, and less inspiration. Brainy people choose to compose. They could be doctors, lawyers—even scientists—but they choose to compose. Which is too bad: They're brainier than they are musical. I don't know what Bruckner would have scored on his SAT. I do know he was a genius.

I also know that there's a lot of pretending among critics and others. They pretend that dreck—especially atonal or politics-tinged dreck—is high art. They have either drunk the Kool-Aid, because life is easier that way, or they know better but are terrified to be thought square. On a naked emperor, people see, or pretend to see, fine robes.

Bless the candid. I regularly ask important musicians, "Who's worth listening to, among today's composers?" In 2009, I put this question to Lorin Maazel, the late conductor (who was also a composer). Immediately, he said, "Penderecki." Then he said, "Um . . . well . . ." He paused for a long time, smiling at me. He was saying, in effect, *Pickin's are slim, aren't they?* Later, he spoke up for Rodion Shchedrin and Aaron Jay Kernis—who are well worth speaking up for.

And Penderecki, yes. Two years ago, I heard a new solo-violin piece by him. I thought it had a chance of making the standard, or semi-standard, repertoire. I was able to tell him so, too, as he was sitting behind me.

Recently, I heard a cantata by Thomas Adès—formidable. I also applauded an opera by Marc-André Dalbavie. And a piano trio by Justin Dello Joio (son of Norman Dello Joio, the American composer who lived from 1913 to 2008). And a tone poem by Christopher Rouse. Like many others, I greatly admire Michael Hersch, who, I must disclose, is a friend of mine, but who should not be penalized for that.

I also appreciate performers who roll their own: who compose their own music, as performers once did, before the split between the performer and the composer set in (about a hundred years ago). These include three pianists: Stephen Hough, Marc-André Hamelin, and young

Conrad Tao (b. 1994). Their music is good or less good. My point is that they're composing, which musicians really ought to do. They're in the game.

Most days, I don't sweat the future of classical music, which has been sweated forever: Charles Rosen, the pianist-scholar, said, "The death of classical music is perhaps its oldest tradition." Music is one way in which people express themselves. It is also a way in which people praise God (and such praise has resulted in some of the greatest music). The creative instinct is unkillable. Beauty, though it may be suppressed, is unkillable. And genius will out.

But may more of it out, soon, please?

—November 19, 2015

Acknowledgements

My great thanks go to Jack Fowler: publisher of *National Review*, friend to all. What an example. And treasure.

Great thanks to Luba Myts, the art director of *NR*. You can see her handiwork on the cover and elsewhere in this book. An artist and friend.

Rachel Levine-Ramirez was my intern. (Great American name, by the way.) Intern? I would be lucky to work for *her* one day. What a whiz.

A deep bow to Fred Schwarz, Ian Tuttle, and Brooke Rogers, my *NR* colleagues. And to Elijah Stevens. I appreciate their help. Seth LeMaster took over indexing chores from Rachel. Much appreciation to him, too.

Rich Lowry is the editor of *NR*. Invaluable. Lindsay Craig is the president of the National Review Institute. Ditto. I am grateful to the rest of Team NRI as well, including Alexandra Zimmern, Charlotte Sawyer, and Charles Correll (a Summer 2016 intern).

May I add that William F. Buckley Jr. started *National Review*, in 1955? I may. Speaking selfishly, he has enriched my life. Speaking less selfishly, he has enriched life, period.

INDEX